The Talon of the Hawk

THE TWELVE KINGDOMS

Books by Jeffe Kennedy

The Twelve Kingdoms:
The Mark of the Tala

The Twelve Kingdoms:
The Tears of the Rose

The Twelve Kingdoms:
The Talon of the Hawk

The Master of the Opera
available as an eBook serial

Act 1: Passionate Overture
Act 2: Ghost Aria
Act 3: Phantom Serenade
Act 4: Dark Interlude
Act 5: A Haunting Duet
Act 6: Crescendo
(the complete novel coming in August 2015)

Published by Kensington Publishing Corp.

The Talon of the Hawk

THE TWELVE KINGDOMS

JEFFE KENNEDY

KENSINGTON BOOKS
www.kensingtonbooks.com

KENSINGTON BOOKS are published by

Kensington Publishing Corp.
119 West 40th Street
New York, NY 10018

All Kensington titles, imprints, and distributed lines are available at special quantity discounts for bulk purchases for sales promotion, premiums, fund-raising, and educational or institutional use.

Special book excerpts or customized printings can also be created to fit specific needs. For details, write or phone the office of the Kensington Sales Manager: Kensington Publishing Corp., 119 West 40th Street, New York, NY 10018. Attn. Sales Department. Phone: 1-800-221-2647.

Kensington and the K logo Reg. U.S. Pat. & TM Off.

ISBN-13: 978-0-7582-9447-0
ISBN-10: 0-7582-9447-6
First Kensington Trade Paperback Printing: June 2015

eISBN-13: 978-0-7582-9448-7
eISBN-10: 0-7582-9448-4
First Kensington Electronic Edition: June 2015

10 9 8 7 6 5 4 3 2 1

Printed in the United States of America

To my mother,
who first read to me and then empowered me to
read on my own.

Acknowledgments

Many thanks to Veronica Scott and Susan Doerr who suggested the perfect way for me to use the iron dress in this story. I don't think I would have gotten to it without your ideas.

Special thanks go to Anne Calhoun, for helping me sort through Ursula's angst and listening to so much of my own as I questioned where this story took me.

Heartfelt love and gratitude to the rest of my critique partner/cheerleading squad—Anna Philpott, Carolyn Crane and Marcella Burnard. There aren't many people in this world willing to read nearly 130,000 words in less than a week and who are then able to provide such brilliant, thoughtful feedback. I'm eternally indebted to you all.

An extra-special thank you to my agent, Connor Goldsmith, who picked up representing me after this trilogy was sold, as this book was in process, and has worked tirelessly on both this series and my behalf. All the French 75s to you, baby.

Huge thanks to the Kensington team for midwifing this trilogy into the world and being so awesome at every turn, especially my editor Peter Senftleben, awesome production editor Rebecca Cremonese and her myriad minions, publicist Jane Nutter, and communications diva Vida Engstrand.

I don't know how to express my deep gratitude to all the readers and reviewers who have loved on these books and shouted that love to the world. All year I've been hearing how much you couldn't wait for Ursula's book. Both tremendously gratifying and terrifying. I hope I did her justice for you.

I'd like to send a very special note of thanks in particular to the reviewers and staff at RT Magazine, for all you've done in championing these books and supporting me as an author.

Always, I send love to my family, who listen patiently to my long explanations, pretend they know which book I'm talking about and who don't complain when I sneak off on holiday visits to write at Starbucks.

Finally and forever, love and gratitude to David, who's there every day, feeds me, heals me, and makes everything possible.

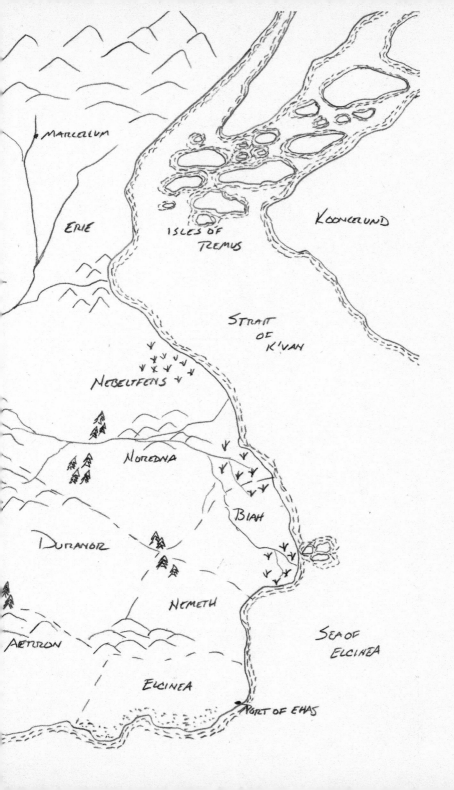

1

The bright pennants of Ordnung, High King Uorsin's rampant bear topping them all, snapped in the cool breezes from the high mountain peaks. Those pristine white towers, the banners of the Twelve Kingdoms gathered under one, all symbolized my father and King's greatest triumph. One I believed in with all my being.

Or had once believed in.

From the ravages of internecine wars and crippling enmities, Uorsin had united the kingdoms, bringing them together in lasting peace, capped by the shining castle he built on the ruins of the past. Always, no matter in what condition I returned home, I'd felt a surge of elation at the sight, pride in my legacy and sacred duty.

Not this sick dread.

As we rode closer, the formidable grandeur of Ordnung only mocked me for my many failures of the past months. Soon I would stand before my King, and I had no idea how I would explain myself and my actions. Or what price he would exact.

"Nervous?" Dafne, riding on her gentle palfrey, studied me with serious eyes. A scholarly woman with a quiet manner, she asked with complete sincerity what might sound like a taunt from another.

"Being nervous would imply that I'm uncertain about the confrontation to come," I told her. "I am . . . readying myself for King Uorsin's sure disappointment." And his rage. Never forget the bear's towering fury. As if I could.

"You don't need me to tell you, but you did the right thing, Your Highness. I wasn't sure which you would choose—love or duty."

"Think you I could have ripped a newborn from my baby sister's arms, with her barely recovered from believing her daughter dead, hard upon the heels of her husband's murder?"

Dafne considered the question with due gravity. Which made her interesting. No court sycophant she, with ready answers to most please the people who governed her fate.

"Before I answer, I'd like to make clear that I don't agree with the word 'murder.' You did not kill Prince Hugh in cold blood, but rather in the heat of battle. More self-defense than anything."

Remembering the sickening feel of my sword cutting through Hugh's neck, realizing I'd killed my sister's husband, I knew better. All of it had happened so fast—Hugh lunging to kill Rayfe, my other sister Andi thrusting herself between them. I'd acted without thought, though hardly without consequence.

"Self-defense means defending one's own self. I was in no danger. He was my ally and did not deserve to die by my blade. Nor for me to compound my guilt by fobbing off responsibility for it onto Andi and the Tala."

"Queen Andromeda was right to insist on taking the blame. If Princess Amelia hadn't taken it as a reason to incite Avonlidgh to civil war, Old King Erich would have."

"Which is happening anyway. Warring over an infant heir." The disgust and frustration that had ridden me these past months leaked into my tone. Speaking to Dafne, though, and surrounded by my loyal Hawks, I could say what I normally would not. Ami and Hugh's son belonged neither to Uorsin nor to Old Erich, though you wouldn't know it from the way the two kings be-haved, both claiming him as heir. If I hadn't killed Hugh, we wouldn't be in this particular battle. One the Twelve, already plagued with problems, could ill afford.

"That's on Erich, not you. As for the question of murder, I'd put forth that defending your sister is the same for you as defend-ing yourself. Both of your sisters are part of you on a profound level. In a way that even Queen Andromeda and Princess Amelia don't fully appreciate."

A legal scholar's mind, there. Always useful in a companion for someone in my position. "And the answer to my question?"

"Yes," Dafne decided. "I think you would and could do any-thing. You're certainly capable. *If* you believed it to be the right thing to do."

"Obeying the High King is the right thing to do," I replied, knowing full well I hadn't done so. The grind of guilt and failure made my bones ache. "Semantic arguments aside, the High King commanded that I bring Amelia's son to Ordnung. I could have and did not."

"Some truths exceed the law of man."

"But not the law of the King."

"The King is but a man."

"Don't let High King Uorsin hear you say that, librarian. You won't long keep your place—or your head—speaking that way."

"Would you report me?" She cocked her head, brown eyes sparkling with curiosity. No trepidation there—only apparent genuine interest. As if she had already gathered her information and predicted my actions. The answer I gave her would simply confirm or deny her theories.

"Have you no fear at all, Lady Mailloux?" I asked, instead of feeding her the insights she sought. Let her continue to speculate.

She transferred her gaze to the castle, imposing on its rise, framed by the snowcapped mountains. The corners of her soft mouth tightened. "It's always strange to me to see it as it is," she commented. "In my mind's eye, I still see Castle Columba, though it's been gone nigh on thirty years. I don't know if it's fear or something else that digs at me now."

"And yet, you return, for a second time."

"It seems to be my fate." She gave me a wry smile. Amelia was right that Lady Dafne Mailloux often failed to observe courtesy. Not that it bothered me. So did my Hawks and the other soldiers I regularly trained, traveled, and fought with. Something about focusing on a greater purpose relegated the bowing and scraping to the negligible category. "Besides, I owe you. When we thought Stella dead, you wanted to spare Princess Amelia the pain of it, to let her rejoice in having Astar happy and healthy. I expected you to be angry with me for forcing the truth into the open."

She would be the one to lay it out there, when others would avoid the subject. Those had been dark hours, Ami near death from birthing the twins, then finding the girl, Stella, dead in her cradle. At least the boy, Astar, had stayed strong.

"I was wrong to conceal it from her." I shrugged, using the motion to loosen my shoulders. Not that it worked. "Not only because she had the wit to see through the trick that I did not."

"I saw Stella's dead body, too," she reminded me. "That black magic fooled us both."

Enough that we'd even buried her, giving someone enough time to abduct little Stella. Everything in me champed at the bit to be searching for my niece, to be helping Amelia instead of riding into Ordnung. Infinitely preferable to facing the High King with the news I brought. Nevertheless—and though it had nearly killed me—I'd followed my duty and returned home. Though we'd traveled fast, a messenger could have caught up with us. I kept expecting one, saying they'd recovered the babe. With each passing hour that the news failed to arrive, my dread and uneasiness that I'd made the wrong decision grew. Lately what had once been black and white had shaded into disturbing grays.

"I disobeyed a direct command," Dafne persisted. "You would have been within rights to kill or dismiss me for it. So I owe you."

"I should have given her credit for needing to know the truth, for being strong enough to stand up to the pain. You owe me nothing."

"Nevertheless, I have an idea of what you'll have to deal with at Ordnung, and I couldn't live with myself if I let you face it alone. Returning with you was the least I could do."

She meant that well, in all earnestness, so I didn't comment. Didn't say that no one and nothing could spare me my father's wrath. I'd learned that lesson early.

We'd passed through the outlying farms and rode through the extensive township that surrounded Ordnung. People moved about busily, with the many chores of summer at hand. They acknowledged our passing with respectful bows and salutes—and something else. A sense of wariness that made the hairs on the back of my neck stand up.

We did not travel with fanfare. Out of long familiarity with my comings and goings, the people did not dote as they might have on the rest of the royal family, so I did not expect effusive greetings. I preferred it this way—in part because it relieved me to dispense with the pomp and formalities when not necessary, but also because it gave me opportunity to take the measure of the people of Mohraya, the small kingdom that housed Ordnung.

Uorsin saw to his own first, so the Mohrayans generally fared better than the other eleven kingdoms, regardless of the swings in harvest yields and other variable producers of wealth. No matter how severe the troubles in other parts of the Twelve Kingdoms—some I'd seen too much of lately, sorrows that weighed on me—I could usually count on at least Mohraya to be doing well.

Not so, it appeared. One more problem added to the precarious pile that threatened to topple over onto us all.

No, things were not right here. The town burst at the seams, crowded with people. Overly so, despite the increased activity of the warm season. The farmers and livestock growers ought to be out on their land, tending to those concerns.

Perhaps I'd lost my count of days and they'd come into town for market or a fair. But I didn't think so.

For a start, many of the people gathering in the squares were neither buying nor selling. I'd never expect to recognize all the faces, but the citizenry teemed with unfamiliar looks. More men than usual. Tall ones, light haired, with broad, exotic features.

I called over my lieutenant. "Marskal." I kept my tone easy, conversational, so he wouldn't go on alert. "What am I seeing here?"

"Seems the population has grown during our travels, Captain," he replied blandly. He'd been taking note, too, then. Part of why I relied on him.

"What do you put it down to?"

"We've long heard of the increasing conscription rates."

"Those are foreigners, not raw recruits and new conscripts."

"True," he agreed.

"I've read the people of Dasnaria across the Onyx Ocean described as such," Dafne, still riding on my other side, observed. "Tall, fair-haired, strongly built."

"Is that so," I replied. Both of them, knowing I did not ask a question, remained silent. I misliked it, foreboding crawling up my already aching spine. They could only be here with Uorsin's knowledge, which made no sense to me. But then, so much of his behavior had become erratic. Ever since Andi rode home with the Tala on her tail. Absolute loyalty to my King and father meant I should not question him. As his heir, it fell to me to give him my unqualified faith and support.

I hated feeling that erode, even in the quiet depths of my heart, where I harbored doubts I spoke of to no one. That I could hardly bear to examine myself.

The nearer we drew to the castle walls, the more of these exotic men we spied. All hardened warriors to my eye, all heavily armed. Uorsin had dropped hints about having other resources beyond the somewhat questionable loyalty of the Twelve. Ordnung's guards manned the outposts and the usual positions on the walls—and then some. I counted surreptitiously, lazily turning my face to the sun. More than twice the standard posting. Looked like he'd dug into those other resources after all.

The conflict with the Tala and the overall unrest in the Twelve had made the High King wary. Understandable. But these changes edged past that into paranoia. Along with an expense we could not afford. More fears I'd never give voice to.

"Jepp reported no alert, correct?" I asked Marskal. I knew our scout hadn't, but it never hurt to confirm.

Jepp, at Marskal's head tilt, jogged her agile mountain pony closer. "Captain." She nodded at me. "I checked only at the guard gates, and they gave the all clear. No mention of . . . this."

"Pass the word to be on alert, then."

Jepp saluted and fell back. Not that I needed to tell my Hawks that something was awry in Ordnung. They knew it as well as or better than I did. As much as we could not be less than on alert, telling them so meant that they pulled in closer, taking long-rehearsed positions. Dafne remained placid, a pleased smile on her lips, though she had to be aware of her vulnerability.

"You might have done better to stay at Windroven, after all," I commented to her.

"I'll stick with you, if that's all right. Right with you. I'll keep up."

Before we undertook this journey, I had doubted that. Now I felt certain she could keep up with the best of my Hawks. Unless we fled flat out and it was frankly too late for that. Even if I hadn't been honor bound to return to Ordnung to face the King with the bad news, my instincts warned we'd have to fight our way free—impossible odds, not to mention a traitorous act.

On that thought, guards stepped up to bar our passage into Ordnung. More of the foreigners, their helms making them look even taller.

"Who approaches Ordnung?" one demanded in our Common Tongue, though his accent twisted the words.

I stared him down, showing my great displeasure at being questioned, transforming the deep unease into righteous fury. "Who dares raise a blade to a Princess of the Realm, Heir to the High Throne of the Twelve Kingdoms?"

Jepp and Marksal drew up closer, their battle readiness almost an audible buzz in my ears. For a moment, it seemed it might come to that, the foreign guard undaunted, scrutinizing me for some sign that I was who I claimed to be. I flexed my hand on the hilt of my sword, edging Dafne more behind me.

A series of shouts in another language relayed from the walls and my challenger cocked his head, nodded, and stepped aside. "Welcome home, Your Highness." He bowed but did not apologize. I ignored him and rode forward, not feeling welcome at all.

We passed through the outer gates, the shadow of the walls passing chill over me.

2

We rode into the outer courtyard of Ordnung, the eyes of the castle guard continuing heavy on my back. Since when had our usual guard been replaced with foreigners who knew so little of our realm that I would be regarded with such pointed suspicion? I would have to discuss this with Lord Percy. Unlike him to man the walls with no one to recognize when important personages approached the gates.

All we needed now was a diplomatic incident because a noble of the Twelve got skewered on our doorstep by an untrained guard.

Unless this wasn't a mistake and the High King had publicly disinherited me already, upon hearing the news of Astar's birth. Or declared me a traitor as I had neither rejoined our forces poised at stalemate with Erich's nor returned with the babe. His spies would have long noted that Ami did not ride with me and that we moved at a pace too rapid for an infant. He'd never directly ordered me to join his army encamped near the river east of Lianore, but normally I would have. The last I'd heard, Uorsin's army had not moved to intercept Erich's on the march to Windroven to "celebrate the birth of Avonlidgh's heir."

Both preserving the fiction that civil war had not yet begun in earnest.

I straightened my spine, wishing the ache away. For all the good that did. Too much time in the saddle or sitting long hours in bad chairs while I contemplated the awful possibility that Amelia might die. The rest of the Hawks looked tense to my eye as well, though I doubted a more casual observer would notice. They called out greetings to the watchful guard and joked among themselves, creating the illusion of a pleasant homecoming. The appearance of victory could be as vital as the actual accomplishment.

We dismounted in the inner courtyard, the young grooms dashing up as usual to take the horses. That much hadn't changed. But I did not recognize the guard at the door, which I absolutely should have, and my ladies did not appear to persuade me to bathe and change into a gown before greeting King and court. I would have refused, but they always made the attempt.

I'd been gone quite a long time. Perhaps that explained it.

Dafne raised her eyebrow, ever so slightly. No expression of interest now. She'd marked the changes, too. *Nervous?* Her question echoed in my head, as if it had been a warning.

Danu take them all, this wasn't right.

"Your Highness?" Marskal saluted me and the rest of the Hawks echoed the movement. It marked the transition for me, from warrior to princess. I never much liked this moment, but it wouldn't do to enter my father's court flanked by my specially trained team of crack soldiers. Though I might need them. Especially with the cold whisper of a traitor's fate breathing down my neck.

"Well ridden, well fought," I replied, placing my clenched fist over my heart, returning the salute. "You're dismissed."

Marskal slid a glance at the castle proper and lowered his voice. "Captain, should we—"

"You've earned your ease," I interrupted. "I shall see you all at supper."

I hoped.

They didn't like it, but neither would they argue. In private, maybe. Not in public view. With a final salute they dispersed. I pretended to oversee their departure, steadying myself, gathering my courage.

A scuffle of feet inside the shadowed entrance. Derodotur, Uorsin's aide and closest adviser, emerged and bowed formally. "Your Highness Princess Ursula, welcome home."

"Thank you, Derodotur. It's good to be home."

"King Uorsin requests that you attend him immediately."

Not a good sign at all. Sending Derodotur to give his messages? I peeled off my metal-embedded leather gloves. My hands felt cold and I rubbed them together.

"I should change first."

Derodotur negated that with a bare shake of his head. "King Uorsin and the court await you, Princess."

I managed a smile and nod of acknowledgment, though my bowels turned watery. By all rights Uorsin should have met with me privately, to allow me to give him all my news informally. Once he would have done exactly that and we would have discussed how best to present it to the courtiers. With this, he was forcing me to either prevaricate in public or share sensitive information with potential enemies. At any given time, the court included several ambassadors from the eleven kingdoms outside Mohraya, if not one or more monarchs themselves. At least several sympathized with Erich and should be present, unless tensions had escalated even more than I knew.

The only one I could count on not being there was Erich of Avonlidgh himself. Danu take it, we were practically at war—what *was* Uorsin thinking? And how to plan my strategy, not knowing?

I had no more answer to the questions than I'd had before, and delaying would only exacerbate the King's uncertain temper. Nothing to be done about it.

"I'll go straightaway. Shall we, Lady Mailloux?"

"I'm at your disposal, Your Highness."

The librarian could be all that form required, when she set her mind to it. She put me in mind of those lizards from the desert reaches of Aerron that changed skin color to match whatever you set them on. She trailed behind, as demure and discreet as any of the ladies assigned to me.

Court is simply another sort of battlefield or dueling ground. Anyone who implied otherwise was either not paying attention—Andi—or focused entirely on the social whirl—Amelia. Though I had to give my sisters credit for coming a long way in their political understanding of late. Granted, they'd been forced to in the heat of their own particular battles. I, however, had been learning the rules of this sort of conflict since I was five years old.

When Queen Salena, my mother, failed again to produce a son and Uorsin's eye fell on me.

Girding myself appropriately, I cleared my mind of all else but the duel ahead, as Danu taught. No emotion. Nothing but the moment. Defend, parry, attack, retreat, regroup.

Tension rode thick in the air, the courtiers unusually silent, so that my bootheels audibly echoed on the golden marble as I entered the throne room, the metallic braces of my leather armor clinking. High above and behind me, the rose window of Glorianna cast a pink haze. All faces turned toward me, cautiously bland—neither welcoming nor condemning. Being careful. They didn't know which way Danu's breath blew either.

Uorsin sat on the High Throne at the end of the long center aisle, flanked by the empty thrones that had always belonged to me and my sisters, along with the one to his immediate left, which had remained vacant all these years since Salena died. I'd heard the jibes enough times—both intended for me to overhear and not—that Uorsin had never felt the need to remarry, since I suited him better than any queen might. That was truer than people knew.

After all, he'd trained me to be exactly what he expected from early on. Danu knew I'd tried my best. Seemed to be unable to stop trying.

The smooth topaz in the pommel of my sword warmed the palm of my hand. Just a brief touch to my mother's jewel before I made myself move my hand away. One simply does not approach the High King with hand on sword, even if he is your father.

Particularly my father.

I studied him during that long walk, taking his measure. Enraged, yes, but not yet boiling over with it. He'd noted the lack of a babe in my arms, though that information would indeed have flown ahead from the moment I dismissed the Hawks and only confirmed what his spy network would have relayed. *Oh, Amelia, I hope you appreciate what I'm doing for you.*

A man stood near the empty throne at Uorsin's right hand— my seat—and though he didn't have the audacity to sit in it, he had a proprietary air. As if he belonged there. Another of these foreign men, he stood a good half head taller than I and his reach would likely outstrip mine by a forearm's length, if not more. A muscle-bound giant with a warrior's keen-edged poise. I could only hope that his bulk would slow him if it came to a fight. He caught my assessment and smiled, a bare tightening of the lips, a grim promise that his mind, at least, was not slow.

More bad luck. Danu stacked the challenge deep for me today.

I bowed, showing the respect I felt for my father, my King, and the throne on which he sat, that kept the peace of the Twelve Kingdoms.

"So." Uorsin's voice came out in a low rasp. "My eldest daughter, at least, returns to me. But strangely empty-handed."

Defend. "High King, I—"

"No!" He slammed a fist on the arm of his throne, making me jump inside, though I'd long since trained myself not to show it. Uorsin respected strength, and like the bear whose standard he carried, he turned more aggressive at any sign of fear. Something my sisters had never quite internalized. But then, I'd always shielded them from the worst of it. If nothing else, I'd succeeded in that. "Spare me your excuses. I don't wish to hear the long, sad, sorry tale of your recurring difficulties in following simple instructions. I want to know one thing and one thing only, understand? The next words out of your mouth, Daughter. Where is my grandson?"

Dangerous in this mood. He would not like the exact answer, but he'd grow angrier if I gave him anything but that. "With the Princess Amelia," I answered, crisply. A good soldier.

"Aha. An honest and exact answer. And where is the Princess Amelia?"

I sent a swift prayer to Danu and met my father's eye. "I don't know, my King."

He stared me down, deceptively calm. "I believe you don't know. Do you know why?"

Certainly not because he trusted and believed in me. "No, my King."

"Because"—he said the word softly, hissing the final syllable— "*nobody knows where she is!*" He finished on a shout that pierced my temples. I had to relax and widen my eyes to keep from wincing. The foreign warrior watched me while appearing not to, still assessing. I held my ground, keeping my sword hand relaxed at my side, and did not reply to Uorsin, as he had not asked me to.

"Perhaps"—Uorsin dropped into the rasp again—"you could find it in your heart to offer me a crumb of information. *Perhaps* you could tell me where they are *not?*"

Danu get me through this. "The Princess Amelia is neither at Windroven nor with King Erich. Nor has she, to my knowledge, taken refuge at any of the temples of Glorianna."

"Is that so?"

"Yes, my King. As last I knew."

"And what precisely do you know?"

Parry. "I attended Princess Amelia's lying in. The labor was a difficult one, but I'm happy to report that both she and your grandson came through in the blush of good health." All true. Fancy foot- and bladework to cover the lies of omission. That Amelia nearly died. That a half-breed Tala escaped convict and rogue priest of Glorianna—also apparently her lover, Danu take us all—saved her life with forbidden magic. That she'd actually borne twins, the other a daughter no one but a handful knew about. That she and her lover, Ash, even now pursued the Tala renegades to recover Stella. That I hadn't done what my heart and sanity urged and gone with them. Instead I'd come here, so I'd better make sure I played it correctly.

"She named him Astar," I added, with a bow to my father, "and sends you her love and regards."

An outright lie, that last, but one Uorsin would want to believe.

Uorsin tapped blunt fingers on the arm of the throne, frowning. He wore the crown of the Twelve Kingdoms, the sharp metal edge digging into his brow. Though he'd long complained of its discomfort, he would not allow it to be softened.

"Prince Astar. He should be named for me."

I allowed a slight shrug for my sister's whims. *Attack.* "Princess Amelia has always had a fanciful bent. She does not take my counsel."

He did not smile in fondness for his favorite, as I'd hoped, my attempt to open his guard neatly deflected. It could be that Ami had at last put her dainty slipper a bit too far over the line.

"She need not take your *counsel.*" Uorsin sneered the last word, dripping with contempt for my opinions. Very bad indeed. I wanted to stretch, to relieve the strain up my spine, but I held myself still. The foreign soldier's gaze flicked over me, as if he'd noted my discomfort. I returned the look with studied boredom.

"I do not want Amelia's regards, as she well knows. I want my thrice-cursed heir and I want him here!" Uorsin's voice thundered impressively, and all in the court quailed, a shuffling of feet and a nervous cough betraying them. All but the foreigner. Nerves of steel there.

"They must be sought and returned to me," Uorsin demanded.

Retreat. "As you command, my King." I bowed, giddy with relief. All my instincts had shouted at me to escape Ordnung while I could, to seek out and assist Ami. Now I had not only permission, but a public command to do so. The convict Ash fought impressively, but I'd feel much better guarding her and Astar my own self, with my Hawks at hand. Danu smiled on me. Far more than I'd hoped for. "I shall set out immediately."

"Not you."

Uorsin's negation rattled me, slicing out that momentary relief and replacing it with wariness. Bad, bad, bad.

"My King?" I let my voice carry all my unspoken questions.

"How can I be sure of you?"

The reaction, nearly inaudible, ran through the assembled court and nested in my pained gut. Here it was. The accusation I could not defend myself against. I could only reposition, entrench.

I took a step forward, to demonstrate I felt no cringing guilt. Another lie of omission. The guilt might break me. "I am, and ever shall be, your loyal subject. If you can be sure of nothing else, you can be sure of that. I would never take action against the crown. Or my father." My throat closed on that last. I wanted it to be true. I'd long since come to terms with the reality that I could never measure up to Uorsin's ideal of the son he never had, but I still cherished, somewhere in the depths of my foolish heart, the feeble hope that he might someday love me. He'd never wanted my love, but at least I could give him the unwavering loyalty he deserved from his heir.

Despite it all.

"What say you, Captain?"

For a startled moment, I formed a reply, before I registered that Uorsin spoke not to me, but to the foreigner. Of course. The Hawks called me captain. My father would not.

The foreign warrior bowed to the King, remarkably fluid despite his bulk. Danu save me if it came to hand-to-hand with him. I would have no physical advantage of any kind.

"High King Uorsin." His voice, baritone deep, pronounced our Common Tongue with a twist of accent, strangely lyrical from such a brute of a man. "Her Highness Princess Ursula has not yet shed her fighting gear, nor shaken the dust from her boots. Is it not traditional among your people, as with ours, to welcome the wanderer home? A feast to feed her, an opportunity for news to be exchanged."

I could hardly be called a wanderer. And the way he phrased that—"feed her"—as if I were livestock to be fattened for slaughter. What game did this man play? My palm itched for my sword. Uorsin nodded, gave the man an actual smile. As if at any moment he might clap the fellow on the shoulder. "An excellent idea," Uorsin proclaimed, waving a generous hand over the court. "A feast it shall be. Do you agree, Daughter?"

Regroup. I inclined my head at my King, added a nod for this foreigner who claimed such power over my father's opinion. "I would like nothing more."

He harrumphed, giving me a suspicious eye. "I think there's much you do not say, Ursula."

My name, at last. *I* had been named for him, his firstborn and, ostensibly, still his heir. Ami might be flighty in some ways, but she wasn't insensitive. She never would name her children after Uorsin, since I already bore that mantle. The only one who didn't see that truth sat on the High Throne, giving more weight to the carelessly proffered opinions of a foreign warrior than to the daughter he'd groomed to replace him.

I knew why. Not my recent failures, though they didn't help. No. Because of what failed to dangle betwixt my thighs. Such a foolish thing by which to judge a person and yet the one thing I could not learn, train for, or otherwise acquire, even to please my father.

There was a time—perhaps even still, in the quiet corners of my heart—when I would have done anything to change what made me so deeply flawed. To achieve the impossible. Danu knew I'd attempted any number of challenges to win Uorsin's approval, short-lived though it always was.

I'd only ever refused one.

And for that, he would forever damn me.

3

"There's much to say, when you have the opportunity." I couched my words to the King in a neutral tone, though the ambassadors ranged just behind me would be keen to pick out the least nuance. Hardly a state secret, however, that I'd have observations to communicate to Uorsin in private. And questions. Many, many questions.

His eyes gleamed. Tempted. He loved nothing more than privileged information and the game of debating and predicting repercussions. We often agreed, and when we didn't, enjoyed the argument. For long spaces of time during those conversations, he'd forget what I lacked and engage with me entirely as another duelist. In our shared love of strategy, I always felt closest to him, that I measured up.

I met his gaze steadily, asking him—as much as I could afford to—to give me that time with him. Things had changed when King Rayfe of the Tala had sent the message claiming Andi as his contractual bride. It bothered me that I still didn't quite know all the reasons for it, but I believed we'd return to normal, once we'd resolved this crisis and all of the subsequent repercussions. I had to believe it.

I doubted that Uorsin would truly set me aside for my nephew. He taunted me with the possibility just as he'd so often knocked me down with the flat of his sword: to teach me to get back up again. I simply needed to prove that I could.

"Perhaps tomorrow. Go so that you might better present yourself tonight. Try to look like a Princess of the Realm, Daughter, rather than a foot soldier."

I bowed, taking the extra effort to ensure I kept the movement fluid, not stiff with the humiliation that threatened to burn its way through to my face. The foreigner's sharp gaze flicked over me, but I ignored him. Uorsin had not seen fit to introduce the man; thus he would remain beneath my notice. If he thought Uorsin's barbs made me weak, then he'd be committing a grave tactical error.

My father was a great King. A peacemaker and leader of men. He'd made me strong.

I strode back up the aisle, keeping my head high and strides confident, allowing myself to rest my hand on the sword hilt. Now a gesture of power. The faces of the courtiers remained studiously blank, but many tipped heads in acknowledgment. I held rank still and they knew it.

More, they needed me. Particularly if Uorsin's erratic behavior had only escalated, as it seemed it might have.

An odd figure caught my eye. Another foreigner, of the same breed but female. She wore a cloak the color of banked coals and sported the same sunny looks as her countrymen. Her eyes, however, burned dark—a startling contrast to her fair skin. She stared hard at me, which was how she'd caught my attention. My skin crawled and the hair rose on the back of my neck. Much as in the presence of the Tala and their dark magic.

Hers, however, made me think of death.

Refusing to hasten my stride, I nevertheless realized as I made my escape that I'd neglected to look for Dafne before exiting the room. Not that she couldn't take care of herself, but I'd meant to and the strange woman had rattled me enough that I hadn't.

I needed to settle myself before the feast or I might lose my hard-won composure.

A hot bath could do the trick. I rarely indulged, but the warmth might loosen my back and I needed to bathe regardless. Just outside the throne room doors, I nearly ran over Madeline Nique, chatelaine of Ordnung.

An imposing woman, she rarely presented as flustered, though she came close at the moment. "Your Highness." She curtsied. "Welcome home."

"Thank you. You heard?"

"I wished to confirm with you. A feast for the entire court, a few hours from now?"

"Indeed. Can you manage?"

"Barely. I'm not entirely unprepared, but . . ." She rolled her eyes and made the circle of Glorianna, asking the goddess mutely for assistance.

Uorsin never gave a thought to such things. He could provision multiple armies and plan food supplies to outlast an extended siege, but it never seemed to cross his mind that Ordnung's daily activities required similar management.

Nor had he needed to, as I'd stepped into my mother's shoes in making decisions for such things even before Salena died when I was ten. I'd trained Madeline myself when her predecessor retired, and I knew her to be an efficient, competent woman. No doubt the kitchens would already be in an uproar over such an undertaking on this short notice.

"He called for formal, so that gives you an extra few hours. Do we have any entertainment we can tap?"

"No minstrels, of course."

Ah, right. Uorsin's ban on song. He'd thought slowing the speed of news would impede any colluding amongst the rebel kingdoms. An interesting strategy, though I'd argued against it. People liked their entertainment. Taking it away only made them feel slighted, quicker to anger, easier to coax to fighting. Besides, it seemed like insult piled on injury to me, the hardships they suffered and now no songs or storytelling to ease their minds at the end of what had to be grueling days.

"What about the castle ladies—surely they have some summer play or dance?"

"There's not so many without you or your sisters in attendance. The ladies who did not accompany the Princess Amelia to Windroven have largely returned to their families."

It hadn't occurred to me how the social life of Ordnung would deteriorate under these conditions. If only I *had* been born male, I could have married and left this sort of thing to my wife. "Bad luck—entertainment would allow us to serve nibbles for an hour or two longer, along with copious wine. You'd have more time and a happier, more forgiving crowd to serve."

"There are these . . . acrobats," she tendered.

"Acrobats?" I turned the word over in my mouth.

"Some of the Dasnarian mercenaries. It's a sort of exercise they do. Twisting and tumbling. Quite amazing. The best among them don colorful costumes and compete."

Mercenaries. Danu save us all. I had hoped for another explanation for the presence of the foreigners. Though what it might have been, I didn't know. Another demonstration of the foolishness of relying on such a flimsy thing as hope. One day I would learn.

"Then Ordnung might as well get its money's worth. Can you arrange for it? What else can I do?"

"You've done it, Your Highness. Thank you." She curtsied again and gave me a sincere smile. "It's good to have you back. Things will be done as they should be now. I'll arrange for the acrobats and will be in the kitchens, should you think of aught else."

I took the shortcut to my rooms, through the arcade, mulling her words. *Things will be done as they should be now.* Mercenaries, in Ordnung, with their captain waiting attendance on Uorsin. Weariness crawled through me. Perhaps I'd forestall a bath and lie down, see if I could manage to sleep. Madeline would need nothing more, I felt sure. She'd been handling everything without my direction in my absence. Taking over those responsibilities for my mother, I'd quickly learned that finding the best people was key.

Mother had deteriorated in those last years after Andi was born and particularly during her pregnancy with Amelia. I understood more now than I had then. Andi had borne the mark that made her our mother's successor in Annfwn, as Queen of the Tala, and Salena had desperately wanted to take her there. But she'd done her duty and waited the five years to strengthen enough to bear her third daughter.

She would have left then, taking Andi and Ami with her, but she'd died before she could. It would have been better for my sisters, if she'd managed to. Not that it would have made much difference in my life. Even if she'd tried to take me, too, which I highly doubted, Uorsin would never have let me go.

It hadn't been easy, being both son and queen for my father, but I'd risen to the task. Until recently. *You will again,* I told myself. *You're just tired.*

"Your Highness." Derodotur's voice called out as he hastened up the arcade. Facing a private grassy courtyard, the white marble arches let sunshine into the hall, with urns of tumbling flowers at intervals. The quickest way to my rooms, it became impassable in winter. Derodotur was one of the few who'd know I'd go this way. He sketched a bow and scratched his nose. "Did you see that the armory has been updated as you directed?"

I suppressed a sigh. Of course he'd have information to impart, that I'd want to hear before facing Uorsin and the court again. It shouldn't take long, and then I could bathe and take a few minutes. Shaking off the weariness, I nodded. "I had not had the opportunity. Let's take a look. Court has adjourned, then?"

"Yes. Everyone is looking forward to your welcoming feast."

Oh, yes. The one that a foreign mercenary suggested—making it suspicious right there.

We moved briskly through the formal areas of Ordnung, quieter now that the courtiers had made themselves scarce in hopes of better fortune in the relaxed atmosphere of the promised feast. No doubt also planning to seek me with petitions they'd saved for my return. Troops drilled in the barracks courtyard. No sign of these acrobats, however. It would be interesting to assess their abilities. I highly doubted that mountain of a captain would be twisting or tumbling.

Derodotur made a show of pointing out the additions to the armory—slight—and made sure I got a good look at the additional ranks of mercenaries in the barracks—substantial—before closing the door behind us in the blade-sharpening room and turning to face me.

Buried in the ground and lined with stone, the chamber made an ideal location for Derodotur's confidential conversations with me. I'd been nine when he first brought me here, giving me insight on dealing with my often irascible father. He'd been Uorsin's page in the Great War, long before he met and married Salena. Having survived this long as the King's closest adviser, he also knew well the importance of never showing fear.

Seeing that emotion in Derodotur's face cemented the dread. Things were bad.

"When did they arrive?" I asked him, point-blank.

We both knew exactly who I meant. Derodotur shook his head. "I argued against it. You know that. At first—" He laughed at himself, a bitter edge. "At first I thought he was joking. But no. Uorsin sent for the Dasnarians shortly after you departed for Branli. He's determined that only they can be trusted not to defect to the loyalties of their home kingdoms. They've been at Ordnung just under four months."

"I'd heard nothing."

"You wouldn't have. No one has been allowed to leave the castle proper or the township. The minstrels departed long before that."

"The township? How does he prevent— Ah." That explained the foreign soldiers' idleness in the village. They were guards. And, with no open decree to prevent people from traveling *to* the township, as people were wont to do in warm weather, the population would keep increasing. We could sustain the situation into early autumn, but once the snows moved down from the mountains, we'd be hard-pressed to feed and clothe everyone. Disease would follow. It made me feel ill to contemplate it. Ugly ways to die. Give me the sword instead. "He must have a plan."

Danu tell me he has a plan. That he's not . . . I stopped myself from even thinking the words.

Derodotur's eyes shifted to the side. "He has not confided such to me." The closest I'd ever heard him come to expressing doubt in his King. Very bad indeed.

"How is he paying them?"

"He has promised a share of any spoils, should it come to war."

The smooth surface of the rounded topaz under my thumb grounded me enough that I resisted rolling my head to loosen my tightening neck. Even alone with Derodotur, it would not do for me to show weakness. "And if there is no war? The aim has been to settle this without conflict."

"He is certain there will be."

Uorsin could make war happen, regardless. Still. "But what provision if there are no spoils to be had?"

"He has promised to levy taxes and up conscriptions to a similar level."

"Conscriptions? How will . . ." I trailed off, understanding the fear. "Slave trade?"

"I don't *think* so." Derodotur shook his head, unhappy, uncertain. We'd be thrice damned if we allowed the people of the Twelve to be sold into slavery. Uorsin must have a plan. He'd nearly died uniting the Twelve. My mother had sacrificed her own throne, certainly her happiness, to assist him. He couldn't betray the people and that peace.

"I shall find out the details," I assured Derodotur, squeezing his shoulder. He'd grown frail in the last year, now shorter than I. "You know how Father loves to strategize. He'll have a plan."

Derodotur nodded again but did not seem convinced. "I'd never say this to anyone but you, Princess, but I worry that—"

"No, don't say what can't be unsaid. The unrest will be settled and the Dasnarians sent home with pay. You'll see."

"There's one more thing." Derodotur swallowed hard. "A woman among the Dasnarians."

"I think I saw her in court."

"Yes. That's her. There are whispers . . ."

"There is always gossip in court."

"Not like this." Derodotur's eyes flicked from side to side, as if expecting attack from the shadows. "The King has entertained her privately."

Uorsin entertained many women privately. Always had, even before Salena died. Nobody blinked over it, usually. I raised my eyebrows and waited, ignoring the curl of foreboding.

"She is . . . not wholesome," Derodotur finally whispered.

"Are you saying she holds undue influence over the King?"

"No. Well, yes. You see, she—" He broke off and shook his head.

Had he grown so old that the dementia of age had touched him? "She . . . what?"

"'Tis unnatural, Ursula," he said in a rush, seizing my hand, horror lurking in his eyes. "I'm afraid of what the days shall bring."

His hands on mine trembled and he seemed about to tumble over. "Don't fret so, Uncle." I hadn't called him that since I was a girl. "I'm home and I shall look into it. No one is stronger than Uorsin. I will talk with him. Amelia will turn up. We'll settle the matter of the heir to everyone's satisfaction and restore peace. Uorsin will see his throne secure and will send the Dasnarians home."

Derodotur nodded and, shocking me, bent over my hands and kissed them. "If anyone can save us now, you can."

I only wished I believed that.

4

Too unsettled to rest now, and since I was already in the barracks courtyard, I decided a light workout might do me the
most good. Burn off some nervous energy and maybe loosen up
my back muscles.

With the afternoon waning, most of the troops had cleared the
practice yard. Finding an open corner, I stood quietly for a moment, centering myself and asking Danu's blessing for a clear
mind and a bright blade.

Drawing my sword, I held it upright before me, hilt down and
point up. This moment always gave me a measure of peace, the
gathering pause before the flow of motion. Danu's spirit filled me
and I moved into the first and simplest of her sword forms.

Most children begin with her first form, Midnight. I'd learned
it younger than most, at five, clonking myself regularly with the
wooden practice blade. Salena had just given birth to Andi and
Uorsin had been raging through Ordnung in the hours since.

I'd heard his bellowing summons long before he burst into the
nursery. Though I remembered little else about that time—other
than feeling bereft, summarily dismissed from my mother's attention—that memory blazed bright in my mind. My father, who al-

ready frightened me more than a little, standing like a giant amidst the miniature toys of the nursery, his red-gold hair bright and blue eyes blazing.

"Curtsy for the High King," my nurse prompted, poking me with a shaking hand, but I'd stood frozen, clutching the doll my mother had just given me, so I would have a baby to play with, too.

"What is this?" Uorsin yanked the doll out of my hands and threw it across the room. With contempt, he took in the little table and tiny teacups I'd set out for my doll and me to share and dashed a big hand through them, sending china shards flying. "You are my heir, Ursula, whether I like it or not—and here you are fussing about with dolls and fripperies."

Even then I knew better than to let him see me cry. Mother told me to save the tears, tuck them away, and take them out later. They were for me, not for him. She did the same.

"Come with me, Daughter. It's high time you learned something useful, if you're to be a credit to the throne. Do you know how many people died so you can sit here in your pretty rooms playing with pretty things?"

"No, my King."

"Thousands. Tens of thousands. Are you worthy of their sacrifice? Of *my* sacrifice?"

"No?"

"No. But you can be. Your mother has a new daughter now and has cast you aside. I'm all you have. Understand?"

I did understand. Then and in the days since. He took me down to the practice yard and started teaching me how to hold a blade. When I tripped over my dress, he ridiculed me. When I fell, he made me get up on my own. My dolls and dresses were packed away, replaced with practice daggers and wooden swords, pants and shirts better suited for drilling.

While Uorsin continued to oversee my progress, another instructor took over my daily training. A priestess of Danu, Kaedrin taught me the twelve sword forms, starting with the Midnight form. My father's brute-force techniques would never serve me well, she said. Kaedrin showed me how to use the strength of my lower body, the speed and flexibility of my lighter physique.

The twelfth form—the most complicated and demanding—finishes at Noon pose, one that took me two full years to master. It's one of Danu's tests that she demands the most strenuous postures and intricate maneuvers of the blade after you've already executed eleven other forms and your muscles are weeping from exhaustion.

I held Noon pose, up on the toes of one foot, the other leg poised in front of me to protect and deflect with a snap kick, my sword high above and behind, ready to slice into Snake Strike, my other hand palm out, steady. Danu's salute.

My back sang with the strain, but I refused to drop before the count of twelve, as Kaedrin would have expected of me. As I lowered body and blade, my gaze snagged on the intent stare of the Dasnarian captain. He showed no sign of overt aggression, but I moved my sword and self into a defensive posture, ready. A slight smile twitched at his somber mouth. He raised his short blade—a wide, bevel-edged hunting knife—and held the flat against his forehead.

Then he strode away, leaving me wondering. Challenge or salute—or both?

But the sun declined in truth now, and even with the delayed hour of the formal feast, I would run out of time if I did not move quickly.

When I at last achieved the sanctuary of my rooms, Dafne awaited me in the outer chamber. "I'm out of leisure time for conversation, librarian," I told her. "Can it wait?"

She followed me into the bedchamber, watching as I unstrapped my sword and laid it on the bed. "Apparently I'm the one to wait—on you. You have no ladies to tend you and I have no chambers any longer. Ordnung is bursting at the seams, so you get to be stuck with me."

I took her measure. "You are no lady-in-waiting."

"Nor do you take much tending."

I snorted at that and ran a hand ruefully through my sweat-drenched hair, which I'd chopped short to better fit under my helm during the campaigns of the recent months. "I do, however, take a fair amount of work to be made suitably feminine for court."

She made a wry face. "As for that, one does not spend any amount of time with Princess Amelia without learning an extensive amount about grooming and beauty tricks."

"You'll be relieved to know I don't aspire to beauty—adequate to pass the King's muster is a high enough bar. If you can assist, I'd be grateful."

"I have hot water readied for a bath, if you care to start there."

"Make that eternally grateful."

She had arranged for wine and food, too, and I felt sufficiently drained to avail myself of hearty helpings of both before I stripped off the travel-worn fighting leathers and submerged in the tub.

"Too hot?" Dafne sent a maid off with my clothes for cleaning.

"Not at all. Could be hotter. No, don't trouble yourself to—"

"I had the maids heat extra." Dafne poured in enough to make me hiss, then turned to examine my bookshelf. "You struck me as someone who'd like the extremes. Plus, you might be in far better physical condition than I, but that ride from Windroven was grueling. I feel I could fall over and never get up again."

"You'll have to bathe next."

"I already did. Have a good soak. After you're set, I need to find myself something to wear tonight."

"If you're too tired, you could skip the feast."

She came round the end of the tub and gave me a long look. "I don't think I should. There's much to witness, wouldn't you say?"

I closed my eyes against her inquisitive stare. "Much, yes, that I cannot tell you. Except that they are Dasnarians as you surmised. Mercenaries."

"I did hear of the moratorium on leaving Ordnung."

Cracking an eye at her, I confirmed what her voice revealed.

"It won't apply to us. Once Uorsin is reassured of my loyalty, we'll be off to assist Amelia. Make no mistake of that. If she's not back at Windroven already."

"You and I both know full well she won't go to Windroven. Especially not with Erich there."

I sat up and soaped my hair. The short length made that infinitely easier. "Think you she'll take the girl to Annfwn first?"

"Yes. *Stella*," she added with emphasis, as if I needed reminding.

"Even if she leaves the girl to foster with Andi and her Tala brethren, continues to keep the girl a secret, she'll return with Astar. It would be best for all if she came here," I mused.

Dafne laughed. "You may be a brilliant strategist in a fight, Your Highness, but you do not predict your sisters as well as you might."

I ducked my head, enjoying the sting of the hot prickling on my scalp. Being in the field meant bathing in a lot of cold lakes. Necessary, but I'd come to savor the luxury of warm water. Dafne had the right of it—my sisters never seemed to do the predictable thing. Very likely Ami and her convict would chase the child's kidnappers into Annfwn. If they survived the quest—the alternative nearly unbearable to contemplate—she couldn't stay there with Astar. Even Andi and Ami would know that much. If not, I would inform them in no uncertain terms. They might think I'd prefer Astar away from Ordnung and no competition for the throne, but they should know me better.

All I really cared about was seeing the High Throne secured and the Twelve thriving in peace. Too many people had died to see that happen—including Salena. I'd die myself before I'd let their sacrifices be in vain. The populace depended on us, on me. I would not let the people down while breath remained in my body.

"Did you note the woman—the female Dasnarian?" I asked Dafne.

She looked grave and turned down her mouth. "I did. Though I did not have the opportunity to speak with her."

"Impressions?"

"I should say that I did not *try* to speak with her. She . . . unsettled me."

"Me also."

"That's even more unsettling. I thought nothing frightened you."

I laughed. "Fear is like pain—it alerts us to a danger. That woman strikes me as dangerous. Though my sources did not explain more than that."

"I can do some research," Dafne offered. "Not until tomorrow, but there should be some scrolls and texts on Dasnaria in the collection."

"That would be most appreciated. Everything we can know about them will be advantageous."

"There's one problem."

"Which is?"

"As you may or may not recall, the High King—at Andi's behest—removed the contents of Ordnung's library and sealed them in her rooms, part of the condition of her good behavior."

I should have remembered that. So much had happened in a short time. And I'd been away, alternately chasing my sisters, various armies, and rogue Tala. "Are they still there?"

"I believe so. The last time we visited, the doors were still locked and no one knew otherwise. I couldn't, of course, ask directly, and Andi naturally never returned, so . . ."

"Uorsin will not be best pleased to be reminded of such, if he has in fact forgotten."

"No. The books are as safe as they can be, if they're still there, but if we want to access that information . . ." She raised her brows at the problem.

"I'll mull it over and we'll discuss in the morning."

"Thank you." She nodded, then headed into the other room.

"Don't thank me until I've found a solution," I said, more to myself than to anyone else. I leaned back, sinking deeper into the water, willing my back to relax. If only I could take my own advice and rest tonight. The heat seeped into my bones, lulling, soporific.

"Do you only have pastel gowns?" Dafne called from the other room, startling me from the edge of sleep.

"Oh, for Danu's sake—you don't have to do that!" I yelled back, then made myself get out of the tub. If I stayed too long, the warmth would make me groggy, and I'd spent any napping time running Danu's forms. I felt the better for the exercise, however. If the Dasnarian thought he'd spied my secrets from observing my workout, he did not understand Danu's way. "I can pick out my own thrice-damned dress."

"Can you?" Dafne reemerged and gave me a dubious look. "Then why does your wardrobe consist of gowns that look as if they belong to Amelia?"

"Most likely because Amelia picked them. The idea was to reduce my harsh angles with softer colors and fabrics, as I recall." That had been before Amelia married Hugh and moved away, when I'd been intended as his fiancée. They'd fluttered about for months trying to make me into proper princess material, Ami and all the ladies. A well-intentioned effort. As Andi had remarked, however, all such attempts to adorn us was wasted with Amelia, the most beautiful woman in the Twelve Kingdoms, in the room. There's a reason you can't see the stars when the sun is in the sky. "I doubt I've worn even a third of them. If you want any, help yourself."

"I'd have to take up the hems and waistlines by a good eight inches," Dafne mused, holding a buttercup yellow silk confection, "but I might just do that. This color would be terrible on you."

"You *did* spend too much time with Ami."

Dafne made a face. "All knowledge is worth having. My education shall now benefit you. You are still heir to the High Throne, and tonight you should look it."

I finished toweling my hair dry. "I may not be as well read as you, librarian, but I've noticed that my father holds the throne just fine without a pretty outfit to wear."

"Oh?" Her voice came muffled from the other room, so I

pulled on a robe and followed her in. "Let me ask you this—why did the King wear his crown today?"

"He was holding court and he's entitled to."

"Though he rather famously detests wearing it and frequently holds court without."

True. Even I'd noted that his wearing the crown today meant no good for me, that he saw the situation as meriting a particular level of splendor. "I see your point."

She emerged from the wardrobe with a red velvet dress. "This. Have I ever seen you in it?"

I frowned at it. "It was for a Feast of Moranu. But even I know not to wear midwinter gowns in summer."

"This is the one. The claret will be perfect. And if you're wearing something the other ladies aren't, even better. You made an impression of one kind this afternoon. Tonight you'll underscore it. Today the noble weary warrior returned home. Tonight Her Royal Highness shines like a jewel in the heart of the Twelve. But first, let's trim your hair."

"My hair is already short." But I obediently sat, bemused by her take on things. Danu taught that no trick should be neglected in battle. If primping would help me hold my own, so be it. "There are those braid supplements my ladies use, to make it look like my hair is put up instead of just short."

"No offense, Your Highness, but it's obvious what the intent is. It fools nobody. Everyone knows your hair is short. By wearing the hairpieces, you look as if you're apologizing for it. You're extraordinary as you are. Your strength lies in being exactly that."

Fringes of my hair fell on the white robe as she worked, looking like spatterings of old blood, deep red like the gown.

"You've apparently given this a great deal of thought."

"Ami—Princess Amelia, I mean—and I discussed it. She learned a great deal on her journeys about disguise and appearance as a method of displaying and holding power."

"Ami—and you might as well call her that when we're alone,

since I know you do anyway—has made a science of being beautiful. If I stick with my strengths, that's not one."

"Where is your circlet?"

I swallowed a groan. "Don't make me wear that thing."

"Formal feast," she reminded me. "You'll wear the Heir's Circlet. Think of it as another kind of battle helm."

"Jewelry chest should be in the bottom of the wardrobe, if no one's moved it. You've been in my rooms longer than I have."

She went rummaging for it while I pulled on the gown and servants came in to light the lamps. The sunset chant went up from Glorianna's Temple, bidding the day good-bye. By rights we should hear the song for Moranu's moon, but none at Ordnung observed her worship, at least not openly. It had been interesting, those weeks at Windroven, to hear the rites for all three goddesses. Ami was intent on restoring the balance of the Three, though I didn't quite understand why. But if she thought I'd missed the changes she'd been making in Glorianna's church, then she didn't know me well enough.

More likely she counted on my not caring. Which, in all truth, I didn't. Glorianna, with her pretty pink roses and promises of life everlasting, had never held much significance for me. The High King had declared Glorianna's worship supreme in the Twelve Kingdoms, and as long as Ami's actions upheld his law, I had no problem with her machinations.

For myself, I privately looked to Danu, goddess of high noon and the bright blade. All the warriors did, no matter the time we spent bending a public knee to Glorianna.

With the great exception of Uorsin, who'd declared Glorianna's church preeminent, but rarely gave her worship more than lip service. He had his reasons, no doubt. Still, it had pierced my heart in an odd way at Windroven, the sound of the "Song of Danu" at high noon. Something I hadn't heard since the day Kaedrin left.

"Good goddesses," Dafne exclaimed. "You keep the crown jewels in the bottom of your wardrobe?"

She had the little chest open on a side table and she drew out a glittering strand of rubies.

"Salena's," I explained. "They came to me upon her death. I was ten and more interested in swords, so they meant little to me. Recall that we weren't to mention her name, or her very existence, for quite some time. I didn't know what to do with them and that seemed like a safe place. It's not as if anyone would steal them."

She held up a pair of teardrop ruby earrings. "If only because everyone has forgotten they exist." She handed them to me and also the coil of the necklace.

"I'm not wearing them."

"Yes, you are. Along with this matching bracelet and"—she made a frustrated noise as she untangled the gold circlet from a nest of silver chains—"your circlet, once I've had it polished. I'll be right back."

Amused to find myself obeying, I donned the glittering stones. In an odd way, the Lady Mailloux reminded me of Kaedrin. Perhaps just because my old teacher had come to mind this afternoon. But, for all her scholarly ways, Dafne had a style of direct confidence that Kaedrin shared.

It wasn't exactly true, what I'd said about stuffing the jewels away. There had been days in those lonely years after Salena died, before Andi grew up enough to leave the nursery, when I'd locked myself in these very bedchambers and pulled all the treasure out. I knew how every piece fastened, how to make the earrings pinch my ears the right amount so they wouldn't fall off.

Once, I'd put everything on at the same time and preened in front of the mirror. Until I observed how silly I looked, a too-thin girl, drowning in the cold glitter of a dead woman's unwilling gift.

"This is better." Dafne carried the flat gold circlet on a black cloth, then paused, eyes going bright. "Oh, Ursula, you look positively queenly. Sit and let me put this on. Then you can see."

She worked the circlet into my hair, fluffing and smoothing it. "There! I think you'll be pleased."

Because she wanted me to, I went to the mirror in the outer chamber. A lingering shadow of that memory made me half expect what I'd seen that long-ago day. Instead, the woman in the mirror took me by surprise. The way Dafne had shaped my hair, it lay close against my skull, coming to fine points in front of my ears, making my cheekbones look higher and sharper than usual. The gown and rubies matched my hair, surprisingly, within a few shades. The Heir's Circlet, which I'd received in a ceremony when I was twelve—the proudest and most awful day of my life— was a simple gold band that crossed my forehead; I'd worn it rarely over the years, but it looked fitting tonight. Bolstering.

"See, Your Highness?" Dafne sounded well pleased with herself. "Queenly."

I could only hope my father would be as pleased.

5

Dafne hastened away to tend to her own preparations, cutting short the questions that I had planned to ask her. Clearly the librarian acted on some agenda of her own. I did not believe for a moment that anyone had assigned her to be my lady's maid. No, she'd made herself my ally in this, which I supposed she'd declared on the journey here.

I would not turn down whatever help Danu sent.

Making my way to the feast hall, I took note of the surprised looks and recovered manners of those I passed along the way. I held myself to a stately pace—queenly—made easier by the odd sensation of the heavy skirts swirling around my legs. There was a knack to it, of staying inside the circular swing, so I wouldn't tangle in them or step on the hem.

The absence of my sword tickled at the back of my mind, nagging me with the sensation that I'd forgotten something. More than one court wit snickered that I slept with it, that I was naked without it, and other such bawdy insinuations that arise when a woman has no apparent lovers. In truth I felt exposed without a weapon. I'd learned early that I would never have my father's brute strength, but by Danu, I also knew a blade evened my odds considerably.

I never went completely unarmed, and I had good reasons for it. So I'd compromised by digging out a dagger with a ruby-jeweled hilt, elaborate enough to be considered more decorative than defensive. In the banquet hall, Uorsin sat already at the High Table— nothing unusual there, as he often arrived early, which allowed the courtiers the opportunity to circle by, share a toast, and discuss in conversation matters not suitable for either informal or formal court. However—gratingly unusual—the Dasnarian captain also sat at the table.

I made certain to give no sign that I'd taken note of it, as many sets of eyes scrutinized me to see if I would. The seating arrangement of the High Table echoed that of the throne room, with the King's chair—the largest and heaviest—at the center. My chair had always been to his right, Salena's long-abandoned chair to his left, with Andi's after that and Amelia's next to hers. When Ami married Hugh, a chair was added to her left. Now, though my seat remained empty for me, another chair had been added to the right of mine.

Uorsin's penchant for preserving empty seats for the missing members of the royal family had long caused logistical issues. The arrangement put Andi and Ami far out of speaking distance, even if the King didn't attend. My mother's empty chair felt like the bleeding hole of a wound that never healed over, and I secretly hated the sight of it. That distaste naturally extended itself to the spaces left by my sisters' more recent absences.

I thanked Danu for Uorsin's odd habit this time. If the captain had been sitting in any of our chairs, I might have had to kill him on the spot.

Instead, I managed to serenely make my way to my seat and did not even put a hand to my dagger when the Dasnarian captain stood and held the chair for me to sit. Uorsin, deep in conversation with Laurenne, the ambassador from Aerron, who stood on the other side of the table, her ancient face set in lines of disappointment, took no note. No one had assisted me in such a way that I could recall, though Hugh had unfailingly treated Amelia to the courtesy. I wondered if the Dasnarian would have done so had I not been wearing the gown.

No sense tipping him off that he'd surprised me—several times now—so I thanked him, with a queenly nod that should have pleased Dafne, and sat.

"We have not been properly introduced, Your Highness," the Dasnarian said, in that deep baritone. If a boulder could speak, it would sound thus. "I am Harlan, captain of the Vervaldr, at your service."

"Vervaldr?"

"It translates roughly as 'seawolves' in your Common Tongue."

"Not a very believable creature."

He lifted a shoulder. "But a vivid image, Your Highness."

I accepted the goblet of wine from a server, using the moment it offered to order my mind on how to speak to this man. Uorsin clearly held him in high regard, so I could not be openly rude. Nothing, however, required me to be especially friendly. Particularly after the incident at the gates.

"Your man challenged my right to enter Ordnung."

"Ah." His tone conveyed regret I doubted he felt. "My deepest apologies, Your Highness. We are still newcomers to your realm and you had not been in residence since we arrived. This afternoon you appeared somewhat unlike your formal portrait."

He said it with such blandness for the understatement, I nearly snorted. The paintings of my sisters and me had been done some years ago, and the artist had taken pains to exaggerate what little loveliness I possessed.

"I shall have him apologize formally, Your Highness, and will personally ensure you are not insulted again."

"Addressing me as 'Your Highness' can become cumbersome. You may call me Princess Ursula."

"The former has two fewer syllables than the latter." His face did not move from its stern lines, but I received the distinct impression of amusement from him—along with the recognition that he had surprised me indeed. He had to know that no one expected a man who looked like the side of a cliff to be articulate or clever.

"As you wish—either is appropriate," I replied, deliberately casting a bored-seeming eye over the assembly as I lent half an ear to Uorsin's conversation. Laurenne chewed on an old bone, ever unhappy with the crop tithes. Privately I didn't blame Aerron for their concerns. The southern drought continued, expanding the desert by leagues each year, eating into the fertile farmland. They weren't the only ones struggling to produce, however, and we needed every grain they owed and then some. From the tenor of her complaints, however, it sounded as if Uorsin had recently increased the tithe, which seemed most ill-advised.

"No dispensation for a less formal accolade in conversation, then, Your Highness? What do your men call you?"

I turned and met his eye, allowed a slight smile. "Captain."

He laughed, as resonant and booming as his voice. "Touché, Captain."

"Are we fencing, then?"

"I witnessed your practice today, as you know, Your Highness. It would be interesting indeed to match blades with you."

"And yet we are allies, it seems, so such a scenario is unlikely to occur."

"You do not spar?"

"Rarely. Only to teach." *Only with my Hawks.* "Are you asking for lessons, Captain Harlan of the Vervaldr?"

He grinned, and it belatedly occurred to me that the remark, which I'd intended as mildly insulting, had possibly sounded salacious.

"I enjoyed the display this afternoon and would be delighted for you to show me more." He leaned in as he spoke, dropping his voice to a soft rumble. I refused to look away, much as I wished to. Amelia would have had a charming quip to sweetly set him back on his heels. Andi wouldn't have gotten into the conversation in the first place. I settled for a steely glare. "Though you are equally beautiful this evening, Your Highness," he continued when I did not answer. "The gown and jewels become you. You exceed your portrait in every way and make an impressive Heir to the High Throne."

"Drumming up business for the future?" I inquired, using the excuse of taking up my wine goblet to tear my gaze away.

From the corner of my eye, I saw him refill his goblet and drink from it. He let the silence stretch a beat too long for courtesy. "Do you object to my profession, Your Highness?"

"On principle? Yes, I do. Loyalty should be earned, not purchased."

"Purchased loyalty is the only kind you can depend on."

"Until a better offer comes along."

"Isn't it the same, Your Highness, with your version of loyalty?"

"My *version*, Captain?"

"Yes. Loyalty simply means adherence to the law. In a contractual arrangement, the law is far more precise than in one governed by emotion."

"But emotion can't be bought."

"Aha—but it can be swayed. You imagine that more money would buy my loyalty, which it would not, by the way, as that's a serious ethical breech within my profession. With emotion, the next great orator, the more sympathetic cause, the wrenching tale of the martyr—all of these can redirect loyalty in a flash. And with no ethical prohibitions against it—after all, how can you deny a shining truth?—then the emotional contract is forfeit."

"And nothing trumps your contractual agreements?"

Something flickered in his gaze. "I wouldn't say 'nothing.' "

"Then what could—"

"Do not let that one draw you into a debate, Daughter." Uorsin set a heavy hand on my shoulder and Ambassador Laurenne strode away, anger in the line of her back. I'd missed the rest of their conversation, distracted by the Dasnarian. Though I would no doubt hear it from her directly. Multiple times. "He is as nimble with an argument as he is with a blade."

"Surely he is no match for you, my father and King."

He snorted but looked pleased. Then his gaze sharpened, hardened with hot fury, flicking from the earrings to the necklace to the bracelet. "Where did you get those?"

The accusation thudded into my gut and set my heart to racing. Forcing myself not to cringe away, I hardened my aching spine. "I've had them all along. It seemed appropriate to wear them tonight."

His face flushed scarlet, the metal of the wine goblet bending in the clutch of his fist. "They are witch's jewels."

I scrambled for a reply. But a shout and a blast of music grabbed his attention. With a series of calls like animals and birds, a group of young men tumbled across the floor. They wore costumes made of silk scarves, some reminiscent of feathers, others scales—all vivid colors not of any nature I knew. Their somersaulting leaps resolved them into a line and they bowed to us, to Uorsin and me evenly, executing the maneuver with an unusual flourish.

The youngest spun into a whirl and ended up directly before me. Beneath the table and before I'd known it, I'd drawn my dagger, the adrenaline shock ratcheting up the high alert triggered by angering my father. The lad, with hair so fair it gleamed nearly white, smiled angelically and presented me with a flower, one of Glorianna's pink roses.

I managed to take it, after sheathing the blade without anyone noticing.

No one except for the Dasnarian captain.

He said nothing, but he refilled my wine goblet, sliding it toward me. "A traditional gesture," he said, as the young man impressively reversed the spin that had brought him to me. "Our acrobats study the art to improve flexibility and speed—not for assassination."

Beside me, Uorsin had sat back to observe the show, clapping his hands as if nothing had transpired between us. I knew the confrontation was only postponed, and possibly would be worse for it. *Stupid, stupid, stupid.* I should have known he'd hate the sight of Salena's jewels. I had known it. That was why I'd kept them hidden away all these years. How had I lost sight of such basic common sense? I stared ahead blindly, trying to summon Danu's centering mantra, struggling not to show how my breath wanted to shudder in and out of my strained lungs, how cold sweat dripped down my spine.

The goblet nudged against my hand, which was curled around the posy, crushing the stem.

"Drink, Your Highness. 'Tis but a fragile blossom that's done you no harm. It was intended as a pleasure to you."

I stared at the Dasnarian, feeling somewhat wild, desperate to leave the table and my father's presence, knowing I could not. Wishing that Amelia would appear to distract and appease him. Or that Andi would be on the other side of him, rolling her eyes. Captain Harlan returned my gaze steadily, calming somehow, something of sympathy in it. His eyes were not blue like those of the others, but a very light gray.

Very nearly I told him to save his pity. But that would be admitting there was a reason to feel sorry for me. Instead I took the goblet and drank, fortifying myself for later.

The feast lasted several hours, with course after course arriving once the acrobats finished. Madeline had outdone herself. I tasted none of it, using up every ounce of self-control to keep from crumbling. No matter how many years intervened, no matter how accustomed to command under dire circumstances I became, in the face of my father's displeasure I somehow always reverted to my five-year-old self, as brittle as the fragile toy teacups.

"Attend me, Daughter." Uorsin delivered the command at last, heaving himself up from the table. Captain Harlan came to his feet with remarkable agility, holding my chair as I arose. I ignored the gesture, especially when Uorsin made a sound of disgust. His son would not have elicited such chivalry.

"Your Highness." The Dasnarian touched my sleeve as I passed him, his gaze serious. "Good luck."

He said it as one warrior might to another, as she headed into battle, taking me aback. With a solemn nod, he lifted one hand, tipping two fingers back against his forehead, much as he'd done with the flat of the blade that afternoon.

"Good night," I told him. And I strode away as quickly as I could, to face my father.

He went for his private rooms, naturally, sending his attendants scattering so we would be alone. To my knowledge, neither Andi nor Amelia had been inside them. I had gone to lengths to prevent that. Normally he conducted family conversations in his private study.

With me, however, it had always been his bedchamber. An intimacy he shared with very few.

Unlike mine, Uorsin's private chambers were not divided into smaller spaces. Located in the dead center of the castle, the room had no windows and was sealed with three sets of doors. The stone walls, an arm's length thick, allowed no sound through. Once closed, the room became as impregnable as any prison.

The King's final fortress.

"So." He poured wine for us both. A picture of careless indolence. He handed me a goblet, face weary as he studied mine. "Speak to me truly, Daughter. Do you challenge me for the throne? Wearing the Heir's Circlet? Flaunting the queen's jewels in my face? Must I look for betrayal from even you?"

The dredging sorrow in his voice made my heart ache. Few people knew him as I did, understood how lonely holding the High Throne could be. He might be difficult to deal with at times, but he carried a heavy burden. He was everything I aspired to be, my King, my father, my hero. I loved him despite everything.

"No, my King," I answered, wanting to say more, knowing too many of the wrong words would only push him back into rage.

"No? No, you did not wear the circlet or your mother's witch jewels?"

"I did not wear them as a challenge or to flaunt them."

He waited to see if I would say more. Another technique. When I was younger, the expectation, the stinging silence, would get to me and I would inevitably blurt out something more. More for him to chew on. Eventually I learned to hold my tongue and I held it with all my might.

"I know why you wore them." He clasped my shoulder, eyes sympathetic. "You fear for your position as heir. Your ambition is understandable. I've groomed you for this all your life. It bothers you that I intend to give it to my grandson instead."

"My King—the throne is yours to decide. I wish only to honor it and you."

"Yes." He sat, heaving a sigh, and pulled off the crown, tossed it on the table, where it clattered against the wood. "It's a heavy burden, that crown. Have you ever wondered why I never let them soften the sharp edges, make it more comfortable?"

"You told me before it was so that you wouldn't forget what you suffered to bring peace and so that the weight of rule would never become too comfortable."

Uorsin eyed me. "Did I say as much?" He huffed, sounding like the bear he was named for. "Then you understand why I must make this choice. I cannot have someone unworthy as my heir. Someone who is not strong and clearheaded enough to remain loyal."

"I am loyal."

"A pretty lie, I'm afraid. You've been conspiring. I see it all clearly. You plot with your sister and those demons she consorts with to overthrow me. That's why you let her go, why you did not bring her back. Did you murder your nephew, too? Perhaps my beloved Amelia, as well? Do they even now lie moldering in the ground, in some pauper's grave, victims of your overweening ambition?"

Each accusation hit me in the gut, blows as painful as if they had been physical punches, all the worse that he spoke in such a coaxing, reasonable tone, the sorrow of betrayal in his visage. Each stole more of my breath, forcing my heart to labor.

How had it come to this—and why hadn't I seen it? It made a horrible sense, the way he put it together. The same way he'd struck at my sisters. An invidious logic I could not argue against. I had no proof otherwise. Other than that I would never be disloyal at all, let alone in such heinous ways.

Purchased loyalty is the only kind you can depend on. Uorsin must believe that. That was why he'd sent me to Branli, on what I now clearly saw as a fool's errand. There were no other routes into Annfwn not blockaded by Andi's wall. But Uorsin thought I conspired with her, lied about the magical barrier. If I'd returned with a way in, or with my nephew, my loyalty would not be in doubt. I'd known I'd face this, but not to this extent. No wonder he'd contracted with the mercenaries.

"You do not deny it, Daughter?" The question came so softly I almost didn't catch it.

"None of that is true." I kept my voice as clear and emotionless as I could. Disaster if I wept. So weak. So female. *Put the tears away.* "I cannot prove my innocence, except by bringing Amelia and Astar to you, safe and unharmed."

"Something you could have done already, had you wished to." He poured more wine, only for himself this time, and drank. "I thought I'd done my best by you, Ursula, my namesake. I taught you everything I knew. Perhaps I've been hard on you, but everything I've done, I did for the High Throne and the peace it stands for. I thought you understood that, believed in it, too. Now I have to wonder—do you want the throne so badly that you deprived me of another heir?"

My spine ached and my gut churned far too much to risk drinking the wine. I had to find a way to get through to him. "My King. There is something you need to know before you judge me. A secret I dared not reveal before the court without your permission. May I tell you?"

He sat silent as I fretted. Finally he groaned, as if in physical pain. "Tell me."

"Father, Amelia bore twins—a girl and a boy. At first we thought the girl did not survive the night, so I kept her birth a secret. The boy child was healthy and strong and the Twelve did not need the additional grief when there was so much to celebrate. Amelia, once recovered from childbirth, however, discovered that we had been fooled by a . . . simulacrum and that the girl is still alive, but taken by Tala rebels."

As I spoke the story, in the stale silence of Uorsin's bedchamber, pinned under his penetrating gaze, it sounded more and more absurd to my own ears. I would not have believed myself. I wrestled down the desire to say more, to fill that deadly quiet, to beg my father to believe me. My nails, even as short as they were, dug sharp into my palms.

"And *how*"—Uorsin's voice dripped contempt—"did pretty little Ami see through a trick that fooled you?"

I certainly could not say that it had been a magical vision from our mother. Or that Amelia's ex-convict, Tala half-breed lover had assisted. Danu taught that the greatest strength came from taking responsibility on yourself. "I made a mistake," I replied.

He rose and came around the table. Not raging. Deadly quiet. "Look at me and say that again."

I raised my chin and looked my King and father in the eye. "I made a mistake."

His fist blasted my cheek with pain. A hard enough blow that my brain darkened a moment, swimming to stay alert. Fortunately it had been a fairly casual backhand. Far from the first he'd dealt me over the years. Not that it made them sting any less. Though no more than the sting of admitting my failure to him.

"You made a mistake."

"Yes, my King." I clenched my teeth against saying more, and in case he chose to strike me again. A censure I richly deserved. *I saw my dead niece, but it was magic. Ami was beside herself with grief and I couldn't say no to her. I stood by while she opened the tomb, saw for myself that the blanket held only twigs and leaves. I could not take her son from her, after all that, so I let her go into the Wild Lands with him.*

Now a greater mistake stared me in the face. I should not have come back here, to face the King. This rage and betrayal went deeper than ever before. I cringed inside, where he couldn't see, and hoped to survive to prove myself to him. My eye socket throbbed, but I dared not put a hand up to touch it.

Uorsin stared at me, stark points of ice blue in bloodshot pools. "Where is Amelia now?"

"She chases the kidnappers to retrieve her daughter."

"My pretty Amelia. You would have me believe that she's raced off into the Wild Lands, burdened with an infant, to fight rebels all by herself."

I hardly would have believed it myself. But Ami had grown up in the last half a year. Hugh's death had, instead of crushing her, polished her to a high sheen. She had a certain indomitability about her these days. A surety of purpose she'd lacked before. One I envied at this moment, as I wondered where my own had gone. Uorsin glowered, expecting an answer this time.

"She took her personal guard with her, including an expert huntsman and tracker. I believe her to be well protected."

"Yet, you ask permission to go after her."

Would he let me go? "To ensure their safety, yes." *To prove myself to you.*

"A safety that did not concern you before this."

"I knew you would be expecting word. That your army remained poised to intercept Erich. I knew you needed to know, from me, that Astar was not in jeopardy of being taken by Erich's forces."

"I think you'd say anything to have the throne for yourself."

Desperation gnawed at me. "Then disinherit me. Send me off in exile. Have me executed. The High Throne requires a worthy heir. If I don't meet your measure"—I sucked in my stomach muscles to steel my breath so it would not waver—"then I don't deserve to be your daughter."

"Empty words." Uorsin stood, walked away, and emptied the flagon of wine into his goblet. "Have you more to explain why you abandoned your mission in Branli and somehow ended up at Windroven?"

"I sent you a missive with my report."

"Tell me again," he said, tone deceptively soft as he paced around the room.

"We spent months following the rumors, looking for the other route into Annfwn." It hadn't been an easy task, combing the pubs and chatting up shepherds, ferreting out anyone who'd heard the old stories of pathways over the mountains into paradise—without directly inquiring. "I kept a list of the roads and paths we followed, some no better than deer trails. None led us anywhere but deeper into the Wild Lands."

"Did you reach the sea?"

"No." I'd tried, hadn't I? I'd tried everything I could think of to bring him the answer he wanted, not letting myself contemplate the eventual impact on Andi, should I succeed.

"Then you did not go far enough."

We had gone far enough, and found ourselves circling back on our own tails. More Tala magic. When we'd stood at Odfell's Pass and Andi gave her demonstration, though I had seen that the land beyond the barrier bloomed with summer, my Hawks later told me that they had seen only snow, that she and the Tala had disappeared from sight on the other side. Perhaps she hid the barrier from me also now, reflecting us away as if from a mirror. I'd tried to explain this to Uorsin once before, but he'd flown into such a rage that I knew better than to say it again. I'd hoped he'd calm over the ensuing months.

Instead he'd only gotten worse. *Danu give me strength to know what to do.*

"We did not go far enough," I agreed, aching with the failure of that, too.

"And then your sister sent for you and you threw all else aside to go to her."

How to tread this path? "I knew you placed a high value on securing her child, should it be born a boy. I sought to serve you in that, Father."

The sound of the flagon hitting the wall clanged like a broken bell against my nerves.

"But. You. Failed." The King bit down on each word. Each as bad as the physical blow.

"Yes, my King." I thought a tear escaped me, but it was blood, I realized, leaking from my forehead where the Heir's Circlet had cut in. I put up a hand to wipe it away.

"Give me that."

Pulling off the circlet, with a sense of the inevitability, I placed the thin gold band in his palm and for a long and dreadful moment faced him, forcing myself to hold steady.

"Allow me to correct my error, my King. I'll go and find them, bring them here. Or die trying."

"You shall not wiggle free so easily, escaping the consequences of thwarting me as your mother did. You need not retrieve my grandson, because Amelia will bring him here—if she truly lives and your tale is true. She, at least, dotes on her old father and will want to see me happy. You denied me one heir. I won't stand by and let you do it again."

His words hung between us, the scorching accusation that I deprived him of the happiness he sought. He left it open, waiting for me to offer what I knew he most wanted.

I couldn't. I never would again.

"You will remain inside these walls. See that your behavior is beyond reproach. Formal court in the morning."

6

I took the shortcut back to my rooms, the night-blooming flowers filling the air with sweet scent, as if Ordnung had not become my prison. At least the corridors were empty, with none to witness my humiliation. In my rooms, I removed the thrice-damned rubies and put them carefully away. The gown took some doing, but I struggled out of it. Further proof that Lady Mailloux made a terrible lady's maid, as she should have waited up for me.

Thank Danu she hadn't.

Her absence gave me time to clean the blood from my face and gown, though the deep color barely showed it. Something to remember.

Knowing I'd never sleep, I changed into a set of soft leathers and strapped on my sword. The familiar weight grounded me, settled some of the roiling energy that came of being stymied at every turn. Funny that I'd never felt truly trapped until this moment. All along I'd thought the sense of being surrounded would ease off, that we'd ride out soon. Now I needed to move, to burn off this near-desperate urge to escape. I headed for the courtyard off the arcade. No one would go that way and I could work off some of this emotion until I felt centered enough to form a plan.

Danu's priestesses kept few temples, and those were mainly on the mountain peaks. Unlike Glorianna—or Moranu, I supposed, though I didn't know—Danu had few prescribed prayers or rituals. The sword forms and her other martial exercises were the core of her teachings. Work the body to temper the spirit. With Glorianna, a worshiper could mouth the words and be smiled upon. Danu required sweat and blood.

Though my body protested, I started the Midnight form. My knees groaned from riding since before dawn, the earlier workout, and then sitting through the banquet. If I exhausted myself enough, I might be able to stop thinking, perhaps even sleep a few hours.

Defend, parry, attack, retreat, regroup.

The situation with my father was a battle like any other. I had defended myself, parried his attack, and retreated. I simply needed to regroup. He'd been angry about the jewels—understandable—off-balance with worry over Amelia, and more than a little drunk. I should have realized he'd see my wearing of Salena's jewels as aligning myself with her, which had come to mean with Andi, Rayfe, and the Tala also. The last year had tried us all. Uorsin had poured his life into creating and preserving the peace of the Twelve Kingdoms. Of course he could allow no threat to it.

If he believed I'd done as he thought, then I'd deserved his censure.

I needed only prove myself.

I couldn't let myself dwell on the more sinister implications, that my father's behavior had gone from angry and erratic to something I hesitated to put words to. What would become of the Twelve Kingdoms if the High King was . . . No, I wouldn't think of it. Taking the circlet might not mean I was no longer heir. He hadn't stripped me of it publicly. And surely he'd only meant for me to stay close to Ordnung for the moment, not forever. Tomorrow would be better. We'd both be calmer, clear of thought, and we'd discuss. Even when he'd been most unhappy with me, we'd always managed to meet mind to mind, for the good of the Twelve. We'd do so again.

Danu make it so.

My blade whistled through the Whirlwind into Heron Strikes, and my back grabbed hard. I swallowed the cry of pain easily enough but had to pause, half hunched over like an old granny, catching my breath and waiting for the thrice-damned muscles to let go.

"Here, now." That baritone rumbled, and a warm hand settled on the small of my back.

I started to spin and turn, hissing at the spike of agonized resistance. "Danu take it!"

"You'll get nowhere forcing it." The merc captain said. "Hold still a moment."

He worked a series of knuckles into a spot lower down on my hips.

"That's not where it hurts."

"Hush. I'm helping you."

"I didn't ask for help."

He chuckled, warm and low. "Believe me, Your Highness, I'm fully aware of that. However, you need my help, lest you add yourself to the statues that decorate this courtyard."

I didn't reply to that. The spasm would have let go eventually. They always did. But whatever magic he did with his hands—pressing into places that felt bruised and somehow extracting the soreness as he withdrew—worked far faster. If he declined to take advantage of my momentary injury and instead elected to put me back in fighting form, so be it. And, oh, Danu, the release from that spasm felt sweeter than a summer's day.

Straightening, I moved tentatively, rather astounded that my body responded so easily. I turned to face the Dasnarian, using the movement to step outside of weapon's reach. He noted that, of course, eyes glinting colorlessly in the moonlight.

"Better?"

I nodded. "Yes. My gratitude. What technique is that?"

"We call it *lifdrengrr,* giving health to the warrior. Excellent tools for quickly returning a comrade back into the fight."

Rolling my shoulders, I agreed. Only a few twinges. I could work through those.

"It is not, however, a long-term fix. You should have your healers tend to you."

"I'm fine. And why are you here? It's the middle of the night."

"I could ask the same of you."

"You have no business asking me anything. This is a private courtyard. You may have the run of the castle, but not the family wing." I pretended to test my sword arm, which gained me another half step of distance. Danu, the man had a long reach on him. "Are you a spy, Captain?"

"I didn't get all of it."

"What?"

"Your back. There's a catch between your shoulder blades still. I can see it when you move."

"It wouldn't stop me from taking you down. Why are you here?"

"As much as I'd love to spar with you, Your Highness, I'd prefer to test myself against you when you're fully recovered. Let me get that catch."

"I'm fine," I repeated, willing it to be true, though the ache he'd spotted sent tendrils of ominous pain up my neck and down my spine. My back sometimes bothered me after long training sessions, but it had gotten worse in the last year. I hated to think it might be age. "I'm going to ask a third time, and if you don't have a satisfying answer, I'm signaling the guards. Why are you here?"

"If I give you an honest answer, will you let me adjust your spine?"

"Why are you so determined on that?"

"Maybe I just want to put my hands on you again, Princess Ursula."

"I'm not certain what game you're playing with me, Captain,

but if you mean to be flirtatious, I can warn you right now that your efforts would be wasted on me."

"I followed you."

So he was indeed a spy. I should be congratulating myself for seeing through him, instead of having to ignore the stain of disappointment. "For what gain?"

Shrugging those big shoulders, he tucked his thumbs in his sword belt. "I had concerns about your meeting with High King Uorsin. So I waited until you went to your chambers. Before I knew it, you'd emerged again and come here."

"And you stayed to watch."

His teeth flashed white in the glow of the moon. "Yes."

"To gain what?"

"That's the second time you've implied I'm motivated entirely by gain."

"You're a mercenary. And from a race of slavers."

"Why do you say that?"

"Do you deny the truth of it?"

He didn't respond to that immediately. "I answered your question honestly. Time to pay the price."

My body sang to alert when he started toward me, and in a flash I'd pressed the tip of my blade to the hollow of his throat. "Perhaps it is you who will pay the price."

"You are blazingly fast," he said in an admiring tone. He seemed entirely unperturbed. Hadn't even twitched a hand toward the hilt of his own sword. "Even with a stove-up spine, you're faster than any fighter I've seen."

"Tell me why I shouldn't slit your throat this moment."

"To begin, the contract with the High King expressly forbids my execution, even at the hands of a disgruntled member of the ruling family—we've learned lessons there. Plus, I've given you no real cause and your honor won't let you slay me in cold blood. Besides which, by paying the price I meant that you'll let me fix your back."

"You're obsessed with this notion."

"I tend toward single-mindedness. The trait has generally been an asset. Rarely has anyone wanted to kill me for it." He returned my gaze calmly, eyes clear as the moonlight glinting off the blade at his throat.

What in Danu was I doing?

I lowered the tip of the blade, keeping my guard up in case he used that reach to lunge for me. "My apologies. I have been . . . on edge."

"Understandable, given what transpired today. Will you sheathe your blade, Your Highness? This fix requires your hands free."

If the cramp that had ascended to burn between my shoulder blades hadn't been growing worse, I would have refused. I slid the blade home in her sheath, noting that he relaxed fractionally. Not so calm as he'd like me to believe, then. Made him more human.

"Fold your arms over your chest, palms on the opposite shoulders. Yes, like that." He moved behind me and I turned, tracking his movement. "Your Highness," he sighed, impatience tingeing the tone. "I have to be behind you. Trust me. I'm not going to harm the Heir to the High Throne in the heart of Ordnung."

Maybe not the heir. Not anymore. The grief and failure of it rode between my shoulder blades, a physical pain that threatened to override all else. But I would not be the one to give voice to it until Uorsin did. No one would notice if I didn't wear the circlet, since I rarely had. Still, I'd keep up a strong front with the mercenary. "If only because your contract forbids it."

"Which it does. We are here as allies, not enemies. You have your version of honor. I have mine."

I would have snorted at that, but he wrapped those bearlike arms around me and I tensed to break the hold.

"Relax, Ursula." His deep voice rumbled through me. "I'm helping you." He crossed his arms over mine, locking one hand around his other wrist and pulling me back against his broad chest. Easily twice as wide as mine. And strong as an ox. If we ever fought in truth, I'd have to avoid being caught in any grip such as this or I'd never wrestle free.

"Drop your head back on my shoulder." His soft laugh against my back reminded me of far-off thunder. "Which means to relax. Surely you know how."

Annoyed with him, I rocked my head on my neck, cracking the bones there, then dropped my head onto his shoulder. Moranu's moon sailed silver overhead.

"Breathe deep. In and out." His dark voice soothed something in me, and leaning against the unshakably strong pillar of his body, I was able to exhale some of the fear and worry.

With a snap of his shoulders, he lifted me off my feet, my spine releasing with an audible pop and a sharp "Ah!" from me. The shock rattled my brain, making my head swim a moment, and though he'd set me on my feet again, he held me until I steadied.

"Wow," I said on a long breath.

"Did that get it?"

"Yes." I started to move away, but his arms tightened.

"Because I can do it again, if not. As often as you like." He spoke the words quietly into my ear, his breath feathering warm across my cheek, clearly intending the double entendre. Something buried deep in me warmed to it.

I twisted one hand up in a knife palm, breaking the hold and stepping free, pleased with how smoothly it went. Mostly because I surprised him. I doubted I could pull that off if he'd really locked down his superior upper-arm strength. He turned the surprise around by snaking a hand around my elbow, keeping me from clearing him entirely.

"Not so fast. I—" He broke off, narrowing his eyes and tugging me closer. "You're hurt."

"No." *Thrice-damn it.* I'd forgotten to ice the forming bruise, hadn't expected anyone to see me. I pulled back, but his grip held this time. "I accidentally hit myself with the sword hilt in practice just now. It's nothing."

His pale eyes glittered. "I bet you haven't hit yourself with your own sword since you were ten years old."

Eight, actually. "Let me go, Captain."

He did. "I was right to be concerned, I see. The High King struck you in his anger."

I hated, hated, hated, that he'd glimpsed that. That I'd forgotten the evidence would be visible. "You have no need to give a thought to me. Or to what transpires between me and the High King. You were hired to do a job. Presumably that contract of yours, the one you rely on to inform your honor and ethics, details exactly what is your concern. I suggest you stick to that."

"I'm surprised you defend him."

I had no choice. My sacred duty to defend the High Throne and the man who embodied it. "You dance perilously close to treason, Dasnarian. I'm sure your contract precludes that."

"You seem uncommonly interested in the Vervaldr contract, Your Highness. Perhaps you should review it yourself." Though his deep voice remained mild, irritation spiked in it. Good to know he could be unbalanced.

"Already on my agenda for tomorrow."

"No doubt."

We stood there, squared off, like opponents before a bout. He didn't move to leave and I was unwilling to break first. The moment spun out, and by the glimmer of amusement crossing his face, I knew he'd keep me there all night, out of sheer stubbornness.

"Good night, Captain."

He swept me a bow, a grim smile cracking the façade. "Sleep well, Your Highness."

I left without bothering to tell him I never did.

7

After staring at the fire for hours, drinking the wine that never did make me sleepy, I finally napped fitfully in my old armchair. Thoughts fragmented into dreams, jumbling themselves together, so that when I woke to the sunrise call from Glorianna's Temple, it took me a bit to sort out what had been real and what had not.

The encounter with the Dasnarian captain seemed like a surreal memory. I'd have put that down to a dream except I didn't think even Moranu would send such a bizarre story and my back felt amazingly better. Looser than in weeks.

"You *do* sleep with your sword," Dafne commented and handed me a mug of hot tea.

Keeping my face turned away from her—though I'd detoured to the deep cellars and grabbed some ice before turning in—I gulped the tea, hoping the burn would clear my head. I hadn't taken off my sword or the practice leathers when I'd collapsed in the chair a few hours ago, waiting for the wine to take effect.

"You don't need to wait on me. I'm used to doing for myself." I sounded grumpy, but better that than . . . what? However I'd been that made the mercenary think he should be *concerned.*

Though in the cold light of day, it seemed clear that had been a ruse to cover his spying. What had he hoped to learn by following me?

"I know from traveling with you that you like to have hot tea before you work out with your Hawks," she returned mildly. "It's no trouble, as I was getting my own, too."

"After our morning warm-up, I'll see if I can't look into getting at the books before formal court convenes. See me there if you haven't heard from me."

Deciding I hadn't been wearing these clothes all *that* long, certainly not the kind of wear my traveling leathers and fighting gear had seen, I gulped the tea and headed directly to the practice yard. By cutting through the arcade and the attached courtyard— banishing the uneasy body memory of the mercenary's strong arms holding me against him—I managed to avoid running into anyone on the way.

Several of the Hawks were already running warm-ups. Jepp ran the twelve sword forms, well into the third. The mercenary captain was also there, setting a squad of his men to sparring with heavy broadswords that matched their bulk. If he thought to intimidate us with the display of brute force, he was deeply mistaken.

"Marskal!" I called out as I approached.

He switched from exercise to a salute so crisply it impressed me. He always paid attention, which was why I'd made him my lieutenant.

"How about a bit of boxing to start the day?"

"Always a pleasure, Captain." His gaze flicked to my swollen cheek and the bluing bruise under my eye, but he said nothing. He'd seen such before and knew better than to comment. They all did. The King was above the law.

We squared off. Over Marskal's shoulder, I noted the mercenary captain positioning himself to keep an eye on both his men and me, and I found myself mentally measuring the slighter Marskal against the Dasnarian's bulk. Good preparation, I told myself, as Marskal and I struck and parried, to imagine how he'd use that power and reach to overcome this guard or that maneuver. After a few exchanges, I dropped my guard and Marskal's fist flew through, glancing off my cheekbone exactly as I'd intended.

The Hawks watching hooted with glee, congratulating Marskal on getting one past me. I clapped a hand over my eye, making a convincing show of pained chagrin. It stung like Danu's tits—far more than I'd expected, which meant Uorsin had really walloped me one—so that made it easy for me to act dizzied by it.

I straightened and gave Marskal the Hawks' salute, fist over heart. He returned it, expression somber. "That's my cue to take it easy today," I said, then took the excuse to signal them to a quiet corner, indicating a meeting. The ones that hadn't been watching the match swiftly convened, gathering around me in a tight knot, Marskal and Jepp front and center. I'd lost a number of the Hawks on our campaigns to relieve the siege at Windroven and attempting to take Odfell's Pass. We'd barely been at Ordnung long enough since to hold trials for new members. I hoped we wouldn't be here long enough this time, either, much as I'd like to build up our forces again. Recruitment and training took time we didn't have.

Only the very best could become one of my Hawks. Something we all were proud of.

I cut to the bare bones of our situation. "Settle in." I hesitated to put it too strongly, as they'd hate the sense of confinement as much as I. Still, they were mine and what applied to me included them. "No one is to leave Ordnung."

They all nodded, with expressions of dawning frustration that echoed my own. Few of them were privy to what had actually occurred at Windroven, but none of them liked that Ami and her son were unaccounted for. Smart warriors all, they'd no doubt pieced together quite a bit.

"Jepp—any messages from your scouts?" I asked, so they'd all hear the answer.

Jepp shook her head. "Nothing, Captain. You'll be the first to know."

I nodded. Even knowing that was what she would say didn't ease the sting of it. Not for any of us, judging by the restless shifting of my Hawks.

"There's no official word on Princess Amelia, either."

"It could be," Jepp tendered, "that I could get better unofficial word than the people I sent."

Since Jepp was the craftiest scout I'd had the pleasure to know, I believed that. And was tempted.

"Yeah—what if someone accidentally slipped out?" one of the other scouts asked, exchanging looks with Jepp.

"That person could not get caught." I tipped my head toward the mercenaries, grunting and clattering broadswords ostentatiously. All I needed was to give Uorsin any fuel to feed his suspicions. He might not remember about books, but he knew soldiers and he'd be alert to the movements of my elite crew.

Jepp's smile sharpened. All of my Hawks possessed a keen love of danger that bordered on recklessness. "Who said anything about getting caught?"

"Come up with some options. Run them by me. In the meantime, stay sharp."

The Hawks returned to their workouts, breaking into groups to spar or run forms and strengthening exercises. Wary of not asking too much of my back again, I resisted Jepp's invitation to run the twelve sword forms. A decision I immediately regretted when—no surprise—the mercenary captain strode over. His keen gaze went to my throbbing cheek. "Mission accomplished?"

"I check in with my Hawks every morning, as a rule, so yes."

"You know that's not what I meant."

"Do I? Perhaps it's the language barrier. Though you speak our Common Tongue passably well."

"Do you routinely ask your Hawks to cover for you in this way? They should be defending you."

"They do. That, mercenary, is true loyalty. The kind that's not for sale." I more than halfway hoped he'd take that bait, but he declined.

"How's the back?"

"I'm feeling very well this morning. Fully recovered from my journeys."

"I'd like to have a word with you before court convenes."

"You're having one now." As close as he stood, I had to tip my chin up to hold his gaze. Taller than Uorsin, even. "Well?" I prompted.

He assessed me, picking his approach. "Last night—"

"We sat next to each other at the feast, yes. The Dasnarian acrobats were most diverting, indeed. Ordnung appreciates your generosity in treating us to the display."

A muscle bulged at the corner of his jaw. He shifted tactics. "Indeed, Your Highness. You also mentioned that you don't spar unless teaching, yet you did with your man this morning."

Isn't that what we're doing now? I waited without reply.

"I renew my invitation." The mercenary deliberately left it open, baiting me this time.

"I reiterate my disinterest."

Nearby, Jepp ran Danu's Dance, the graceful movements soothing and even meditative. The form is mellower in style and physical demand than her sword forms. In fact, some court ladies have been known to perform it at her midsummer festival, entirely as a dance, usually holding lit candles in the palms of their hands rather than the slim, two-edged knives we used in combat.

"A pretty dance, that," he commented.

"Yes. That pretty dance would cut you to ribbons." I indicated the paired fighting daggers I wore at my hips.

His expression sharpened with interest and challenge. "Show me."

"Why should we share our secrets?"

"We are your allies, Princess Ursula. Not the enemy. Even you admitted to that. Your guard is the best I've seen among your people, and that's just in drills. The better we understand each other's skills, the better we can mesh our forces when battle comes."

"There may not be a battle."

He grinned then. "There's always a battle. The only question is when and what kind. Spar with me. Show me what those delicate, sharp edges can do."

"I told you, I don't spar with anyone but my Hawks."

"Ah." He nodded sagely. "Then you cannot back up your claims. I understand."

The Hawks near enough to hear growled low in protest. Now I'd have to let them prove themselves. The mercenary knew it, too, a smug curve to his masculine mouth.

"All right, then. Your pick against mine."

He opened his mouth to protest, then closed it and shook his head. "As you will, Your Highness. Blagor! To me."

One of the men with the broadswords bowed out of his match and jogged over. A big guy, though not as big as his captain. And slow with it. Perfect. I called Jepp and she coiled to a halt, her face lighting in delight. Good enough. I cocked my head and she came forward, borrowing my knives.

"First blood?" I asked the captain and his man both.

The man looked Jepp over with an incredulous expression. "Begging your pardon, Your Highness, but I'll crush her with the first blow."

One of the Hawks barked out a laugh, and Jepp, a head shorter than I and slender with it, grinned easily.

"You'd have to hit her first. And out here I'm just Captain. If you're both agreed, square off."

We cleared a circle around them, mercenaries and Hawks alike gathering in interest.

"You didn't tell *me* I could call you Captain," the mercenary said quietly, folding those massive arms to watch.

"Maybe I like it when you call me Your Highness."

He made a sound that could have been a laugh and it occurred to me that I'd once again said something that might have come across wrong. Something about him. The fighters engaged. With an impressive bellow that would have startled a less experienced fighter, the mercenary swung his broadsword in a skull-shattering sweep. Jepp, in an agile blur of speed, spiraled in and under the arc of it, spinning out to dance away again. He charged at her.

"Hold!" I called, which he did, with admirable discipline.

"Why did you stop the match?" Captain Harlan demanded.

I raised my eyebrows. "First blood."

The fellow with the broadsword scowled, then looked down to see the bright red stain seeping through the sliced leather of his shirt. The expression of consternation on both men's faces was a sight to behold, and I burst out in a belly laugh. The mercenary captain glowered at me, but the corners of his lips twitched. "I concede. You've had your fun with us. A nice trick, but she couldn't do it twice."

"Jepp?"

She gave me a crisp nod and they squared off again. Her opponent took her measure more carefully this time, and they circled each other warily, he staying well back from her.

"Do the Dasnarian women not fight?" I asked the captain.

"No," he replied in an absent tone, attention focused on Jepp. "Such a waste."

"The women might agree. The men don't think so."

His man moved faster this time, which was to say, not fast at all. He thought to take Jepp by surprise, wielding the broadsword in a more intricate maneuver. She sidestepped it, flickered in and out, leaving a bleeding slice down his arm. The Hawks hooted in approval and the bulk of the mercenaries looked impressed. A few exchanged coins.

"That was, if anything, easier for her that time."

"Not true," I countered, signaling my Hawks that they should disperse. "She showed off less. Your man didn't underestimate her a second time, which partially redeems his judgment."

Jepp gave me a cheeky grin of agreement as she came over to return my knives, saluted, and walked off to collect her due. In congratulations and coin. She'd cleaned the blades, but I checked regardless.

"May I?"

I hesitated and the captain observed it, waiting with bland courtesy. And a hint of an ironic glint in his eye for my not wanting him to touch my weapons. Giving myself an internal shake, I reversed the blades and handed them to him by the hilts. He handled them with due respect, holding the blade edge up to play the morning sunlight against it.

"Razor sharp," he noted. "I should likely thank her for not gutting him."

"Jepp has excellent control and doesn't rattle easily. That's one reason I picked her."

"And the other was to prove to me that a woman fighter can best a man."

"Draw whatever conclusions you like."

"You could have proved the same by sparring with me."

"Not going to happen." Unable to stand it a moment longer, I held out my hand for the knives. With a quirk of his lips, he handed them back. "Besides, I have no need to prove anything to you."

"Ah." He nodded as if I'd confirmed something. "But I have a great deal to prove to you—that I and my men are both capable and trustworthy."

"Both of which are impossible to prove definitively."

"You would not get past my guard so easily."

"We'll never find out," I replied easily. "Unless you do fail me if it comes to the real thing, in which case you'd be dead before you had a chance to guard yourself."

"You're so certain you could best me?"

"Not at all." I let him see me scan his bulk. "I have as healthy a respect for your strength as you do for my speed. My best odds with a fighter like you lie in taking you by surprise."

"You already have, Your Highness." The warmth of his tone sent an unaccustomed flutter through me, and I looked away, deciding it was irritation.

"I must be going. I'm afraid I have several appointments more to keep before court. Good-bye, Captain."

"You could call me by my name. It's Harlan."

"I know what it is."

"And you have no intention of using it."

Without bothering to reply, I saluted my Hawks and headed for the castle. I began to see how the mercenary captain had succeeded so well in his profession. He was nothing if not dogged.

8

The man irritated me no end with whatever game he played. No hired mercenary should have an agenda, but he certainly did. A spy for one of the Twelve? Or, a more daunting possibility, for the Dasnarians or some other foreign power, eyeing our state of unrest as an opportunity to step in and annex us to another empire. He thought to manipulate me, to make me question the King by insinuating I'd been mistreated.

That was what came of the mercenary lifestyle. He could not understand true loyalty. Nothing could shake my faith in the High Throne. If I couldn't hold on to at least that much, I didn't deserve to be heir. And him, making all those flirtatious comments, egging me on to spar with him. If he thought me an easy mark, he'd find his man wasn't the only one to make a grave error in underestimating us.

Yet I found my black mood had dissipated somewhat and I felt more clearheaded. The tea kicking in, no doubt. I swung by my chambers to gulp down some more from the teapot Dafne had thoughtfully left for me, and clapped some mostly melted ice from the insulated bucket on my throbbing face. Marskal hadn't held back. As well he shouldn't have. If the Dasnarian knew any-thing about true loyalty, he'd have understood that.

A little more than an hour past sunrise still and the castle mostly quiet, this would be the perfect time to check Andi's rooms. Taking my ring of chatelaine's keys—the set I'd acquired upon Salena's death, along with her thrice-cursed jewels—I headed up the tower to Andi's old rooms.

The lock resisted but then gave with a firm twist of the key, to my great satisfaction. The rooms sat oddly silent, dim and cov-ered in dust. Clearly no one had been in here since the servants packed in the books and draped the windows. I'd been preoccu-pied in those days after Andi fled Ordnung, disguised as one of Amelia and Hugh's entourage of servants. We'd had the after-math of the Tala attack on the castle to deal with and prisoners to question. Though the Tala had retreated—withdrawing far too quickly and completely, it was clear in retrospect—we'd spent days chasing them through the countryside, clearing the forests of stragglers and ensuring the safety of both the townsfolk and the outlying farms.

They'd toyed with us, leaving just enough of them behind to entice us to believe they'd bought the ruse that Andi remained in-side the castle. But they'd gone after her, following her to Win-droven and laying siege before we even began assembling troops.

Uorsin's rage in those days had nearly driven us all over the edge.

The books and scrolls had been piled on every available sur-face and in stacks on the floor, with no apparent regard for order. Dafne would have quite a chore ahead of her, sorting through these. Something she could do far better than I, so I might as well get the key to her.

Nevertheless, I lingered a moment longer, for no good reason. Standing in front of the cold fireplace, I recalled that night I made Andi burn the feather she'd hidden. She'd been so angry at me, but I'd been angrier. And baffled at her disloyalty. The feather had come from Rayfe's bird form. I knew that now. Then, I understood only that something about the King of the Tala called to her, meant more to her than her loyalty to the High King. To me.

I missed Andi. Had started missing her at that moment.

Of course, even if she were here, she would have done her utmost to avoid court and would have failed to pay attention to most of what went on. Still, when she did pay attention, she had excellent insights. I could use that from her. Along with her company.

Shaking off the mood, I locked the door again and descended the steps to my own rooms. Dafne had returned and I undid the mechanism that kept the ring closed, removing the key to Andi's rooms.

"Don't lose this, librarian. I don't have to tell you to be circumspect, correct? Lock yourself in. Don't be seen coming and going. You'll find the books are all over the place. I'd like your impressions on court this morning, but you're probably better doing this while everyone is occupied."

She tried not to look too appalled, but the thought of the rare documents in disarray bothered her. "Would you mind if I put them in order as I look?"

"As a secondary goal, that's fine. Priority is any and all information on the Dasnarians. Bring those here, if you can do so discreetly. As you've likely noted, my chambers are *not* a whirl of social activity." Though, compared to Andi's abandoned ones, they were.

"Speaking of Dasnarians, Captain Harlan pulled me aside to ask about you."

"Did he, now?" I'd known the man was up to no good. "What did he ask and what did you tell him?"

"You needn't interrogate me." Dafne's tone was deliberately mild. "He mentioned that you'd taken a hit in practice with the Hawks earlier and wondered if it happened often."

"And you said?"

"That, yes, like any soldier, you train hard and take your knocks."

"Good answer."

"I would not betray your secrets, Ursula." She said this softly, threaded with meaning. Of course she saw more than she let on. A keen and discreet observer. I was fortunate to have her aid. Along with her discretion. A court like Ordnung's ran on a delicate balance of sensitivity and blind eyes. It would never do to imply the High King wasn't above the law, much like a force of nature. Everyone understood that. Or, if they didn't, suffered the consequences.

"Well handled—thank you." I pulled off the practice clothes and sponged myself down.

"He also asked why you hadn't wed before your sisters and wasn't it traditional for the eldest to marry first."

I made a noncommittal sound, though that was most interesting. Did he wonder about the order of succession? Perhaps he sought to discover more around the circumstances of Andi's defection to the Tala.

"I told him that it had been your choice not to marry."

"True enough."

"I didn't know if it bothers you, that Hugh fell in love with Amelia instead, so I did not reveal that he'd been your intended. Though I suppose it was common knowledge at the time."

I pulled on a serviceable enough court gown—light green, but who cared?—and laughed. "Upset not to marry the golden prince? He was pretty enough, and a decent fighter, but no, we would not have matched well." My mind, however, did not stick to those early days. Instead my hands remembered the heaviness of my blade cleaving Hugh's neck and the emptiness of his eyes staring up at the sky, as his blood stained the snow around him. Ami knew the truth of it now—that we had lied when we said that Andi killed him. Other than my Hawks, Dafne, and a few of Rayfe's men, no one else knew.

I'd killed other men and women in the course of battle, but none I regretted that way. If I had married Hugh as intended, and we'd stood on that pass together, with Andi throwing herself in front of Rayfe to thwart Hugh's sword—would I have acted the same way? Where would my loyalty have fallen then?

It didn't bear thinking about, because I hadn't thought then. Instinct, long honed after all these years of protecting my little sisters, had spurred me to act. Very possibly I could never do otherwise.

I made it to court before Uorsin. A mixed blessing in that it spared me that long walk down the center aisle under the King's scrutiny with the nerve-wracking puzzle of assessing his mood. Captain Harlan, however, had preceded me and stood to the right of my throne as he had the day before, applying his own watchful gaze.

Ignoring him, I stepped onto the dais. Then barely stopped from drawing my sword when he moved to take my hand to assist. Sliding the sword back in the hand's breadth I'd pulled it, I steadied myself by smoothing my thumb over the topaz in the hilt, while the mercenary held up his palms in a mock surrender that only served to point out my nerves.

"That should teach you to touch me without permission," I told him under my breath as I sat.

"Simple courtesy. Your people practice the custom also, I've noted."

"Not with me."

"No. You stand and sit alone, don't you?"

"Don't make more of it than it is." The courtiers and ambassadors mingled, having quiet conversations. Derodotur passed among them, gathering petition scrolls for him to order for the King's review.

"You have cold hands," the mercenary commented, also looking out over the gathering crowd.

"Always have had."

"In Dasnaria we have a saying—'Cold hands, warm heart.'"

I snorted quietly. "Which goes to prove that Dasnarians know nothing."

"Or that we understand more than you realize."

The Dasnarian woman entered the hall then, wearing that same cloak as if it weren't warm weather and us indoors. Even from this distance, her eyes burned like smoldering coals and a chill pricked the back of my neck. The topaz seemed to warm under my thumb, until I forced myself to take my hand away, lest it appear I contemplated drawing my blade against her. Which I did, but it was impolitic for anyone to know that.

"Illyria, Mistress of Deyrr," the mercenary captain said, still speaking for my ears alone.

"One of your company? What is her specialty?"

"Not mine. She's no fighter, which you knew the moment you laid eyes on her."

"Not true," I countered. "With the archers and similar specialists it can be difficult to discern, until they take up their weapon of choice. They are still lethal, under the right circumstances."

"She is dangerous all right, but not in the way you might think."

The woman stared at us, giving me the uneasy impression that she listened to our conversation, though that should have been impossible. I'd learned better, from encounters with the Tala, to reclassify my definition of impossible.

"I'll explain more tonight." The captain turned his face away from her to speak to me, warning clear in his gaze, as if he thought she eavesdropped, too.

"At dinner, yes, that will be fine. I often entertain informal audiences at that time."

He laughed and shook his head. The herald trumpeted the arrival of the King and I turned all of my attention to the matters at hand.

Formal court dragged on without a break until well into the late afternoon. Many of the petitioners, I suspected, had awaited my return to approach the High Throne, in hopes that I might temper the King's rulings. In easier times, I had sometimes been able to. Not with things as they stood now.

The wisest, most experienced courtiers knew better than to bring forth any obviously contentious issues. The unwise quickly learned that lesson. Ambassador Laurenne had not attended court today, which spoke volumes. I was not the only one to carefully track Uorsin's temper and plan accordingly. We all most benefited from biding our time until he calmed or news arrived to alter the current tense situation.

Much as it pained me—for a number of the pleas were important, and denied due to the King's foul temper—I could not afford to appear to be in anything less than complete agreement with my father, on even the most minor of issues. Not that it appeased him. He seethed still, avoiding looking at me or addressing me directly.

Court ended with still no word of Amelia's party. A bad sign that neither Uorsin's spies nor my scouts had found any trace of them, something that deepened the restless dread tightening my spine and further infuriated Uorsin. His uncertain temper on top of my own fears pushed me closer to the edge of losing my equanimity. Ash was a largely unknown quantity to me—but he possessed Tala blood and tricks aplenty. He no doubt enabled them to evade us. They might even be inside Annfwn, as I knew Amelia had found her way past the barrier before. What worried me most was that they'd conceal themselves so well that I wouldn't be able to find them, should the worst occur.

Visions of those possible scenarios plagued my mind and made my heart race with the forced inaction.

Thus, I greeted the ultimate adjournment of court—and Uorsin's precipitous departure—with great relief. My back ached from sitting on the hard throne all day and I envied the mercenary in being able to stand. I'd barely stepped down from the dais, ignoring Captain Harlan's offer of assistance, when my fighting instincts roared to alert, warning me of attack.

My hand went to my sword, but I saw nothing. *Where was it?*

The mercenary captain keyed in to my alert, tensing beside me. I followed his gaze to the seemingly serene glide of Illyria toward us. *Goddesses guide me.*

"Your Highness." The woman curtsied with perfect form but somehow made it mocking. She wore the dark cloak, a deeper red than dead blood, though the crowded hall had grown warm with too many bodies and late-day heat. Her fair hair, nearly a white blond, tumbled in glossy locks only shades darker than her white skin. Beautiful, except for those lusterless black eyes that she flicked at Captain Harlan in implicit demand.

"Your Highness, may I present Illyria, Mistress of Deyrr."

Her bloodred lips thinned ever so slightly at the title. No, they were not friendly, by any stretch. He'd spoken the truth.

"Illyria," I acknowledged. Then waited pointedly.

"I wonder if you might grant me a boon, Princess."

I didn't reply, letting the nerves that shouted to pull my sword translate as impatience.

She smiled, displeased that I made her chase what she hoped to gain.

"I'm interested in an ancient artifact rumored to be found in Ordnung. The Star of Annfwn."

Only iron control kept me from reacting to that. No one but Salena and Lady Zevondeth had ever used that name. Our secret. How in the Twelve did this Illyria creature know about it? Locking down the flare of unaccustomed panic, I kept my hand unmoving on the hilt of my sword and my face as bored as possible.

"I have never heard of such a thing. But then, I rarely concern myself with artifacts. Perhaps you should consult our archivists? You'll forgive my hasty departure. I've a number of things to see to before supper."

Illyria's white face chilled, but she acknowledged that I'd dismissed her with a flicker of her dead eyes that promised retribution. Who *was* this woman?

I strode out of the hall, not the least bit surprised that the mercenary followed, pacing me easily with his longer stride. I stopped at the archway to the arcade, placing myself squarely in the middle, to make it clear that going farther would be counted a trespass. Unfortunately that put me face-to-face with the man.

"What's the Star of Annfwn?" he asked in a quiet voice.

"As I said—no idea."

"I think you do know. We must discuss this."

"Must we? I doubt I have time for that." Deliberately, I yawned, though I lacked enough sleep that it overtook me, cracking my jaw. "My pardon. I had a late night."

"Have you reviewed the contract yet, Your Highness?"

"One of the things on my schedule." I hoped. I'd sent the request via page, for that and several other documents that would create the overall impression that I was simply performing due diligence and catching up on the affairs of the Twelve. Which, in truth, I needed to do.

"Good. You can give me your take on it when we meet tonight. Note the section that binds me to act to protect you, if you will."

"I doubt that will change my mind—about anything, Captain."

He caught my elbow as I turned to leave, as he had the night before, angling away just enough that I couldn't jab it into his gut as I'd been halfway to doing. Absorbing the energy behind it, he used my momentum to propel me against him. I recovered fast, but he made a show of steadying me. "Watch your step, Your Highness. Meet me again tonight in the courtyard," he added under his breath.

"Thank you, Captain." I gave him a steely look that had leveled lesser men. "When Danu grows pink roses." I turned my back and strode away, aware of that low, nerve-caressing chuckle following after.

9

With no word—official or otherwise—about Ami, Ash, or any of them, I resigned myself to waiting as best I could, and I spent a few productive hours reviewing the Vervaldr contract before dutifully descending for supper. It steadied me that the scrolls I requested had been delivered so readily. It indicated that the King had not given any formal orders to cut off my access.

Derodotur had described the terms fairly enough and the document impressed me in its thoroughness and logical clarity. Had the brutish Captain Harlan drawn up the contract himself? It seemed unlikely. Though he might be more articulate than the typical hired thug, I doubted he had that sort of education. Else, why be a mercenary?

Supper was a quiet affair, as Uorsin did not show. Whispers implied that he closeted himself with the Dasnarian witch. I knew well how much the court at Ordnung loved to throw that term around, so I told myself to take it with a grain of salt. Still, from seeing the woman, I wondered how much of that might be accurate. She made my skin crawl. The mercenary captain had called her the Mistress of Deyrr—clearly a Dasnarian term that might not translate to Common Tongue.

She was not mentioned in the Vervaldrs' contract, unless I'd missed the reference. I didn't think so, however, as all other specifics had been very clear. An unusual and concerning omission.

The mercenary captain didn't show for supper either, for all his insistence on talking with me, which meant I sat alone at the head table. Usually I minded that not at all, but the quiet on top of the growing worry over Ami ate at my nerves. Truth be told, I missed the minstrels. They added a welcome distraction when conversation became scarce. And nobody was conversing. As if all possible topics carried too much gravity, given the tension in the air. We all waited for further developments, as if under siege.

I ate quickly, with thoughts of making an early night of it. Some more time with the documents I'd requested—due diligence meant more than an excuse, after all, and I worried over what besides today's petitions might have gone neglected—some wine and peace, and I might be able to sleep. The best option, as I wouldn't be wearing myself out with a late-night workout, since I had no doubt the determined captain wouldn't hesitate to seek me out in the private courtyard again. The contract damnably gave him and his designees access to all of Ordnung, even the family quarters, in the name of personal protection and security.

On one level, it made sense, to use the otherwise idle mercenaries so. On the other, our personal guard had nothing else to do. I couldn't quite wrap my mind around what Uorsin was thinking. Either he played a deep game that I hadn't sorted out, or . . . *Or he's gone out of his mind with paranoia.* The traitorous thought made me feel ill and I left the table without finishing my meal.

It worried me deeply, in a vague, formless dread that added to my uneasy stomach, that Illyria had asked after the Star of Annfwn. Walking through the hallways alone, I let my fingers pass over the round of the topaz embedded in the hilt of my sword.

Mother had given it to me for my seventh birthday. That had been a good day. Andi, still a toddler in the nursery, had stayed behind, and Salena took me for a rare outing, pulling rank to get me excused from the practice yard. She rarely did so, but when the Queen took it in her head to require something, no one stood in her way. Even Uorsin, though he fumed, backed off when she gave him a certain look.

Though no one spoke of it outright, power had hung about her like a rumble of far-off thunder that's felt, not heard. When she pinned Uorsin with that storm-cloud glare, the hair prickled on the back of my neck, standing up as if a lightning bolt might stab from the sky at any moment. Though his face turned signature red, he'd backed up a step and then flung up his hands, ordering us out of his sight, as if that had been his idea all along.

My gut had twisted with a blend of terror at disappointing him and sheer awe that my mother could accomplish what no one else could.

So, for that birthday, I'd had my mother all to myself. The best of her, too. She'd been happy, with her hair brushed and hanging loose. We took a picnic and rode up into the hills above Ordnung. She sang songs in the oddly liquid Tala tongue and told me stories of Annfwn.

"I wish we could go now," she'd said, her gaze focused west. "If I could, I'd take you and Andi and we'd ride over the mountains. You should see it. The water is bluer than aquamarines and as warm as a bath. You can run or ride on the beach for days, whiter than snow and brighter than diamonds. No need to bring picnic food, because you can pluck fruit from the trees."

I laughed. "Fruit doesn't grow on trees!"

"You are so like your father, with all his fire and certainty. I want you to keep the best of him and discard the rest. Do you understand what I'm telling you?" Her gray eyes had turned serious, the air thickening with the ominous pressure of a summer storm, though the sky remained pure, cloudless blue.

I didn't understand, but the way she seemed to look through

me, seeing something else, filled me with apprehension. "Let's go, then," I urged her. "We'll sneak Andi out of the nursery and go tonight."

"Ah, my brilliant and brave daughter. If only it were so easy."

"It can be," I insisted.

"I have to stay this course I committed to long before you were born. One more daughter for the world. And you"—she stroked my hair, long like hers then—"you have to stay in Ordnung, with your father. It won't be an easy path. The one of duty and honor never is. I want you to remember that, in the long years ahead, that I understand what you'll go through, that it's a path I myself chose. In that way, you are the most my daughter. To help you remember that, I have a gift for you, to honor your natal day."

She'd wrapped it in a piece of silk tied with a ribbon, and I untied it eagerly, catching my breath at the sight of the orb. Perfectly round and smooth, flawlessly golden, like the sun at high noon. I held it up to the sky and it seemed like a second star, glowing from within. My mother wrapped my hands around it, folding its light into my palms.

"I brought this from Annfwn. It belonged to my mother and her mother before her, back more generations than I can count. Keep it with you, always. Remember that you are the daughter of queens as well as of a king. A star to guide you. The Star of Annfwn. I hope you get to see Annfwn, but . . ." Her voice caught then, silvery eyes glistening, and for a terrified moment I thought she might break our rule and weep. She stopped herself, however. "But if you don't, you'll have this piece of it. Don't let anyone take it from you. You will need it someday. Follow your dreams when you do. And remember my love goes with you, always."

I did as she asked, keeping it hidden for the most part, carrying it in my pocket. Especially after she died. The warm, round weight reminded me of her, that she really had lived, no matter what that empty throne declared. Then, when little Ami was about six, she ferreted it out of my pocket and—as she did with everything—demanded that I give it to her.

She begged prettily, with wide violet eyes and many kisses pressed to my cheek, a technique that admittedly usually worked on me. I found it difficult to deny her anything. We all did. When I refused, she threw a full temper tantrum, complete with tears and screams, threatening to tell our father to make me give it to her. She was just a little girl, so lovely and so terribly overindulged. I'd gotten angry enough that I came close to slapping her.

Until Lady Zevondeth intervened. She'd seemed old to me then, and that was more than ten years ago. My mother's faithful servant and our adviser on all things for proper young ladies to know, she calmed Ami with another jewel and slipped the topaz away, out of Ami's sight and grasp, promising to take care of it. Days later, she called me to her rooms and presented me with a new sword—the topaz firmly fixed into the pommel. Never since had I been parted from it. Over the years, though, I'd grown so accustomed to touching it that I sometimes forgot to look, to admire its deep and brilliant beauty.

Andi and Ami called it a cabochon and I never corrected them. Only I and Zevondeth knew how much of it lay beneath the surface. My personal star.

I didn't think Amelia remembered that day, though sometimes I caught her looking at the jewel with a speculative eye. I never told her or Andi where it came from. A piece of our mother that was mine alone. Which wasn't fair of me, because I'd had far more of her than either of them had. Andi barely remembered her and Ami not at all. I'd tried to be a mother to them, as best I could, and had not succeeded very well.

My list of failures seemed to be growing of late.

Dafne had left me a stack of scrolls and books, with salient passages on Dasnaria thoughtfully marked with ribbons, Danu bless her. Instead of diving into them, however, and with that long-ago memory heavy in my mind, I took advantage of the solitude to pull the doll Salena had given me from its hiding place. Maybe the Star had some significance I'd forgotten or never known. *Find the doll,* Ami and Andi had both nagged me multiple times, insisting our mother had somehow left them messages in theirs. They didn't know that looking had been unnecessary for me. I'd known exactly where it was, since the day my father yanked it from my hands and threw it across the nursery. I kept it behind some particularly heavy and uninteresting tomes on obsolete shipping laws in the Isles of Remus. Carefully hidden away, so he wouldn't find it and break it any more than it already was.

It was the one pretty thing I'd kept, though she'd suffered from the passage of time. The porcelain hands and feet had broken that long-ago day and had mostly crumbled away. One hand remained with a sharp fragment I used to like to poke my finger with, just to see how much pain I could stand. The little crown on her head had dented but still sat atop her bloodred hair. Though the painted-on features had blurred and faded, her queenly face was vivid in my memories.

I smoothed her dress, made of shining silver, dulled from all the times I'd done that very thing. Why I liked to pet it, I didn't know. It soothed me. Anchored me in a way little else did.

After Andi told me to, though I had been skeptical at the time, I'd of course gotten the doll out and examined it. Removing the gown and petticoats reminded me of being a little girl again, when I'd had many outfits to dress her in. I'd even gone so far as to cut the doll open, searching the packed cotton innards. The slit remained open still, as I hadn't had time or opportunity to sew it up again and I didn't want to hand it off to anyone to fix. The slice had distorted her shape, though, and it annoyed me to see her less than she should be.

To be diligent and thorough—after all, Ami insisted she'd found a message, too—I unlaced the gown, removed the undergarments, and unpacked the stuffing yet again. And found nothing more than I had the other times I'd looked.

It shouldn't make me sad. Ridiculous, the sting of disappointment. After all, Salena had given me other gifts. And she'd told me things to remember, as she'd been unable to with Andi and Ami so young. I didn't need special messages.

I was simply in a melancholy mood. Shaken by Illyria's unexpected question, which annoyed me. Work would help me shake it off and calm my nerves.

Putting the doll back together as well as I could without taking the time needed to mend her correctly, I hid her away again, in the little bed I'd made for her as a foolish girl. Nevertheless, feeling both nostalgic and vaguely silly, I still tucked her in under the doll-sized satin comforter, as if by doing so, I could safeguard us all. Folding the gown neatly beside her, I hid her away again in the shadows behind the big books.

Then I dutifully reviewed the documents I needed to, saving the Dasnarian research for after. Tax revenues. Crop reports. A plague outbreak in Noredna. Deployment of troops. So many recruits sent to Mohraya—where were they all? I'd fallen months out of touch and puzzled over many of the changes. Some of the numbers simply didn't add up. Deep into summing a column of figures, I barely registered a knocking at the door to my rooms.

It came again. Who in Danu's shadow had come to see me this time of night? Any of the likely candidates wouldn't bother to knock, and the outer guards would have stopped any threat or opportunistic courtier. Maybe Dafne had found something interesting and hesitated to disturb me, for whatever reason. "Come in already!" I called out, noting down my last calculation so I wouldn't forget my place. That total definitely did not match the one I'd seen on another report. Where I had I put that?

Someone cleared his throat and I looked up to see Captain Harlan standing on the other side of my desk. Why had the thrice-dammed guards let him in? This mercenary contract had all the protocols upset. I would have to talk to the Hawks about standing duty. People I could count on.

"Did you kill my guards?" I asked.

He indicated his empty sheath. "No, but they did relieve me of weapons."

At least they weren't complete idiots. "How can I help you, Captain? It's quite late."

"I waited for you."

"I can't imagine why. I told you not to."

"Nevertheless. I have several important things to discuss with you."

I sat back in the chair. "So you mentioned. What's on your mind that couldn't be said in court or the practice yard?"

"It needs privacy."

I gestured at the quiet rooms. "This is as private as it gets, inside Ordnung."

He hesitated, angling himself so his back wasn't entirely to the door. "It's not inappropriate—for me to be alone with you in your chambers?"

I couldn't help it—a laugh bubbled from deep within. "No, Captain. If there ever was a time that anyone fretted over my virtue, it has long since passed. What are your Dasnarian women like, that they don't fight and they can't be trusted on their own?"

"Not like you, Your Highness," he said with a wry smile, casting his gaze over the unruly piles of scrolls and books on my desk. "You're doing paperwork? Don't you employ scribes for such things?"

"I'm not much for hired help."

"Or trusting anyone else."

"That, too," I agreed easily. "Certainly not blindly."

"And yet you won't give me the opportunity to prove myself."

"Why should you care what my opinion is? I have no need to rely on you. It's not my name on this contract." I nudged the parchment with my quill.

"You did read it."

"Of course."

"And your conclusions?" His expression dared me to express doubts, knowing full well I'd found nothing untoward. Except the raw fact that Uorsin had never hired mercenaries before.

"I concluded that this Illyria, Mistress of Deyrr, is not mentioned."

"*Deyrr*," he corrected, rolling the r. "In your tongue it means 'death,' after a fashion."

Not news to relieve my worries. "What can you tell me about her?"

"What can you tell me about the Star of Annfwn?" he shot back.

"I told you I don't know what it is."

Harlan made a growling sound, a rumble of growing impatience. "Your problem, Your Highness, is that you put faith in all the wrong people."

"I don't recall soliciting your opinion on the matter."

"Well, you get it. If Illyria wants it, whatever it is, that can't be good. She won't give up."

"Why don't you give me a reason to put faith in you by telling me what you know?"

He looked grim, gestured at the wine goblet on my desk. "It's not a comfortable tale. Have any of that to share?"

10

I contemplated him a moment. It had been some time since I'd indulged in a late-night conversation over wine. Since before Andi left. Perhaps he'd have something useful on this Illyria. "Why not? Make yourself comfortable in the sitting room. I'll fetch the wine."

He chose one of the chairs by the fire—not my favorite chair, which made me wonder if he'd noticed the signs and made the choice out of consideration—and accepted the goblet I handed him. I settled into my chair, stretching my feet to the fire. Though the days stayed high-summer warm, at night the snow-cooled air slid down from the mountain peaks, adding a chill. The blaze felt welcome.

"I've served a number of royal families in my career." The mercenary likewise made himself comfortable. "I have never known a princess who keeps no attendants and pours her own wine."

"I like my privacy, when I can have it. And there's not much luxury in the field."

"I expected grander chambers, also."

I shrugged a little. "They've been mine since I left the nursery. I had no interest in moving."

"Shouldn't you have taken over the queen's rooms?"

"You've been quite busy, watching and drawing conclusions."

"You like to imply that I'm a spy. Understanding the politics in a given situation can be crucial to being on good working terms with a client. One disadvantage of being a mercenary is coming into conflicts with many unknown parameters. I like to know what I can."

I mulled that over. A legal scholar's brain inside that thick skull. He probably had written that contract, after all. Besides, anyone could—and likely would—give him the answers he sought. "Fair enough. Yes, I could have taken Salena's rooms. I chose not to. They're Amelia's when she visits now—appropriate for her rank as regent mother."

"Queen Andromeda would outrank her, would she not?"

"Yes. But that presupposes Andi would ever return to Ordnung, which she won't. And, if she did, she'd prefer her traditional chambers, as I do. Ami will have the throne of Avonlidgh soon enough, regardless, as Old Erich can't have many years left." Particularly if he persisted in stirring up civil war.

"And when you ascend to the High Throne?"

"That's not something I contemplate and neither should you. Uorsin is High King and I'll do everything in my power to ensure that remains the case."

He didn't comment on that. Rather he took a swallow of wine, studying me. "You're not what I expected."

"You have the advantage of me in that I didn't expect you at all."

"No, you couldn't have. I advised the High King against secrecy, but he seemed quite determined." He shrugged over the vagaries of clients. "You read the contract, so you know we agreed to it. I would have thought he would have communicated our presence to his heir, however."

I elected not to respond to that. Of course he should have told me. I hated how much it pained and concerned me that he hadn't. "I also know that there are omissions in the contract. Glaring ones. As I mentioned earlier."

"Not so much. Illyria is not one of mine, nor did she travel with us."

"Then how did she come to be here?"

He caught my gaze with his. "I don't know. She was here when we arrived. That's one of the concerns I wished to bring to your attention."

I waited for him to say more, but the moment stretched out. The mercenary regarded me calmly. Maintaining his defense against my next move.

"Have you shared this concern with anyone else?"

He shook his head, a slow silent swivel that reinforced how unusual this move was for him. Telling me without saying that there had been no one else before this to speak of it with. What did he intend by telling me?

"I've heard tell that she has been closeted with the High King."

"Even as we speak."

"He's had many lovers. More than can be counted. It's his right."

"She is no simple lover."

"What does it mean, then, 'Mistress of Death'?"

He sat forward, elbows on knees, the empty goblet dangling from his hands between them. I refilled it and he gave me a nod of thanks. "The translation isn't quite accurate, which is why I use our word *deyrr*. It means more the impermanence of life. The fragility of it in the face of a world that falls into decomposition and decay."

"A cheerful lot, you Dasnarians."

"You have no idea. The Practitioners of Deyrr are a . . . sect, if you will, that honors an old religion. They worship a god long since shunned by decent folk."

"A god? Not one of the three goddesses?"

"No. Though Dasnaria acknowledges Glorianna, Danu, and Moranu, they are considered minor deities." He glanced at me, a bit of a mischievous twinkle in his eyes. I didn't bite. "The practices of this group go far back, with roots before King Orsk established the Dasnarian throne, when our ancestors lived in warring nomadic tribes. He is the god of the hunt and also of hunger, of death through starvation. He rules over the transmutation of the living animal into death and death recycling back into life through consumption of the meat."

"I suppose I see the logic there. But that's a fact of life. Hardly dire."

"In most instances, this is true. The Practitioners of Deyrr, however, take his dominion over transmutation to a terrifying place—if the stories can be believed."

Something in his deep voice sent a shiver down my spine that recalled the way I'd felt when Illyria looked at me with her coal-dark eyes. Captain Harlan seemed a most practical man. Though most warriors carried a healthy respect for the whims of fate and the blessings and curses of the goddesses—or gods, in his case—most had a strong grip on the real and relevant.

"Do you believe the stories?" I asked.

"I do. I have reason to. Though the rites are kept secret, tales have leaked from the temples. Blood sacrifices. Torture. Vile arts based in dark magics that muddle the line between life and death."

"I take it we're not talking about hunting deer anymore?"

"The higher the being, the more magic it carries. We're talking human beings."

"And this worship is legal in Dasnaria?"

He sipped his wine, contemplating me. "First, our governance is different. Our king does not hold absolute power. We have a number of ruling bodies that must debate and agree upon the laws. Second, though not precisely legal—kidnapping, murder, and torture of human beings are not—what cannot be proved cannot be prosecuted. The Temple of Deyrr is powerful. As long as they prey on those without consequence and support the ambitions of the ones with it, they are left alone."

"I cannot find that admirable about Dasnaria."

His even stare reminded me that not all in the Twelve Kingdoms went admirably at the moment. But we endured a time of trial that would soon be resolved. The High King would see that and take action soon. I had to have faith in that. If he didn't, I didn't know what I could do.

"I don't disagree," the mercenary finally replied, yanking my thoughts back. "You'll note I am not living in Dasnaria."

"So what are you telling me? That this Illyria is a priestess of this practice and she is here to attempt to start her religion? Glorianna's temple won't sit idly by."

"That's not what I'm saying. The rites gain the priests and priestesses the magic they wield. She seeks to use her power to gain more." And Uorsin made a fine path, he didn't say out loud. His meaning, however, hung in the air.

"How?"

"It's theoretically within her abilities to raise an army by animating the dead."

He returned my incredulous stare, not giving any sign of teasing. In fact, he looked dead serious.

"How is that even possible? I've never heard of such a thing. It sounds like a wild tale to me."

"You have a history of the Dasnarian kings on your desk. You'll find mention of all I've relayed here in the chapter on the foundations of the Orsk dynasty."

Sharp eyes on him. Sharp mind behind it. I would not underestimate him again.

"Presupposing this is true—where would she obtain the dead?"

He rolled his shoulders, shrugging off a tension he didn't otherwise reveal. "Tombs, crypts, mausoleums. I don't really know. I'm guessing at her plans—I am far from being in her confidence."

"Slave trade?"

"Not as far as Dasnaria is officially concerned. The temple does what it may in the shadows. Suffice it to say the dead have little protection from slavery."

"Mohrayans burn their dead," I mused to cover my chill. "But not so in some of the other kingdoms. So she has no other unusual powers—shape-shifting, wizardry, anything like that?"

The mercenary narrowed his eyes, set the goblet aside. "Are those stories of the Tala true, then?"

"Some, certainly. It's not easy to sort truth from hysteria. In the thick of a fight, much can seem mystical that isn't." Except that I'd stood on the opposite side of an invisible barrier that my sister controlled with her mind. "That said, should we battle the Tala again, be prepared for the extraordinary."

"I would say the same with Illyria. I don't know what powers she possesses, but I would put nothing past her. I believe her to be a great danger."

"Have you said as much to the High King?"

He tapped the tips of his fingers together, cocked his head, and studied me. "You know I could not."

"Because?"

"Your father is not receptive to hearing what he does not wish to." He'd phrased it carefully, but more lurked beneath his words. Frustration. Anger, perhaps. The implication that Uorsin favored her foul plans. Surely not. If I could count on anything in the King's increasingly strange behavior, it would be his hatred of magic. Salena might have given him the edge to win the High Throne, but he'd never let go of the resentment. And of the fear, if I gave it honest thought, that she had possessed a power he could not control.

The alternative, however, that he might be blind to Illyria's true nature—or that she somehow manipulated him—was not pleasant to contemplate. If only because it would mean I could not in good conscience go after Ami. What would it take to send Illyria away?

I poured myself more wine, hoping to dull the sharpening

worries I didn't care to ponder. Our conversation could be considered treasonous—certainly by Uorsin, suspicious as he already was—and already I fretted over what I could possibly do to discover more without inciting him further. And yet, for the good of the Twelve, I could hardly ignore such a warning.

"Why are you telling me?"

"She asked you about this Star, and that concerns me. And because, Ursula, you impress me."

Uncertain how to respond to that and uncomfortable under his intent gaze, I drank from the goblet, the wine warm and rich. I didn't feel impressive. And I had no intention of telling him about the Star.

He read it in my face and laughed a little, looking into the fire. "You know, when I signed on and heard that High King Uorsin's heir was a woman, well—" He broke off, shaking his head. "I've said the Dasnarian women are not like you. When you walked into court, I thought . . ." He paused, glancing at me.

"You thought what?" I both did and didn't want to know. Better to hear it, though. Some odd part of me had gone breathless. Fear, perhaps, of feeling those old wounds. I'd long since stopped caring about the sly jokes and innuendos, but there had been a time when they'd cut me to the quick. Before my skin thickened. Something about this man, though, made me feel thin-skinned again.

"I thought you were the most extraordinary woman I'd ever seen." The mercenary said it softly, deep voice as smooth as the wine. "The way you faced the High King was amazing to witness. Nobody that I've seen has handled him so well. You're fearless, flawlessly intelligent, and you have the mind, spirit, and reflexes of a warrior. If anyone can save us from this potential disaster, you can."

I shook myself mentally, the eerie echo of Derodotur's words penetrating the allure of Harlan's flattery. *He's a strategist; of course he knows how to play you. And how to suck up to his royal clients.*

"I watched you deal with him and thought, here is an ally. Here is someone with the strength, the guile, to deal with what the presence of the Temple of Deyrr implies. Which brings me to my other concern." He stared into his goblet, as if seeking an answer there. "About what happened last night."

11

Ice clawed at my heart. Warning me of trouble to come. *Too thin-skinned.* "To what do you refer?" My voice came out as cold as my foreboding.

"Why do you let him brutalize you?"

The shock hit me in the gut, taking my breath for a moment. Blindly I stared at the fire, willing it to chase away the discomforting chill. I poured more wine and took a deep drink from my goblet, willing it to dull the pain of humiliation. Willing him to shut up already.

"Am I supposed to ignore it, like everyone else? Collude to make it appear you earned this injury in honest combat instead of—"

"Instead of what, exactly?" I cut him off, unable to bear any more. "You are an outsider. You know nothing of our ways."

"Your ways? You're quick to criticize Dasnaria, and then you defend this. You wish me to agree that it's simply a different custom for a father to blacken his daughter's eye?"

"For a king to discipline his heir," I corrected, my chest unbearably tight. The wine did nothing to loosen it. "To teach me to get back up again."

"If you believed that, you wouldn't have tried to conceal it."

"It's time for you to leave, Captain." I reached to pour myself more wine, but he startled me by taking the goblet from my hands, seizing them in his own and dropping to his knees before my chair.

"Ursula." He tightened his grip, leaning his weight in and pinning my legs to the chair when I would have moved to tear away. "Look me in the eye and tell me why you let him do it."

Because he's my father. Because it's my duty. Because if I question him, then I will be forced to question everything. The foundation of my world would come crashing down and I didn't think I could survive that. The sound of teacups smashing filled my brain and I couldn't make any of the words come out over the din.

"It's not right, Ursula," he said, the quiet tone cutting through the jangling noise. "You know it's not right. I saw how it hurt your heart as much as your body. It cut me to the core."

"Let me go."

"I want to help."

"I don't want help, mercenary."

Instead of flinching, he smiled. "But it's in my contract."

"Not against the High King."

"Against all threats. Not because it's in the contract. Because I want to."

"My father is not a— What are you doing?"

"Your hands are cold. I'm warming them."

He curled his fingers around my hands, stroking my palms. Shivers of warmth traveled up from his touch, thawing me where the wine hadn't.

"Well . . . don't."

"What are you afraid of, Ursula?"

"You yourself called me fearless." Which wasn't true. My fears hounded me, baying that everything I believed might be a lie. Fear that sickened.

"Then why are you afraid of my touch? If you won't talk to me, let me comfort you, at least."

"I'm not afraid of you."

"Am I repugnant to you? You don't have a lover, according to Lady Mailloux. You're not promised to anyone, and you yourself said your virtue is not an issue." He lowered his head and, turning my hand, pressed a kiss to my palm.

I gaped at him, struggling to assimilate this shift in the world, the fiery sensations traveling to my heart, my groin. Thawing deep cells long since frozen over. This had never happened to me. I had no training, no skills, to counter it. The romantic posturings of my barely enthused suitors had been easy to ignore, to snip off neatly and early. Not so this visceral attack that no doubt penetrated because my defenses had fallen so low. "Are you trying to seduce me, Captain?"

He smiled, sensual and slow, then pressed a longer, lingering kiss to my palm. "How am I doing?"

"I—I have no idea. I don't think anyone's ever tried before." I'd never let anyone get this far. Why him? Why now? And with so much else tearing at me.

"And you scoffed at the Dasnarian women. What are your men thinking?"

A dozen overheard jokes and bawdy songs flew through my head. None that I cared to repeat, though surely he'd heard them. Harlan's hot mouth traveled up my index finger, pressing a kiss to the tip, and the words melted away.

"I love that you have sword calluses," he murmured, dark voice buzzing over my skin. "I have this idea of how your hands would feel on me, strong and soft, rough and caressing, all at once." He drew my finger into his mouth and the fire became lightning. Heat ran over me in waves and I suddenly seemed to be out of breath.

Unable to pull my thoughts together, I drifted on the furling flames that licked through me. This, then, was what it felt like, that drove everyone so. I'd been forever outside, looking in the window through a thick pane of glass and not understanding. I'd seen people eating at the banquet table but hadn't smelled the food or tasted it. Now the glass had shattered and I found myself starving.

For what I couldn't have. Would never have.

"I can't possibly do this." Though I said the words, I couldn't pull my hands away from the stirring sensations his mouth awoke in me. He'd worked his way to my pinky finger and nipped the tip with his teeth, so I gasped, my core clenching. Only hands, and yet . . . "I mean it. Stop this."

With a show of reluctance, he lifted his head, still holding my hands, rubbing my palms with his thumbs, a deeper echo of his kisses. "I think it's not me. Do you prefer women?"

I wished I did. It would be so satisfying to say so. And yet, I couldn't quite make the lie come out. I also couldn't tell him the truth.

"What's wrong?"

I shook my head, unable to find words. "I don't . . . I don't *do* this."

"Why not?"

"It's not who I am." It didn't matter that I was broken, so deeply flawed. I yanked my hands from his grip and pushed him away, easily extracting myself, as I could have at any moment, had I had the wit to make the effort. My head swam. Too much wine.

"You're a woman who finds me attractive. I'm a man who wants you. Uorsin has his lovers. You can, too. Your right as much as his." He leaned in, put a hand on my knee, hot through my silk court gown. "It's not more complicated than that."

"I don't have the luxury of taking lovers."

"I won't get in your way. Our goals are aligned. Protect the High Throne of the Twelve Kingdoms."

"Only you're paid to do it."

"Thus you know exactly where I stand."

"Is this part of the service you provide—did you pleasure the other princesses?" The anger flared in me and I stood, pacing a safe distance away from his seductive touch. "Were they locked away by their daddies and thrilled to have a hot man between their virgin thighs?"

He didn't pursue, didn't show any sign of being bothered by my slicing remarks. Instead he shifted to sit, back against the chair and one knee drawn up, massive thighs flexing. "Is that who you are, Ursula?"

I laughed and it came out harsh. "Don't be ridiculous. Just because I eschew lovers doesn't make me some blushing virgin. I simply have better things to do."

"Do you? Like anesthetizing yourself with wine and working your body to exhaustion just to get a little sleep?" His pale eyes stayed on me, clear and calm; he never raised his voice, but he tested my guard with those taunting feints. "You keep your head down and lock yourself in your lonely chambers, pretending that you're not as much your father's prisoner as any of those princesses you so detest?"

"You know nothing about me. I don't need rescuing and I've already asked you to leave once."

He didn't move. "I know more about you than you want me to, which is the problem. You trembled when I touched you, heating willingly to my hand; thus, I know you want me. You wear the bruise on your face that your father dealt you and pretend to me and the world that it's not so. You tell lies to yourself and you expect me to believe them, too. I don't. You think it's your job to protect everyone else. Perhaps you should consider protecting yourself."

I tapped the hilt of the sword I still wore, the topaz smooth and warm. "This is my protection."

"Only if you use it," he retorted. "If you won't take care of yourself, then it falls to me." He tipped his head toward my desk. "Contract."

Wrapping my hand around the hilt, I pulled the sword an inch, feeling more balanced with it in my grip. "Time for you to leave, mercenary."

"Will you draw on me?" He didn't drop his voice, but it still somehow grew deadly quiet.

"If necessary."

"You won't admit me to your bed or meet me on the practice ground in an honest match, but you'd have me believe you'd draw your sword, knowing me to be unarmed. Your honor won't let you."

"You don't have much room to call me on questions of honor, mercenary, since yours is available to the highest bidder."

"I imagine you think that if you keep saying such things, you can convince yourself you don't want me as much as I want you."

My temple throbbed and I pressed a finger to it, wishing I hadn't drunk so much wine. *Anesthetizing yourself.* That was the only reason I let things go this far. "I apologize if I gave you the wrong impression, Captain. But I'm truly not interested. There are a very many good reasons I don't take lovers. The first and foremost is I can't possibly compromise the High Throne. I look to Danu, and many of her priestesses are celibate."

"Yet you've taken no such sacred vow."

"I can't. I would have." Kaedrin would have sponsored me. Hoped to salve my hurts that way. Not long after she suggested it, Uorsin had declared Glorianna's temple supreme and all Danu's priestesses—including Kaedrin—unwelcome in Ordnung. I followed Danu's teachings in my heart, where it wouldn't offend him. He accepted her as a patron of warriors, at least. "But there is always the possibility that I will need to marry, to serve the High Throne and the Twelve Kingdoms. I won't be foresworn to my goddess, so I am celibate in practice only." I let out a long breath, rolled my head on my shoulders. That was mostly true. Close enough to serve as the truth. I would never marry.

"Come and sit." Harlan patted the floor between his spread knees. "Let me rub your neck at least. Relieve your headache."

"I'm fine. It's late and you should leave."

"Afraid to let me touch you again?"

Yes. My starving body still throbbed, full of yearning to sate myself at the banquet table. A feast that had always been easy to ignore until now. He'd awakened a hunger I hadn't known I was capable of, one I needed to lock away again.

"You could probably break my neck with your bare hands."

"But I won't. If you won't let me be your lover, let me be your friend."

"I have friends."

"Do you? I see you with your subordinates, the people who turn a blind eye to what you suffer. I have not seen any friends."

"My sisters."

"And what do they say about how your father treats you? Ah." He nodded, though I hadn't replied. "They don't know, do they? You protect them, too. Shield them from the truth—and from being hurt also."

"Look . . ." I had no idea how he had seen through so much so quickly. It left me off-balance. Not myself. Terrified that he'd see my worst shame. "Would you please leave?"

"Let me rub your neck and I will. If you won't let me pleasure you with sex, then let me do that much. You felt better after I worked on your back."

It was true. So much so that the prospect of him loosening my neck appealed far more than the promised seduction. I knew where that would lead, the shame and pain of it. But this—I wanted this bit of comfort, as weak as it might make me. "And you'll cease bothering me?"

"I'll leave and let you get some sleep."

I didn't miss that he hadn't quite promised what I'd asked. "Fine."

"Do me a favor and leave the sword behind."

"Now who's afraid?"

"Justifiably cautious." His lips twitched in a wry smile and he patted the floor in front of him.

I unbuckled the sword belt and sat cross-legged between his knees. "I still have my daggers."

"I know you do."

His hands, always so warm on my skin, settled on the base of my neck and dug into the tight muscles there, much as he'd massaged the palms of my hands. He worked them up the tendons to the base of my skull and a groan escaped me at the delicious feeling of release. He laughed, low and dark. "Ironic that you make no sounds when I kiss you, but you melt under my hands for this."

"This is better," I lied. "Where did you learn these techniques?"

"Most Dasnarian warriors do. It's considered as much a part of our training to maintain our bodies as any other exercise. Our bodies are our first weapon, the one that cannot be lost in the heat of battle, the one we take to our graves—or that will take us there if we fail to keep it honed and in the best possible working condition."

"I'd never thought of it that way."

"See? We have much to learn from each other." His voice, deep and vibrant, loosened my nerves like his deft massage rubbed the knots from my muscles. So much so that I nearly forgot to pay attention to the meaning behind the soothing sound of it.

"I'm sure there are plenty of court ladies willing to entertain you. Go learn from them." I meant it to sound tart, but my voice came out sleepy. The sheer pleasure of his hands on me wound with the heat of the fire and the warmth of the wine, conspiring to blur my mind.

"If I wanted entertainment, I'm sure that's so. I want something more."

His hands lightened, still rubbing my neck, but changing tenor, stroking me with touches like sueded leather. With the softer caresses, his own sword calluses made themselves known, scraping from tough to velvet, depending on the angle. *I have this idea of how your hands would feel on me, strong and soft, rough and caressing, all at once.* I understood now what he meant, and my body went taut with expectation, thrilling to the imagined sensation of him touching me in far more sensitive places.

"It's you I want, Ursula." He said it in a rough voice, as if continuing the words he'd left off some time before. Those strong, rough-soft fingers feathered down the sides of my throat, from the tender hollows under my ears down the shallow artery to my collarbone. "Any way I can have you. Even if only this much. You're satin and steel under my hands. Like a finely balanced blade, beautiful, sharp, deadly. Seductive. No one else will do."

His hands drifted lower, and I froze, my stomach clenching. Pulling away, I scrambled to my feet, putting distance between us. He regarded me with a slumberous gaze, relaxed and predatory. Hungry, too. Then he climbed to his feet, downed the rest of his wine, and toasted me with the empty goblet.

Pausing at the door, he looked back and smiled in his serious way. "I'm very good at waiting, Ursula."

12

I awoke early after a fitful sleep in which I compared columns of numbers that never quite added up and chased after a cloaked woman who left bloody footprints in her wake. Though I caught up to her, my sword had become a quill pen and she laughed as I slashed at her with it.

Putting my hand on my sword, I felt better knowing I had it still. Only a dream. A common one at that. The Hawks often joked about such dreams, of riding into battle naked or with feathers instead of blades.

I dressed in my practice leathers, smiling to hear Dafne's step in the outer chamber, bringing me tea. "Good morning, Your Highness," she called out, as if I might expect someone else. Had the guards or someone else mentioned Harlan's late-night visit? Despite what I'd said the night before, people might gossip. Or was that my guilty conscience?

"Danu," I growled at myself. "Nothing happened." And nothing ever would.

Dafne had set a pile of books on my desk and looked weary, dark circles smudging under her eyes. She waved a hand at the collection and handed me the key. "I think that's everything to be had."

"Did you stay up all night going through them? You needn't have."

"I felt I did. Better to extract what I could before I lost the opportunity."

I studied her, sipping the hot tea, grateful for the warmth that diffused the lingering frost of the nightmares. "What aren't you telling me?"

"Nothing specific." But she shook her head, unhappy. "Ordnung has a very strange feel. It's nerve-wracking to be forbidden to leave like this."

"Like being under siege."

"Yes," she said on a long, considering breath. "Very like that."

"I know you worry about Ami and Stella also."

"Still nothing?"

"I haven't talked to Jepp yet today, but she'd have sent word if there was any. However, I've learned something else that has me worried."

She winced in dismay. "I am afraid to ask."

"Did you read much, about the Dasnarians?"

"Only enough to find the correct passages and mark them. I don't really know where to begin. Why?"

"I had an extended conversation with Captain Harlan—twixt thee and me—and he told me some interesting details about Illyria. I'd like to know your perspective, from a more objective standpoint. If you want to start researching, look for the Orsk dynasty and the Temple of Deyrr."

"Deyrr?"

"A Dasnarian term. I won't prejudice you by giving you the Common Tongue translation. I'm not convinced the mercenary's interpretation is correct." Nor the rest of his dire warnings.

"I'm not going to like what I find, am I?"

"I doubt it. But well-armed is well prepared."

"Speaking of strange events, had you noted that Lady Zevondeth has not been at court since we arrived?"

I frowned, replaying the images in my head. "True, I don't think I've seen her. But she's not required to be present. Perhaps she's unwell."

"Perhaps." Dafne sounded unconvinced.

"I shall check on her. Before court commences, if I can."

The Hawks and mercenaries alike were out for early morning practice and warm-ups. To my surprise the two groups mingled extensively now. Jepp appeared to be showing several of the mercenaries the opening stance of the Midnight form. Not that it was forbidden to share, but that she wanted to had me rethinking.

These Dasnarians had a way of using charm to sneak under your guard.

Of its own accord, my eye found Harlan's bulk easily. The rising sun caught his fair hair, gilding him with a crown of light. He talked with Marskal, several other Hawks, and another of his men. Then threw back his head, showing the strong column of his throat and letting loose that booming laugh. He spotted me and raised a hand in greeting, his smile warming in a different way for me.

Marskal grinned and saluted. "Captain! We're offered a demonstration of Dasnarian wrestling. They seek to redeem some of the pride Jepp cut away yester eve."

"Oh?" I made sure to keep my stride casual, my tone slightly bored. This irritated me also. "Are we meant to coax our enemies into the ring and pin them until they cry mercy?"

Harlan's eyes glinted and I knew he restrained a pithy—and lascivious comment—in response. I gave him a hard look, to forestall any undue familiarity on his part. If he thought I would cut him any slack, excuse any rude behavior, he was mistaken. The bawdiness of soldiers was one thing. I had the dignity of rank to uphold.

Instead he bowed, showing perfect respect. "You are absolutely correct, Your Highness, that this technique would be rarely used in battle. As a last, and most dire, resort, perhaps. Much like your blade forms, our wrestling is intended to build strength, endurance, and character. We believe the most confident fighter, the most determined, will carry the day."

He just loved to layer in multiple meanings, his words deferential, even bland, but somehow suggestive of the previous night's encounter. And his declared intent.

I shrugged. "Do as you will. I have a workout to get in before court. I'll leave you gentlemen to your games."

"Ah, badly timed, then," he replied, then turned to the other men. "Not this morning. We shall save the demonstration for when Her Highness is less pressed for time."

He kept good discipline, as the mercenaries showed only a hint of their disappointment. Marskal and the other Hawks, however, did not manage to be nearly so polite.

"Captain." Marskal gave me an odd look. "We already placed bets—only awaiting your arrival."

Danu take it. He knew full well I should have wanted to see this. Now I'd only made him wonder about my hesitation, knowing I otherwise loved any opportunity to witness a new fighting style. Especially if it gave us insight into our unwelcome guests. Besides, my Hawks would be as restless as I with our comfortable imprisonment—I should be happy for them to find distraction where they could.

I inclined my head. "You have the right of it, Marskal. I can spare the time. You may proceed," I said to Harlan, and he seemed amused by the regal command.

Yes, it had sounded stiff, but I needed all the formality I could muster at this point. Create and keep distance. That would be key going forward, to manage his expectations. And discourage further advances.

Two of the mercenaries marked off a circle with twine, roughly twice a man's height in diameter, while Captain Harlan and another man began stripping off their shirts and pants. To keep from watching, I pulled up a bench and set to polishing my sword. Not that I hadn't seen plenty of men unclothed—field outposts and battle left little room or reason for modesty—but Harlan's muscled physique seemed unduly attention-grabbing.

His all-over golden tan hinted that he often went unclothed outdoors, and his fair hair barely showed, leaving the rippling cuts of his muscle plainly defined. He seemed more lithe, more like a male animal, without the hardened leather armor he typically wore. Fortunately he and the other man retained strips of cloth over their groins, though their buttocks were bared.

Unfortunately, they commenced applying some sort of oil, the morning light catching it and making Harlan's golden skin gleam over taut muscles. I resheathed my sword when I came close to slicing off a finger, Danu take him.

"Now, *that*," Jepp said, coming to straddle the bench next to me, "is a fine way to start the day."

"I thought you were teaching those mercs the Midnight form."

"This is much more interesting. Everybody is coming to watch."

Indeed, the other female Hawks had drawn quite close, expressions avid with more than casual interest. Marskal circulated, taking more bets, no doubt, but everyone else watched Harlan and his man. At the far end of the practice yard, Madeline and some of the maids and kitchen ladies gathered, their giggles carrying on the air like birdsong. The castle ladies would likely be sorry that they were not early risers and had missed the spectacle.

"Nice of you to grab us a ringside seat," Jepp continued, sounding entirely too casual, "but then, this is staged for your benefit, isn't it?"

I was sorry I'd put my sword away, as I had nothing to do with my hands now and seemed to be unable to look away from the glistening display of Harlan's masculine form. "Yes. Marskal knows I'm keen to learn more about how these Dasnarians train and fight."

"Oh, Captain, we are *all* keen to see more," she drawled.

"No consorting," I snapped, without thinking it through. Always a bad sign.

Jepp gave me an astonished—and terribly disappointed—look. "You can't mean it."

She leaned in on the pretext of drawing her knives to polish and dropped her voice. "If we're to get out, it will be through them. I'm working on making some *special* friends."

"Duly noted. But you needn't do anything you don't wish to."

"Not exactly a sacrifice." She boldly eyed the near-naked men. "I don't mind fucking one or two. Or five. Possibly all at once." The two men in the ring circled each other, thighs flexing in their half crouches, backs rippling, as they flexed muscles in display. "Do you think they all look that good under their clothes? I need to know. Call it scouting. Postcoital glow is excellent for extracting information from a man. Danu, I love my job."

"You worry me, Jepp."

"I won't touch the captain, but say I can try a few of the others. Please?"

"Danu. Fine. Have any of them—even the captain. I don't care. Just watch your own glow and what gets extracted from you."

She tore her gaze away to cast me a quick, delighted grin. "You're flustered. I've never seen you flustered."

"Shut up, Jepp."

The men connected, grappling, their hands sliding off the oiled skin of the other before catching to hold. They strained to master the strength of the other, their muscles hardened and impossibly bulging.

"I missed my workout is all," I added. "All this waiting and wondering. It's making me restless."

Harlan flipped the other man and they went down in a tangle of limbs, the oil gleaming bright. The other man slipped partly free and Harlan laughed, exultant, scrambling to lock him into another hold.

"Uh-huh," Jepp breathed. "I feel exceptionally restless this morning also."

The maids and kitchen ladies had made bold to press through the ring of onlookers now—else they wouldn't have been able to see through the crowd—and cheered wildly, cheeks pink and eyes bright. No one blocked our view, however, much as I wished they might.

"We'll have a crop of Dasnarian-made babies in nine months," I predicted. "And likely no Dasnarian fathers about to help feed the lot."

"Mmm," Jepp hummed, not listening to a word I said, fascinated gaze locked on the men as they tumbled over each other. Harlan had the other man pinned, facedown, locked so that he could barely struggle. Another mercenary counted in what must be Dasnarian, slapping the ground on a shout.

Thankfully that ended the match—the mercs, Hawks, and overexcited ladies cheering alike. Even Jepp leapt up from the bench, squealing in most un-warrior-like fashion. Harlan and the other man rose to their feet, now swarmed by the onlookers with much congratulating and slapping of backs.

"Not bad for a little rabbit!" The loser clapped the mercenary captain on the shoulder, shaking his head as he did.

Jepp turned on me with a stern, expectant expression. "You can count on me, Captain. I swear to extract as much as womanly possible"—she couldn't suppress her grin at the thought—"and hands off Captain Harlan. Fair?"

"I told you, I don't care if—"

"I'll report!" She gave me a distracted salute and sauntered over to the man Harlan had defeated, a saucy sway to her trim hips. Harlan used her arrival to deftly extract himself from the cluster. For a big man, he moved with slick precision, and came toward me.

I stood to go, but he stepped into my path.

"Not bad for a rabbit?" I echoed his man, raising my eyebrows.

Abashed by nothing, he grinned. " 'Harlan' means 'rabbit' in Dasnarian."

"Not very auspicious."

"I don't know about that. What did you think?"

"An interesting sport," I commented, keeping my eyes on his, pretending that he wasn't standing nearly naked in front of me, glistening with oil and sweat. "As you noted, not terribly useful on the battlefield."

"Did you like what you saw, though?" he pressed.

"Not enough to be further interested."

He smiled easily. "You're not tempted—not even a little?"

"Tempted?" I had gone for arch, not breathless, Danu take it.

"I think you are. We could trade lessons. You'd enjoy it."

"You're mistaken." I deliberately looked at the sun, pretending to gauge the time. "I have no interest in learning a new sport; nor do I have free time to squander on pointless activities."

"Never pointless, if done well."

Over his shoulder, Jepp had her hands splayed on the other man's pecs, as if measuring, gazing up at him with a bright, teasing smile. Madeline had corralled the maids into heading back to their duties, but more than one gazed back longingly. We'd be in for a bumper crop of babies, indeed.

Harlan turned, following the direction of my gaze. "Shall I order the men to keep hands off? They are accustomed to exercising that discipline."

"As are you?" I riposted, seizing the opening and regretting it instantly.

"As well you know, Your Highness," he returned in that smooth, deep voice, a caress in it that reminded me of the feel of his hands. "I would never press an undesired advance. Nor would my men. But yon ladies look most willing. The men will resist any and all invitations, however, if I instruct them so."

"No need," I sighed, thinking of Jepp's ulterior motives and enviable enthusiasm. "I'd have every woman in Ordnung out for my blood. But make sure they behave themselves—and that they pay up for any babies they start." That should have been in his almighty contract. Docked pay for each child left for us to raise.

"There won't be any."

"You're so sure?" In my skepticism, I made the mistake of looking at him, his blond hair dark with the oil, the thick neck and corded shoulders. For some strange reason, my fingers itched to do as Jepp was even still—run my hands over the shape of those muscles, to feel that strength for myself, to discover if his skin was as smooth as it looked. I shouldn't want that. Had never felt that desire.

He knew it, too, Danu take him, eyes glittering with answering invitation. *This is staged for your benefit, isn't it?* "We have methods for preventing unplanned babies. Our women are always safe with us. No Dasnarian man would have so little care for his lover as to expose her to that danger. I should have made that clear last night. It didn't occur to me that it was one of your concerns."

"I have many concerns—none of them to do with you. Believe me, Captain, I haven't given you or your . . . offer the least bit of thought."

"Liar." He leaned in close to murmur the word, so I scented his skin. Man, sweat, and sunlight. "How did you sleep? I tossed and turned myself. I kept thinking of you and the way you taste. Imagining how your hands on me would feel."

Calling it a strategic retreat, I stepped back, removing myself from the temptation to touch him, to run my fingertips over his oiled muscles. "How unfortunate for you," I replied. "I had far more important things to think about and still do. Excuse me, Captain."

Satisfied at having set him back on his heels, I strode away, ignoring the fact that his amused laugh once again followed me.

13

~

It was missing my workout that had put me in such a foul mood. Harlan and his machinations had made it so I'd have to sit in court all day, enduring the stagnation as my blood slowed and muscles stiffened. Was it so much to ask to be left to my own devices?

Apparently so.

Dafne softly snored from her adjoining bedchamber and a pang of envy stabbed at me for her deep and easy sleep. I tried to be quiet for her sake as I pawed through the gowns, looking for something feminine to please Uorsin, formal enough for court and yet suitable for my state of mind. Dafne had a point about all the pastel pretties. I might as well drape my sword in silk scarves and call it a rose of Glorianna.

Grabbing one at random, I pulled it on, giving up my boots for a pair of satin slippers. Protection from nothing. The floofy skirt bunched up in a weird way when I buckled on my sword and it irritated me that I had to fuss with it. The topaz caught the sun as I turned, gleaming with tawny gold as Harlan's skin had. I didn't know what to make of him and this strange flirtation. *The way you faced the High King was amazing to witness. Nobody that*

I've seen has handled him so well. Harlan's words echoed in my mind and I turned them over, seeking the truth in them. I rubbed my thumb over the Star, taking a moment, wondering about the jewel—why Illyria wanted it, how she knew of it, and why my mother had given it to me.

Had I learned handling Uorsin from Salena somehow? I certainly had none of her Tala magic. That had all gone to Andi and, it now appeared, also to Amelia. I'd always been glad not to have it, knowing well how much Uorsin hated Andi for her strange and skittish ways. It had relieved me to be so thoroughly his daughter. Despite everything else, I'd always had that.

But I'd protected my sisters. Harlan had that much right. I'd never regretted that choice.

Lady Zevondeth might know more about the Star. I should have gone to seek her out as soon as I arrived. She could be tedious in her old age and her rooms unbearably hot, but I owed her a visit. Good thing Dafne had reminded me. Odd thing that I hadn't thought about her. I emerged from my dressing chamber to find Derodotur waiting for me.

"The High King wishes to see you in his study," he said, "before court commences."

Biting back a sigh, I nodded. Visiting Lady Zevondeth could wait. Would have to. "Is there news of Amelia?" I followed along with him.

He hesitated. "Not exactly."

The summons boded well, in truth. That he meant to consult privately with me. Perhaps my initial punishment had ended and we could return to reasonable speaking terms. Danu knew we had plenty to discuss. Uorsin sat behind his great desk, poring over a scroll so fresh from the road that it shed dust on the glossy surface.

"My King." I curtsied, glad I'd worn the gown. Captain Harlan, formally attired now, turned from the window he'd been gazing out of and gave me a respectful bow, marred by a slight frown. I ignored him, keeping my focus on the King.

Uorsin tapped the scroll without looking up. "Erich has sent me a letter. Can you imagine what it says?"

Hopefully not a declaration of war. "Inquiring if Amelia and his grandson are at Ordnung?"

He made a noise of disgust and tossed the scroll at me. "No, Daughter. Guess again."

I scanned the letter, then backed up and read more carefully. "This makes no sense."

"It makes no sense on any number of levels, but mainly because Old Erich is an even older and greater fool than I took him for. And I had figured him for quite a bit of both."

"How can he think you'll pay this kind of ransom for Astar? Even if we thought he had him—and he has to realize we know he doesn't—Astar is Avonlidgh's heir as well. Erich can't turn him over to the High Throne, even for the price of Avonlidgh's freedom. Who would succeed him on his throne if he did? Erich can't mean to get more children at his age, especially when Hugh was the only one to survive to adulthood. And I can't see him giving Avonlidgh to anyone not in his direct line. It's a bluff."

"It's only a bluff if he doesn't truly have Amelia and Astar."

"He doesn't."

Uorsin narrowed his eyes, studying me. "That's only true if you haven't lied to me, Daughter. He knows full well I'd never release Avonlidgh."

He wasn't blazingly angry, however, or he would have conducted this interview in private. Much as I hated having witnesses to him questioning my honor, I'd rather face him like this, across his desk. "What would it have gained me to prevaricate? I would much rather have brought you the news that Amelia and your grandson were safely ensconced in Windroven than tell you the truth, that I don't know where she's gone. I wanted to bring them here, but knowing them to be there would have been my next preference. Had she in fact remained there, I could have arranged to hold the castle and bring your forces in to defend it against any misbehavior of Erich's."

"If that's so, then Erich thinks me the fool and, further, believes that I don't know otherwise. Why would he think that?"

I glanced at Harlan, who watched and listened with apparent impassivity, but I began to read him well enough to detect his interest in the conversation. Choosing my words carefully, I said, "Amelia left only with her private guard and the child, spirited out of Windroven in secrecy. He has to be guessing that you don't know where she's gone either."

"Or he's recaptured her."

I nodded, thinking. "Possible, yes." Though I seriously doubted it. I might not care for Ash's background, but he was a fierce fighter and dedicated to my sister. They would not have been easily captured. "Did he offer any sort of proof?"

"No. It would be interesting to ask." He nodded at me, and like that, we were in sync again. Always it came back to this, that my father and I thought the same. Today he'd settled, seemed more himself. His best self.

"It would tip our hand," I pointed out. "Asking would reveal that we, in fact, don't know where they are either. This could be a test. Perhaps he suspects she's here and is seeking to confirm that. If we deny the ransom, he could take that as affirmation that his heir is in Ordnung."

"Perhaps he's heard rumor of this girl child."

Through dint of great will, I did not look at either Harlan or Derodotur.

"My King?"

"You may speak freely in front of the Captain, Daughter." Uorsin sized up the man. "He is, after all, bought and paid for."

Harlan's easy expression didn't change and I resisted the surprising urge to defend him. Hadn't I, after all, accused him of the same thing?

"I don't see how he could have. Nobody knows except the Lady Mailloux, myself, and those in Amelia's party." And now the other two men in this room, though I was sure Derodotur had been informed immediately. It was a hedge. Amelia's midwife also knew, but we all agreed she'd likely been taken along with the infant princess. Pray Danu she didn't pop up somewhere else. Like back at Windroven, spilling her guts to Erich. "Until we have the infant princess safe, I think the fewer people who know of her existence, the better."

"They should be here. This is where they belong. Here, in Ordnung, where they will be safe."

"I agree, my King." Would he let me go? Did I dare go with Illyria lurking? At least the Star went where I did. "My Hawks stand ready to—"

"Not you." He cut me off. "Don't make me repeat it. Captain Harlan?"

He snapped to attention, bowed, and straightened. "Your command, High King?"

"Prepare a detail of your best men and lead them into the Wild Lands. You will ascend Odfell's Pass and enter the Tala kingdom. Find King Rayfe and his wife. You'll no doubt find my grandson with them."

Though he spoke to Harlan, Uorsin watched me for reaction, cagily waiting for me to argue. Which I wanted to, with every fiber of my being. Only the sure knowledge that he laid a trap for me with this gambit kept me from speaking. Folding my hands behind my back, to keep them off my sword hilt, I made myself wait calmly.

"Your will shall be done, High King." Harlan bowed again.

"Nothing to say, Daughter?" Uorsin ignored him and needled me.

"You believe Amelia is with Andi and the Tala?" I kept my voice neutral.

"Yes." Uorsin stood. Leaned on his desk. "Don't you?"

"No."

"Why not?"

Still a trap, but I could hardly refuse to answer. "Because they can't enter Ann—the Tala kingdom. No one can." Amelia had—a secret from our father. She'd refused to tell me much about it. I knew only because she'd slipped up and referenced talking to Andi. As near as I could piece together, she'd snuck out of Ordnung and made the arduous journey to Annfwn, somehow convincing Andi to let her through the magical border. Where little Ami had gotten the courage and fortitude to pull that off, I didn't know.

It also truly impressed me that she had. Though it had been a disobedient, even traitorous, act, I couldn't condemn her for it. If it ever came to light that she had done so, I'd find a way to take the blame. It rightfully belonged to me anyway. If I hadn't killed Hugh, she could have cozily lived with her true love in Windroven, raising their babies and staying out of trouble.

Therefore, I would not be the one to betray her actions—which Uorsin had strictly forbidden—to our father. Not only to protect her. Preserving Uorsin's great affection for his youngest daughter would go a long way toward preserving the peace and stability of Ordnung and the Twelve.

"Because Amelia knows we'd worry—and that her and Astar's extended absence would only heighten political tensions."

"Bah." Uorsin dismissed that idea with a flick of his hand. "Amelia is a beautiful and sweet girl, but not that bright. Thinks of no one but herself. Such things would never occur to her."

I tightened my jaw to hold back my reply to that.

Uorsin tapped his blunt fingers on the desk thoughtfully. "It could be, however, if your tale is true, that the baby was taken as bait to lure her into the Tala's grasp and that she is, in fact, a hostage."

"Why go to the trouble of faking the child's death, then?" I pointed out, knowing I might regret provoking him. Better than insisting on Andi and Rayfe's good intentions. "We were not meant to see through the subterfuge."

"If you think yourself so clever," Uorsin growled, "where *do* you think she is?"

No good answer to that. "If you agreed to let me go look for her, I would cut through the Wild Lands at a diagonal and attempt to pick up her trail from Ordnung."

"And if you should not return, as she has not?"

"I would return to you and Ordnung as long as I had breath in my body." Hadn't I done that already? I'd come to Ordnung instead of going with Amelia. "My place is by your side."

He eyed me, a glimmer of something in his eye. "I want to believe you're loyal to me. I need to be able to count on that."

I met his gaze with a rush of relief. He praised me rarely, but when he did, all was worth it. Here was the King I knew. We could come through this and all would go back to normal.

"Yes, you'll stay here, and Captain Harlan, you'll take your men, see what you can find."

I took the chance—a final bid—and leaned my hands flat on his desk, holding his gaze as steadily and fearlessly as I could. "But, my King, Captain Harlan and his men have never faced the Tala. They don't know what the demon folk are capable of. The Hawks are experienced. We very nearly won Odfell's Pass—any of them can verify—and would have taken it but for the magical barrier."

"Then you shall advise him."

A sound in the antechamber, a crawling up my neck. The door opened and Illyria, with her dead eyes, entered. Uorsin's gaze went to her, locking on with a ferocity that seemed unnatural, even from a man who'd built an empire out of sheer force of will.

"Leave us now," he commanded.

As I turned to go, Illyria glanced at me, lips curving in a blood-red smile.

14

Court should have already convened, but indications were that Uorsin would not be arriving anytime soon. He hadn't given official word either way, which wasn't entirely out of the range of his normal behavior. In better days, we'd all welcomed the break. In recent months, the reprieve had given me time and opportunity to do what I could to ease the growing troubles outside Ordnung's white walls. Thus, instead of sitting on my throne, I took a seat in the antechamber, which made me available for consultation and able to quickly take my formal chair, should Uorsin suddenly appear.

It did not surprise me that Ambassador Laurenne pounced upon the opportunity first, Stefan, one of the princes of Duranor, with her. Between them, they'd cooked up a plan to take water from the Danu River and divert it to the farmlands bordering the desert that encroached on both their realms. Never mind that the river ran entirely through Avonlidgh in that area. They clearly expected Old Erich's rebellion to soon end in his demise. Stefan, a cruel-faced man who'd made a halfhearted attempt to court me once, seemed to think I wouldn't see that he cared nothing for the starvation in Aerron and took this opportunity as a way to gain a foothold in Avonlidgh, with an eye to ultimately assimilating it. While I suspected Aerron, along with Elcinea and Nemeth, would throw in with Old Erich if they saw things going his way, it had always been clear that Stefan ran on his own agenda.

As Duranor had started the push to create an empire of the Twelve Kingdoms back when Uorsin was but an Elcinean conscript, it wasn't difficult to guess what that agenda might be.

Still, I sympathized with Aerron's plight, and the aqueduct plans looked as likely as I'd ever seen. Keeping them out of Erich's pocket would also be a benefit. Short of magic, Ordnung could do nothing to alter the drought. Some things were not in a ruler's power. I finally agreed to put it to the High King, when I found the right moment.

By the close of the morning, my head pounded from the parade of bad news and my heart ached at the litany of misfortune. People did not hesitate to share with me the disasters that they'd soft-pedaled for the sake of Uorsin's temper.

I did take the opportunity to inquire after Lady Zevondeth's health but received the same answer from everyone I asked—that she'd been scarce at court since midsummer, at very least. Several people seemed surprised that I'd mentioned her, as if they'd forgotten her very existence.

Captain Harlan would be out with his men, planning their journey, and I wanted to speak to him about it. I doubted that he'd leave before morning, but the chance that they'd set out this afternoon remained. I needed to give him advice, whether he asked for it or not. Uorsin didn't believe in the magical barrier, but I knew it to be very real. They'd never get through unless Andi allowed it. Captain Harlan needed information.

And to take at least Jepp with him.

Though a few of the Hawks hung about the practice yard, none of Harlan's men were in evidence, besides the supplementary guard on the walls. With a pang of dread, I thought they might have already departed. Harlan and his men would be sitting ducks for the Tala's tricks. I understood Uorsin's stubborn determination, but he'd faced the Tala. He knew full well their capabilities. Danu take it, he'd been married to Salena and, if stories ran true, had used every bit of her power and influence to win the Great War and unite the Twelve Kingdoms.

Perhaps that explained his fascination with Illyria. With so many troubles plaguing the Twelve—to an extent he had not confided to me—the King might feel a desperation to take extreme measures. People looked on Uorsin and saw the trappings of power but not the relentless responsibility of it. They didn't understand him as I did.

"Looking for me, Your Highness?" Harlan called out, coming from one of the secondary barracks. He looked terribly pleased with himself.

"Not for the reason you think," I told him in an undertone.

"I thought perhaps our imminent separation had caused you to reconsider your previous decision."

"No. Nothing ever will."

"Nothing at all?" Far from seeming daunted, he grinned. "And yet, you sought me out."

"I need to speak with you before you go on this venture. As you well know."

"You're speaking to me now."

Several of his men emerged from the barracks and went over to swap tales with the group of Hawks. More than one glanced over at us with interest, causing me to wonder what Harlan had said about me. He followed my line of sight and—more uncomfortably—the direction of my thoughts.

"They only wonder about what commands you relay. I've said nothing to cause anyone to speculate. What's between you and me stays between us."

Oh, they speculated, all right. Or, as in Jepp's case, leapt to assumptions. But that was the way of fighters, so absorbed with the physical. Fighting and fucking, two sides of one coin.

"I need to speak with you privately—and don't smile like that. Only to ensure we won't be overheard. There are things you must know before you leave, and not all for everyone to hear. When do you depart?"

"We leave at daybreak. I'll come to your rooms tonight."

I was already shaking my head. Daybreak. It should be me going. They'd be slaughtered and I'd have their blood on my hands. "No. Not there."

He raised his brows. "Weren't you the one to say that's the most private place possible?"

Too damned private, it had turned out. But he had the right of it.

"Don't you trust me to abide by your wishes?" He frowned. "Or is it yourself you don't trust?"

"Believe me, Captain, your offer holds no interest for me." I held his gaze, letting him see the truth of it. "While I appreciate your healing hands, they do nothing more for me than that."

He smiled, slow and certain. "Then spar with me."

I gestured to the dress. "I'm not exactly prepared for that."

"Go change, then. I'll wait. I'm good at waiting."

I ignored that intimate reminder. "Why are you so determined to spar with me?"

"Perhaps I seek a way under your guard—one way or another."

"Be frivolous all you like, Captain. I seek to give you the tools you'll need if you're to succeed and return alive."

He spread his hands, showing open palms. "Our interests there align, Your Highness. Do you prefer the courtyard? Some other location?"

Unfortunately I could think of nowhere else that I could be certain of not being overheard. I would simply have to ask Dafne to stay. She knew all the secrets already. "Fine. Attend me in my chambers after supper."

"I look forward to it." Slowly, with a sparkle in his eyes, he gave me that salute of his, something in it that unsettled me.

Several responses popped to mind, none that promised to daunt the irrepressible merc. So I turned and left him there, ready to put him out of my mind until after I met with Lady Zevondeth.

"Is she unwell?" I demanded of her maid.

The girl blocked the doorway, tacitly refusing me entry. Heat leaked out from behind her, baking like the Aerron desert, and she was flushed with it. "Lady Zevondeth grows frail. She sleeps now, Your Highness. She's really not fit company. Perhaps—"

"I'll see her."

"Your Highness, I—"

I merely raised one eyebrow, and she wilted, knowing full well I could have her bodily removed if I wished. She stood aside, waving me in. If possible, even more braziers burned than before, heating the rooms like one of the sauna huts the Branlites used to ward off the chill winds of the Northern Wastes.

The bedchamber was stifling, but Lady Zevondeth nevertheless lay under a pile of blankets, a slender skeleton of a woman, deeply asleep. For a terrible moment, I thought she might be dead and this goose of a maid not noticing. But there, her chest rose and fell, her head turning slightly on the pillow.

Then her eyes popped open.

Milky white, they usually seemed sightless. Other times, like now, they fixed on one like the gaze of the keenest predator. She grinned, suddenly and unexpectedly. "Ursula! You've been back days without coming to see me."

I sat on the side of her bed, taking the hand she wormed out from under the covers. It shook with the palsy that had overtaken her in recent years. "My apologies, Lady Zevondeth. There has been much to do and I've neglected you terribly."

"What's terrible is that dress. Pink does not suit you, certainly not with your sword disturbing the hip flounce."

"I know. I shall commission new gowns. Will that please you?"

"No." She closed her eyes and turned her face away.

"No?"

"You shall not be here long enough for them to be made. You shouldn't be here at all. Death walks the halls of Ordnung." She opened her eyes again, staring sightlessly at the ceiling. "No one can plan for death."

"Death?" I tried to sound amused and indulgent, but she'd have none of it.

"You know who I mean. Uorsin is a fool to court her. Salena was more than he could control—look where that got him—and now he wades even deeper into the swamp that will drown him. He's not just stupid; he's lost his mind."

"Don't say that." Not only were her words treasonous; I hated that she put voice to my own misgivings. "The King has a great deal to handle at this time."

"Ha!" Zevondeth's hand shook harder in mine. "You, my girl, are no fool. He's barking mad. His obsession has robbed him of the last of his reason. He'll destroy what little he managed to build. Now he seeks to buy what he could not cultivate."

The King might be on edge, but he was hardly mad. Instead I feared that fate had fallen to Lady Zevondeth. "The mercenaries are a temporary solution. Soon gone, you'll see," I soothed her. "Amelia had her baby. A fine boy, as you predicted—Astar."

She smiled, managing to look cagey, even with the few teeth she still possessed. "And the girl?"

"You knew? You never said."

"Eh, I don't tell all I know. Little Ami needed to untie that knot herself. I promised not to interfere."

"Who did you promise?"

Zevondeth sobered, gripping my hand tighter. "Salena. She saw, you know, some of what you girls would face. But not all. She was sorry for what he did to you. I am, too."

Nausea curled in my gut, icy shards of shame. I tried to pull my hand away, but she hung on with surprising ferocity. "It couldn't be stopped, do you understand? When she saw things, it was because they were inevitable."

"I don't think I believe that."

"What you believe is irrelevant. She saw something else, dis-guised in the shadows of death. So she gave you the Star of Annfwn. To keep it safe, to guide you through. Do you have it still?" She dug in her nails, a frantic light in her eye. "Promise me it's safe!"

I tapped the topaz. "Right where you had it set for me. Why did Salena give it to me—do you know?" I wouldn't tell her Illyria somehow knew about it and sought it.

"You'll know when the time comes."

"The time for what?"

"To kill the King."

15

The ice penetrated out, freezing my joints in place. "What?"

"You should have killed him then. But you were so young. You're not too young anymore. It's your destiny, Ursula. He knows it. He seeks the soldiers you cannot kill, to save himself from your avenging sword. But he won't escape it. It's his destiny and yours."

I dropped her hand and stood. "You're talking nonsense. Hallucinating. I won't stand by and listen to this."

Her gaze glittered, as bright as a bird's. Not entirely sane. "You worship him so. Even when he's tried to crush you under his heel, you crawl back to lick your own blood from his boot."

"The High Throne, the peace of the Twelve—those things are more important than my bruised feelings."

· "But the Twelve are dying. What will you do about it? It falls to you, Ursula."

"Della!" I called the maidservant. She cringed her way into the room and curtsied and stayed down, biting her lip. "How long has Lady Zevondeth been out of her mind like this?"

"Your Highness." Her voice trembled. "I did try to send you away."

"I know you did. I'm not angry at you." I took my hand off my sword hilt and, for lack of anything else to do with my hands, adjusted the flame under the teapot at Zevondeth's bedside. "When did she start talking crazy?"

"I'm not crazy, girl!" Zevondeth muttered.

Taking Della by the arm, I led her out of the room and shut the door. "Talk."

"After the Dasnarians arrived."

"Did something in particular occur?" Zevondeth had some powers of foresight and possibly other tricks she cleverly kept out of sight. Had she run afoul of Illyria? She'd been here first, from what Captain Harlan had said.

"No, Your Highness." Della wrung her hands, wide eyes shimmering with tears. "Not that I witnessed or that she mentioned. She declined bit by bit, not wanting to go to court and sleeping more." She glanced at the closed door. "Saying crazy things."

"Has anyone else heard these remarks?"

A few tears escaped her lids, trickling down her cheeks. "Your Highness, I've kept everyone away but you. Please don't execute her. She's just a frail old lady. My gran went this way. Thought everyone was a shape-shifted Tala demon wanting to drink her blood. You can't take what she says seriously."

"Oh, for Danu's sake—I'm not an executioner and I'm hardly going to drag her before the High King for judgment. Have the healers been to see her?"

"I didn't dare, Your Highness. With her treasonous talk and all, I—"

I held up a hand to stop her. "I understand. And I'll take care of this, okay? You did the right thing, but we need to help her."

Della burst fully into tears and dropped to her knees, gathering the hem of my gown in her hands and kissing it. "Thank you, Your Highness. I didn't know *what* to do."

"There, Della." I patted her curls, feeling awkward. No one tries to kiss the hems of pants.

With a few more reassurances, I extracted myself, the much

cooler summer warmth of the corridor nearly a shock. Surely it couldn't be good for Zevondeth to overheat so. Or perhaps she'd do better in a warmer climate. If we could get her well enough to travel, I could send her with Ambassador Laurenne's retinue. With Erich pulled back into Windroven, it might be safe enough.

Certainly safer than leaving her here, where Uorsin would inevitably get wind of her traitorous bent.

Casting an eye at the afternoon sun, I calculated that I'd have time before supper to catch up on the reading Dafne had marked for me. She'd awakened and sat at my desk, looking through one of the histories and making notes. Glancing up, she either frowned at my dress or retained an uncomfortable thought from what she'd been reading. Remembering herself, she jumped up from the desk.

"I visited Zevondeth," I told her, forestalling any tiresome apologies or conversation about presentation.

"Truly?" She raised neat eyebrows in surprise. "I asked around a bit and heard that she hasn't been taking company. That maidservant of hers is as loyal as a dragon."

"Rank has its privileges." I smiled thinly. "Though it turns out to have been a smart move on her part. Zevondeth is bad off. Who do we have for healers for the elderly who can keep his or her mouth shut?"

"Most healers are discreet," Dafne pointed out. "Part of their vows."

"I need someone who won't be tempted to curry favor with Uorsin."

"Oh?" She kept the question carefully neutral and brought me a pot of tea.

I frowned at the text she'd been reading, not seeing the elaborately scripted words, Zevondeth's crazed screed rolling through my mind. "She actually talked about me killing the King." I would have laughed if the thought weren't so very wrong, so deeply horrifying to me. "Can you imagine me doing such a thing?"

Dafne didn't reply and I looked up to find her frozen in place, a truly stricken look in her eyes.

"Don't fret, Lady Mailloux. Nobody but Della and I heard her say it—and now you. None of us will point a finger at her for her demented talk, but you can see my point that the healer must have discretion. Maybe someone from outside Ordnung? Or Mohraya entirely? A priestess of Moranu, maybe. I understand one tended Andi and kept *her* secrets well enough. Though someone from outside would find themselves trapped here and they might not appreciate that kind of summons."

"Ursula." Dafne gathered herself and sat in the chair across from me. She started to reach across the desk, as if to take my hands, but several books were in the way.

I raised an eyebrow at her somber expression. "Dafne," I said, in the same tone of voice.

"What if—" She broke off. Then folded her hands in her lap. "What if she's not crazy or demented?"

Now I did laugh, rolling my head on my tightening neck. Thought about having some wine. Too early to start. "Don't say things to me I'd be honor bound to act on. *You* I could never pass off as out of your mind."

"Tell me this, Ursula, as a citizen of the Twelve—is Uorsin a good king?"

Out of habit, I glanced to be sure the door remained closed, some young and fragile part of me certain that he'd come crashing through at any moment. "That doesn't matter."

She gaped at me. "How can that not matter?"

"Because, Dafne, he *is* the King." I held up a hand when she opened her mouth. "No, there's nothing to argue past that. If nothing else, I'm a warrior and that demands adherence to discipline, to order. Uorsin is the High King. More than a man, he embodies the power of the High Throne. Without that, we have chaos. He's not subject to our analyses of good and bad any more than the goddesses are. I cannot pass judgment on him any more than I can on the drought that eats away at our most fertile farmlands—it simply is, and all we can do is work around that reality.

"You said some things are beyond the law of man, and I happen to agree. The King is a law unto himself, one that we abide by. Now, will you look into it for me—finding Lady Zevondeth a healer?"

"Yes. Yes, I will." She stood and turned to go. Then glanced back at me.

I caught the movement and looked up from the text. This was the bit about the Orsk dynasty all right. "Something else? This is interesting. Thank you for digging it out."

"You're welcome." She seemed to be searching for something else, and I waited, semipatiently, for her to get it out. Finally she shook her head slightly. "I'll get right on that."

I went down to supper late, I'd gotten so absorbed in the Dasnarian texts. Captain Harlan had relayed the information with impressive accuracy. The Orsk dynasty—which inaugurated the history of Dasnaria, it seemed—came into power with the overt and possibly covert assistance of the Temple of Deyrr. The writer employed a clever style, implying much, definitively stating very little.

However, the tales of those battles contained many references to an army that fed itself, that could not be stopped or killed. King Orsk participated in some sort of temple ritual—that much was clear. Opposing forces fell before his irresistible soldiers and then—if the text could be believed—were recruited and made to fight against their former brethren.

None of it, however, spelled out the absurd idea that these armies were formed of the resurrected dead. No doubt a profound sort of superstition came into play. Some sort of mystical brainwashing, perhaps. Or possibly wizardry akin to shape-shifting. It bore contemplation.

And Illyria bore watching.

I hadn't ruled out the possibility that the Dasnarian witch had somehow poisoned Lady Zevondeth. I needed to find a way to

show Uorsin some of this information. Whether that would penetrate whatever hold she had on him would have to be seen. The
texts didn't spell out what had happened to King Orsk. Certainly
his dynasty continued for some time, but the man himself seemed
not to have survived much past the establishment of his throne.

My mind full of the implications, I hurried down to the banquet hall, the final summons ringing through the empty halls.
Good thing I'd resisted the urge to change out of the flouncy
dress—it would serve well enough for supper, and finding a new
gown would have made me unforgivably late. How Amelia could
bear all the primping I'd never understand. I just thanked Danu
no one expected it of me.

Most everyone had already seated themselves, with a few
courtiers milling about still, having muted conversations. I nodded
at the long table where my Hawks sat, and Marskal gave me a sober
look, along with the hand signal for being on the lookout for unexpected danger.

Strange.

Scanning the hall, I saw nothing amiss, until my gaze fell on
the head table. Uorsin, already seated, naturally, was deep in conversation with a woman next to him. Sitting in my mother's chair.

Illyria.

My heart grabbed, sending a burst of blood to my brain, the
edges of my vision going red. Grief, rage, shock. Greasy cold filled
my veins, allowing me to continue to walk. Pretending nothing
had happened.

The courtiers I passed glanced surreptitiously at me, assessing
how I'd parry this fresh attack. Ambassador Laurenne caught my
eye, a look of grave sympathy on her parchment face that only
stung the heart wound. I looked through them all.

Being brave in the face of disaster often meant locking out the
softer emotions.

Captain Harlan stood as I approached the table, and for once
I felt grateful for his archaic courtesy, holding my chair and offering a steady hand as I lowered myself into it. I hated that my legs

felt weak enough that I might have faltered without the support. I could only hope he hadn't noticed the lack of steadiness in me.

I eyed the wine jug, desperately wanting to pour myself a goblet or twenty, but not if my hand would shake. The courtiers gazed with avid interest, their own troubles forgotten temporarily in the drama playing out. Uorsin, shoulder to me, had yet to acknowledge my arrival, speaking in deep tones with Illyria, resplendent in emerald satin.

"Your Highness." Harlan had filled my goblet for me, briefly touching my hand to get my attention. It made me jump, like a skittish deer hearing the crack of the hunter's footstep, and my gaze swung to him. Surely such a small thing wouldn't break me, after all I'd been through. Just a bit of first blood, a ringing blow that slipped through my guard. I needed only gain some room to move, retreat long enough to clear my head and regroup.

Sometimes, however, the press of the battle prevents retreat.

"Daughter." Uorsin turned to me, sliding his chair back somewhat, eyes glittering with that unholy light he gets when he's winning. He held Illyria's hand in both of his. "Have you been properly introduced to Illyria? Illyria, my eldest daughter, Ursula."

No honorific for me. She smiled, full of confident triumph, white skin smooth, glossy hair tumbling, and those dead eyes burning deep in her skull. Did Uorsin not see? Did he choose not to or had he been blinded? Regardless, it would take careful maneuvering to open his eyes.

"I know much of your exploits, Ursula." She smiled coyly, a rasp under her sweet tone, like the echo of hissing snakes. "I hope we shall be fast friends."

"You shall be much more." Uorsin spoke in answer to her, but smiled at me, making it clear he delivered a command. I knew him well. Could anticipate the flat of the blade coming to knock me down.

Defend, parry, attack, retreat, regroup.

"I have an announcement!" Uorsin stood, drawing Illyria

along with him. My eyes snagged on Derodotur, looking miserable, as if he might be ill at any moment. The courtiers held their collective breath. Everyone knew what was coming. As absurd, impossible, unthinkable, as it might be. "I am making Illyria my wife and Queen. All hail your new Queen."

Well trained and obedient to his will, we all stood, cheering and applauding. Harlan put a hand to cup my elbow, though I thought sure I didn't sway on my feet.

Sometimes, not only was retreat impossible, but the press of the enemy became so great that there was nothing to do but endure the onslaught. Praying to survive to fight another day. At last we sat again.

"She should have the royal jewels, don't you think, Daughter?" Uorsin gave me a boyish grin, full of lethal pleasure. "Since you were so good to remind me of them."

"Of course," I managed to say, amazed that I kept my voice steady. "I shall bring them to court in the morning."

"Oh." Illyria pouted. It should have been pretty. I'd seen Amelia pouch her lips the same way a thousand times, always with devastating effectiveness. On Illyria, it made my skin crawl. As if by holding her mouth that way, something awful might come slithering out. "I'd so hoped to have them now—to celebrate."

"You shall have them, my love." Uorsin lifted her hand to his lips and kissed that white skin, which I more than half expected to sizzle at the touch. Over his bent head, she smiled at me, and I realized how hard I gripped the hilt of my sword.

Retreat, retreat, retreat. The alarm claxon sounded in my head, and I stood so abruptly the backs of my knees banged the chair. "I'll go get them."

"Don't be silly," she cooed. "Send one of your ladies to fetch them. We have so much to discuss." Then she clapped a hand over her heart, in apparent feminine distress. "Oh! Forgive me. Do you not have any ladies-in-waiting? I know you're not much for womanly ways."

Her dead eyes burned through me and the sound of all those

songs and jokes chorused up around my ears. I wanted to hunch my shoulders to keep them out. *More like a sword than a woman.*

"Here is Lady Mailloux, Your Highness." Captain Harlan's deep voice broke the spell, and I felt like the mouse fleeing the snake's hypnotic gaze. He gave me that calm, deceptively placid look. Backing me in the fight. No friend of Illyria's, he. Something to remember, if I could trust it.

Dafne curtsied, the picture of elegant grace. "I shall retrieve the rubies immediately, Your Highness."

"Thank you," I told her, infusing the words with all my appreciation for her support and craftiness. Illyria would have seen only the rubies, as I'd foolishly worn them that first night, and Uorsin was not a man to remember all of my mother's jewels.

"This is so delightful." Illyria clapped like a girl a third her age and Uorsin smiled dotingly on her. "Shall we have a special feast, too? To celebrate our engagement!"

"Of course. Whatever you desire shall be yours." Uorsin waved a hand, willing the feast to materialize.

Oh, Danu. Each minute spiraled into another level of disaster. My back ached and a headache throbbed low at the base of my skull.

"Perhaps we should order the engagement feast for tomorrow night." I tried to keep my tone light, enthusiastic. "That will give us the opportunity to prepare something truly extraordinary for you." Or anything at all.

"Oh, but the dashing Captain Harlan leaves on the morrow and I know he wants to be here to enjoy the celebration."

Harlan nodded to her, the picture of politeness, forever inscrutable, but I began to know him well enough to sense his tension.

"The servants already carry out the supper platters," I persisted. Underscoring my words, a great platter of meat was set before the King.

Illyria frowned at it. "Why, this looks like an ordinary meal. Not special at all."

Never mind that we ate a hundred times better than ninety-nine percent of the rest of the Twelve tonight, Ambassador Laurenne glowered from her table. How to save this situation? "To prepare a great feast—"

"Of course we'll have the feast now," Uorsin assured her, giving me an angry glare. "Do you insinuate, Daughter, that Ordnung, seat of my power, the crown of the Twelve Kingdoms, cannot provide a worthy celebration at a moment's notice?" He laughed, with a cruel edge. "I suppose that, if the Tala attacked, you'd ask them politely to wait until tomorrow night, also?"

Illyria laughed gaily, pressing a palm to his cheek. "Oh, my lord King—so witty you are!"

"Send back those platters!" Uorsin called out, waving his goblet so the ruby wine splashed on the white table covering, like fresh blood on snow. "Bring out a feast worthy of my bride-to-be!"

The servants took the platters and scuttled back to the kitchens—in some cases pulling plates away from people who'd already begun to eat—and the room fell into uneasy muttering. The minutes stretched out. I sipped my wine, thinking what to do. My earlier analogy of the King being like the drought haunted me. How to handle this?

"Send out the cook!" Uorsin commanded. "We shall tell her what we want."

The headache rose to circle my eyes. *Think, Ursula.*

Madeline emerged, stately and composed, curtsying before the King. "How may I serve you, High King?" she asked in a clear voice. The cabochon topaz, hot from my hand, pressed smooth into my palm.

"What will you have, my love?" Uorsin asked Illyria.

"Lobster!" she declared. "And duck in pastry. Flavored ices, too, don't you think?"

"Whatever pleases you. It shall be done." He waved a hand in that imperious way of his, and Madeline, to her vast credit, barely blinked.

"My King," I said quietly, unable to think of any other way to salvage the situation. "We'd have to acquire lobster from Kooncelund or the Isles of Remus. It would take days to—"

"Silence!" Uorsin's hand pounded flat on the table with such force that my goblet turned over, adding to the spill of growing red. "Do you say"—he turned his glare on Madeline as if I hadn't spoken—"that Ordnung is unprepared?"

She didn't flick an eye at me. Simply sank to her knees and bowed her head. "The fault is mine, High King. I cannot do as you require."

The vast room went still, apprehension thick as smoke in the air.

"Do I ask so much?" Uorsin's quiet words fell, stones crashing to the marble. "I am Uorsin, High King, Uniter of the Twelve Kingdoms, and I cannot give my chosen bride a simple meal."

Madeline remained where she was. Across the hall, Dafne froze in the doorway, the rubies glittering in her hands.

"Send for the executioner," Uorsin growled.

Someone sobbed. Not me. I was made of ice. My thoughts frozen. I had to stop this, somehow.

I opened my mouth, willing Danu to give me the words, but Harlan put a hand on my knee under the table, squeezing in warning. The executioner strode in, wearing his black hood, carrying his great axe.

"Behead this miserable excuse for a cook." Uorsin pointed at Madeline.

The room seemed to take a long, slow spin. The topaz burned fire into my palm. I shook off Harlan's hand. That was the coward's way. Madeline was mine to protect.

"High King Uorsin," I began, "perhaps exile would—"

The back of his fist crashed against my face, shattering my nose. My head snapped back, hitting the metal-inlaid back of the chair so hard my vision went momentarily black. Blood poured down my throat, turning my stomach, and bright tears filled my eyes. I scrambled to orient, wondering why my head took so long to clear, how everything had so suddenly spiraled out of all control.

The executioner strode forward and with a casual swing of his axe lopped off Madeline's head where she knelt. Blood poured out on the golden marble, red as the spilled wine, as the bright spatters on my pink gown, as that day on Odfell's pass when Hugh's wasted death stained the pristine snow. Several ladies fainted, and more than one person retched. I made a sound, the surprised oomph of a gut-wounded warrior.

"You were saying, Daughter?" Uorsin smiled at me. Daring me.

"Nothing, my King." My voice came out in a croak, and Illyria, who'd been staring avidly at the pooling blood below us, turned to give me a smile also. And licked her lips.

"Are those my jewels?" She pointed at Dafne in the doorway.

Suddenly terrified to bring anyone else into range, I struggled to stand. "Yes. I'll get them for you."

"Let me, Your Highness." Harlan pressed something cool into my hand. "You spilled your wine." His eyes held that same warning, as if we waited together in ambush, the enemy creeping closer. *Stay calm. Stay steady.* I pressed the damp cloth to my nose and mouth, pinching into the pain to stop the flow of blood.

He strode across the hall, an imposing figure, took the jewels from Dafne, and dismissed her so neatly it seemed planned. Returning to me, he placed the box before me and opened it, as if asking for my approval. The rubies. A few other things. Not all of it. Dafne should have brought them all. I didn't care about the jewels.

They didn't matter. If Uorsin noticed, I would say I'd hidden the rest, for fear of theft. And then I'd go get them and tell Dafne to run. I'd rather he cleave my head from my shoulders. Far more bearable than watching Dafne die, too. "Your Highness?" Harlan inquired with grave courtesy.

"Thank you, Captain," I managed. "The jewels, my King."

I waited, too full of sapping grief to be tense, as he presented them to Illyria. She cooed happily, adorning herself with Salena's jewels. My vision fogged and I pinched my broken nose, staunching the blood and using the pain to keep myself alert.

"But there's something missing." Illyria sounded disappointed. And accusing.

Oh, Danu. I cleared my throat of blood.

"The Star of Annfwn," Illyria continued. "It should be here."

Uorsin frowned. Anger rising. Not for me, though. Not this time. "We don't speak that word in this court."

Illyria hesitated slightly. Laid a hand on his cheek. "But, my love, I—"

"There is no such thing," he thundered, anger spilling out. "I would have had it, if so." He pulled her to her feet and lifted her in his arms. "Since there is no meal forthcoming and you have your engagement and your jewels, I'll have what you promised me."

She giggled, ringing false to my ears—and her dead gaze caught and held on mine. For once, though, Uorsin did me a favor, ignoring her laughing protests, and carried her off.

Leaving a dead body and a horrified court in his wake.

16

"Come, Your Highness." Harlan cupped my elbow still, urging me to stand, his deep voice grim. "You need tending."

"Wait." I stopped him. Madeline's first assistant stood riveted by the doors to the kitchens, staring at the headless body, white-faced and shaking. "Lise!" I spoke sharply to cut through her shock. Out of habitual obedience, she hastened to me.

"Your Highness." She wiped tears away, immediately replaced by a fresh flow. "I don't know what to—"

"People need feeding. Not here. I'll have the Hawks take care of Madeline and clean up. Send the word round that everyone can dine in chambers if they can stomach it. Plate up what you were planning to serve. Any delicacies that can be created quickly should be sent to the High King. Can you handle that? I need you to maintain."

"My men will help clear the hall and notify everyone," Harlan added, and I didn't protest. Lise nodded and fled to the kitchens. Servants, mercenaries, and pages moved out, speaking to the ambassadors and courtiers and shaking them from their stunned silence. Gradually they rose, filtering out of the hall. Marskal, as ever alert, had already moved forward with a detail to retrieve Madeline's body, his quiet face filled with regret.

"Captain," he said under his breath, "we're packing to flee. We await your word."

Harlan, still holding my elbow, gave no indication he heard, though he had to have.

"I'll let you know my status," I answered.

"Come, Your Highness," Harlan repeated, and this time I let him lead me from the hall.

We didn't speak on the way to my rooms. The halls were distressingly empty, a pall hanging over Ordnung. A team of my Hawks guarded my chambers, crisply saluting me, faces grim. Dafne sprang up when we entered.

"I have a washbasin and ice ready," she said, and Harlan guided me to where she directed. I trailed along dumbly, the image of Madeline's blood pouring across the floor bright in my mind. She'd trusted me and I'd failed her. I might as well have wielded the axe myself. No one was safe if I had no power to protect them. I had no power to save any of them—not the starving, not the plague ridden. I was down to rescuing one person at a time, but by Danu I'd do at least that much.

"Run," I told Dafne. "I'll send a few of the Hawks with you. Go prepare your things." I glared at Harlan, daring him to object to their escape.

"We'll discuss it. Sit," Dafne said.

I was about to remind her who gave the orders when Harlan pressed me into the chair and Dafne replaced the pressure of my hand with an ice-filled cloth, making my eyes water anew. "Tip your head back. How badly is she hurt?"

"He broke her nose, I'm sure of it," Harlan replied. "Probably concussion, as hard as her head hit the chair. Her eyes aren't focusing right."

"I'm fine." I gasped as Dafne fingered the back of my head and laid more ice on the lump forming there. "I've had worse injuries."

"Good." Harlan moved in front of me, peeling the bloody cloth away and grabbing a new one from Dafne's pile, pressing it into my hand. "Then you'll stay steady for me to straighten your nose."

"Do you have to?" Dafne sounded appalled.

"Better to do it now, before she swells." He put a hand behind my neck and reached for my nose. I stopped him by grabbing his wrist. Harlan simply raised an eyebrow at me. "Can't have a broken nose marring your lovely face, Ursula. Bear with it a moment more."

I laughed without humor at his joke, the blood thick in my throat. "Fix it," I croaked. Crooked noses made it hard to breathe.

Holding my gaze, he laid thumb and forefinger on either side of the bridge of my nose.

Then yanked.

A bright flash of pain. A sharp cry and blood gushed out of me. I clapped the clean cloth over my nose and mouth to staunch both.

And found myself sobbing.

Pain, grief, and guilt wrenched at me, convulsive. I tried to hold it all in. Failed utterly. I could no more stop the fountain of it than I could the bright red blood.

Strong arms came around me. I pulled away, but they tightened. "It's okay, Ursula." Harlan's deep voice stroked my shattered nerves. "Let it out. Let me help you."

"I fell apart," I gasped, choking over the tears and blood and sheer horror of it all. "She was my friend and I let her die. I couldn't stop any of it. I'm worthless."

"No. Never that." His chest rumbled under my ear as he murmured that and other soothing nonsense.

The paroxysm lessened and I gradually managed to get ahold of myself. "I'm all right," I told him, pulling away.

He let me that time, moving to a chair across from me, then handing over a wet cloth. I wiped my face with it, hissing at the painful swelling around my broken nose. Dipping the cloth in the basin of water, I saw the blood eddy out, rustier now. The dregs of my tears added no color. Physical injuries leave evidence where emotional ones don't. When the cloth washed clean, Harlan handed me the ice again. We seemed to be alone. Now that I'd recovered from my outburst, embarrassment crawled up my spine. How weak he'd think me.

"Thank you," I said, meaning for all of it. Wishing I could tell him he could go without sounding ungracious.

"I'm sorry about your mother's jewels."

"Things. Only things." *At least she didn't have the Star.* "Where did Dafne go?"

"She's giving you a bit of privacy."

"I notice you're still here."

"Yes."

Apparently I didn't get that much privacy. "She needs to flee. It's not safe for her to stay in Ordnung. I can't watch another—" Danu help me, I still had no equilibrium. My voice caught on the prospect of watching Dafne die, too. "Tell me your men won't prevent that."

"She's packing for you both. We'll leave as soon as you're ready."

I gaped at him, my brain still far behind. "I'm not going anywhere. I can't leave. The King specifically forbade me."

He sighed, the first sign of real impatience I'd seen from him, and braced his elbows on his knees, clasping his hands together. Such big hands. Fiercely strong, rough with calluses, yet amazingly gentle when he'd comforted me.

"Ursula." He said it sharply enough to get my attention. "You're in shock and your head is swimming with concussion, but *you* cannot stay in Ordnung."

"You heard him." Was that voice mine? I sounded ten again. No, five, and he'd shattered the teacups. I struggled to drag my thoughts back, to focus. I set the ice down, tired of holding it.

"He'll kill you next. Do you understand me? Illyria will see to it. We must go now, tonight, while they're occupied with each other and before he thinks to change my orders. This is our window of opportunity. It might be the last one."

"I cannot fail the Twelve Kingdoms by running. And I cannot defy the King's will. I'm honor bound to stay." I knew that much.

Harlan took a cloth, dipped it into the water, and began cleaning the blood from my hands. So much blood. "You owe it to the Twelve Kingdoms to get out with your life," he said quietly. "Your people will look to you to save them in the days ahead. They love you. You are their hero—we all can see it. You cannot be that, however, if you get yourself killed. You are still the only viable heir. Protect yourself as such."

It sounded so unlikely. Ridiculous, even, that they'd love someone so weak and foolish. The mercenary sought to flatter me, yet again. "Some hero I am. Nearly knocked unconscious while waiting for dinner. I couldn't even block a lousy sucker punch."

"You didn't try."

"What?"

"Ursula." He tossed the bloodied cloth aside and took my hands. "I sat right next to you and saw the whole thing. You're one of the fastest fighters I've ever seen and you didn't raise a hand to stop him."

"He's the King."

"For a smart woman you have a huge blind spot when it comes to your father."

I narrowed my eyes at him, pulled my hands away, and stood. Then had to brace myself on the back of the chair, my head swam so. He might be right about the concussion. "Not blindness. Loyalty. Something you wouldn't understand, mercenary."

He shook his head. "We're not having this conversation right now. Regardless of all else, we need to flee."

"I think you're right about Illyria. She must have him under some kind of spell. Influencing his mind. That's the only way this makes sense. I need to talk to him, find a way to get through to him."

"What is this Star of Annfwn?" Harlan asked suddenly. Hoping to trip me up?

I resisted, barely, putting my hand protectively over the gemstone, and shrugged, not trusting my voice.

"Your Highness." Harlan sounded entirely out of patience now. "Part of my contract is protecting you as part of the royal family. I can't leave Ordnung knowing you to be in grave peril, if only from the Mistress of Deyrr. It would be smartest to take this thing she wants out of her reach. But, regardless, you're coming with me whether you wish to or not. If necessary, I'll get your Hawks to help. They see the need to flee, even if you don't."

"Is that so? Do you plan to knock me over the head and carry me bodily out of the castle? If you think that, you'll get this fight you've been spoiling for."

He cracked a grin. "In your current condition I might pull it off, but it would be far from the test of skill I want. Don't make it come to that. You know I'm right. You can meet up with your sisters, assure yourself of the youngest's safety, secure the next generation of heirs—more important now than ever—and make a plan of action with them. Perhaps take this 'star' back to Annfwn."

"Even if you're right—which I don't agree that you are—I can't violate the King's law and my father's directive. Neither can you, as your contract explicitly states that you must uphold the King's law."

"It also states that we are here to uphold the peace of the Twelve Kingdoms and protect the royal family from all threats. I interpret that to take precedence in this case."

"Honor is not a matter of interpretation! You can't bend the rules to suit the desire of the moment."

"You do."

"Thrice-damned if I do!"

"You lie to me without blinking. Is that honorable? You bent your precious rules for your sisters, didn't you?" He glowered at me. "If you'd followed the King's edicts, you would have brought

Queen Andromeda back from the Tala border or killed one of you trying. And you would have brought your infant nephew here with or without Princess Amelia's agreement. Don't you sneer down your broken nose at me, Your Highness. At least I'm honest about my choices."

My legs felt weak and my head mucky. Easing myself around the desk, I sat. Then, giving up all pretense of pretending my skull wasn't pounding, I dropped my face in my hands. Danu, how could this mercenary be so right? Misstep after misstep. "I can't think."

"You don't have to." He'd followed me, and his hand brushed over my hair. Then he pressed the ice into my hand. "Let me take care of things. Just for the next few hours. You're injured. Your life has turned upside down. No one expects you to handle every damn thing, Ursula."

"I expect it." My voice had no strength, though. "If I don't have my honor, I'm nothing."

"That's not true. You have everything you are. Heir to the Twelve Kingdoms. So many people are counting on you. Right now, you have one responsibility: live to fight another day."

"He's right, Your Highness," came Dafne's voice. "Please listen."

I raised my head to find her just inside the doorway, face pale and eyes dark.

"I did what I thought best for my sisters at the time, yes. But I wasn't going directly against my father. Walking a fine line, maybe." I glared at Harlan, who only smiled, thin lipped. "But now you both stand there and ask me to betray my King, to abandon him when he's under threat. That's a big, fat line to cross."

"If he's under Illyria's influence as you suspect, then he's compromised," Harlan pointed out. "That's not a betrayal, but a strategic retreat."

Defend, parry, attack, retreat, regroup.

"Surely that's part of your ethic," he pressed.

"Retreat and regroup," I said, feeling dulled by it all. Could he be right? Or was I rationalizing because I so badly wanted out of this imprisonment and to get to Ami? I rubbed my temples, which did nothing to relieve my headache. Or heartache.

"That's right, Ursula. Retreat and regroup." He stroked my hair. "Did you get the remaining jewels?" Asking Dafne, not me.

"Everything I could find. I don't know if any would fit the definition of a star. I did pack up what books and scrolls I could on the Tala and Annfwn—we might find something in there."

"I hate to leave anything within Illyria's reach that could give her more power. And she's unlikely to want something so much for any other reason."

I levered myself to my feet. "Don't worry about it. I know where it is. I have it." I returned Harlan's accusing glare evenly. "It will be safe."

"Fine." Harlan nodded, accepting my word for it. A faith in me I didn't understand. "And your decision?"

Closing my eyes, I sent a brief prayer to Danu for guidance. Once upon a time, everything had been so clear, so simple. Or had that, too, been an illusion? "We go to Annfwn. If it will have us."

He looked satisfied. Maybe even relieved. "Then let's plan our strategic retreat."

It didn't take much plotting to betray my King. It helped that Harlan's men had so thoroughly replaced the usual palace guard that they simply obeyed his command to let all he designated, including my Hawks, pass through the gates.

I tried not to let that rankle too much.

I also had the disturbing realization of how thoroughly Uorsin had handed over the defenses of Ordnung to these contracted soldiers and how much of the familiar guard seemed to have disappeared. Another manifestation, perhaps, of Illyria's machinations.

We left in the predawn darkness. Moranu's moon had set and

Glorianna's sun was still hours off. Riding only by the light of Danu's stars, we headed at a stately pace out the main gates, a force under the King's orders. Then we switched back to follow the paths that wended up the hills behind Ordnung.

Harlan hadn't argued too much about my decision to ride my war stallion. Not much choice there, as the paths we'd follow didn't allow for wheeled vehicles, even if I would have consented to be stuck in one. He rode close by, keeping an eye on me and pretending not to.

"I'm not going to tip out of the saddle like a raw recruit who's had his skull rung for the first time," I said to him, keeping my tone mild.

"I never doubted it for a moment," he replied, unruffled. But he stayed near.

I'd done something like this to Amelia—badgered her to leave Windroven and ride in a carriage woozy with morning sickness. Then she'd sneakily traversed this path before me. Ironic that I followed in her footsteps now. And in Andi's when she'd ridden too far and encountered Rayfe the first time.

Somehow the Three guided our steps to Annfwn.

Or Salena did.

I didn't much care for the notion that our mother had set up all of this. Had somehow foreseen this dark morning when she gave me that jewel on my seventh birthday. Harlan accused me of lying about it—technically true—but my promise to my mother that long-ago day superseded that point. Perhaps he had a point about layers of honor. The path rarely led as straight as a blade. She'd asked for my solemn vow not to tell anyone, and I hadn't.

Why did Illyria want it?

I suspected that Harlan had the right of it. So far as I'd observed, everything came down to power with her. Surely, though, the jewel carried no magic. If it did, Salena would have gifted it to Andi. Possibly to Amelia. Not to her stubbornly practical, non-magical, mossback daughter.

It could be that she'd given it to me for safekeeping. This

might have been her plan, after all, that we rode for Odfell's Pass and Annfwn. If nothing else, I could offer the jewel to Andi. If it truly belonged to Annfwn, then it should stay there. And if Danu smiled on me, Amelia and the babies would be there also.

Annoying that I'd be following the mercenary's advice, but consulting with my sisters would be helpful. With them I never wavered on the right decision.

Everything would be clearer in the bright light of day.

Pray Danu to make it so.

17

None of us had slept, so we needed to rest a while before pressing on. It would not do for any of us to encounter the Tala and their tricky ways with anything less than our best. Andi and I had not spoken since that bitter day on Odfell's Pass, when we parted ways, she going to her new loyalties while I carried Hugh's body back to Amelia. We weren't at open war with each other, but neither were we exactly at peace.

Who knew what might be set against us as we approached the border this time?

While the weather remained pleasant enough for everyone to comfortably sleep outdoors, it seemed wise to conserve our food supplies for deeper into the Wild Lands, where I knew from experience we would not have the luxury of shelter. So we continued through to midmorning, to the last guard outpost, to take advantage of their reserves instead of hitting ours.

We'd not yet encountered patrols, as we should have, and I'd half feared that Jepp would find the guard station abandoned. Instead she reported that the outpost appeared to be occupied as usual, but seemed unduly silent.

Which made me even more uneasy.

Harlan had never been asked to cover anything outside of Ordnung and the township, so these should be guards out of Ordnung under my authority. Odd that they weren't following established protocol, however.

"This falls to me, then," I said, and Harlan nodded. Relieved that he didn't balk, because I had enough energy to hold off the headache and look commanding, but not enough to burn his ears back, too, I agreed to let him accompany us.

Jepp and Marskal flanked me a horse length behind, Harlan bringing up the back point of our diamond, as we rode up to the outpost.

"Ho to the guardhouse!" I called out once we approached close enough.

No immediate response. Then a guard stumbled out, sleepy and disheveled though the sun had risen quite high. He raised a negligent hand, then goggled upon seeing me. Belatedly he snapped to attention, then bowed.

"Your Highness! We did not expect—That is, we had no word that—How may we serve you?" He called back something through the darkened doorway, and the sounds of barked orders and mad shuffling drifted out.

"We ride on a scouting mission," I informed him, "and require a hot meal, a few hours' sleep. Where is your lieutenant?"

More shuffling, and another man, one I recognized, pushed through the doorway. The former captain of the gate guards at Ordnung. I lifted my brows in surprise. "Captain Hammet. Do you customarily lie abed all day?"

"Your Highness." He gave me the salute of the palace guard. "My deep apologies. We have all been ill and our messages for relief from Ordnung have not been answered."

"What illness?"

"A food sickness. When we ran out of provisions, we supplemented one of our leaner stews with mushrooms. Apparently the wrong kind." He grimaced. "Glorianna blessed us in that no one died, but more than one of us prayed not to live a couple of times there."

"Why did you run out of provisions?"

"Your Highness—we don't know. Our regular rotation, which always brought fresh supplies, has not arrived in more than five seven-days. I worried that something had happened at Ordnung." His gaze lingered on my battered face. No doubt I sported two black eyes by now. "I've sent three men. None have returned."

Because of the edict that none should leave Ordnung but the mercenaries, no doubt. Still, provision should have been made for the outposts. It seemed like such a huge miss. What about the other outlying guard stations and patrols?

"Are you certain this ailment is not contagious?"

"I make no guarantees, Your Highness. We have only our best guess that the mushrooms were the culprit."

Worse luck there.

"We shall not risk it," I decided. "You are unlikely to receive relief from Ordnung anytime soon. I cannot explain why and I apologize for that. However, we cannot continue with such lax posting. At best it shames the might that is Ordnung, Mohraya, and the Twelve Kingdoms; at worst, it places us all in grave jeopardy. I shall leave additional troops and supplies with you. Mobilize the healthiest of your subordinates to clean this place up and make arrangements to quarantine those still too ill to work."

He flushed, even at such a gentle setdown. The man I'd known at Ordnung would never have let the situation go so long, or allowed himself and his guard to grow so shabby. Illness alone could maybe produce what I'd seen, but this had gone on much longer.

"Captain Harlan, to me." I reined up after we'd gone some distance, pointing Jepp and Marskal to rejoin the rest of the group. "Can you explain?"

"You read the contract—outposts were not included in my responsibilities. Only Ordnung proper and the township."

As I had recalled, but wanted him to confirm. He returned my stare calmly, not evincing any guilt. "What provisions were made to continue manning the outposts?"

"To be frank, I don't know. I was given to understand that anything not under my command would be otherwise handled."

"How did you determine who staffed the castle walls? Who did you work with?"

"You needn't treat this like an inquisition." He finally bristled a little. "The High King told me to disperse my men as I saw fit, according to the contract. I don't concern myself with what's explicitly not my responsibility. That would be overstepping."

"But your men would stop anyone from leaving Ordnung under the current restrictions."

"Without proper authorization, yes."

"Who can authorize?"

"The High King, of course. The King's adviser, Derodotur, would convey messages."

I barely restrained my frown, covering it with a crisp nod. At least that partially explained why Hammet had been exiled up here. "Did you have occasion to know Lord Percy?"

Harlan did not attempt to disguise a frown of puzzlement. "No?"

"All right, then." I urged my horse back to our company. Why hadn't it occurred to me until now to inquire after Percy? He should have been coordinating the guard and the outposts. But I *had* thought of it, when the gate guard challenged us—and then bizarrely forgot. Even without that, it would have been my habit to check in with him early on, if only to get status and another perspective on the mercenaries. Instead I hadn't thought of him again. Or Hammet. Not until I saw him.

"I need volunteers," I said to my Hawks, glancing at Harlan, who nodded assent. "Hawks and Vervaldr both, to supplement the guard post and get patrols back up. Some men and women with decent command abilities and better-than-average hunting-and-gathering skills. And a strong constitution." I grimaced. The smell emanating from the barracks had been enough to turn my stomach without the fresh skull rattle.

We sorted out the stay-behind crew quickly enough. It hurt to leave them with a good portion of our supplies—quite the opposite of what I'd planned—but we'd be able to forage. Harlan's man, the one he'd wrestled for my benefit, offered to stay, and Jepp jumped on that wagon fast enough, giving me pleading puppy-dog eyes when I scowled at her.

I had other scouts. She was just my best. Which meant she would serve the Twelve well setting up the patrols to protect them from this section of the Wild Lands, but it annoyed me to lose her. I wanted the best for finding Amelia. If she'd crossed into Annfwn, however, Jepp would be cooling her heels at the pass, so she'd be better staying at the outpost.

On the other hand, Dafne stubbornly refused to stay, as I would have preferred, but I would not command her to do so.

Harlan, though he showed little of his irritation, wasn't best pleased to lose his man, either. We lost an hour to the organizing—including the few minutes I stole to debrief Hammet. Sure enough, Percy had taken him off command of the gate guard when the mercs arrived and sent him up here. Then fell silent nearly two months ago. Fresh rotations had continued to arrive for a couple of seven-days, then dropped off.

Most unsettling.

And now I couldn't return to Ordnung to determine what had happened. Too many fights on too many fronts. Danu taught that a warrior must remain single weighted. Me, with one foot in Ordnung, another with my sisters—with each of them, truly, except I did not have three feet—defending my back from Illyria, the Tala, Old Erich, facing my father and the multiple problems plaguing the Twelve—I was so multiply weighted that I'd be doomed were it a physical fight. As if sealed in a fortress besieged on all sides, I could do nothing to help those trapped outside.

And yet, how could I alter any of this? Already I was in retreat, slinking away like a chastened hound dog, if not in outright rebellion. There—another example of my lack of single focus. How could I be in a castle under siege, a beaten dog, and a defiant rebel all at once?

"You're worried," Harlan commented quietly to me after we'd ridden for a time, still unrested and fed only from our much-reduced provisions.

I gave him a sidelong glance. "Being worried would imply that I lack confidence in our forces. I am . . . thinking."

He made a snorting sound. "Not much of a distinction. How's the head?"

"Fine."

"You've lost color. You need to rest."

"Thank you, Mother."

Harlan raised his brows at me. "Shall I cuddle you on my lap and sing you a baby-sparrow song?"

My turn to snort. "What in the Twelve is a 'baby-sparrow song'?"

"Eh, not in the Twelve. I don't know your word for it. A soothing tune, usually with a lot of silliness, that you sing to infants to make them sleep."

"A lullaby, we call it."

He nodded, once, filing that away. Truly his command of our Common Tongue was excellent. He showed flexibility in substituting phrases for words he couldn't translate. An admirable skill. "Sing me one of your lullabies."

I had to laugh. "Danu, no. You do not want to hear me sing. Unless we're attacked by wolves—then it might serve to drive them off."

"Perhaps sometime I'll convince you to sing for me when we're alone, then."

"Not happening. And before you ask, I mean both that we'll never be alone and that I'll never sing."

"I haven't given up on persuading you."

"Save your energy. We'll need all of it before this is done.

Everyone would do well to remember that," I added, thinking sourly of Jepp's bright-eyed interest in her man-mountain.

"It's good for people to take joy in each other. Brandur is most taken with your Jepp. He commented that she's unusually flexible and . . . inventive."

Only years of controlling my emotions kept me from reacting to that. I was less successful at preventing the image from blooming in my mind, a naked and limber Jepp scaling her personal mountain. It chilled my gut even as some part of me warmed to it. One more example of how I had lost my single weightedness. Conflicting emotions caused hesitation or, worse, paralysis.

It made no difference which front, which battle—all of life is a war, and I could not afford to be less than my best in any arena.

I needed to find a way back to the place I'd comfortably occupied before all this. I'd long ago reconciled myself to a life without sex and, most likely, any kind of intimate relationship. It had been an easy choice, compared to the alternatives. The mercenary captain brought a foreign element to my world in many ways, so I hadn't had adequate guard in place for his unusual moves.

I would learn how to counter him.

"He thinks your dagger forms and the physical training they bring lend themselves to it," Harlan continued. "Also, it's new for him to have a lover who is also a warrior, so that adds an unusual level for him. Apparently she can do this thing where she arches her spine, bends back, and—"

"Captain, I do *not* want to hear this."

"Embarrassed or titillated?"

"Neither." *Both.* My head throbbed in time with my pulse, but I couldn't use that excuse. "I simply am not interested in this conversation."

"Why does it bother you, to think of them together like that?" Harlan asked after a brief silence.

Our company had strung out at this point, the midday sun making already tired people move more slowly. Some napped in their saddles, trusting in our scouts and lookouts to alert them if trouble arose. I knew my Hawks would come instantly alert and trusted that Harlan's men were similarly well trained. Nothing moved in the open landscape other than us, giving me no excuse to tighten up our formation.

Danu frowned on wishing for action, but it would end this discussion. I would have to find another way. Harlan only intensified his attempts to get through my guard when faced with a direct defense. A more subtle deflection might work better.

"It doesn't bother me. I'm happy for her to enjoy him. Otherwise I would have forbidden it."

"But you don't understand her wanting to."

"Oh, I understand. Jepp approaches everything in life with lustful enthusiasm—fighting and fucking both. It makes her who she is."

"What makes you who you are?"

"What you see is what you get."

"Oh, now—that's just not true. What I see is what you want everyone to see. I'm asking to know more."

"I'm saying no—and asking *you* to respect that."

"I respect that you think you want that, but I've come to the conclusion that you could use a friend. I want to be your friend, Ursula. Let me in a little. Tell me a story."

"Even if I did—which I have no intention of doing—this is not the time or place for that kind of conversation."

"Then you acknowledge that there could be a time and place for it." He grinned at my narrow glare. "That works for me."

I sighed, indulged in rubbing my temple when I really wanted to massage the pounding lump on the back of my head. "You weary me, mercenary."

"So much for you being fine. When will you rest?"

"There's a spot not too far ahead where we can stop. More defensible than this open meadow."

He studied the landscape. "I've seen little so far of concern. What lurks out of sight that would attack a party this size?"

"This is why you needed us with you. Just wait and see. For now, the danger is less, this close to Ordnung." Unless our skeleton staffing had encouraged the Tala to venture closer. Unless Uorsin sent troops after me. Neither of which I could control. "Still, the Tala have penetrated this far and farther. With our defenses so lean, they might have grown bold."

"Surely your sister would not sanction attacks on the Twelve?"

No, I didn't think so. But I also didn't care to discuss Ash's dire comments that Andi and Rayfe contended with discontent internal to Annfwn. Or to rehash our recent disagreements for the foreigner's amusement. I hadn't heard from Andi, except via Ash, and I considered him an unreliable messenger at best. Even if she denied us passage across the border, at least I could see her and make sure that she fared well.

She loved and trusted Rayfe, I knew.

But I didn't.

We stopped an hour or so later, on one of the aprons where the acid-green meadow grasses gave way to soft, moss-covered soil that abutted a sharp cliffside. With our backs to it, we needed only guard to the forward of our group, not above or behind. Remembering to watch for attack from above was key when dealing with the Tala, I told Harlan, and I was gratified to see him pass the word among his men.

I tended my horse and made sure everyone had instructions and something to eat before I made my way to where Dafne had set out my blanket roll for me in an alcove against the stone. She gave me that same half-sympathetic/half-exasperated look Harlan had.

"You're waxy, Your Highness," she said, with a shake of her head. "I'm making you a healing tea, but you need to rest." She and Harlan, singing the same tune.

"That wasn't your opinion when you convinced me to flee my home with no sleep."

"I regret that, but we had to get out and you know it. Now we have breathing room. You saw to it that you won't be missed for some time. When you are, there's no one with the skill to catch up to you and your Hawks—something else you know full well. Take care of yourself, Ursula. We need you." She handed me a steaming cup.

Obediently I took it, sat on my pallet, and sipped, humbled by her caring. The brew backed the headache off almost immediately, making me even more guiltily grateful. "I apologize. I hate feeling less than my best. It makes me irritable."

"I understand that." She sat beside me. "I wish I'd been able to bring ice. The swelling is, if anything, worse."

"Second day is always worse. It will start going down soon. And we'll hit pockets of snow before long. I'll grab some of that."

She looked a bit aghast. "We'll hit winter weather even in late summer?"

"There's a reason those peaks are white, librarian. But no—most of our way should be warm and clear. In these mountains, though, old snow can linger in shadowed clefts of the north faces. Near the top of the pass is anyone's guess. While I have you away from the others, tell me—did you see Lord Percy while we were at Ordnung?"

"Well, of—" She looked up and to the right, as if mentally scanning one of her documents. "Wait. No. Come to think of it, I didn't. I should have. More, I should have noticed I hadn't seen him. He's a longtime personal friend and always at court in some capacity or another, or about in the halls. How is it possible I didn't miss him?"

"You were occupied a great deal," I pointed out.

"Not *that* much. Interesting, because I didn't think to look for Lady Zevondeth, either, not until I ran into a reference to her in the books in Andi's rooms."

"And I didn't think of her until you mentioned her. Just as it never occurred to me to look for Percy."

"Which you always would have," Dafne replied, looking

somber. "It was always your habit upon return to Ordnung to visit with him and confer on the status of Ordnung's defenses."

"I'm surprised you know that."

She shrugged a little. "I pay attention."

"So I see." My jaw cracked with a yawn, stretching my bruised face so my eyes watered. "In your reading, did you find that the Practitioners of Deyrr had unusual powers of persuasion?"

"As in, being able to make us forget about people?"

Or to influence a king. "Yes—anything like that?"

She thought about it. "Not directly, but I brought what I could with me. I'll look with that in mind." She paused, looked out over the waving grasses below, so brightly green even this late in the season. "I don't much care for the notion that I can't trust my own thoughts."

"I'm with you there." I yawned again. "Suddenly I can't keep my eyes open."

Dafne took the mug from me with a pleased smile.

Too pleased.

"Danu take you—you sedated me?"

"Not very much," she retorted. "Very mild painkiller and soother. The fact that it's hitting you so hard confirms how badly you need to sleep."

"Tell Marskal that whoever is on watch should wake me in four hours. We can make more time today." I had more, but I lost it in the fog of drowsiness. Had to lie down. "And remind me to discuss insubordination with you later, Lady Mailloux."

"Yes, Your Highness." She sounded not in the least worried, covering me with a blanket. "Sleep well."

She disobeyed on that, as well, was my first thought when I awoke to full dark. We would have a serious conversation about this.

"You're awake? Good." Harlan rumbled, a darker silhouette against the starry night sky. "Some food and tea for you."

I sat up, scrubbing my hands over my scalp to clear the dregs of the heavy, dreamless sleep. The headache had backed off considerably, which I appreciated, but not enough to let Dafne off the hook.

"Now *you* are my lady-in-waiting? I know that's not in your contract." Taking what Harlan handed me, I sniffed the tea suspiciously.

"No sedative this time," he said. "Though you look better for the sleep."

"Do you have cat's eyes that you can see in the dark?" I muttered.

"I could observe that much before the sun set."

"Then why in Danu didn't you wake me earlier? Why didn't Marskal? I'll skin Dafne if she didn't pass along the message."

"She did," he returned in that mild tone, surprisingly soft for all its deepness. "I overruled your order."

"Listen, mercenary, you don't have the authority to—"

"Countermand you in most situations," he agreed. "Unless I perceive that impaired judgment is leading you to endanger yourself. It's in the—"

"Yes, I know what your thrice-dammed contract says."

"You seemed as if you needed reminding."

"A reminder that my authority is compromised by a hired hand who makes cavalier decisions about whether my judgment is up to his standards? No, I remember that quite well."

"What bothers you most, Ursula?" He asked the question almost philosophically. A soft whisking sound told me he sharpened his blade. He sat with his back mostly to me, gazing out into the night. Guarding me, even still. "That I'm paid to do my job—which I'm very good at, by the way—or that you can't push me around?"

"Oh, I think I could if I tried."

"I look forward to it." Harlan sounded as if he meant it.

"Where is everyone?" Less groggy, I peered into the dense night, listening for movement.

"I sent them ahead to scout and hunt, replenish our provisions."

"Your men don't know the dangers that—"

"Marskal and your other Hawks do. I tasked him to lead the group. Your lieutenant is a good man."

He had the right of it, but I seethed over his autocratic decision making nonetheless.

"We shall catch up, then."

"In the morning, yes."

"You think you can keep me here against my will?" I loosened my blade in the sheath.

"Tell you what: if you can take me down, we'll leave."

"Another gambit to get me to spar with you."

"As you like. I'm betting that you're in no shape to do it. You were stretched thin enough to break and slept like the dead. So, yes, I intend to see you get a full night's sleep. When was the last time you had that?"

Not since Rayfe had turned our world upside down, certainly. I'd grown accustomed to less sleep over the years since Salena died, however. Some nights had been better than others, but never the same again. As if losing my mother had robbed me of some essential peacefulness. Maddening that thinking of her still grieved me so. Even more aggravating that this mercenary saw this essential weakness. "I don't need much sleep."

He didn't comment, his silence damning enough.

"What's it to you?" I needled him, fed up with this entirely. "Oh, right—a paycheck. How could I forget."

He stilled. Set the blade he'd been sharpening down. Turned and looked at me, face shadowed but his slow-boil anger palpable.

"Keep pushing me that way and you will find out."

18

≈

"Is that a threat?" I asked, a bit on the loud side, to cover the sound of my gathering myself to spring, ready to defend, then attack.

"You'd like it to be, wouldn't you?"

"No. I'd like you to cease interfering, however well-intentioned you think it to be."

"Put down your sword. I'm not your enemy, Ursula, even if you feel on firmer ground treating me like one. You asked what it is to me. Is it so impossible to believe that it's important to me because you are, because I have come to care deeply about you?"

I thought I'd been ready, but I hadn't seen that coming. A sucker punch to the gut that stole my breath.

"You're paid to care."

"That blade grows dull with overuse. I've served many ladies without loving them. If anything, the contract is what brought us together, not what dictates my heart."

"You hardly know me."

A curve of Moranu's moon topped the tree line, gleaming on Harlan's face, silvering his pale eyes. Enough that his wry smile showed. "That doesn't seem to matter. I started to fall in love with you the moment I saw you striding through the court, so tall and proud, determination and anguish in your eyes."

I was not equipped for this. Amelia would know how to flirt or gently put him off. My thoughts spun without traction. No defense to this.

"At least I've rendered you speechless," he commented, his tone echoing his smile. "Is it such a shock? I made my intentions clear before this. I invited you into my bed, after all. You knew of my desire."

I found a way to parry that one. "Yes, but that's hardly a declaration of . . . deeper feelings."

"Won't even speak the word in my presence, I see."

"Look at Jepp and Brandur," I persisted, feeling a bit trapped, needing to break out of this corner. Rebalancing, I angled myself so I could step out of his reach as soon as I gained my feet. "Their liaison is hardly an emotional one."

"True, but you are not her, are you? And I am not him. You and I are much alike in that. We are not people who take 'liaisons' casually."

"I'm certainly not. I don't know about you, Captain."

"Harlan," he rumbled, shifting his weight and edging into my reach. He'd know that I'd feel the pressure of his proximity. Deliberately making me feel cornered.

I refused to budge, to give him the satisfaction. Sometimes reaching a détente with an enemy required refusing to be the loser. Until we tested each other, either of us might be the winner or loser. I could never beat him strength to strength. My best strategy lay in speed and surprise. Which I could not exercise in my current position. For the moment, I'd have to rely on bravado. "I know your name."

"Then use it, Ursula. This conversation is between you and me, not our roles in the world."

"See, that's where you don't understand me at all, mercenary. You have a profession, which you may do very well, but you do it for pay. I *am* my role in the world. There is no separation of selves. I can't escape that, even if I wanted to. You may be a man first and a mercenary second, but I'm the Heir to the High Throne and because of that a warrior for my kingdom and only incidentally a woman. The last is the least important."

"Only because you don't put the woman first," he countered.

"What you don't understand is that I don't care to."

"Then explain it to me." He leaned on one elbow. "We have time and a place now."

"Yes, you certainly made sure of that."

"I did. So if you care to condemn me for it, I'll accept the sentence on those terms. But first I want my prize. What I did this for. Tell me about your other lovers and why they left you so cold."

When Danu raised the moon. "No. And I'm not cold."

Faster than I expected, his hand snaked out and grabbed mine. "Cold," he repeated.

"If that's your seduction technique, it wants improvement." I tugged my hand away, but he simply scooted closer, as if I'd drawn him in. "Keep your distance."

"Which is it, Ursula—do you want my seduction technique or my distance?"

My back hit the cliff wall, Danu take it. "Your distance." I hardened my voice into command. "Don't think I won't cut your throat."

He stayed where he was—far too close—and rubbed his thumb over my palm. "I'm sticking. I need the reason, to understand how you can want me and still refuse me at every turn."

"I don't want you." A last-ditch effort to escape his relentless attack.

A weak one and he knew it, pressing his advantage. "Let's dispense with that artifice. You like what you see when you look at me; you warm and soften when I touch you. That's not the problem. What is?"

"Some of us don't have the luxury of indulging in everything that takes our fancy."

"What's the harm? I'm a simple mercenary who poses no threat to the throne. I won't get you with child. We're alone for the night. I'm bought and paid for." A smile in his voice, he pressed a kiss to my palm, and I shivered before I locked down the response. For an unhinged moment, I entertained the possibility. To touch and be touched in return. To have this sweet warmth run all through me, like a spring thaw.

But I knew where this led.

I yanked my hand away, scrubbing the kiss away on my pants. "I can't."

"Why not?"

"I—" I shifted restlessly, needing to pace. To escape this questioning, which laid my heart open as surely as a flaying knife. "I just can't."

"Are you a virgin?" he asked, careful and quiet.

I laughed at that, jagged. If only. "At my advanced age? Hardly."

"Rape?"

His voice came out harsh enough that before I squelched the impulse, I reached out to touch the hand that automatically went to his sword. "No. Not that. Never think that. I was willing."

"Then what happened?"

I shrugged. Holding off the memory of that night. Making it stay quiescent. "Nothing to speak of. I agreed. I tried it and I didn't care to repeat the experience. Ever."

"Only once?"

"Believe me, once was enough." Enough to keep me awake for years until I learned to set it aside. Where I should have left it. What about this mercenary made me dredge it up again?

"Who was it?" Suspicious anger ran deep in his voice. "Did he hurt you?"

Yes. Oh, yes, it had hurt. And I had broken my rule and wept. Told him to stop, that I'd changed my mind, but he hadn't. I'd come away from that night wounded in some unhealable way, where the blood never dried, broken inside. So strange, the injuries of the invisible self. I'd take a physical hurt over that any day.

And now . . .

Now these questions brought back those memories I'd thought dulled by time, their edges as sharp as the dagger that slices, leaving you bleeding out before you feel the pain.

"I'm not talking about this." My words came out on a gasp, my chest so tight I had no breath. "I have to move. Let me out."

Thank Danu, he moved out of my way and I lunged to my feet, gulping in deep lungfuls of the sweet mountain air. Head swimming, I leaned my hands on my knees, head down, willing my heart to stop its frantic pounding. Forcing the tea to stay down.

A hand on my shoulder made me spin, my dagger in my hand before I knew it, pressing the point to the soft spot at Harlan's throat. He held up his palms in surrender, expression full of some sorrow.

"I'm not the enemy, Ursula," he said gently, as if I didn't hold his life in my hands. "I'm not him."

"He's not—wasn't the enemy either."

"That's a matter of debate. He hurt you. That makes him my enemy."

I sighed. Sheathed the dagger in a slow, deliberate movement. "It's ancient history. Go slay dragons for some other princess."

"How many times must I say it?" He settled big hands on my waist, testing my reaction, then cupping my hips when I didn't protest. I flattened my palms on his muscled shoulders, holding him off as much as I could muster. We stood eye to eye and worlds apart. "I don't want some other woman. It's all about you. I want you."

"Surely even you know we never get everything we want."

"That doesn't mean we give up trying."

"I can't give you what you're asking for. I can't talk about this. Don't ask me to."

He let out a long breath, the sense of strategic retreat palpable.

"All right. I'll let it go for now. And I'll take whatever you're able to give. Even if this much of you is all I can ever have."

"Don't make promises you can't keep, mercenary." I tried for a dry tone, but I'd gone breathless again. In a different way this time. My heart pounding another rhythm. The way I'd felt seeing his golden skin gleaming with oil and sweat.

"I always keep my promises." He edged me closer. "So here's one for you: tell me to stop and I will. No matter what. Always."

He leaned in. I readied the words on my tongue, but he did nothing more than brush my cheekbone with a kiss, as light as a butterfly's wing. I held my breath, waiting for the awful to rise up.

It didn't.

Harlan waited, too, then, with a deep hum that I felt more than heard, he kissed my other cheek, at the high point just below the temple. Warmer this time, a tingle of heat that filtered into my bloodstream. Both energizing and comforting.

"Does this hurt?" he whispered, and I realized he meant my bruises. Of course he meant those, not that other, invisible wound.

"No," I breathed, surprised to find that was true of both, that I'd changed my grip so that I no longer held him away, but curled my fingers into his shirt, absorbed in the sweetness of his mouth on my skin.

"May I kiss you?" He'd already trailed several more soft kisses down my cheek, to the line of my jaw, to the corner of my mouth. But he hovered there, waiting for me to decide. He meant more than he had already. A real kiss. Like lovers do. Like I never had.

"I don't know how," I admitted, hating that I had to, certain that I should say so. A concession in that it revealed so much about that other time, that awful night. So many skills I'd perfected, and yet I'd never kissed anyone, mouth to mouth. Amelia had awakened her lover that way, with a deeply sensual kiss that had stabbed me with a strange emotion. At the time I'd put it down to suspicion of Ash's motives. Now I wasn't sure what it was. Envy, perhaps.

More, I'd wanted to know how that felt, if only once.

"Let me show you," he murmured, lips a breath away.

"All right." I braced myself and he chuckled, low and deep, running his hands up my back in that sensual, soothing way.

His mouth feathered against mine, exquisitely gentle, barely there and gone. I sighed out, breath mingling with his, and it seemed we created a web that drew our lips together again, lightly caressing, sweet, almost innocent.

My heart softened, thudding with lulled beats.

"More?" he asked.

"More," I agreed.

He changed his angle, careful of my broken nose, and kissed me again. Deeper this time, lips moving over mine with leisurely heat, opening and inviting me to do the same. Vaguely surprised at myself, I wanted to taste more of him. The inner edge of his lips possessed a velvety texture, a contrast to his man's mouth and the slight scrape of stubble on his face.

Then his tongue touched mine. His hands soothed me before I realized I'd tensed. Another kind of stroking, this. But one that went to the core of me, the hot glide of his mouth on mine. I made a sound, something incoherent, needy, and he pulled away, surveying my face.

"Still okay?"

"I don't know." An honest answer, if an unsteady one.

"Let's sit." He took my hand, lacing his roughened fingers with mine, and coaxed me back to the pallet.

"I don't think—"

"Shh. Don't think." He tugged me down to sit beside him. "Only kisses and only if you want to. I won't hurt you, Ursula."

Taking my hands, he pressed his mouth into each palm, in that place he'd found me to be so vulnerable, and this time I let the shiver take its course. A delightful fire that shimmered through my blood, heating me throughout. He drew my hands behind his neck, then slowly lay back, guiding me to lie atop him, steadying me with his gentle hold on my hips.

"Kiss me, little hawk," he urged. "Your mouth is like the finest wine."

"You can save the flattery and compliments." A line I should draw, though the muscled bulk of his body under mine made me even more breathless. I might as well be some seaside recruit newly arrived to Ordnung's heights, as much trouble I seemed to be having keeping my breath. "I'm not a woman who needs romance."

He brushed my cheek with light fingertips. "On the contrary. I think you need it more than most. You've had so little of it in your life. Kiss me."

I studied his mouth, picked my angle, and settled my lips on his, anticipating now the delicious shock of contact. My breath rushed out in a long sigh, and he swallowed it, hands roaming down my back, never dropping below the line of my hips.

Softening with the sensation, not caring that he'd called me on that very thing, I relaxed against his reassuring bulk, sinking into his scent, taste, and texture. I lost myself in him, in the long, slow moments of tongue glide and sweet caress of lips. Restlessness built in me, like a hunger for more food after a few tastes. Like I wanted to take bites out of him, or lap him up. I shifted, moving to deepen the kiss, and he flinched, making a pained sound.

"What?" I pulled back, seeing nothing, then scanned the moonlit meadow for danger.

"Your sword, darling Ursula." Harlan laughed and moved me off him, pressing a hand to his groin. "The hilt caught me in a sensitive spot."

"Oh." Chagrin cooled me. What had I been thinking? I knew enough of the vulnerabilities of male fighters to have paid attention to that. I unbuckled the belt and set it next to me, edging away as I did so. "I apologize."

"Don't pull back." He caught me by the hand, drew me down by his side, settled me so that my head lay on his muscled arm, the bulge as mounded as any pillow, our faces close together. He brushed the hair back from my temple, then stroked my cheek. "You are so beautiful in the moonlight."

"Because the shadows hide the bruises and swelling, no doubt."

"On another woman, that might be so. But your beauty is of a different sort—in the set of your jaw and the fire in your eyes. You burn with a strong, clear light. Like the stars in the sky. Remote. Glorious. Exotic."

"Don't tease me. I don't need your lies, as poetic as they may be."

His thumb rubbed over my bottom lip, tracing the edge. "This is the truth. I know beauty when I see it."

"So do I. When your younger sister is ten times more beautiful than you are and the youngest ten times more beautiful than *that*, you quickly learn how such comparisons work. And it's not important to me. I don't need beauty to accomplish what matters most."

"And what is that?"

"Upholding the legacy of my mother and father. The peace that so many sacrificed so much to obtain."

"You don't mention your mother often."

"No. It's . . . painful still. Even after so much time."

"We never stop grieving some people. How old were you when she died?"

Odd that I didn't mind speaking of it right then. The shadows wrapped around us, bodies close together, intimate and quiet. With long caresses, he followed the line of my throat and collarbone, light, chaste touches that I relaxed into.

"I'd just turned ten years of age. Andi was five and Amelia barely born. I was lucky—they hardly knew her at all."

"Lucky to know her. Hardest on you because you did."

Maybe so.

"I heard she died from childbirth?"

Because he'd stroked down to my waist, smoothing his hand over the curve of my hip, I touched his chest, intrigued to feel the play of muscle beneath. He sighed a blissful breath and closed his eyes. Pleasurable, then, too, to feel him soften under my hand. I began to understand why he liked it from me.

"That's the story. It may be true. I have reason, though . . ." I hesitated, but he said nothing, staying pliant and quiet. "It wasn't right away. Maybe the fever took her."

"But you don't think so," he murmured, shifting back, so my fingers brushed the skin inside his open shirt. Surprisingly soft, with a scattering of crisp hairs. He made that deep humming sound as I explored that texture, too.

"I don't know," I admitted. "The alternatives are . . ." *Unthinkable.* "Salena was this amazingly powerful woman. Some say Uorsin won the Great War because of her and the Tala magic she brought to the battlefield."

"Did she love him?"

"No." I'd answered too quickly, lulled by the moment. By the seductive scent and feel of his skin. I pulled my hand away and he caught me by the wrist, putting it back.

"Don't stop. You feel even better than I imagined. And I'd imagined a great deal."

Ah, yes. He'd mentioned those fantasies of my hands on him. I flushed, hoping the darkness covered it, but resumed caressing him. Even moving his shirt aside so I could follow the fold at the crease of his shoulder.

"Why do you suppose she did it, if not out of love?" he asked after a time.

"Others than you would like to know that answer. Salena kept her own counsel. But, in the end at least, she hated Uorsin. I remember that well."

"She doesn't sound like the sort of person who could be forced."

"True. She married him—and stayed—for reasons of her own." *It won't be an easy path. The one of duty and honor never is . . . a path I myself chose.* "She told me once that she did it out of duty and honor."

"Ah. That's where you get it, then." Harlan closed his hand

over mine before I could pull away again, opening his eyes to stare fiercely into mine. "All that extraordinary strength and power."

"I'm my father's daughter."

"You're hers, too."

In that way, you are the most my daughter.

He unbent his elbow and leaned up, slowly gathering me against him, giving me time to consider. To say no. I didn't. Instead I tipped my head back, anticipating the drowning kiss that followed. Waves of it swept over me, melting, tumbling. This time I touched him back, his skin hot under my hand, corded neck enticing me to dig in, to take more.

19

After an eternity of drifting on that sensual sea, I blinked dreamily at him when he pulled away, brushing my hair back with a sweet affection I wasn't sure how to handle. I felt not wholly myself, as if the boundaries between us had somehow blurred with the physical intimacy.

"Why did you stop?"

"You need more sleep. And you're finally relaxed enough to do so."

I frowned. "I already slept. I should take first watch."

"You chose a good place. We are protected on all sides but one. You and I are both well trained enough to wake at any disturbance." He drew his sword and laid it on my other side beside mine, turning me so I lay with my back nestled in the curve of his body, our blades between us and the rest of the world. Side by side, as we were. "We'll both sleep."

"I thought you wanted sex."

His laugh rumbled through me and his arm around my waist tightened. "I want you, Ursula. And here you are. I told you— whatever you're able to give. I meant it."

"*This* is your seduction technique. To leave me wanting." Not just that, but needing in a way I'd never thought possible.

"I can be patient. This is enough, to hold you against me, to have the scent of you in my head, the flavor of you on my tongue, and the feel of you under my hand. I want you, yes, but not frightened and panicked. And not until you're sure of me. One day you'll want me enough to overcome what went before."

"I'm not afraid of you."

"No. I never imagined that, my fearless hawk. We have time. Time enough for you to heal inside and out. I told you I don't mind waiting. One day you'll tell me what happened and we'll proceed from there."

"I don't want to speak of it."

"Don't tense up. I won't have only part of you. Only once you trust me with your wounds will I know it's time to take this further. I am a patient man."

I had no doubt of that. He gathered me closer and, for once, it didn't rankle so much that he saw that in me, the bleeding wound that no one else knew lurked there. Still, I blinked out at the night, unsure what daylight would bring. His breathing deepened and slowed.

I doubted I would sleep before dawn. Though his broad body curled around mine lulled me with its protective warmth. Restorative in its own way.

Still I worried over it all. *Enough to overcome what went before.* I hated that it had become a big deal between us, especially since I'd never thought of it as one. *I tried it and I didn't care to repeat the experience. Ever.* I meant that when I said it. Though physical intimacy held greater appeal now than it ever had, I would not pay such a high price as discussing that terrible night. The awful humiliation of it.

"Relax, Ursula," Harlan murmured, stroking my flank. "I'll sing you a lullaby."

I laughed. "I don't need that. I'll keep watch."

Instead of replying, he sang, low, deep, and soft, a song in his language of blurred syllables and the cadence of the ocean. The dark melody wrapped around me as surely as his arms, and after a time, I forgot what had worried me so.

I must have drifted off, because birdsong wakened me, a chorus of calls greeting Glorianna's sunrise. The events of the night returned in a rush at the same moment I became aware that an iron-thewed arm held me down. Startled, I tried to leap away, but Harlan pulled me back against him, laughing sleepily.

"I should have known you'd come awake all at once. Don't run yet."

"I'm not. It's dawn. Time to move on."

"Not just yet." Stretching his big body, he rose on his elbow, coaxing me onto my back and studying my face.

"What?"

"You look better," he pronounced.

"I'm so relieved," I replied in a dry tone. "Does that mean my captivity is at an end?"

"Almost." He smiled and leaned down, brushing my mouth with one of his gentle, searching kisses. It sighed through me, delicious, tingling and soothing both. "Good morning, Ursula."

"Hi." I felt absurdly shy suddenly. Something I hadn't felt since I got over being a too-tall, awkward girl. I shifted restlessly, turning my head to see the growing light, anxious to be on the move. Sifting through all I had revealed the night before.

"Shall we have a workout before we ride?" He loosened his hold on me, though his hand fell intimately to my hip. *The feel of you under my hand.*

I rolled away and stood, my body stiff from the long sleep. "Yes. Danu knows I need it."

"You look good to me." He grinned, unrepentant, when I pinned him with a glare, then shrugged one shoulder. "I can't help it. If I started falling in love with you when I first saw you in court, watching you run that sword form of yours cemented it. Never have I wanted a woman so much."

I picked up my sword and pointed it at him. "You should stop saying these things."

"Not speaking of my feelings won't make them go away, Ursula."

But I'd be less self-conscious. Something he no doubt knew and wielded against me, another weapon in his vast arsenal.

When I returned from answering the call of nature, he'd stripped down to his small clothes and had already worked up a fine sweat, grunting through a series of push-ups. Deciding to ignore him to the best of my abilities, I settled into the Midnight form, letting it clear my mind and body of the dregs of sleep and seduction.

Much as I hated to admit it, and despite my injuries, I felt better than I had in days. Maybe longer. Muscles and ligaments growing elastic, my body sang as I moved through Danu's ritualized forms, the first blending into the second and on through the twelve. Blood coursing, heart pounding, breath flowing—not with emotion, but with honest exertion—I moved faster and faster, exultant, powerful.

When I finished, holding the last pose for an endless, still moment—always my favorite part—I realized I'd forgotten Harlan's presence. He sat nearby, expression rapt, eyes glittering in the way I'd discovered meant desire.

"You should do that for me naked sometime," he commented.

"I don't think you need any more encouragement for your prurient fantasies," I replied, tartly enough to slice through his trance.

He only grinned at me. "Don't worry. I have the fantasies with or without the encouragement."

"You are a strange man."

"Ah, my lady love sees through me." He clasped a hand over his heart, imitating a court minstrel. Then stood when I laughed and, heedless of my sword, snagged me around the waist before I could step away. "Kiss me, Ursula."

"I already did—a number of times."

"Not enough." His mouth captured mine, not so gentle this time, but with a searching hunger, hot, urgent. Hands harder on me than they had been thus far, he pulled me tight against him and wrapped me in a bear hug, one big hand cupping my neck as his mouth and tongue moved over mine. Like answering a swifter attack, I responded in kind. He'd pulled on his clothes at some point but left the shirt unlaced, so my hand bracing on his bare chest encountered the shocking heat of his skin. Without thinking, I dug my nails in and he growled, low and rumbling.

Gasping, unbalanced by the rapid rise of heat, I broke away. He transferred his mouth to my throat just under my ear, sending lightning straight into my blood.

"What will be enough?" I laughed, because I wanted to groan. To growl as he was.

Harlan lifted his head, gazing intently into my face. "That's the thing. I don't think there ever will be."

Unsettled, I moved away and he let me go, though with reluctance, hands maintaining contact until the last moment. "I don't know what to say to that."

"You don't always have to have an answer," he replied easily.

He was wrong on that. I did need an answer.

We rode out soon thereafter, the day bright and warm. I had to remind myself that we weren't on a pleasure jaunt, that danger awaited. Somehow, though, the pressing worries of the day before seemed less grim, less looming.

Sleep always helped. That was all it was.

Marskal had left markers for me to follow, secret signs the Hawks used. After a time I realized the Vervaldr must have done likewise, as Harlan made directional adjustments before I indicated the path marked for me. I made a game of it, following the direction of Harlan's eyes, seeing if I could determine what he looked for.

"The flat gray stones." I raised an eyebrow at his surprised look. "The number indicate their pace and the alignment the reverse of their direction."

"Well done. I've not yet determined your system."

"And you never will. Trade secret."

"We'll see about that." He nudged his horse closer and caught my hand, pressing a kiss to it before I pulled away. "I have ways of extracting your secrets."

As he had the night before. "Look," I said, "I don't want the others to know anything about—"

"I know how to be discreet," he interrupted mildly. "Though they know already."

"Know what?" I had to work to keep my tone even. "There was nothing to know before this. There's still nothing to know." Only a few kisses had passed between us. That hardly qualified as more than a pub flirtation for most of my Hawks. Though saying as much to Harlan would be baiting the bear in a way I did not care to.

He slid me a look, amused and annoyed, perhaps divining my unspoken thoughts. "You know better. This may be an unusual arena for you, but that's not so for my men or yours. Warriors are sensitive to the ways of the body. The desire between us is not something they'd miss."

The desire between us. I tore my gaze away, to stop the unexpected surge of heat, as if by speaking it, Harlan had evoked it. Had I shown desire for him? I didn't think I had. I hadn't even recognized it for what it was. I'd never really believed in it before, I now realized. Standing outside that pane of glass, watching the bizarre motions of people feasting on a meal that had no smell or flavor for me. On some level I'd imagined them all to be pretending, indulging in a lovely fairy tale that had nothing to do with real life.

"I haven't decided what I'm going to do about this," I finally said, pleased that my voice remained steadily neutral.

"About me, you mean?"

"Yes." About his determined pursuit and my surprising, growing interest in tasting more. I couldn't remain indecisive for long.

"Do you have to decide?"

I risked a glance at him, to find him watching me with that expectant look, as if he knew he'd be entertained by whatever I said next.

"I think it's important to have a plan, yes."

"I'm not a battle for you to strategize, Ursula," he said mildly.

"I'm not so sure of that."

He laughed, velvety, strumming my nerves. "I look forward to being plundered, then."

"Don't get your hopes up," I retorted.

"Too late for that." He sounded ridiculously cheerful. "My hopes are high indeed. I never thought to find a woman like you. Now I believe all sorts of things are possible. It's a fine place, your Twelve Kingdoms. I thank your goddess for guiding me here."

"I highly doubt Danu had anything to do with it."

"You're her faithful warrior. Is it any surprise she rewarded you for it?"

"With you?"

"Yes, my valiant hawk. With me."

"That remains to be seen."

"Yes. That's exactly what I've been telling you."

He had a legal scholar's turn with arguments, using banter to draw me out, his words as flirtatious in their way as his teasing touches and lavishly bestowed kisses. In the final analysis, however, it mattered not at all. Our idyll had come and gone. Trouble lay ahead and I needed to focus on that.

No more being multiply weighted. A consolidated, single purpose would see me through. Gain the border to Annfwn without casualties and confer with Andi to set the next course of action.

Harlan could entertain himself with his pursuit. I had more important things to do.

We caught up to the others by early evening. They'd paused to eat, roasting a couple of deer the archers had brought down. Good timing, as we could have our fill and carry the scraps with us on the morrow. Hunting opportunities on the pass itself would be scarce.

"Captain!" Marskal clapped his fist over his heart in the Hawks' salute, then nodded at Harlan. "Scouts report no trouble. No sign of anything untoward, at all."

I studied the steeply rising hills, the peaks sharply jagged, with the cleft where the pass ran through. "Odd."

"We thought so, too. Perhaps we'll see that change tomorrow, as we come closer to the ascent."

"Keep the scouts on a short leash. I don't want anyone going up the pass too far ahead of the main company." I gave Harlan a pointed look and swung down from the saddle. "That goes for your men, too."

"So be it." He relayed the order as he handed off his horse. "Why?"

I appreciated that he obeyed first and asked second. We made our way to the campfire, our mingled guard greeting us as usual. No smirks or sidelong looks as I'd dreaded. Either Harlan was wrong and no one suspected a thing, or good discipline won out.

"Though we're some distance from the actual border, the Tala should be tracking our approach by now. They like to play tricks to make us uneasy—spooking the horses, stealing supplies. All part of a strategy to turn casual interlopers away. It will get more intense as we get closer, but I'm surprised the scouts have encountered nothing yet."

"Perhaps your sister eases the way for you."

I raised an eyebrow at him. "And me with a small army of mercenaries, along with my elite guard? I don't think so. Rayfe is no fool, even if Andi would assume my visit to be affectionate rather than aggressive."

"And is it?"

"That all depends on what they know of Amelia and the babies."

While Harlan consulted with his lieutenants, I found Dafne settled under a pine tree on a rise, surrounded by books and scrolls. She gave me a cautious smile as I approached.

"How much trouble am I in?"

"Unfortunately I have no prison cell handy."

"Lucky for me. I apologize, however, for being insubordinate. Marskal took me to task—it hadn't occurred to me to see it that way."

I sat beside her and looked out over the camp. "You're not a soldier, Lady Mailloux. I don't expect you to behave as one."

She winced. "That's almost worse than an actual reprimand."

"Just be wary of drugging me insensible and leaving me with strange men in the future, yes?"

"Since I'm not a soldier, I'll argue there. Captain Harlan is not a strange man. He's sworn to protect you. And cares about you beyond that."

"He has a business contract to do so. Not the same thing."

"I'm not sure I agree."

"It doesn't bear debate. Have you found out anything about our mutual and suspicious absentmindedness about certain key personnel?"

"I have." She unrolled a scroll I hadn't read and ran her finger down the crabbed lines.

"Is that in Dasnarian?"

"No, thankfully. I'm still limping along in their language, though a number of the Vervaldr are literate and have been helpful."

"You haven't shown them exactly what you're researching, have you?"

She wrinkled her nose. "Give me more credit than that. I've pretended to an interest in Dasnarian marriage customs, playing my spinster card. Alas, though no man in the Twelve will have me, perhaps I can snare a foreigner." She sighed dramatically and batted her eyelashes.

I snorted. "From what I hear, you wouldn't much care for life among them."

"From what I've read, too. No, this, Your Highness, is Old Elcinean—pre–Common Tongue—and is far more forthcoming on the subject of the Practitioners of Deyrr than any of the Dasnarian texts. In fact, you've already seen pretty much everything there is to see there. Either what was in our library is heavily edited or the Dasnarians themselves have little information."

"The mercenary captain indicated as much. Most of his insights alluded to rumors and other tall stories."

She glanced at me, seeming about to say something, but simply turned her attention to the scroll. "It says here that an invading force of Dasnarians arrived in Elcinea several hundred years ago. Their ranks included—get this, 'fair-haired giants with bloodthirsty broadswords'—and a group of wizards, mostly female, who wore black cloaks and who could cloud the mind."

"Anything more specific about this mind-clouding business?" I easily picked out my personal fair-haired giant moving among the troops. As if feeling my gaze, he looked up, touching the backs of two fingers to his forehead. I hadn't observed him exchanging that particular salute with his men, only directed toward me. If it meant something flirtatious, we'd have to discuss. I refused to acknowledge the gesture, as always, and he grinned.

Cocky son of Danu that he was.

Dafne cleared her throat. "Nothing exact, no. But there *is* mention of sailing ships returning and the captains asking to report to people who were subsequently discovered to have disappeared."

"And no one noticed until that moment."

"Exactly."

"Interesting."

"I thought so, too."

I mulled it over. "So if there is some sort of magic at work, it's localized. And affects mainly active memory. You thought of Lady Zevondeth when you read a mention of her."

"Do you think Illyria is doing this?"

"Entirely possible." Relief from one worry at least flooded through me. My father wasn't unstable, just bespelled in some way. "And one convenient aspect of magic workers is that they're as mortal as any of us."

"But she's the King's fiancée."

"Not if I kill her."

Dafne blanched. "You don't mean to."

"I do."

"Have you considered how King Uorsin might retaliate?"

She seemed frightened, so I sought to reassure her. "He will be initially angry, no doubt, but I truly believe her sorcery is to blame for his current behavior. Once the cloud of her dark magic has cleared, he'll return to being the High King we know and love."

"And if he doesn't?" she demanded. Not fear but anger. "Will you allow him to destroy you?"

I studied her, uncertain where the anger came from. "My fate is unimportant."

"No, Ursula—that's where you are so thrice-damned wrong. King Uorsin is not more important than you are. Why can't you see that?"

"I value your advice, librarian." I measured the words slowly, managing the anger that wanted to rise to match hers. The smells of roasting meat wafted up from the camp below, strangely unappealing to my sour gut. "And I want you to be able to speak frankly to me. Therefore, I won't censure you for your words. Be wary, though, of encouraging me to treason."

"What if that way leads to your death?"

"Then so be it. I would never betray my King to save my own life."

"I don't understand how you can think this way."

I glanced at her, gripped her shoulder. "Don't fret so. Danu will guide my sword."

"I can only pray she does," Dafne muttered, gathered her scrolls and took herself off.

It wasn't something that bore examining. Being loyal to the King formed the core of who I had to be. It didn't bear thinking that I could have been wrong in this, all these years. It would mean Salena let him destroy her year by slow year for nothing. That I had let him do the same to me, not because he was more important and above the law, but out of blind cowardice.

Why do you let him brutalize you?

It made me ill to contemplate what the true answer might be.

20

After we put out the cooking fires and everyone began to settle in for the night, I sought out Harlan as he returned from checking with our watch outposts. "I need to consult with you a moment."

His pleased smile flashed white in the rising moonlight and he ran a hand down my arm, on the side away from our people. "I hoped you'd seek me out."

"Not like that." I stepped out of reach. "But I do have several things to discuss."

"As you command," he replied, not at all daunted. Then he turned and began walking into the trees.

Setting my teeth, I lengthened my stride to catch up. "Where are you going?"

He lifted a shoulder, let it fall, and glanced over it at me, still moving. "You could have spoken with me publicly at the camp-fire. I assume you prefer this conversation to be private."

We could have been out of earshot and still in public view and well he knew it. He moved behind a dense thicket of trees, deft and silent, despite his bulk. I followed, careful to stay well back.

Not careful enough, because he snagged me with an arm

around my waist, pulling me against him and kissing me in that spot below my ear. I meant to push off, had my hands in place, but that delicious melting sensation had me hesitating, then lifting my chin and humming a little before I got hold of myself.

"Let me go."

"Mmm," he rumbled. "I missed you."

"Nonsense. You've been with me all day."

"It's not the same."

"Well, stop it anyway. I need to talk to you."

"So talk." He spoke against my throat, mouth moving down the thin skin covering the vulnerable artery there. My brain fogged and I nearly forgot the actual reason I'd sought him out. Not for this.

I pushed off, taking a step back, glad that years of training kept me steadier than my head would have.

"Illyria."

"Ah." He leaned back against a tree, folding his arms. "That name will dampen any man's ardor."

"We never discussed what happened the other night at Ordnung."

"No. I didn't think you cared to."

"I still don't, but we must. First, let's discuss your loyalty."

"Do you have reason to question it?" He sounded irritated. Good.

"You know I don't believe a contract equates to true loyalty."

"And you know I believe a contract does far more to guarantee loyalty than fickle emotion."

I nodded, confirming to myself. "If it came down to a test between the terms of the contract and protecting a fellow Dasnarian—what would you do?"

He didn't move, but something about his posture told me he'd come to full attention. "What are you saying?"

"Dafne uncovered some information—from our texts, ones you wouldn't have seen—that indicates Illyria may have the ability to change how we think. I believe she made me forget about checking in with Lord Percy, even about his existence entirely, as well as other people."

He didn't comment, so I forged on.

"If she can do that, then the King's behavior can be ascribed to more such witchcraft. Freeing him of her influence may require her death. I want to know—if I kill her, will that destroy her spells? What other repercussions might there be? She's not in your contract, but what of your personal feelings? What of any political connections she might have?"

Again, Harlan let the silence drag out. This time, I waited on his answer. Finally he sighed. "Let me ask you something, Ursula."

"I'd prefer you answered my questions."

"Too bad. I'll follow your commands, as I've repeatedly demonstrated, but this is just the two of us—private, as you wished. Tell me this. Were you surprised that the King struck you, either time?"

"He's never hit me in court like that before." Never anything I hadn't been able to conceal from my sisters, disguised as fairly earned bruises from training.

"That's not what I asked you."

"Of course not." My stomach, still unsettled from my earlier thoughts, clenched that Harlan brought up exactly that. Danu taught that coincidences were patterns not yet made clear. "He's a warrior to the core and a sailor before it. Those aren't gentle professions. They require strength and mettle—qualities his heir must also possess. I've met the flat of his hand—or his blade—many times. It's to be expected. To make me strong."

"I've never struck anyone, man or woman, outside of combat. It's not expected. *You* should not expect that. It doesn't make people strong—it grinds them down."

"We're getting sidetracked and you're not answering my questions."

"I'm questioning your fundamental assumption. What if the High King's behavior is not due to Illyria's influence? It's my understanding he's executed people for little reason before. Along with torture, imprisonment, and various other excesses."

"Never in front of the whole court at dinner."

"Merely an escalation. And I haven't mentioned how he's treated you and his other daughters."

"What happened to your contractual loyalty?" I accused. "It's remarkably flexible, it seems."

"I'm loyal to the representative of the High Throne," he returned in a quiet tone.

"As am I—the High Throne is Uorsin and he is the High Throne. It's not my place, or yours, to pass judgment on him."

"You're thick skulled is what you are." He sounded uncharacteristically impatient, an echo of Dafne's anger. "Can you kill her? I have no doubt you possess the skill. Would anyone in Dasnaria, including the Temple of Deyrr, seek to avenge her? Possibly. Will her death change anything? Probably, but not what you hope it will."

"That's somewhat helpful." Something to work with, anyway.

"Ursula, even the best monarch can go bad. Power corrupts."

I wasn't having that conversation. "What do you know of it?"

"More than you think."

Determined to keep on track, I ignored the bait. "I'm focusing on Illyria's corruption first. You should know what we'll face as we ascend the pass tomorrow. It's very likely we'll hit foul weather at the barrier—and we won't be able to cross into Annfwn. I'd like to leave a contingent here and at the base of the trail, before it narrows. Only a small party should attempt the border."

"All right. But I will be with the group that ascends."

"I think it would be more strategic if—"

"You can order me to stay behind, but I'll just follow."

"So much for you abiding by my commands."

"That's the upside of flexible loyalty—it allows me to justify many decisions."

"I don't understand you, Captain. Loyalty cannot be flexible." I had to unclench my jaw to continue. "Fine. But I cannot control whether you can cross the border. You might find yourself awaiting my return for some time."

"I don't mind waiting." His voice held an intimate reminder of his other promises, which I also ignored. "Is that everything you wished to discuss, Your Highness?"

"Yes. Thank you." I turned to go, but he stepped up behind me, quick and deadly silent. Should we ever truly cross blades, I'd have to be careful never to turn my back to him. He enfolded me, big arms around my waist, and pulled me against him, mouth pressed hot to the back of my neck.

"Stay awhile," he coaxed.

"I can't."

"You're riddled with worry and tension. Let me melt you a little."

"I thought we weren't doing this."

"Just a bit of love play. Let me tempt you."

"I don't want this." I steeled myself against the slow blurring, reaching for that place of clear determination.

"Why not?"

I groped to remember, my mind already clouding with the pure pleasure of his touch. "It's distracting."

"Oh, yes." Harlan practically purred his agreement, stroking down my hips, teeth nibbling the muscle at the juncture of my neck, so that I wanted to tip my head and purr also. "Deliciously so."

There I was, melting again. This was why Danu's priestesses took vows of chastity. Not out of a lack of interest, but because the desire could become so overwhelming. Taking away good sense and resolve. A vow served to shore up one's will when temptation presented itself. I'd never thought I'd need that kind of help, but I could admit to it. Learn from my mistakes.

If I didn't have my willpower, I had nothing. Single focus.

No more indulging.

"I'm not doing this." Breaking his hold—albeit not difficult, but I did it with a bit of satisfying force—I stepped well out of his reach. "No more."

"All right," he agreed. "All you have to do is tell me to stop."

"Well, I'm telling you. Not for just now, but for always. No more," I repeated, cementing the promise to myself and Danu.

"What are you saying?" His voice had gone flat.

"A final no. I'm not doing this. Leave me alone, Harlan. I can't afford any distractions. Put a hand on me again and I'll cut it off."

He was silent a long time. So long that I nearly caved and said something more, instead of waiting him out as my ultimatum required. Any good negotiation depended on holding to one's lines in the sand.

"What changed?" he finally threw out. A gauntlet between us.

"Nothing." I kept my voice even, proud of myself. "I considered your proposition and have decided against it."

"This isn't a negotiation on water rights, Ursula." He grated out the words.

"The principle is the same. You made an offer—repeatedly and with various attempts to sweeten the deal—and I've given it fair thought, weighed the options, and have decided against it."

He cursed, something that sounded most foul in Dasnarian. "You've done nothing fairly. You refuse to speak honestly with me, to give me the least measure of your trust. You stand there and lie to me about having considered what I've offered you— someone who will love you without reserve or judgment—and you blithely claim you feel nothing even while your blood pours hot in your veins from my mouth on you."

"There's more to life than sex. All of it more important."

"You don't know that because you've never had it. No"—his voice shot out of the dimness—"don't you dare claim that you have, because whatever happened to you had nothing to do with love or desire or real intimacy between two people. You're just afraid and dressing it up as something else. You deny yourself the least happiness out of blind adherence to some ideal that doesn't exist."

His words stung, far more than they should have. Danu! Such a viciously targeted strike. He'd opened the way to this wound, breaking the scar tissue with his questions, flattery, and attention. A weapon so finely honed I'd never felt it going in. I'd been fine, all of that squarely in the past. Now he'd made that old injury seep with blood and pus once more. With pain. I nearly staggered from the ache. Of course that scared me. I couldn't keep bleeding like this.

"Fine. I am afraid. You called me fearless and you were wrong about that, also."

"Also?"

"You thought you could cozen and seduce me. It will never happen."

"Ah. I understand. I never figured you for a coward, Ursula."

"Think what you like. I'm not interested in having the good opinion of a mercenary." I hauled myself back, almost regretting that last attack. A clean slice, meant to hurt enough to end this dance between us once and for all.

He absorbed the strike silently, a warrior to the end.

"Be ready to ride out in the morning," I said, and turned to go.

"Ursula," he called after me.

Unwilling, I stopped, looked over my shoulder into the shadows. "What?"

"Do you realize that's the first time you've used my name? And you did it to break my heart."

I steeled mine. "Then you know I mean it." With that, I strode off to take first watch. He would get over it soon enough.

Better now than later.

We packed up to leave at first light, the squad I'd picked to establish a camp at the base of the pass to await us moving more quickly than the ones resituating to wait us out in this spot.

"Your Highness?"

I raised an eyebrow at Dafne. "This must be serious if you're using my title."

She actually flushed lightly, bearing out my suspicion. "I'd like to ask a favor."

"I'm not taking any more of your potions—I slept fine," I told her, though I hadn't. After first watch, I'd lain awake, alternately missing the reassuring warm bulk of Harlan's body and fuming over his accusations. Ridiculous. All my life I'd slept alone, and I sleep next to a man one night and find some lonely part of myself longing to have it again. I'd made a choice I knew to be the right one, then spent a sleepless night dissecting our argument. All the ways he'd muddled me.

Good thing I'd cut his pursuit short when I had. I should have nipped it in the bud.

"This is for me." Dafne took a breath, clearly squaring her resolve. "I want to come with you up the pass."

"No." I checked the saddlebags and moved a few things to a pack I'd wear on my back, just in case I became separated from my horse.

"Your Highness." Dafne looked less hesitant, more determined.

"What? You asked, I answered. It's not safe. There's a reason I'm leaving most everyone here or at the base camp. We're not going on a picnic, librarian. You'll stay here."

"Don't insult me," she snapped back. "I'm aware of the dangers and will be responsible for myself. This is important to me and it's my life to risk. Didn't you say much the same thing last night?"

"It doesn't work that way. Anyone not a trained fighter will be a liability. Your presence would force the rest of us to focus energy on your safety instead of keeping our attention where it should be, on ourselves and the mission. I can't afford any distractions. You're staying behind."

"I'll be responsible for Lady Mailloux." Harlan's smooth baritone grated on my nerves. Tempting not to look at him at all, but I would be better than that. And would have to practice, regardless. I gave him a cool, dismissive glance, making my displeasure at his interference clear. He returned the gaze with apparent neutrality, his expression set as it had been when I first saw him standing guard at Uorsin's side. But I knew him better now. A glint of anger in his pale eyes, challenging me. A hunger, too.

Part of me answered to it, warming, and I ruthlessly froze that away. I would not feel it.

"You're lucky I'm letting *you* come along," I informed him, taking a savage pleasure in goading him with an imperious tone. "Don't forget who you answer to here, mercenary."

"Shall we confer privately, Your Highness?"

"No. We need to set out and there's nothing to discuss. Lady Mailloux stays with the main group."

"You're being stubborn for the wrong reasons, Ursula." Harlan's eyes glittered with building emotion, that impassive shell showing cracks. "You can't shut us all out."

"Actually, I can do that very thing. Lady Mailloux understands my decision."

"No, she doesn't." Dafne stepped between us, making me abruptly aware that we had closed on each other so we stood nearly nose to nose. Not good that I'd forgotten something as basic as maintaining a perimeter outside his reach. If it came to a fight between us, I needed to be outside that range to have a chance of winning. He'd lulled me into forgetting those boundaries. Repeatedly. Reestablishing my distance, I gave Dafne my attention.

"Do we need to have that conversation about insubordination after all?"

"You said you didn't expect military obedience of me." Her brown eyes snapped, brimming over with more emotion than I'd seen in her before. "Have I ever asked you for anything?"

I considered her, how her petite body vibrated with the strength of her feelings. And no, she'd really asked nothing of any of us, but had given a great deal. True loyalty. To Andi, then to Amelia, and now to me.

Blowing out a long breath, I acknowledged to Danu that I'd

let the situation with the mercenary affect me too much and prayed to her for clarity. "Why do you want to go so badly?"

"I want to see Annfwn."

She phrased it simply, but her fingers had knotted together, her voice full of a lifetime of yearning. So much more than simply wanting it.

"You might not be able to cross the barrier," I told her gently, not liking how hope suffused her face that I seemed to be relenting.

"If I can't, then I'll know and go on with my life. But I might never get this close again. Please, Ursula—let me try. I truly don't care if I lose my life in the attempt."

"You have a lot of life still ahead of you."

She laughed, a bitter sound that came out of a deep unhappiness, stabbing at my own raw heart. "An empty life. A meaningless one in most ways. Sometimes I feel like a ghost living on the edges of everyone else's lives—yours, Amelia's, Andi's, even the people in the books and histories. I have no family, no prospects, no real value to anyone. The only thing I've ever really wanted was to see Annfwn."

"You have value to me."

"I could make a life of that, yes—be Derodotur to you, give my days to that service and be happy doing it. *If* you survive to take the throne. But I want to make that choice, not be forced into it because I have nothing else, because I believe nothing more than that is possible for me."

I pretended to think, studying the brightening cloudless sky, using the moment to master my own turbulent heart. Why her words affected me so, I wasn't sure. I certainly didn't want Harlan's far-too-keen gaze to see how unsettled I felt. He'd no doubt think it had to do with him and it didn't. It couldn't.

"Fine." I nodded. Then had to look away again from the bright joy that flooded her countenance. I fixed my eyes on the mercenary instead, annoyed that my fingers itched to touch him, that the hard look in his eye pricked my conscience. Let him be angry. I'd withstood worse. "You're responsible for her, Captain Harlan. See that you don't fail me in this."

A muscle in his jaw flexed, but he simply bowed. "As you command, Your Highness. I would never fail you, in any way. Maybe one day you'll do me the honor of not questioning that."

I glared at him, torn between calling him out for his barbed words and refusing to give him the satisfaction of an answer.

Dafne looked back and forth between us. Stepped back as if easing herself from the line of fire. "I'll go get my things and be ready to leave."

Neither of us replied—or even glanced at her.

"Your move, I believe," Harlan said. A smoothly voiced taunt.

"I don't know what you want from me, Captain."

"Yes, you do." Now he let the desire show, the love he claimed to feel. Naked and raw. It thudded into me like an arrow, piercing, unexpected. Somehow I'd lost the ability to shield myself against him.

Determined to master this situation, I took in a long breath. Centered myself. "I'm sorry if your pride is offended. Surely a woman has turned you down before."

"Don't give me that, Ursula. This isn't about pride. I gave you my heart and you tossed it back like so much rotten meat."

"Because I don't want it. I never asked for it."

"Because you're terrified you want it too much."

"That sure sounds like pride to me," I snapped back.

He fingered his sword and I swiped my thumb over the topaz in the pommel of mine. Warm, smooth, and reassuring. "Do you plan to draw on me, mercenary?"

"I should. Then you'd be forced to deal with me, one way or the other."

"Don't do it," I warned him. "I will kill you if I have to."

"Do you really believe you could?"

"I'm fast enough."

"No doubt of that." He leaned in, deliberately trespassing on my careful perimeter. "I'm asking if you really think you could bear to strike me down. You might be successfully lying to yourself, but I know better."

"You know nothing about me, mercenary."

"That's where you're mistaken. Tell me what Lady Mailloux meant about there being a question of you surviving to inherit the throne."

The swift change of subject almost caught me off guard, though I shouldn't have been surprised he caught that. "She worries too much. The pair of you are alike in that way."

"I'll guess then. She believes Uorsin will kill you if you carry out your plan to assassinate Illyria. It's logical. Why shouldn't he? Particularly if you deliver your nephew into his hands. Your replacement. The boy he truly wanted all along."

The edges of my vision went gray and I pressed my lips against the tremble that threatened. "He's the High King. Only he can choose who best should succeed him."

Harlan lifted a hand and I stepped back, though he wasn't close to touching me. "I apologize. I meant to make you see, not to hurt you."

"You didn't. You've said nothing I didn't know. Nothing everyone doesn't know. My father desperately wished for a male heir, but more than that, his accomplishments deserve someone worthy to follow in his stead. If Astar better serves in that role, I trust in the King's judgment. I told Dafne and I'll tell you: this is not about me. I don't understand why *you* will not see that."

"Maybe we see what you don't, Ursula," he replied in a patient tone. "As stubborn, hardheaded, and abrasive as you can be, you are the shining star we look to. All of us."

"Save the flattery, mercenary." I managed the dry tone I wanted. "Better get ready to go or I'll leave you behind."

Harlan broke into a small, inscrutable smile and touched the backs of two fingers to his forehead. "*Elskastholrr*, Ursula. When we ride out, I'll be at your back. Today and always."

21

In the end, seven of us ascended Odfell's Pass—two Hawks, two Vervaldr, Dafne, Harlan, and me. I still didn't like having Dafne at risk, but she positively glowed with anticipation. Both of my Hawks knew to keep an eye on her, despite what I'd told her.

Not that I didn't trust Harlan's expertise. He didn't know the Tala like they did. Like I did.

After a few hours of riding, we paused at the last wide spot until the summit, before the path narrowed too much for us to ride abreast. Harlan had been quiet since our exchange at dawn, but he spoke up when I said I'd take the lead.

"Is that wise, Your Highness?"

"I lead from the front," I told him.

"It's my job to see that you're protected also," he pointed out.

"I don't need coddling. I'll take care of myself." I'm not sure what it was that made me enjoy poking at him, but it gave me a perverse pleasure to pierce that implacable expression he used as a shield, just enough that some irritation leaked through.

Dafne gave me a narrow look, then smiled at Harlan. "I'll take any coddling you're up to providing."

"You're most gracious, Lady Mailloux." He gave her a grave

nod. "I propose Dafne rides in the middle, Her Highness's Hawks behind Ursula, my men behind Dafne, and I'll bring up the rear."

The second-most dangerous position. He met my gaze steadily, daring me to argue. I couldn't ride them both, however, so I shrugged, as if I didn't care in the least. "All of you, keep your ears, eyes, and any other sense you possess wide open. High alert from here on out. Just because nothing's happened so far doesn't mean it won't. You notice anything at all, tell me."

I raised a brow at Harlan, daring *him* to argue. He didn't. Instead he gave me that particular look, as he had when I finished the sword form and he'd kissed me like a starving man. Provoking and distracting, if I let it be.

Put it aside.

We rode up and I set a measured pace. The first time I'd made this ascent, full of worry for Andi, forced into marriage and abducted faster than I could follow across this border, I'd hurried too much. That was how we lost two Hawks, and I was determined not to let that happen again.

Now I felt certain that she expected me, that the lack of trouble reflected her tacit, if not overt, welcome. Still, it felt odd to be wary of her. The last time, I'd figured to be battling the Tala to rescue her. This time, Andi was one of them and wielded abilities I had no way to measure. Or possibly even understand. Up through the dense forest that lined the treacherous trail, bounded by a steep cliff on one side and a chasm so deep it might as well be bottomless on the other, the snow-clad peaks rose, daunting in their remoteness. Above their sharp white crests, the sky deepened into the achingly clear blue the high altitudes brought.

The sense that I somehow looked into Andi's gaze unsettled me greatly.

Birdsong rustled through the trees, followed by a sinister shadow sound that crawled across my nerves. Glancing over my shoulder, I noted that none of the others had heard or sensed anything. Harlan, of course, caught me checking and raised his brows, scanning the woods for the threat. I shook my head slightly and he returned the gesture, a bare dip of the chin, speaking as clearly as if he'd said it, as if we'd been working together for years, not mere days, that he had sensed nothing but readied himself to act on what I had.

The higher we rode, the greater the sense of pressure. It seemed that a storm loomed, lightning poised to strike, though the sky remained cloudless. Keeping my spine straight, I refused to hunch against it. My stallion's withers flickered with the same foreboding.

A shadow in the trees.

There and gone.

"Captain?" Lynn asked. Second to Marskal, who I'd left in charge of the base camp, she had a levelheaded seriousness I appreciated. Which made the fact that I'd stopped without warning or apparent reason more embarrassing. It hadn't gotten to me this way on the last trip.

"Nothing," I said, sending a prayer to Danu that I spoke the truth, and urged my stallion into motion again.

A whisper of warning brushed against my skin. My sword leapt to hand, but the thing—whatever it might be—flowed over and around me like a cloud of birds, shrieking in my ears, bypassing me entirely. Unable to turn my steed, I spun in the saddle, standing as I did so. Ready to fight.

Too late.

The two Hawks and two Vervaldr had disappeared as if they'd never been. A stunned Dafne and murderously grim Harlan met my gaze.

"What happened?" he demanded.

"I should ask you the same."

"If you ask what I saw, it seemed a cloud of starlings suddenly descended, then lifted, and our men were gone. It makes no sense."

"Tala magic," I snapped.

He glowered at me, as if I'd done it. "Where are my men?"

"With mine!" It grated at me that I might have lost two more. We both had to put it out of our heads.

Harlan nodded, seeming to hear my thought, and scanned the now silent trees. "So I take it we three have been selected to continue?"

"One would hope," I replied in a dry tone, glad at least that nothing had happened to Dafne. She gave me a shaky half smile, a toast to mutual survival.

We continued on, and though no further magic occurred, it seemed that ghosts plagued me. Hugh had taken second position on our last trip, so determined to serve Andi by rescuing her. Being back in this place, I imagined he rode behind me again. I fancied that I might turn and see him, pure of purpose in a way I'd never been. Full of noble good intentions.

And I'd killed him for it.

The memory, the guilt I'd never shed, lodged like steel fragments in my spine, making it ache. Amelia might have forgiven me. Andi might have taken the blame. But I couldn't forgive myself. The impulse of a moment.

I knew the clearing the moment we entered it. Recognized it but did not expect the assault of such vivid memory. That day had been full winter chill, freezing to the bone. And Hugh, after I'd slain him, had lain in the snow, bleeding crimson across the white, spilled like Madeline's blood, pooling on the marble floor of Ordnung. Their ghosts chased me, skeletal fingers of foreboding plucking at my nerves.

Today, though the ground cover bubbled frothy and green with late summer, I spotted the shrine Ami had mentioned. She'd seen it as an incongruous living flower in the dead winter landscape. For me, it shimmered in the same way the shadows had, as blue as the mountain sky, vivid and luxuriantly alive. Nothing moved. No Tala forces awaited us, as they had before, as I more than half expected this time. Wind soughed through the trees like a man's heavy breath, the timber creaking. I dismounted and crouched to see the blossom—the forget-me-not under a dome of magic.

I tapped it, unsurprised when my hand did not pass through. The same material as the border barrier. It would be nearby, probably reflective. I'd touched the barrier only the once, when Andi invited me to try it. All those times nearing it in Branli, I'd had that same prickling across my skin that I did now, but we'd been bounced away, time after time.

If I'd managed to find a path through on that side, I might not have to be here, facing my past self. The turmoil of guilt rising to choke me, my joints aching with the cold.

"What do you look at so carefully?" Harlan crouched beside me.

"You don't see anything?"

He studied the lay of the grass. "Nothing of note."

"Hidden by magic, then. It's a memorial. To my sister's husband, who I murdered." I managed to say it baldly, for what it was. Taking the responsibility as I should have to begin with.

Dafne made a sound of protest, and he gave me a long look, searching my face. "Knowing you, it couldn't have gone down that way. Your honor would never permit it."

"She did it for me."

I spun, sword leaping to my hand, and Andi stood there. Garbed in a silky white slip of a gown, hair falling around her in a glorious rusty black cape, and eyes like a summer thundercloud, she looked so like Salena she took my breath away, the grief flashing sharp through my other tumbling emotions. So much sorrow tied to her—losing my sisters, my mother. I wanted to beg her forgiveness and rage at her for betraying us.

"I apologize for the disappearance of your fighters," she added. "I promise they're fine. Just . . . relocated for the moment, as I did not care to have other witnesses." Andi held out her hands, an invitation, a question. "Ursula, I'm so, so happy you're here."

Sheathing the sword, I strode to her. Then bypassed her hands and, impulsively, overcome, seized her in a hug. She choked a little in surprise—had I really so rarely embraced her?—then squeezed back, tears wet on my neck.

Wiping her tears away, she put her hands on my cheeks. Belatedly I recalled the broken nose, the vicious bruising. "What in the Twelve happened to you? I assume whoever did this is dead now. Did he die fast or slow?"

"It's nothing." I brushed her off, automatically. "I failed to block a parry swiftly enough."

"King Uorsin did it." Harlan moved to my side, giving me a sidelong accusing look. I glared back coolly. We would have words about this. Andi should not be burdened with such concerns.

Sure enough, she blanched. Not, however, I observed with interest, in fear, but in uncharacteristic rage. At least, not within her previous character. Another way she'd changed. "Moranu take him," she hissed. "Say it's not so."

"It is so." Dafne moved up on my other side. "The entire court witnessed it this time, among other distressing developments. Hello, Queen Andromeda. It's so good to see you again."

Andi stopped her curtsy with a hug. "Don't 'Queen Andromeda' me! I'm so happy you're here, too. I've missed you so and I have many things to tell you." Her gaze slid over to Harlan, a subtle change coming over her as she studied him, the magic gathering about her more dramatically than her cloak of dark hair, reminding me again, forcibly, of our mother. Long-forgotten memories of Salena surged up, triggered by the woman Andi had become. "And you are?"

"Captain Harlan of the Vervaldr, late of Dasnaria," I told her, before he could reply. "The High King contracted them to provide extra security." I raised an eyebrow at her, on the side away from Harlan, and she gratified me by widening her eyes fractionally. An old gesture, one she used instead of rolling them, because I'd make her run ten laps around the stables for doing it.

"Captain Harlan." She inclined her head, far more regal and self-possessed than my little sister had ever been before.

"Queen Andromeda." He bowed deeply, then straightened. "Forgive me for not speaking to you with the proper respect previously. You are much like your sister, so I should have known who you were."

Andi and I exchanged bemused glances. Even the most glib court minstrel had never attempted to compare us.

"You don't think so?" Harlan rumbled with amusement. "The problem with your people is they fail to look under the skin. I imagine when I meet Princess Amelia, she will also have that same shimmer of power about her, will share the way you are all more vividly colored than the rest of the world."

Andi reassessed him, contemplating. "*When* you meet her?" She phrased the question neutrally, so I wasn't certain if she meant that he should have met her already, which indicated Ami wasn't in Annfwn or an otherwise known location, or that meeting her would be an unlikely event.

"Captain Harlan, Dafne—would you excuse us a moment?"

"I'll step away," Harlan replied, not sounding happy, "but I'll keep you in my line of sight. Apologies for any implied insult, Queen Andromeda."

"You believe I'd want—or be able—to harm my sister? Despite her many efforts, Her Highness was never able to make much of a fighter of me." She smiled, amused, but also interested that he'd implied as much.

"From what I understand, you wield magic as easily as Ursula does her blades. I'd be failing in my responsibility to protect her, were I not to take that seriously."

"Captain Harlan suffers from the delusion that I need protecting," I commented.

"As it's not the appropriate company to discuss the various delusions you suffer," he replied, "I shall withdraw for the moment. Lady Mailloux?"

"He called you by your name," Andi mused, after they moved out of earshot. "And teased you."

"Yes. These Dasnarians are an incorrigible thorn in my side. What news of Ami? Are she and the babies alive?"

She gave me a look that made me think she would not drop the subject of Harlan so easily, then sighed. "I suppose your questions are more pressing than mine, so I'll answer yours first. But promise you won't brush me off later?"

"I wouldn't do that."

"You would if I let you. We'll discuss this Captain Harlan and our father, both."

"There's nothing to say about either."

"Ah, now I'm sure there's plenty or you wouldn't be clamming up like that. Besides, I knew there was something between you just from looking—which is why I let him approach." Andi smiled with genuine affection, but sadness in her eyes. "I hate that Uorsin hurt you. And I'm going to be very angry if I discover this wasn't the first time and you hid it from us."

"Never mind that. Is Ami all right?"

She pushed her hair back off her shoulders, allowing the topic change and settling into the business at hand. "She's alive and so is Astar."

Cold dread sank my stomach, then crept back up my spine. "Danu," I whispered. "What are you not telling me—what of Stella?"

"I'm telling this badly. Let me summarize. I think you know part of it. A rebellious contingent here stole Stella and her nurse, attempting to bring them over the border to Annfwn. Of course, I knew the moment they met the barrier, though feeling Stella took me by surprise."

"Of course," I murmured, and she flashed me an owlish look, acknowledging we both felt the chagrin at her much changed status.

"The nurse couldn't cross, having no Tala blood. Even *I* can't adjust for that, prepared or not. The Heart has its own agenda in that way. Don't give me that look, or I won't tell you the rest. The group left her at the border and brought Stella with them. Though I caught up fairly quickly, I couldn't see where they went. More than one of the group is wise to my abilities. Later Amelia came through, along with Ash and Astar."

"How could you know all these things without being present?"

She tilted her head slightly, reminding me of Harlan when he considered how to translate a concept. "You know how it feels when someone touches your skin? With most people, it's kind of a nonevent—you notice it, but it registers as nothing more than that. But with people connected to you, ones who are part of you in some way, it goes deeper, like it crosses an internal boundary as well. Do you understand what I mean?"

"On one level, yes." I wouldn't think of the way Harlan's slightest touch seemed to go right through me. Andi meant people with true connections. By blood or love. Not lust.

"It's like that. Anyone who comes close to the barrier brushes against my awareness now. Like an itch, a bug that should be shaken away."

"Like you did with me in Branli."

She smiled, close lipped and enigmatic. "I couldn't say. Had my sister Ursula been interested in crossing, I would have paid more attention than I did to a troop of soldiers on one of Uorsin's missions."

She hadn't called him father or king, a choice I made sure to note carefully. "And what did you imagine King Uorsin's mission to be?"

The smile fell away and she visibly hardened. "Let's not mince words between us, Ursula. We both know Uorsin lusts for Annfwn with an unholy hunger. Our mother sacrificed her life to stop him from having it. I could hardly do less."

"She lost her life to complications from childbirth."

"Lady Zevondeth implied differently."

"Yes, but she's never come out and said what happened, has she?"

"Did you ask? You came from Ordnung, I presume. Did she offer you a trade, some of your blood for information, perhaps?"

I shuffled the puzzle pieces in my head. "No. She was . . . un-well. But you gave her blood, didn't you? I'm guessing Ami did, too—she hinted as much."

"Ami has come a long way in understanding the power our blood carries."

"Yours and Ami's."

Andi tilted her head at me. "You are also part Tala, sister of mine."

"I am my father's daughter. A warrior. I have no magic." *In that way, you are the most my daughter.*

"You mean you don't believe in the magic you have. Else you'd see through the barrier as easily as you saw the memorial."

I laughed. I couldn't help it. "Tell me another tale. And you're dodging. Give me the rest. How bad is it?"

Sobering, she shrugged, a bit restless. "There's not much more to tell. I know they crossed—both groups—and we haven't had any success finding them since. They're all in Annfwn still and all still alive; I know that much."

"Did you interrogate the nurse?"

"I had an escort take her home."

"Danu! She might have been in collusion with them. How could you let her go?"

"She told us what she knew, which was scarcely more than we already did. They grabbed her to care for Stella and abandoned her in the Wild Lands without a qualm. We owed her better than that."

Andi was likely right, but still it grated. I'd hoped to find Ami and babies safe and sound. Hearing they were all still at risk knifed at me. I should have stayed with her and never gone to Ordnung. So many bad decisions. *But. You. Failed.* My father's voice redoubled the throbbing at my temples.

Focus. "How have you gone about searching?"

"We're not idiots, Ursula. You needn't make it sound like

we're bumbling about. Annfwn is a large and varied territory—ocean, cliffs, forests, and mountains—we're looking systematically, but we haven't succeeded in triangulating on any of them."

"You need me. I'll find them." Make up for my failures.

Andi nodded. "Good. I could use your help. We'd welcome it."

"Does King Rayfe feel the same?" I'd phrased the question neutrally, but Andi narrowed her gaze in warning.

"I do feel the same." Rayfe stepped up to her side, appearing as if from nowhere, gaze going immediately to the movement of my hand to my sword, putting a hand to his own. A tall, dark-haired man with keen warrior's eyes, he moved like a wolf, fast, silent, and potentially lethal.

"I thought we spoke privately." I glared at Andi.

She folded her hands calmly, unapologetic. "I never promised any such thing. You assumed. I have no secrets from Rayfe." The look she gave him then sent that odd twist through my gut. Full of love. I'd known she loved him—had told Ami as much—but it still threw me. How much of what she'd done had been to spare civil war and how much out of desire for this man?

"Forgive me the subterfuge, Your Highness." He bowed but didn't move his hand off the hilt of his blade. "We were uncertain of your motives and it seemed best for me to stand back for the moment." His tone made it clear he, at least, still harbored suspicions.

"King Rayfe." I tilted my head with the polite respect I'd give any of the subordinate kings, no more. He noted the shading, dark blue eyes glittering.

"Do you have need of me, Your Highness?" Harlan stepped up to my side, hand on his blade also. He and Rayfe took each other's measure, tension thickening.

I was saved the indiscreet moment of having to say I'd told him to stay back by Andi's exasperated oath.

"Moranu take you all," she huffed. "I *will not* have a repeat of our last confrontation. Nobody else dies here and I'll take steps to prevent it. Do you all understand me?"

She seemed to have grown in height, though I knew it to be a trick of the eye. Still, her presumption got under my skin. Salt in the wound of my guilt. "I know better than most what crimes I committed here, Queen Andromeda," I snapped.

Instantly, regret overcame her. "That guilt doesn't belong to you, Ursula. I caused Hugh's death through my actions and I know it well."

"If I may." Dafne stepped into the space between the four of us. My Derodotur, indeed, bridging the gap. "Hugh met his death through his own actions. To claim otherwise diminishes what were truly noble, heartfelt intentions."

We all looked toward the shrine Andi had made, the shining blue forget-me-not.

"Well said, librarian," I murmured and sent a prayer to Danu to give him wings. Still, I knew I would carry the burden of his spilled life with me for all eternity, no matter what any of the others thought.

"I think we are at a truce, then." Andi looked around the circle. "King Rayfe and I invite you into Annfwn, to aid in the search for Amelia, Ash, and the children. I will ask for your oath that you will not use this opportunity to cause harm to Annfwn or the Tala, or allow it to be caused through inaction."

"A sweeping vow," I observed, feeling a tug of reluctant admiration for her strategy.

"A perfectly reasonable one, we believe," Rayfe returned evenly. "Surely you would expect no less, Princess Ursula."

"Can any of us pass your barrier, however?" I asked. I'd been looking at Rayfe, but to my surprise, he deferred to Andi.

Her storm-gray eyes focused on us each in turn, seeming to look through us in that uncanny way she'd always possessed but that had sharpened and strengthened in a way that made my skin crawl even still, though I made certain not to show it. Beside me,

Harlan shifted slightly, as if he felt an itch he dared not scratch, and I knew he perceived it also.

"Ursula can pass easily, of course. Dafne—"

"Easily?" I questioned. "I could not before."

A look of mischief crossed Andi's face. "I may have tilted things against you. It was important at the time that you believe you could not enter—nor bring Uorsin's army with you."

"And now?"

She sobered. "Now it's more important to have you here. And you have no army."

"I still fight for the High King."

"I know you do. Though I can't understand it." She sighed. "Nevertheless. Dafne, you have enough Tala blood that I think I can ease you through without much difficulty."

"She does?" I surveyed the librarian, who showed none of my surprise.

"The Mailloux family shared borders with the Tala for many generations." She raised her eyebrows at me. "It would be more surprising if there were not some intermixing."

"Captain Harlan will be more difficult," Andi continued.

"He can stay behind," I said.

He put a hand on my arm. "Not a chance."

Glaring at him, I shook it off. "We agreed that you would wait at the border."

"Only if it proved impossible for me to cross. If there's a way, I'll take it. It's my duty to go with you, to aid your mission and protect you."

"It's too difficult." I gave Andi a steady look, so she'd see that he needed to stay behind. She returned it blandly, though her gaze intensified as she studied me and Harlan in turn.

"Not impossible." She gave me a smile as she said it, with sweetness I didn't buy into for a moment. "I believe that with me present, we can use his connection to you to bring him across."

"He has no connection to me." I laid it out flat, willing her to understand. Harlan didn't move or look at me, but his seething displeasure impinged on my awareness anyway.

Andi raised her brows, deliberately misunderstanding the message. "Of course he does. The bond between you is very clear to my eye. You're obviously in love."

22

Dafne studied the hem of her gown, attempting to avert her face so her smirk didn't show and failing miserably. Harlan gave me a long, considering look, one that I refused to acknowledge as I concentrated on not showing any reaction to Andi's ridiculous assertion.

"I'm not judging," Andi added, brow creasing in concerned puzzlement. "Far from it. I think it's wonderful that you've found someone to love. Someone to watch over you, for a change. And it will make possible what otherwise might be impossible."

My temple throbbed and I ran my thumb over the jewel for comfort. It felt unusually hot, perhaps because I'd had my hand there so long. "We've simply been working together on this journey. Shared dangers will create that sort of bond."

Andi glanced at Dafne, and they exchanged some sort of look I couldn't read. Rayfe set a hand on the small of Andi's back, under her long, loose hair, and she leaned toward him, regathering herself. "Regardless, he should be able to cross and we need him, too. It works best if I'm on the other side. Rayfe and I will step through, then Dafne. Captain Harlan, you will have to carry Ursula through."

"My pleasure."

"Wait. No—that will not happen."

Harlan shot me a look, mostly impassive but with amused irritation beneath. Andi put her fists on her hips in pure exasperation, then pointedly looked the mercenary over. "Seriously? Do you propose to carry him?"

"Does one have to be carried?"

"Yes." She glared. "Do I tell you how to plan your battles? I know how this works. Full-body contact. More is better."

"What about the horses?"

Rayfe smiled for the first time. "All animals are welcome in Annfwn." He murmured something in their liquid tongue and the horses trotted happily through, even my stallion uncharacteristically docile. Taking Andi's hand, Rayfe kissed her palm. "My queen?"

She smiled back at him with a passionate warmth that had me looking away. Unfortunately into Harlan's pale, discerning gaze. Danu take them all.

Andi and Rayfe took a few steps, then disappeared from view, as if walking through a mirror. Dafne threw me a glance, excitement clear in her bright eyes. "See you in Annfwn," she said. She walked forward, holding out her hands. At first she seemed to hit a wall; then her hands passed through, slowly, as if through mud. Then the resistance lessened and she passed through and disappeared.

Harlan tilted his head slightly, challenge glinting in his gaze. "Our turn."

I wanted to roll my shoulders, shake out some of the tightness there, but he would notice that, for sure. "Fine." I moved behind him at the same moment he started to put an arm around my shoulders, reaching the other for the backs of my knees. We collided and I jumped back. "What are you doing?"

"I was going to carry you," he replied, using that tone of infinite patience.

"Not a chance," I shot back, aghast at the thought of being helplessly carted about.

"Would you have me carry you over my shoulder like a wounded soldier?"

"I'll climb on your back."

"I've wanted your legs wrapped around my waist." He let his gaze travel down my body. "It's not exactly what I had in mind, but it gets me closer."

"Stop that," I hissed, turning so my back was to the barrier and I blocked as much of his voice and expression as I could. "They can still hear and see us."

His gaze flicked over my shoulder and back to my face. "Your sister already perceives the feelings you refuse to admit. This is a secret from no one."

"She *perceives* what she wishes to. The idea that I could somehow be in lo— It's absurd."

"Still can't say it, can you?" Harlan's mouth twisted in that grim smile. "What is it about me, Ursula? Are you ashamed of wanting me? Do you feel like you'd be lowering yourself to admit to it, that you're attracted to, that you might love, a mere mercenary? Because if that's the case, I'll walk away and never importune you again. If it's about getting over the past, I can wait, but if you truly hold me in contempt, tell me right now."

He'd kept his voice low, for my ears alone, but his words hit me like fists, intense and full of wounded fury. If he brought this powerful rage to the battlefield, he'd be a fearsome opponent. More so than I'd even thought.

"I don't hold you in contempt." I tried to speak in a level tone, but my voice cracked over the last word, my heart swelling with an unbearable ache. Too much. All of it.

"What, then?"

I swallowed, held it in. "It's not about you. I already said this. I can't be this person you want me to be! Danu take your ultimatum. I can't speak of what happened. I can't—" To my utter horror, what I thought would be a break to breathe in, to think of the right words, came out as a sob instead. I clapped my hand over my mouth, as if I might stuff the traitorous sound back inside. Harlan's visage instantly transformed from wounded anger to deep concern.

"Here, now." He pulled me into an embrace that I couldn't manage to resist. "Don't weep, my fearless hawk."

"I'm not." Because it was there, and because it was better than letting him see my weakness, I buried my face in his shoulder, hating that I felt better for doing so. "Oh, Danu—they're all watching me fall apart. I can't bear it."

"There's no shame in feeling emotion. It doesn't make you weak. Strength is in bearing our wounds, living through them, and carrying forward regardless—not in pretending they never existed."

"I don't know what's wrong with me," I whispered. I needed to pull away, to stand on my own feet. Not lean against this man who somehow cut me open with a few words.

"Nothing is wrong with you. You've been alone for years. Most of your life, maybe, and the accumulation of being eaten up from the inside out is more than even you can withstand."

His analogy took my breath away. I was hollow inside. A brittle shell over a rotten core. Thin skin over a festering sore. "Bad timing for me to break now."

"You won't break if you'll only bend a little." His lips pressed against my temple. "Bend a little, my brave hawk."

It sounded fine in theory. "I don't know how."

"I'll help. Let me carry you."

Weary beyond belief, I couldn't fight him anymore. He must have sensed my tacit agreement, because he swept me up into his arms, carrying me like a bride over the threshold. The barrier resisted, palpably buzzing against my skin, so I wrapped my arms around his neck and touched my cheek to his. The barrier gave with a pop and we stepped through. As we did, the jewel at my hip flared, sending a startling jolt through me, so that I had to bite down on a yip of almost-pain.

"Is Ursula injured worse than she said?" came Andi's worried voice.

"Injured, yes. And exhausted," Harlan answered for me. "She's been through a great deal. Give us a little time here."

"No." I struggled and he set me down, giving me a look that said he saw through me. I scrubbed my hands over my face, grateful that the swollen bruising would hide any sign of redness or tears. "I'm fine to go on."

Andi shook her head slightly, as if answering some silent question. "It's late and you've traveled since early morning. We have a camp nearby so will spend the night there."

"We don't need to—"

"Yes, we do," Andi interrupted. "Rayfe has already taken Dafne there."

Which proved how off my game I was, that I hadn't noted their absence immediately.

"We'll go the rest of the way in the morning, to the capital city. But first—do you have something on you? Something"—she flicked a cagey glance at Harlan—"unusual."

The Star of Annfwn. She'd felt it, too. By dint of will I didn't touch it and managed a casual affect. "I don't know what you mean."

She narrowed her eyes, scanning me. "I think you do, but we'll speak of it later."

"I will keep your secrets," Harlan inserted. "Especially as I suspect I know what it is already. And, if so, it concerns me also." A reminder that I had never answered his questions about it.

I stared them both down, refusing to give any reply. Mother had only told me never to speak of the stone to anyone, not what I was meant to do with it. I'd have to give thought to how to handle this, as well. My head throbbed. I ignored it.

"Later," Andi repeated. "Meanwhile"—she gestured with open palms, a proud light in her eyes—"welcome to Annfwn."

She had a right to be proud. Our mother's homeland was as extraordinary as the stories she'd spun about it. Her voice whispered in my head, her longing as palpable now as then.

The horses had been unsaddled and turned out while Harlan and I argued, so we all walked to the lakeside camp, a short distance away. Relieved for some distraction from my ragged state of mind, I took refuge in observing the landscape.

Near the barrier, the forest seemed much like the one along the pass we'd ascended, except that late summer in Annfwn felt softer, with more moisture in the air. The pine needles grew longer, more luxuriant, and flowers in astonishing colors gleamed under the trees and swelled into profusions of jewel tones in the meadows. Birds flitted overhead, some natural to Mohraya and its surrounds, others with trailing feathers like rainbows or the richest gowns of the court ladies.

As I watched, a flock of birds landed in the meadow and—in an undetectable transition—became a herd of white deer, falling on the acid-green grasses with enthusiasm. Harlan made a surprised noise next to me and Andi turned, giving him an impish smile. "Staymachs," she said, as if that explained anything. "Ursula—you may recall them as the ratlike creatures that participated in the attack on Ordnung. You killed more than a few in that battle."

"It was necessary."

"I'm not criticizing," she replied in a mild tone, the one she used to indicate she thought I was being unreasonable. "I know full well you were protecting me and the castle. They change shape, but out of instinct or when directed by a handler. About as intelligent as horses."

Which meant Andi would have an affection for them. Of course she did for all animals. "I'll try to refrain from slaughtering any more of them," I told her, gratified when she flashed me a more natural grin.

"I appreciate that. They are, incidentally, the creatures that spirited away your Hawks and Captain Harlan's men. Useful for performing minor magics such as that."

"I take it that you're using 'minor' as a relative term," Harlan commented in such a dry tone that I snorted out a laugh, despite everything. He slid me a glance full of ironic humor and touched me on the small of my back, so lightly I almost didn't feel it. I didn't know how to handle his concern for me, but at the moment I appreciated having him there.

Most disconcerting.

"Well, when compared with the magic that keeps Annfwn tropically warm while winter rages an arm's length away? Yes, relatively minor," Andi agreed.

"How does that work, anyway?" I asked her.

"Not telling."

"Is that how it is?"

She gave me a considering look. "Shall we trade answers for answers? Because I have a few questions for you."

"You can ask," I replied, feeling on more sure footing now.

"That's what I thought."

Andi and I exchanged a smile, and for a moment, it felt like no time had passed and we were back at Ordnung, before Rayfe came into our lives. Being honest with myself, though, I had to face that even then the festering wound had been growing. I'd just been more able to cover it up and concentrate on other things. *Eaten up from the inside out.* I couldn't think about it and maintain the command I needed to.

We rounded a bend and the lake spread out before us, mirror bright, reflecting the towering peaks with perfect clarity and ringed with a crown of unspoiled forest. On the near side, on a lush green lawn worthy of Uorsin's exacting standards, a crew of Tala had set up tents and tables, lanterns already glowing in the shadows cast by the lowering sun. The trampled grass between tents showed they'd been in place for possibly several days.

"How long have you been waiting for us to arrive?" I asked
Andi.

She lifted a shoulder. Let it fall. Far too casual. "Since I knew
you were on your way."

"That's hardly a definitive answer."

"You don't expect me to reveal the extent of Annfwn's spy and
defense network, do you?"

"I didn't expect you to have grown canny about strategy, no.
You never paid attention to those lessons before. What changed?"
I knew the answer before she spoke it. Already her gaze and attention had found Rayfe, wild black hair streaming down his back as
he pointed out sights to Dafne. Though he spoke to the librarian,
his eyes had found Andi as soon as we came into view, and the
connection that vibrated between them hummed like a plucked
harp string. I could nearly see it and wondered if this was what
she meant.

Andi touched my hand. "I found something that mattered."

It stung. "Ordnung should have mattered to you."

"You can't force loyalty, Ursula. I never felt the way you did."

"I know." And I hated it. Uorsin, though, had always treated
her with suspicion. Much as I'd tried to coax her into toeing the
line, into being a daughter he could trust, I'd also been glad
enough for his shunning her. Better that than a more unpleasant
sort of attention.

"We'll talk more later. For the moment, come and eat. Rest.
I've called someone to tend your injuries as well."

"I don't need—"

"Thank you, Queen Andromeda," Harlan cut me off. "We appreciate that."

She laughed, taking us in. "First Ami, now you. Annfwn is
magical, indeed. I'll fetch the healer."

"Whatever that means," I muttered darkly, scowling after her.

"I think you know." Harlan ran a hand up my back, reminding
me of the way Rayfe had touched Andi. "You'll feel better to have
at least the concussion tended."

"I'll feel better not to have you all nagging me to death."

"That, too."

The Tala healer did not inspire much confidence. Looking like a feral version of the Moranu priestess I'd met at Windroven, she wore her white hair long, in unkempt braids, and possessed light green eyes similar to Ash's. He'd saved Ami's life, I had no doubt, though I'd been banned from watching exactly what he did. The eye color might indicate the healing ability, as it seemed they didn't all have it.

She stepped into the tent I'd been given—surprisingly luxurious within—and stopped immediately upon entering, sucking in a breath so abruptly that Harlan nearly drew his blade. Her gaze fixed on the sword I still wore, then flew to my face.

"Of course she gave it to you," the priestess murmured, almost to herself. "We should have known. Welcome home, Princess Ursula, daughter of Salena, Star of Danu—we've awaited this day more years than I care to count." Her brown hands wove a complicated pattern in the air and she knelt, pressing her forehead to my feet.

Harlan hadn't missed a detail, settling himself back on the cushion he'd appropriated to oversee the proceedings, with half a smile for my discomfort and a pointed glance at my sword. No, he hadn't missed a thing. Danu take him for his stubborn refusal to leave me unguarded. As if I needed guarding.

Before I found a way to urge the woman up, she uncoiled with fluid grace and studied me, all professionalism now. "Returning to Annfwn has helped, but you've more healing to do," she pronounced. "Please sit."

Figuring to get this over with quickly, I complied, steeling myself not to flinch when her sure touch found the still substantial lump at the back of my skull.

"You took quite a hit," she observed. "Cracked the bone."

"And here some claim it's so thick, too." I flicked a glance at Harlan, who seemed grimly unamused. Magic gathered around the priestess, both like and unlike Andi's. Greener and sparking with life, streaming into me, the pain lessening.

"The nose has been decently reset and should heal clean," she continued, soothing over my cheekbones and brow arches. "The headache is somewhat from the concussion and the rest from that which eats you up inside. Your back, too." She stood before me, lifting my face to gaze deeply into my eyes. Mesmerized, I couldn't seem to look away. "Those injuries are not ones I can heal. Because the pain can't find its way out of your body, it lodges in you, crawling into your bones and muscle to hide. Only you can lance the wound, drain the poison. But you must. You will not be able to do what lies ahead if you are not whole."

"How am I supposed to do that?"

"Feel. Allow yourself to feel and then release it."

I groped for a reply, but my brain fogged through, sizzling with the fire of her magic. Dimly aware of her lips pressed to my forehead—a benediction that infiltrated my bones with the ache of memory—I lost time for a bit.

So much so that I didn't see her leave.

23

"Back with us?" Harlan inquired.

I shook my head to clear it. Noted that the sunset light slanting through the tent flaps had declined half an hour at least. "This is one of the many reasons I'm not fond of magic," I commented.

"Understandable." He rose. "People like you and I prefer what we can lay our hands on." Drawing me to my feet, he framed my face with his big hands, as if in demonstration. "If I hadn't witnessed the results myself, I wouldn't have believed it. The bruising, the swelling—all gone as if it never was." His thumbs smoothed over my cheekbones as the priestess had done, but my blood leapt to the caress in a different way, hot, needy. Yearning. "How does your head feel?"

"Better," I managed, focusing on his mouth. Something about the magic had lit me up from within, and I longed to have his lips on me, his hands. I shouldn't want it, want him, but in the exotic intimacy of the tent, I couldn't quite remember what made having him such a bad idea. The clamoring need drowned all else.

His face grew intent, full of lambent desire. "Ah, my hawk. Don't look at me like that."

"I didn't mean to."

"That makes it worse. I don't want to make things more difficult for you."

"I think—" I had to stop. Try again. "I think I need you to kiss me—would you do that?"

With a groan, he brushed my lips with his, sweet, gentle, tender. The touch burned through me, laying me open as he always seemed able to do. It wasn't enough. I moved in, pressing myself to his muscular body, every pore starving for more. Sliding my hands behind his thick neck, I dug my nails in, drinking in his increasingly hungry kisses in great ravenous bites.

We devoured each other, my hunger feeding his, his fueling mine, his hands roving over my body, me pressing against him as if I might somehow pull him inside of me. Through my skin and into me, into that cold, empty, lonely space.

"Ursula," he said against my mouth, trying to pull back. I wouldn't let him, nipping his lip to show my displeasure and holding him there to drink from his hot mouth again. He groaned, kissed me back with urgency. Then wrenched himself away, holding me by the shoulders at arm's length.

"What?" I demanded, hurt and determined to cover it. "I thought you wanted me."

"More than any woman I've known," he ground out. "But not like this."

I looked around. "In a tent, you mean?"

Impatient frustration clouded his brow. "You know full well what I mean, Ursula. I won't touch you until I know what happened."

"Nonsense. Danu take your excuses and your ultimatums," I snapped.

"It's not like that," he fired back. "Stop calling it an ultimatum."

"I won't be pressured into talking about something I don't want to. It's in the past. It doesn't matter anymore."

"You heard what that priestess said, and even I can see how the poison of it works on you."

"I don't know that's what she—"

"Of course it is. Maybe it's not the only thing, but it's the worst. Else you'd tell me and be done."

"You don't need to know. It's private."

He held out his hands, palms up, showing me something I couldn't see. "What if I do what he did? How can I touch you, not knowing how he hurt you, what might turn pleasure into pain? Don't ask me to do that."

"It wasn't the pain." It hadn't hurt nearly as much as some of the blows I'd taken. Even the flat of a blade hadn't made me feel ill that way.

"Then what?" He cursed softly in Dasnarian, framing my face in his hands again. "You go so pale when you think of it. Don't you see that the only way to drain the infection is to let the light in? As a soldier you know that an undrained infection can kill. Sometimes slowly, but all the more lethal because of it. Just say the words."

It sounded easy, put that way. Just say it. "I—" A burst of laughter from outside caught me. "Not here. Not now."

To his credit, he didn't comment on the irony that I would have shared my body, but not my words, where we could be overheard. Instead, he nodded, in confirmation.

"After we eat. We'll walk down to the lake where we can be private."

My stomach knotted at the prospect. *Only you can lance the wound, drain the poison.* I had faced worse than telling a simple story.

Still, at the moment, I'd rather face an army of Tala wolves and dragons than that.

Andi and Rayfe sat at a table on a rise, drinking wine in the golden evening, deep in conversation. They rose as Harlan and I approached, Andi smiling as she surveyed me.

"Much better," she said in a relieved tone. "Sairah said the blow bruised your brain. You'll tell the story while we eat. Captain Harlan, will you join us?"

For once he seemed uncomfortable. "I don't wish to intrude."

I raised an eyebrow at him, reminding him he'd shown little such reserve with me.

"The Tala do not much stand on ceremony," Rayfe said. "The consort of my heart-sister is welcome at my table."

I drew in a breath to correct him, then stopped myself. If I'd had my way, Harlan would have become my lover mere minutes ago. Whether or not that came to pass, I would not shame him by pretending otherwise. He seemed surprised, then nodded, a small smile on his lips, and held my chair. "Your Highness."

Andi seemed terribly amused and I narrowed my eyes at her as I sat. "Dasnarians are big on courtesy, I have discovered."

"Among other things," Harlan agreed easily.

"No more evasions." Andi poured me wine. "Tell me how it came to pass that Uorsin beat you before the entire court."

"That's putting it strongly." The wine tasted delicious—like sunlight and magic.

"Tell it truly or I will." Harlan stared me down. "Or we can call over Dafne, who witnessed it also."

"You all act as if I've never been injured before, giving this incident more weight than it ought to have." But I gave them the report of the evening as we ate, chary of security details here and there. No sense giving Rayfe of the Tala an advantage, should he decide to attack Ordnung again. I doubted that would come to pass, since he'd won what he sought. Still, Andi might act as if we were merely sisters sitting down for an al fresco dinner with our consorts—something I'd never envisioned for us—but I would not forget that we remained on opposite sides of a contested border.

"Have you heard of these Practitioners of Deyrr?" Andi asked Rayfe when I finished, flashing me a stormy glance before she turned to him, making it clear we had not finished discussing our father. Danu save me.

Rayfe picked up a lock of her hair and wound it thoughtfully around one finger. "There are tales. Some say that certain wizards among the Tala have dabbled in such, black magic, death magic. None do so openly, as it would mean banishment from Annfwn."

"Hardly a dire punishment," I commented.

His blue eyes darkened. "On the contrary, Heart-Sister. The Tala dread nothing more. Many would prefer death to separation from our homeland. You knew Salena better than your sisters— surely you saw what she suffered."

I drank from my wine to cover the cut of that, the remembered bewilderment of watching our mother decline. As a child, I hadn't understood. Even as an adult, I didn't see how not living in Annfwn, lovely though it might be, could make the difference between health, sanity, and . . . whatever you would describe as our mother's behavior in those last years.

"So." Andi tapped her fingers on the table, clearly still mulling the tale. "This Illyria has designs upon the High Throne. Even should she succeed in marrying Uorsin, that would not change the succession."

"Except that the High King has already indicated he would put Astar in the role of heir," I pointed out. "Arguably he sees Astar as the better choice, the son he should have had. What's to prevent him from getting a boy out of Illyria? That would make her queen mother and potentially regent."

"Particularly if Uorsin executes you," Harlan inserted.

Andi stilled, that thundercloud sense gathering. "Is it that bad? I knew you weren't telling us everything."

"No, it's not that bad." I glared at Harlan, regretting the impulse to have him join us. He returned my stare evenly.

"Regardless of the High King's motivations," he spoke to Andi and Rayfe, "Lady Mailloux, Ursula's own lieutenants, and I all agreed the situation had reached such a level that it seemed wisest to extract the heir as hastily as possible, despite injuries that made travel a poor decision."

"Which is why we must find Amelia and bring her and Astar

to Ordnung," I stepped in, determined to divert the course of this speculation.

"Is that the best idea?" Rayfe interrupted. "If your life has been in danger, surely an alternate heir's would be also."

I was already shaking my head. "I'm not further discussing internal politics with an erstwhile enemy of Ordnung. Annfwn has no stake in this situation. I'm updating my sister on events in her family and appealing to you both to allow this rescue mission."

"This has everything to do with Annfwn, Ursula!" Andi's magic snapped with her temper. "You might not think you need help, but by Moranu, you have it. The High Throne of the Twelve belongs to you by right—and by our mother's sacrifice. There are good reasons she laid the plans she did."

"How do you know her plans weren't for Ami's son to take the throne?" I pointed out to her. "Salena waited out those years for her third daughter to be born. She'd had you, born with the mark to fulfill her obligation to her people." I nodded toward Rayfe, who inclined his head in tacit acknowledgment. "Perhaps her plan had been to birth Astar's mother all along. We can't know what she meant to do that the childbirth sickness prevented."

"That makes no sense—you were born to be heir," Andi insisted.

Unless Salena had seen how flawed I was, how unsuited to follow in my father's footsteps. I let the wine ease that ache. So many ways I'd failed.

"Besides"—Andi took a deep breath—"I'm convinced that Uorsin killed our mother."

I set the goblet down. Andi held my gaze, waiting. "That's a horrifying and treasonous accusation."

"He's not my King," she replied.

As if I needed reminding that she'd defected. "You have no reason to think it."

"Don't I? Ami thinks so, too. Lady Zevondeth knows the truth. She's been trying to tell us, in her way."

"Zevondeth is old, possibly demented from age and illness. Her words cannot be relied on."

"Ursula!" Andi reached across the table and took my hands. "I know you think Uorsin is a great king, but he's a tyrant. He's abused his power and now I think he's treated you worse than ever we guessed. How can you defend him?"

"He is the King. I'm loyal to that. It's my duty to be. It's not my place to judge him."

"Loyalty does not have to be blind and deaf," Andi insisted.

I shook her off. "Coming from someone who discarded her filial loyalty to pledge herself to the enemy, that's not a convincing argument. Keep to Annfwn and the Tala, Andi—this has nothing to do with you anymore."

She made a sound of incoherent frustration.

"What about the Star of Annfwn?" Harlan asked.

Rayfe sat upright, as if stung, and Andi and I both rounded on the mercenary. She with astonishment and me with righteous anger. He stared me down, not bothered in the least. "Illyria sought it in your mother's jewels. I told you that I—and I feel I can safely speak for Dasnaria—would have a concern over anything the Temple of Deyrr pursues so diligently. It occurs to me that Annfwn would also have a stake in something named for it."

"You have the Star of Annfwn?" Rayfe demanded.

"That's what you brought through the barrier," Andi said at the same time.

Rayfe rounded on her. "You knew, Andromeda, and didn't tell me?"

"I didn't know what it was," she returned. "Don't pull that attitude on me. If you want to be helpful, you can explain the significance of it."

"Why don't *you* explain, Uorsin's heir?" Rayfe focused on me. "How came you to have this jewel?"

"Jewel?" Andi echoed. She knew, then. It showed in her face though she avoided looking at my sword, having at least that much discretion still.

"I've never seen it." Rayfe's intent gaze swept over me. "I thought it a myth, in truth. It's described as perfectly round and smooth, light amber in color, and shines as if lit from within." He touched Andi's chin then, lifting it so she met his eyes. They exchanged a long moment of wordless communication.

"What power does it hold, then?" I made the question sharp enough to break the moment, and they swiveled to look at me.

"Let me see it," Rayfe returned.

"No. I came to have it because our mother gave it to me. And told me to keep it secret. That hasn't changed."

"I remember seeing it now, as Rayfe describes it," Andi whispered. "But so long ago. You never said you had something from her."

The old guilt crept in. "It felt wrong to throw it in your face. I had more of her than you or Ami did. And I had that, too."

"I notice you kept it anyway," Andi replied, in a dry tone I recognized as an imitation of mine.

"She told me to."

"What for?"

"I—" *Remember that you are the daughter of queens as well as of a king. A star to guide you . . . You will need it someday.* "I don't exactly know."

"Our queens were said to pass it from one to the next." Rayfe picked up Andi's hand, kissed it. "It belongs to Andromeda, by right."

"No." Andi denied the assertion almost before he finished speaking. "Ursula is more queen than I. I might be in Annfwn, but she's the one meant to be queen of all the Twelve—even of the Thirteen." Her voice echoed eerily with prophecy, enough so the hair crawled on the back of my neck. Even Rayfe seemed taken aback.

The words reverberated with a hum in the air, gradually fading.

"What are you saying?" I said into the quiet.

Her eyes nearly glowed in the lamplight, both dark and bright at once. "I told you once before, Ursula. Your reign will be extraordinary."

I remembered that day. "You said then you didn't know what the future holds." Certainly not what had transpired lately.

She glanced at Rayfe, back to me. "Not precisely. But some events I do see. Rarely in much useful detail. None are certain, though some are more inevitable than others."

"Are there futures where Ursula does not take the High Throne?" Harlan asked.

Andi turned to him. "Nothing is certain," she repeated. "You, however, Captain Harlan, are a part of this. A crucial one."

Though he didn't show it, I knew she'd surprised him. "Is that so?" He said it slowly, measuring her.

Abruptly she smiled. "It is so. I'd long wondered who in the Twelve and Annfwn you might be. Such a fascinating twist that you're not of us at all. I wonder what that means for our future." Leaving him to ponder that, she focused back on me. "It's safe where it is. Keep the Star. I'll find out what I can about it, now that I see more."

"I don't like it." Rayfe glared at me, as if I'd been the one to say it. I steeled my spine against the wolfish stare, ready to draw if necessary. Trying not to think past that, of taking the blade to another of my sister's husbands.

Andi laughed, leaned in, and kissed him. He visibly softened at the caress, then intensified it. Like a spring squall, the moment passed. She pulled back and stroked his cheek. "I'll make it up to you."

"Yes, my queen," he replied. "You absolutely will."

I had to look away from the exchange, uncomfortable, and found Harlan watching me with that implacable gaze.

She stood and Rayfe rose with her. "We'll leave you. I'm sure you have much to discuss." She slanted me a sly smile and they went off, her arm threaded through his, heads bent together.

"It bothers you, to see them together?" Harlan asked, as I poured us both more wine.

I took my time answering, sorting through my thoughts, the still-roiling emotions of the conversation and all that had gone before. All I'd learned and observed. "Not exactly. I never truly contemplated what marrying him would mean for her."

"Sharing his bed?"

That discomforting heat again. I sipped the wine to cool it. "I suppose. She seems content, though. I'm still not happy about it, but he's a surprisingly good match for her. They . . . suit each other."

"As you and I do?"

"I don't know about that. Don't let Andi's vague prophecies go to your head."

He chuckled. Picked up my hand now that they'd left and turned it over to press a sensual kiss to my palm. In the lamplit darkness of the warm night air, it felt more intimate, more dangerous. Restless, I shifted, and he let me pull my hand away, settling back in his chair.

"It can't be easy, to want what's best for your realm and for those you love—especially when they seem to be in conflict."

"That's why I rely on the tangible—vows of loyalty and duty."

"You don't think you operate out of love? And yet you made a number of decisions, as I've pointed out before, for love of your sisters."

The restlessness niggled at me. I shrugged it off. "What you call love, I call duty. Our mother died. They've had no one else to look after them."

"No one until now," he pointed out ruthlessly. "Queen Andromeda, at least, has found a partner who cares deeply for her."

"Ami, too," I replied, thinking of how she'd kissed Ash, turned to him for aid and comfort. Finishing off the wine, I reached to pour more.

Harlan put his hand over mine. "The wine won't calm what disturbs you."

"Oh?" I gave him my frostiest tone, but his touch penetrated as always, warming. Disturbing in its own way. "I imagine you think that either sex or spilling my guts will."

He didn't rise to the bait, instead tugged me to my feet. "Or something else."

24

"It's late," I said as he led me around the edge of the lake, my hand firmly tucked in his, my stomach knotting with dread. Yet, I didn't actually balk or refuse to go, which puzzled me. "Tomorrow will be a long day and we should get some sleep."

"You're buzzing like a lightning storm, Ursula—you'll never sleep when you're this worked up."

"You think you know me so well." Though he had a point.

His laugh rumbled low, his thunder to my lightning. "I'm beginning to, yes. You're not so difficult to decipher. A bit of study and my strategy seems clear."

"I'm not some castle for you to besiege."

"An intriguing metaphor. I've scaled your walls—the lower ones—and penetrated the outer courts. Now, how to find my way into the heart of you?"

"If you're planning to make me talk, you'd have done better to bring the wine."

"To extend the analogy, a heavy-handed method like a catapult will not work in the close quarters of the inner courtyards. That requires a more delicate approach." He stopped in a clearing ringed by trees. Unbuckled his sword belt and set it aside.

I cleared my throat of the rattling nervousness. The overwhelming tide of desire I'd felt earlier had receded, leaving sharp rocks behind. This was delicate? "Harlan, I, ah—"

He stopped me with an annoyed look. "I don't plan to throw you to the ground and have my way with you, Ursula. Give me some credit. And take off your sword."

"Why?"

"We're going to spar."

I laughed. I couldn't help it. "You must be the most single-minded man under Danu's gaze."

"Yes." In two strides, he had his hands on my hips, unbuckling my sword belt. "I'll have your respect, Your Highness. If only as a fighter."

Unbalanced, I braced myself on his muscled shoulders. "I respect you."

"Not enough." He pulled the daggers from the sheaths, tossed them carelessly aside, and ran his hands up my waist, down over my hips, then settled, flexing. "Not the way you need to. What other blades do you wear?"

Taken aback by his ferocity, my heart accelerated. The way I needed to? "Will you strip me of all my weapons?" My voice came out throaty.

"Not possible. You need not tell me, then. It shall be my pleasure to search you."

Firmly, thoroughly, he ran his hands over my hips and down each leg, removing the short blade I strapped to my left thigh and the set of throwing knives at my right ankle. Bemused, I let him draw off one boot, then the other, so I stood barefoot on the dew-damp grass. Away from the lamplight, the stars above glittered diamond sharp, a dazzling array of light and color as bright as moonlight, such as I'd never seen, lending to the unreality of the moment.

Working his way back up, he loosened my shirt and smoothed hot fingers over the skin of my back, then over the material down my arms, finding the second set of throwing knives at my left

wrist and discarding them. Back to my shoulders, he slid calloused fingers of one hand behind my neck and set the other in
the hollow of my throat, holding my gaze and pausing there for a
long moment while my breath accelerated. Preparing for the
match to come, I told myself.

The thrill, though, of his finger slowly trailing downward over
my breastbone had nothing to do with fighting.

"Anything else?" His pale eyes glinted in the starlight.

"No." I could barely speak for the tightness of my lungs as he
caressed the skin at the opening of my shirt, down between my
breasts. They weren't something I thought about much, except to
bind them, to keep my sword arm free. But now they ached, tight
and full. Part of me wanted his big, rough hands on them, but
somewhere inside I tensed, afraid of that very thing.

He seemed to read that in me, because he stopped, the hand at
the back of my neck kneading the tendons there with that magical
deftness. Then he stepped back, handing me a blunt-edged practice dagger. "Ready?"

I was. He called it correctly—the tension and emotion of the
day begged to be burned off.

I'd spent enough time assessing his reach to situate myself well
outside it. I picked my spot, level ground without loose rocks or
limbs, and moved my weight into the balls of my feet. The restlessness and worry settled into keen anticipation. Weighing the
light bronze in my hand, I found its balance and planned my
strategy. "What are the rules?"

"You take me down, you win. I take you down, I win." He
pulled off his shirt and kicked off his boots, then flexed, muscular
chest rippling as he settled into a ready stance.

"And the forfeit?"

He grinned, sending a bolt of answering desire through me. "I
think we both know that."

He launched himself at me.

I spun, easily dodging the expected move. Men nearly always
tried to grab, and I'd paid attention to how he wrestled. I hadn't

expected him to spend any time waiting for my blade to find him. His best bet lay in grappling me, and mine would be slicing him before he could get there. I evaded him, moving out and away, but— faster than I'd anticipated—he turned his momentum, rolled and grabbed me by the ankle, taking me down. He'd been watching me, too, to know where I'd plant that weighted foot.

Changing my fall into a dive, I reversed and neatly twisted out of his grip, arcing over to come up behind him. I'd done it fast enough to get the blade up near his throat, but he'd anticipated me in turn, rolling so his meaty shoulder deflected the blade, then continuing to surge to his feet, dodging the undercut I'd thought to bring under his guard and dancing back with surprising grace.

"So fast, my hawk," he said in admiring tones. "Come a bit closer."

I laughed, blood humming. "Not a chance, rabbit."

"You don't know the hares of Dasnaria."

He leapt. How a man that size could spring so far, I'd no time to contemplate. Inside my perimeter in an unexpected flash, he seized me, pinning my dagger arm to my side in an unbreakable bear hug, taking me down and rolling so my head spun. He'd miscalculated—or been too soft on me—by taking the brunt on his shoulder and flattening onto his back instead of crushing me beneath him.

It gave me enough room—barely—to get the blade between his heavy thighs to press the flat against his man jewels. Not a killing strike, but one few men could fight through. Feeling it, he stilled.

I allowed myself the moment of triumph and smiled at him. "I win."

"Do you?"

Before he finished the words, he'd broken the grip, clamped his hand over my wrist, flipping me and simultaneously pinning the knife hand over my head, crushing me as he should have to begin with. I didn't bother to fight it. With an opponent of his strength and bulk, I'd truly lost the moment he managed to pin me.

"If I'd had my sword, you'd never have gotten close enough," I panted. Oddly out of breath, given how quickly the match had ended.

"Had you used the dagger as you meant to, I'd have been in no condition to trap you like this," he conceded. "As it is, I believe you've lost and are now my prisoner."

"Do you plan to interrogate me?"

"No." He stared into my eyes for an endless moment. "I plan to enjoy the spoils of war."

His mouth closed warmly over mine and I welcomed him in, the heat of the fight flashing into the heady need I'd felt earlier. Instead of threatening, his heavy weight roused me, stirring my blood, pressing all along the lines of my body. And when his hand slid up my side, to clasp my breast as I'd imagined earlier, my mind rolled into some dreamy place where all that mattered was him touching me and me wanting more.

"Harlan," I moaned.

"Yes," he answered.

The dagger must have fallen away, because my hands were running over his short hair, soft like the pelt of a rabbit, then found his broad shoulders. Those muscles flexed under my hands and his mouth left mine, letting me catch a breath, stealing it again as the heat moved down my throat. He sank teeth into the juncture of my neck and shoulder and I cried out as it jolted through me. Unstoppable, unbearable. Undeniable.

With a sound like a growl, he slid down, pulling open my shirt and finding the cloth I used to hold my breasts tight against my body. Sitting up, he pulled a short knife from the small of his back, bringing the sharp edge against the binding cloth where it ran flush against my ribs, glancing at me for permission.

"Why did you get to keep a blade?" I whispered through otherwise held breath. The moment should have frightened me. Instead I wanted him to cut the cloth away, to touch me in truth.

His face tense with desire, he smiled, feral and intent. "In case I needed it."

The material gave, parting with a hiss under the razor edge, baring my breasts to the warm night air and his avid gaze. My nipples tightened and, abruptly self-conscious, I covered them with my arms. Harlan cupped my cheek, all gentleness again. He leaned down to kiss me, bracing himself over me now, lightly brushing and nibbling at my lips until my breath sighed out.

"We can stop any time," he murmured against my mouth.

"Okay."

He lifted his head. "Okay you want to stop?"

"No—okay, I know that." Screwing up my courage—something I'd thought would never fail me—I unwound my arms and slid them behind his neck. "I don't want to stop. Yet," I added. He settled a hand at my waist and gave me a smile so tender, something in me shredded.

"You are so incredibly beautiful," he whispered. "A shining star." He sat back, cupping my breasts like birds that might fly away. No one had ever touched me that way, and my skin came to life under his hands, filling me with sweetness. With consuming need. I arched my back, wanting, demanding, more, and his fingers tightened, moving with greater urgency, his roughened thumbs flicking over my nipples. The deep, dreamy heat sharpened, zinging into my blood, and I gasped at it, digging my nails into his thighs where my hands had fallen.

He relaxed the grip, softening it and stroking me. Around my breasts, down my ribs to my belly, tracing the scar I'd gotten when I was sixteen and failed to step back fast enough from my opponent's blade. Then relentlessly back up, circling my nipples, watching my face as I shifted under him, close to begging for more, afraid to ruin the moment by allowing this to go too far.

So far none of it had felt like that night, but those memories— oily and jagged—lurked beneath. For the time being I had them locked away. Still they made themselves known, pressing against my control, softly hissing, the buried threat implicit.

I wouldn't let them poison this. *Lance it and let it go.*

Harlan bent his head, following the path his hands had taken with his mouth, so hot on my skin, sending the steaming heat into me, like the bubbling springs beneath Windroven, molten from the earth's core. When his lips closed over one aching nipple, the pleasure so transfixed me, I held his head to my breast, making soft mewling noises I'd never made in my life, too rapt to care how I might sound.

He moved to my other breast and I thought I might not be able to stand much more. The stars wheeled above, bright jewels seeming to circle with the stroking of his tongue. I was hot, aching empty between my legs, and I wanted him there. I needed him to touch me there, to salve the hollowness, to fill me. I wanted to open to him. With all the bright, delightful desire riding through me, it felt so good and real and possible that this could work. I shifted, offering, inviting.

His hand stroked over my thigh, sliding along the outside and, following my movement, up the inside, cupping my mound.

The walls imploded, old poison pouring through, and—Danu help me—I shattered, bursting into tears.

With a soft Dasnarian curse, Harlan rolled onto his back, drawing me against his naked chest and stroking his hands up my back. I pushed against him, suddenly desperate for distance, and scrambled away. I didn't make it far, though. Covering my face to stop the flow of tears, bearing down to quiet the wracking sobs, I pulled my knees up tight against my chest and buried my head against them.

"Ursula—" Harlan sounded wrecked, but I shook my head furiously.

"No. Go away. Don't touch me."

"I won't touch you, but I'm staying right here."

"Give me a minute." I battled against the tide of old feelings, determined to wrest back some control. He stayed quiet, blessedly giving me that time. The tears, however, would not abate. My stomach rolled and the spike up my spine drove knives into my temples. I clenched against the need to sob out the pain, my ribs aching, my lungs burning. I needed to be alone. "Please go away," I managed, completely humiliated.

"No. You've been too much alone in this and it's solved nothing." His arms came around me then, and I struck out, wildly. He absorbed the blows like the mountain he was, easily holding me and pulling me onto his lap. The feel of his skin under my hands seemed to unravel the last of my fragile control, and the tears came harder, the sobs escaping my rigid grasp, heaving out in ugly, awful gulps. I couldn't fight it and him, too. "Let it go, my love," he murmured, rocking me. "Cry it out. No one will ever know. I'll keep watch."

As if unable to resist the command, I came apart entirely. Burying my face against his chest, I let him rock me as I wept. It seemed I cried for hours, for all the years I hadn't. As delirious with the overwhelming grief as I'd been with desire, I wept for the girl I'd been, for my mother, for the shattered teacups. For all the sorrows, great and small.

Eventually, like a storm subsiding, the wracking sobs eased, relinquishing their brutal grip, softening and gentling. The tears still flowed, an endless river, but less urgently, no longer fountaining under the pressure of the awful ache in my heart. I became aware of Harlan's heart, steadily thumping beneath my cheek, that his skin skidded wet from my weeping and that he sang that Dasnarian lullaby, a profound vibration in his chest, deep voice wrapping around me as surely as his strong arms.

"What does it mean?" I croaked, my throat torn apart by the ugly, grating sobs.

"Mostly nonsense," he answered softly. "About the songbirds in their nests and the mother cat who nuzzles her kitten. That we are safe and warm from the winter winds. That all will be well and the sun will rise again."

"Beautiful, though."

"As are you, my fearless hawk. As are you."

I wiped my face, not knowing what to say. Embarrassed at how

I'd behaved. Uncertain of how to explain. "I hate that this hap-pened," I finally whispered.

"I know." He kissed my hair.

I took a deep breath that shuddered only a little. "I want to apologi—"

The sudden tightening of his arms stopped my words. "Don't." He sounded suddenly, brutally angry. "Don't you dare apologize for this, Ursula."

I stayed silent awhile, his anger palpable in the ripple of his muscles. Yet he continued to hold me with what could only be called tenderness, protecting and comforting me both.

"It was him, wasn't it?"

The question didn't surprise me. Nor that we both knew who he meant. Inexpressibly weary, I leaned into Harlan, relieved at least that he hadn't made me say it out loud.

"It's so hard to explain so that you'll understand."

"What's to understand about a father raping his daughter?" His voice cut like a blade, implacable, slicing open the gray areas.

"It wasn't rape."

"Don't give me that. How old were you?"

"Twelve."

He cursed, viciously, that Dasnarian one he reserved for the greatest extremity. "How can you not call that rape? You were a child still."

"I had my woman's courses and breasts." I hadn't been a child for years by then. "The management of Ordnung had fallen to me and I'd handled it. He'd made me his heir that day, given me the Circlet. I was not a child, but fit to hold the High Throne. Do you know how huge that was for me?"

"I can guess."

"When the King explained . . . When he—" I tripped on the words. Bore down. "It made sense."

"How?" Harlan growled the word, meaner than I'd ever heard him sound. "How did it make sense?"

"My mother was gone. Uorsin needed a queen. A male heir. If I'd been a boy, I might have been perfect. My blood, his blood— if he could get a boy on me, then together we'd hold the High Throne."

"And you believed this."

"He's the High King." Always I'd had faith in that. "He is above the law that governs everyone else. I've always understood that."

"How many times?"

I didn't have to ask what he meant, though my throat went dry around the answer. "Once. Just the once. It wasn't rape, because I agreed."

"He hurt you."

"I didn't know what to do. It didn't hurt that much." But it had made me feel ill and awful, bent over his desk while he lifted my coronation gown and thrust himself into me. The tearing stretch while I tried to pretend it was another training exercise, praying to Danu that I wouldn't cry. *Don't cry. Don't let him see your tears.*

My face grew wet, though I hadn't realized I'd started crying again. Going to wipe them away, I discovered the tears weren't mine this time. Astonished, I followed the trail up, seeing Harlan's face contorted with sorrow as he wept for me.

"Oh, Harlan, no. Please." I wiped the tears from his cheeks and he turned his face to bury his lips in my palm. "It's all right. Don't cry for my sake."

"Someone should," he responded roughly, pulling me harder against him. "I'm going to kill him for this."

"Don't say that." My chest froze in fear, in dread.

"He should die for this crime."

"No. That's not for me to judge." *You'll know when the time comes.*

"Even though Queen Andromeda believes he may have killed your mother?"

"I don't know. Maybe even then."

"Who do you think should hold him accountable—tell me that much."

"Nobody! The High King is above the law. Besides, I agreed to—"

"Stop saying that." His hands tightened on my arms and he pulled back to look in my face. His was ravaged with emotion, reflecting all those feelings I'd poured out against his skin. "You were a child, in his power as both his daughter and his subject. He abused you in the worst possible way. An abomination against all that he should have been to you. Why else do you think it hurt you so? Poisoned you all these years."

"Because I failed him. I didn't have the courage." The way his seed had trickled down my thighs, soaking into my underskirts as I walked back to my rooms, sore, bleeding mostly on the inside. "And I—I thwarted him."

"How do you mean?"

"I didn't get pregnant, first off. Then I wouldn't do it again."

"Did he try?" Harlan's voice was measured, even. Didn't fool me for a moment.

"Not really." I still amazed myself, feeling both triumphant and terrible about it. "I told him I'd cut his cock off. He believed me."

Harlan laughed, kind of. A broken sound. "No wonder you carry so many blades on you."

"I don't know if I could have done it. I would have, I think, if he'd tried anything with Ami or Andi. Not that I ever let them be alone with him."

"Always protecting everyone else."

I shrugged. I couldn't bear the thought of them going through that. I'd paced the floors all night following Ami's wedding, worrying that she'd be like me, that she'd suffer that way. It had been even worse when I heard I was too late to stop Andi's wedding to Rayfe. At least Ami had chosen hers.

"You never told them. Never told anyone."

"No." My hidden shame. "I didn't want anyone to know, though I think some people guessed. Then he was so angry that his seed didn't take. No matter how I tried to make it up to him, he's never forgiven me for that."

25

Harlan's body hardened, the anger rippling through again. "The ones who guessed, none of them stood up for you?"

"You've been to Ordnung. No one defies Uorsin. Not for long. And no real harm was done."

"I want you to promise me something, Ursula."

Wary, I levered myself away from him, scrutinizing his face, now set in hard lines. "I'm listening." But promising nothing yet.

"Never excuse it like that again."

Not what I'd expected. "I'm just explaining that—"

"No." He interrupted explosively, holding my head in his big hands and forcing me to look into his eyes. "Never. The crime was committed against you. Being who you are, my fearless hawk"—his grip softened and he stroked his thumbs over my cheekbones, massaging into the tight muscles of my jaw—"you put a stop to it happening again. But you never healed."

"I used to think I was broken," I whispered, surprised I wanted to tell him this part. "When the other women talked about it being pleasurable and I'd hated it. Hated it so, so much . . ."

He kissed me when I trailed off, with exquisite tenderness, dropping his hands to run over my naked back and shoulders.

Not sexual, soothing. All this time I'd been sitting there bare breasted, without being aware of it.

"I thought maybe Andi and Ami would be the same. That we'd all somehow inherited this from our mother. That we were flawed somehow. Then I've seen how they are. That they're happy."

"You're not flawed, Ursula."

I let my breath flow in and out. Let the susurrus of his touch infuse me. "Maybe you're right. I liked this. It felt good, up until . . . the one part."

"I'm sorry I pushed you."

"Don't be. It makes me think that maybe I'm not broken, after all. That I could have that, too, someday."

"You are not broken," he murmured, dropping light kisses, like butterfly wings, over my face. "You are perfect and beautiful. You hated what happened because it was a violation. The opposite of what making love should be."

My breath shuddered out. *A violation.* Yes, it had felt like that. Not the lovely, sparking warmth of Harlan's touch. "I can't think about it anymore tonight."

"Then don't." He kissed me on the forehead, holding it, a lingering caress. "We'll go back to the tent, get some sleep."

"It's late," I agreed. Though I knew I'd never sleep. "But I want to do something for you."

"How do you mean?"

"I've been around men and I hear the talk. I know it's . . . difficult for them. When they get close to having sex and stop." Difficult was putting it mildly, the way some of them went on about it.

"Believe me, Ursula," he said, sounding torn between amusement and annoyance, "my physical satisfaction is about the last thing on my mind right now. I'm not laying a finger on you again tonight. Not as raw as you are."

Maybe not ever. The words went unsaid, but I heard them clearly. I might not have been broken before, but what happened had resulted in damage. As if I'd lost some vital limb to an injury turned gangrenous.

"I can just imagine." The bitterness in my voice surprised me. "It can't be very pleasant to have your lover become hysterical when you touch her. I want you to know that I understand."

He made an impatient sound, grasped me by the hips and turned me so I straddled his waist. "Understand what?"

I did feel raw. Impossibly on the verge of tears again, though I shouldn't have had any left. To stall, I ran my hands over his chest, the muscled ridges of his shoulders. "I wish I could be like Jepp," I said, surprising myself at the words, at the deep regret that infused me. "I wish I could be that woman, that I could pleasure you and be joyful about it. That I could have taken you to my bed the first time you asked."

"I'm not in love with Jepp. You're the woman I love, exactly as you are."

"You wanted to please me. I know you did—you took your time about it and that worked. If I were whole, we would have been lovers long before this."

"That doesn't matter to me."

"It matters to me. I can give you pleasure in other ways. With mouth or hands—I've heard stories."

"Ursula." Harlan leaned his forehead against mine. "You're killing me."

"Let me do this. Just consider me a green recruit is all." Experimentally, I kissed his neck as he'd done to me, finding the pulse point under the hard line of his jaw and sucking at the thinner skin there, his blood leaping to pound under my mouth. He groaned, a deep rumble, hands convulsing on my hips. It gave me a heady sense of power, to feel him shudder now, for him to tip his head back, pliant and greedy for more.

"You don't have to—"

"Shut up, Captain," I ordered, feeling stronger all the time. I raked my nails over his beefy shoulders and muscled chest, digging in and indulging as I'd wanted to since nearly the beginning.

The bright firmament of Annfwn's stars lit him as clearly as the moon might. He said something soft in Dasnarian, closing his eyes. Remembering, I softened my caress, stroking his skin with my calloused fingers. "Is this how you imagined it?" I asked.

"Better," he grated.

"What else went into this fantasy of yours?"

He cracked one eye open, surveying me. "This is pretty damn good as is."

"Stop coddling me. I want to do this. What happens next?"

Wrapping his hands around my wrists, he held mine in place and lay back, drawing me with him. "You sat over me, like this. Ran your hands over me like you're doing."

I complied, though it felt as much like indulging myself as pleasing him. His face had relaxed, though, softening into those sensual lines as he watched me through slitted eyes. He slid hands up my arms to cup my breasts, featherlight, careful. "Only you're more beautiful than I imagined. My naked warrior queen."

The image made me laugh. "Only half-naked. Then what?" I knew the answer. His body provided it in the hard line of his up-thrust cock beneath my bottom. Scooting back, I straddled his massive thighs and unlaced his trousers. "Did I do this?"

He released a slow breath, measured, maintaining composure in a way I recognized. "Yes."

I'd seen men naked, of course. The battlefield leaves little room for modesty. Rarely, though, had I seen a man up close like this, and never in such a full state of arousal. Not surprising, Harlan's cock was as big as the rest of him, hard and full, straining against his belly. The starlight shimmered on the fine, fair hair at the base. He held very still, only the glint of his eyes showing how closely he watched me.

I closed my fingers around his shaft, much like taking the hilt of a sword in my hand. A living sword that leapt to life at my grip, throbbing, heated. "Like this?" I asked him, just to see him struggle to answer. I slid my hand up, then down again, letting the calloused tips of my fingers drag over the soft, tender head.

He convulsed, arching his back. "*Luta*, Ursula!"

"Am I doing it right?" I teased, slowing.

"You know you are," he panted, hips pressing down, hands on my thighs, digging in as if to hold me there.

"I think you're *my* prisoner now." I worked him, speeding and slowing, testing to see what got to him the most.

"I'm at your mercy," he agreed. "A happy captive to do with as you will."

"Good." To my surprise, my voice came out in a warm, satisfied purr. "I hope my hands aren't too cold now?"

He grunted a nonanswer.

"Because, if they are . . ." I bent over and closed my mouth over the head of his cock. He made a most satisfying strangled sound of helpless pleasure. Enjoying the velvet-soft texture of him there, I swirled my tongue around, tasting the brine of the seed that leaked from him, salty-sweet, like the seas off Elcinea. His hands clutched at my thighs with greater urgency, so I lifted my head to see his face, smiled at his near-desperate expression. "Am I doing it wrong? I am not skilled, I know."

"Any more skilled," he ground out, "and I would be a dead man. You'll want to back off."

"No. I want to finish you. Make you spill your seed." I paused, slightly uncertain. Gossip was one thing, reality another. "It's the culmination, yes? The most pleasurable part. There's not a reason you don't want it?"

"Gods no, my ferocious hawk. I want it. It's just polite to—" He broke off and threw back his head when I clasped him in my mouth again. Now that I knew for sure the technique I'd heard of worked, I licked and sucked the tip, using both hands to grip his shaft, judging my success by the way he thrashed and groaned under my hands.

He tensed and, with an incoherent shout, bowed up under me, his seed filling my mouth and spilling out to slicken my hands as I slid them up and down his shaft, savoring the way he unraveled for me.

The pulses ran through him for some time after, slowing but not stopping. Not unlike cooling down after a fierce fight, so I stayed with him, stroking and occasionally licking, until he put his hands on my shoulders with a breathless laugh. "Stop now." He urged me up and fitted me against his side, staring up at the sky and catching his breath as I pillowed my head on his shoulder.

It felt good and right, to lie there beside him, to have done the things normal lovers do. Like an oasis in the Aerron desert, restorative, refreshing.

"I've never seen stars like this," Harlan murmured, sounding sleepy.

I looked, too. "It's the altitude."

"I've been in the mountains in other places—the stars were never so bright. Or so colorful."

He had a point. "Annfwn magic, I suppose. Though how it could affect the sky as well, I don't know."

"Perhaps it's enough to know that it does." He turned his head and kissed me on my brow. "Just as it's enough to be with you and hold you close. Don't ever feel you need to give me more than that."

"I liked it," I told him, reflecting on that amazing fact. "And, oddly, I feel better that you know . . . all of it."

"Maybe you can begin to heal."

I frowned. "I don't see why that would make a difference. Nothing has changed. The past is still the past."

His arm pulled me closer as he chuckled, hand caressing my bare waist. Being skin to skin with him this way gave me a sated feeling, as if it fed something deep inside that I hadn't known was hungry. "Even with your practical mind you must understand that emotional wounds drain us of life as surely as physical ones. Don't your soldiers suffer from the deeds performed, the horrific sights they surely must encounter?"

"I suppose. But there's nothing to be done."

"Not true. Part of the healing system our fighters learn addresses that also. Confiding in another, telling the tale, always helps."

"Which is why you were so determined to make me tell you." I wasn't sure how I felt about that. I didn't care for being manipulated.

A soft laugh rumbled in his chest. "You needn't sound so suspicious. I asked out of love, so I could know you."

I had no response to that. Not the one he expected in return, at least. But he didn't seem to mind, simply stroked my skin with tenderness. With his strong arm around me, I felt safe. Cherished, even. Surprisingly, a wave of sleepiness washed through me, and my lids grew heavy. "I feel good with you," I murmured.

"I'm glad, my hawk. May it always be so."

Blinking my eyes at the rising sun, I couldn't determine why I felt so groggy. Too much wine? But I'd slept outdoors. With a rush, the night before flooded my mind and I sat up. Instantly awake and alert, Harlan sat up also, knife in his hand, keen gaze scanning the quiet glen.

"What?" His terse whisper told me all I'd ever need to know about him, that I could always count on him to be ready to fight with me.

"Sorry." I gave him a chagrined smile and crossed my arms over my bare breasts. Away from his body heat, they'd tightened, my nipples going hard and sensitive in the cool dawn air. Not embarrassing exactly, but . . . inappropriate for the moment. "I didn't know where I was, I slept so hard. It startled me."

He grinned and tugged at my wrists, baring me to his gaze and drawing me down again, so my stiff nipples rubbed against his chest, shivering pleasure through me. Another surprise. "You look so deliciously soft and rumpled. Let's stay like this forever."

Surprisingly tempted, I returned his kisses, letting the dreamy warmth linger a bit longer. Then, with a groan, I pulled away firmly. "If only. They'll be looking for us. I can't believe I slept so long."

"You needed it. And, as you observed, today will likely be a long one." Harlan surged to his feet, stretching, joints popping, and his loosened trousers sagged, tenting enticingly over his morning erection. He caught me looking and gave me a cocky grin. "You know I'm always ready to serve you, Your Highness."

I snorted and found my shirt. It felt odd to wear it bare breasted, especially with my nipples already sensitive. I'd have to find another cloth to bind myself, as Harlan had effectively destroyed the other. Folding the cut pieces of fabric, I found myself smiling at the memory, not minding a bit.

By mutual accord, we headed back to the camp at a brisk jog, just to get the blood moving. It would have been good to have a workout, but I doubted we had time. Sure enough, the tents had been struck and some of the camp already packed away. Andi sat at a table, hands wrapped around a steaming cup—tea, no doubt—looking sleepy and somewhat grumpy. Good to know that she hadn't changed all that much.

Dafne sat with her, watched our approach with a pleased smile, though she offered a good morning neutrally enough and nudged the teapot in my direction. Rayfe strode up, leading two horses, saddled and ready to go, and nodded in greeting.

"We're ready to leave when you've all had breakfast," he said.

"I'm working on it," Andi muttered. Then yawned.

"Are you unwell, Queen Andromeda?" Harlan handed me a basket of bread.

"No," I answered for her. "She wakes up cranky. Always has."

Rayfe straddled the bench and smiled. The good cheer in it took me aback, the way it transformed what otherwise tended to be a brooding visage. He and I had been so often on the opposite sides of a battle line that I'd never had occasion to see him cheerful. "Good to know that it's not me. She gave me some bad moments early on. I feared she'd knife me—yet again—the morning after our wedding night."

Andi glared at him balefully. "Keep it up and I still might."

He laughed and ran a hand down her streaming hair. "Have some more tea, my queen."

"So what is your plan for today and going forward?" I asked Rayfe, giving him a nod of respect. If nothing else, I owed him that for the way he clearly treasured Andi. Their marriage may have come about at great cost to us all, but that also belonged in the past.

He sobered, all king now. "We'll reach Annfwn by midday. My scouts report no further news, but we may discover more once there."

"Aren't we in Annfwn already?" Dafne asked, noting something on a scroll.

"They call the capital city and the country by the same name," Andi inserted, wrinkling her nose at Rayfe. "It's confusing."

"I didn't do the naming," Rayfe responded easily. "Depending on the state of affairs there, and what Andromeda may discover through her scrying methods, I suggest we set out again immediately. I understand you're an excellent tracker, Your Highness."

"I hold my own, though I wish I had my best tracker with me."

"I'm highly skilled at it," Harlan said.

I glanced at him. "You never mentioned that."

"You didn't ask."

No, but I'd seen the list of his skills in the thrice-dammed contract and well he knew it. He simply smiled easily at my consternation and, for the first time, I wondered what else I didn't know about him.

"Good." Rayfe tapped his fingers on the table, his thoughts preoccupied. "I'd prefer to use your resources rather than Tala ones, for the time being."

"Ash mentioned that you'd been dealing with some sort of resistance group." I felt my way carefully here, not knowing Rayfe's temper on the topic or whether Ash had been meant to spill this particular secret. Still, I knew and it seemed best to put that out there.

Looking more alert, Andi widened her eyes at me in quiet warning and a scowl settled on Rayfe's face. "Did he now? Indiscreet of him."

"In all fairness"—I bit into an apple, sweeter and crisper than any I'd before tasted—"I guessed part of it and rather bullied the rest out of him under duress."

Beside me, Harlan chuckled. Andi finished her tea and set the cup down with a thunk. "I believe that. Don't go hard on him, Rayfe—you've never seen Ursula when she's truly sunk her teeth into someone. Better men than he have folded under that steely glare of hers."

"I'm not comfortable sharing internal Tala affairs with Uorsin's heir," Rayfe said. "I'm sure you understand, Your Highness."

"King Rayfe." I leaned forward, folding my arms on the table. "What I understand is that your affairs and mine have overlapped. Like it or not, we have become political bedfellows."

"Have been," Andi pointed out, "since Salena left Annfwn to wed Uorsin."

"Before that, even," Dafne added. "Annfwn wasn't always so isolated from the rest of the kingdoms. Princess Amelia believes quite strongly—and from the information she's uncovered, I tend to agree—that the brightest future for all of us lies in opening intercourse between Annfwn and the Twelve."

"This sounds like a ploy of Uorsin's." Rayfe shimmered with dark violence now.

"No." I said it in a thoughtful tone, parsing it through and attempting to defuse Rayfe's building suspicions. "The High King wants to possess Annfwn. There's no doubt of that and no sense denying it. However, he knows nothing of Amelia's thoughts on this. They have not spoken since she visited here, and I can safely say that her sympathies are no longer fully with the cause of the High Throne."

Andi raised her eyebrows at me. "And you didn't cut her down for treason? Color me shocked and amazed."

"Why?" Her response irritated me. "I sit here with you, don't I?"

Harlan touched the small of my back, subtly soothing.

Andi sighed. "You're right. I apologize. I never thought I'd see the day that you admitted our father was less than a paragon."

I must have been still raw in some way, from my confessions in the dark of night, and her words pierced me. Needing the moment, I touched the Star in my pommel, surprisingly hot in the cool morning air. Harlan shifted beside me, but thankfully said nothing. Andi, though, reached across the table and touched my hand. "Hey. I'm sorry. That was uncalled for."

Clearing my throat, I met her gaze as steadily as I could. "It's nothing."

"No." She frowned. "I can see there is something, but we'll discuss it later."

When Danu grew pink roses. I didn't say that, however, and turned my attention to Rayfe. "You cripple us by keeping secrets. If you want our help, we need to know what we face. This little problem of yours has resulted in the loss of a member of the royal family. Here's what I understand. You can fill in the rest as you see fit."

At his begrudging nod, I continued, glad that they hadn't asked Harlan or Dafne to leave, saving me the trouble of going behind anyone's back to fill them in. "It seems that a Tala man named Terin posed as a minstrel to infiltrate Windroven and abduct the infant princess."

"Our uncle," Andi inserted.

"Excuse me?"

She'd shocked me with that and knew it, nodding with a wry expression on her face. "That was my reaction, too. He's the twin brother of Salena's first husband, Tosin. Not a blood relation, but—"

"Our mother was married before?" Another thought occurred to me. "Is this Tosin here, in Annfwn?"

"No, he died before she ever left." Andi looked sorrowful. More to the story than that. It was odd, imagining our mother with another husband, a whole other life.

"Did they . . . have children?" The question was off topic, but I needed to know if there were others. Half siblings she'd left behind and never spoken of.

Andi shook her head, though. "That's part of why she left, why she married Uorsin—to beget us."

"Another reason," Dafne put in, "that Princess Amelia believes Annfwn needs the Twelve as much as we need Annfwn: too much inbreeding."

"We have Andromeda now," Rayfe snapped. "Salena's solution."

"I'm not enough." Andi turned to him with the exasperation of rehashing an old argument, undaunted by his glower.

"And there are other problems," Dafne pointed out with her calm scholarly logic. "The magic in Annfwn has been bottled up behind the barrier—starving the outside."

"Starving?" I questioned. Puzzle pieces shifted and re-sorted themselves.

"Yes." Dafne folded her hands. "Ami was still working on the theory and so didn't bring it up when you visited Windroven before her lying in, but she believes that the encroaching drought, the crop and livestock failures—most recently the plagues—have been growing steadily worse since Annfwn magically closed its borders. Moranu was never meant to be divided from her sister goddesses."

"The problems of the Twelve do not concern Annfwn," Rayfe asserted.

"They concern me," Andi and I said at the same time. She smiled at me, and once again I had to process how much she'd matured.

"They should concern you, King Rayfe," Dafne continued in her implacable tone. "If the theory holds, you've been experiencing the inverse problem—the magic intensifying and perhaps turning in on itself."

Rayfe didn't reply, but neither did he deny it. Dafne nodded to herself and made a note.

"So what is Terin's objective?" I asked, point-blank. "He objects to Andi being less than full blood, but Stella's blood would be even more dilute. He can't seek to set her up as queen instead, can he?"

"This is the question we all have," Andi confided. "Terin himself has what the Tala consider to be weaker blood. He can shapeshift, but only inside Annfwn, and he could not cross the border without my help. Unlike you or I."

Shape-shifting. Though I knew some Tala possessed the ability, it still seemed like a leap to believe it possible. "But you and I can't shape-shift."

"Well"—she smiled and exchanged a look with Rayfe, both intimate and proud—"you can't."

Danu take me. Andi's smile widened in her delight at having shocked me again. "Want to see?"

"No." Of that I was certain.

"Come on—don't be such a mossback," she teased. Dafne smothered a laugh.

I glared at her, which had zero effect. "I know full well that's a Tala insult."

"Don't be mad. Maybe you can still learn. I'll teach you."

"No, thank you. I like my skin the way it is."

"You do it naturally, to some extent." She grinned at me, though I tried to cover my reaction to that. I was determined not to rise to her bait.

Harlan, however, spoke up. "That's why she's so fast."

Andi nodded approvingly. "Exactly, Captain Harlan. It's very interesting. The Tala have a different physicality. Those with pure enough blood, even if they never fully shape-shift, seem to have unusual control of their bodies. Speed, flexibility, strength."

Uncomfortable with the idea of my body as somehow mutable, I changed the subject, glancing pointedly at Rayfe, who'd relaxed some with Andi's good humor. "Anything else I need to know?"

He shook his head. "Unfortunately you now know nearly as much as we do."

"Tell me this. You people have all these varieties of magic. I hear there are all sorts of black arts, also. Death magics, that sort of thing." I avoided looking at Harlan, just barely. "Could this Terin have some sort of nefarious purpose for Stella? To exploit her blood in some way?"

Andi and Rayfe both looked grim. "It's possible," Andi said, quelling Rayfe with a sharp look. "Ursula needs to know this. Stella bears the mark as I do. It gives her certain . . . access to Annfwn's magic. I don't know that it can be exploited or if they mean to keep her until she's old enough to learn. But that's a factor."

"We must find the child," Rayfe confirmed. "All else is secondary."

"Well, then." I stood. "On to Annfwn."

26

It felt good to be on the move again. To be going after Ami and the babies. Though the confirmation of my worst fears chilled my gut, I liked knowing what we were getting into. It gave our mission a clear focus.

Saving my sister, however, still took precedence for me, regardless of the rest.

Andi and Rayfe had an intense but brief argument about blindfolding us for the ride in, which Andi won. Fortunately, as I would have refused to go blind, at point of sword, if necessary. From the carefully neutral expression on Harlan's face, he felt the same.

We skirted the lake and went up the ridge on the far side, following what seemed to be deer trails. The farther in we penetrated, the more the forest altered from the familiar look of the Wild Lands around Ordnung. It must have been due to the moisture, that the trees grew so large. They towered overhead, with fat trunks, some so wide several men of Harlan's size would have to link their arms to encircle them.

Shadows flitted through those trees, some seeming to be birds, others not any kind of recognizable animals. I caught Harlan squinting speculatively after one and he gave me a rueful smile. "Unsettling," he observed, "to encounter guardians such as this." He gestured at the dense forest hemming us in on the barely there trail. "We would be hard-pressed to defend ourselves against an attack under these circumstances."

Rayfe turned in the saddle and raised one eyebrow. "The Tala are not fools."

I didn't comment, though I agreed. They'd once told me I'd never be able to bring an army against the Tala on their home territory, even if we'd passed the barrier. It seemed they had not exaggerated Annfwn's natural defenses.

"I wonder that you feel you need the magical barrier," I commented.

His brows lowered. "Forgive me if I'm unlikely to take advice from Uorsin's daughter."

"You take advice from me," Andi pointed out, and he glowered at her, making me laugh. She flashed me a quick, naughty grin.

"You're happier, being with your sister," Harlan said. "It's good to see."

"Do you have siblings?" It occurred to me to ask him.

Oddly, he hesitated. Barely, but I knew his patterns better now. "I have six brothers."

"Where are you in the lineup?"

He gave me a disingenuous smile. "I am the baby."

I snorted. "I'd hate to see the others, then."

"It's unlikely you ever shall, as they would never leave Dasnaria and I will never go back."

"Strong words. Why's that?"

"A long story. The short version is that there is no place for me in Dasnaria." He sounded uncharacteristically downcast. "I misliked the future others planned for me and so took my fate into my own hands."

"As a soldier of fortune?"

"I possessed size, strength, and determination." He flashed me a grin at that. "So learning the ways of the warrior made a natural fit. Then, as I wished to be leader of my own men instead of general of someone else's army—and because stray armies are not readily available in Dasnaria—I decided to form the Vervaldr."

"You make it sound easy."

"Not easy, no." He nodded thoughtfully. "But far more interesting and rewarding than my alternatives. I started small, with a few men, specific jobs. Each new place its own challenge. The Vervaldr grew in number, skill, and reputation."

"And now you're here."

"Yes. I knew even in those long-ago days that the world must hold something more than what it appeared to offer me. I allowed *hlyti* to guide me to it."

"God or goddess?"

"Neither. More your concept of fate." He gave me an intimate smile. "Though perhaps your Danu had a hand in it."

"Sex falls to Glorianna."

"But the warriors belong to Danu. You do; thus, so do I."

I shifted in the saddle, uncomfortable with that, and he laughed softly. "Look there." The trees had thinned and we broke out of the dense woods, the city of Annfwn before us as if it had appeared from nowhere. Altogether unexpected.

It appeared to be built entirely into an enormous cliff of white stone, rising from the level of the beach to startling heights. Balconies, towers, archways, and sculptures carved into the rock showed that it had been inhabited for generations. It stretched for leagues up the beach, with uncountable door and window openings, glittering with jewel tones of lapis, ruby, and emerald, level upon level up to the very top. Squinting against the sun, I made out structures on the plateau above, as well.

Stone pathways wound up and around, bordered by low walls draped with vines and flowers. At the near end, multilevel dwellings had been built in and around the massive limbs of the trees bordering the cliff. Bridges of rope and wood connected them to the cliff homes. At the base of the cliff, paths dove under and into shadowed recesses.

The sea, gentle and serene as off Elcinea, lapped against the white-sand beach. All in all, Annfwn made a spectacularly beautiful sight. I had never pictured it so, from my mother's stories, but I recognized now what she'd tried to describe. It pained my heart to think of it. Perhaps because I had yet to regrow my thicker skin. On some deep level, though it made no logical sense, I recognized the place. My blood surged and that strange sense of rightness filled me.

Andi, who'd hung back as Rayfe pointed out features to an interested Harlan and delighted Dafne, while I'd been transfixed, rode close enough to nudge my knee with hers. "Breathtaking, isn't it? I had the same reaction."

"How do you suppose she ever left it?" I breathed.

Andi shook her head. "She was like you, I suppose—full of conviction and powerful purpose."

"Is that how you see me?" I asked, bemused.

"You won't stay, will you? You could. This is your home, too, by right. After we rescue Ami, you could stay here, swim in the warm waters, settle down with the handsome and stalwart Captain Harlan, and make babies."

It made me laugh, even as I was shaking my head at the prospect. "I must return to Ordnung. My place is there."

"See? Conviction and powerful purpose."

"Maybe, though . . ." I trailed off, trying to see the path of my future. How it could fall out. Find Ami, rescue Stella, bring them all home to Ordnung. Kill or otherwise dispatch Illyria, send the mercenaries away. If Uorsin made Astar his heir, if I survived all that, perhaps I could return. If only to visit. A lot of ifs.

Andi's eyes had gone storm dark, as if she somehow followed the turn of my thoughts, looking down that path also. I studied her face. "What is the likelihood I'll survive to return here?"

She started, glared at me. "It doesn't work that way. I can't give you betting odds."

"But you do see scenarios where I die."

"I'm not discussing this."

"What if knowing will help me to avoid it?"

Andi looked through me in that uncanny way. "Did you find your doll?"

"There was no finding needed—I always knew where it was. And yes, I looked at it and found nothing more remarkable than ever."

"Did you bring it with you?"

"No. I thought it safer at Ordnung."

"Probably just as well." Her gaze strayed to the Star of Annfwn in the hilt of my sword. "That will guide you. That's why she gave it to you. The doll will help you see and so will Lady Zevondeth. When she asks for your blood, give it to her and do as she tells you, even if it makes no sense."

I nodded, committing the advice to memory. It sounded crazy, but I knew the words came from another place. It also didn't bear repeating that the doll had been empty or that Zevondeth wasn't in condition to do much at all. If she even still lived. All of that fell to the future.

"And, Ursula? You won't want to hear this, but . . ." She shook her head, stopping herself.

"What?"

"No, I can't tell you. If I do, it changes too much."

"That's hardly helpful."

"I know." She looked profoundly unhappy.

"My queen?" Rayfe called out.

"We're coming!" She answered, but her fierce, troubled gaze stayed on mine. Nudging Fiona still closer, she grasped my hand. "I told you before not to trust him, remember?"

We both knew who she meant, though I didn't want to hear it any more now than I had then. I understood Andi's dislike of our father, didn't blame her, as shabbily as he'd treated her, but I couldn't agree.

"I know you don't believe me, but there will come a time . . ." She shook her head, clearly frustrated. It seemed to me that these visions of the future or whatever they were could hardly be all that useful, if she struggled with them so. "When the day comes that you make a choice that seems heinous to you, know that it's the right thing. The worst option is the best one. For all of us."

"That has to be the least helpful advice I've ever received," I remarked.

Either my wry tone penetrated her haze or the grip of the magic eased its hold, because she refocused on my face and gave me a crooked smile. "Well, we foreseers can't make things too easy on our heroes."

"Some hero I am." I laughed and tugged at my hand, but she held it a moment longer.

"You're my hero, Ursula. Always have been." Then she let me go, shook back her hair, and rode up to enter the city beside her husband.

The Tala people, though they noted our passage into the city, showed little more excitement than the folk of Ordnung Township would. In fact, they called out quite familiar greetings to Rayfe and Andi, observing no formal protocol as we followed the winding road up past houses, shops, and gathering areas.

Curious glances surveyed Harlan, Dafne, and me, knowing us for foreigners, who were obviously scarce in Annfwn. Still, we did not create that much of a stir. If I'd been asked to assess the population of the cliffside city based on this behavior alone, I'd have wanted to call them complacent. Obviously well fed, many of them indulged in conversation or artistic tasks that would have been deemed frivolous in most cities in the Twelve.

However, despite their apparent relaxed indolence and studiously careless neglect of our passage, my awareness prickled as if we'd walked into an ambush. We were surrounded by people who could change form at will or perform magics beyond my comprehension. They were like the prides of big cats of Erie, who sunned themselves and watched passersby with lazy, jeweled eyes—and could spring into lethal action in a blink.

"I'd wish to have my men with me," Harlan commented quietly, "if I wasn't sure they'd just be slaughtered also."

I threw him an appreciative glance. "Disconcerting, isn't it, to pass among them, knowing how quickly we'd die if they took it in their heads to do us harm."

"At least you have the advantage of sharing Tala blood. I'm merely a mossback, mortal meat for these lions."

"Perhaps your new fan club will save you." I nodded at a group of young women who hung over a flower-draped balcony ahead, giggling among themselves, clearly admiring Harlan's big form, judging by their enthusiastic gestures.

They'd been pacing us for some time, an exception to the studious nonattention of most of the population, taking advantage of the way the road switchbacked under various ledges, balconies, and bridges. All dark haired, young, lissome, and lovely, they seemed exceptionally taken with the fair-haired mercenary. I couldn't blame them, really.

He'd tanned darker over the last few days of travel, skin gleaming bronze in the gentle sunshine, shades deeper than his blond hair. The warmth had prompted us all to strip down some, and he wore a simple leather vest over a sleeveless white shirt. It set off the impressive muscles of his shoulders and arms.

"Like what you see?" he asked, his voice low, with a sensual buzz I now recognized.

"They certainly do."

As we passed beneath, the group of young ladies shouted something in the liquid Tala language, and one tossed an exotic blossom to him. He caught the flower and halted, bowing gravely to the woman. Then he placed a hand over his heart, shook his head with an expression of dramatic regret, and handed the blossom to me.

The ladies sighed in disappointment, eyeing me and whispering among themselves. Feeling both self-conscious and surprisingly warmed by the gesture, I studied the blossom, never having seen its like before, uncertain what I should do with it.

"Here," Harlan nudged his horse closer, took the flower from my hands, and tucked it behind my ear. "Beautiful."

I couldn't possibly be blushing. The romantic murmurs of the young women above added to the silliness of it all. I urged my stallion ahead, to catch up. "You might as well plop a bow on my head."

"On the contrary," Harlan replied, easily pacing me. "The red of the flower very nearly matches your hair, and the curve of the petals compliments the line of your jaw and cheekbones, the fairness of your skin."

"Just my luck—a romantic mercenary. Who knew?"

"We've had little opportunity for romance," he agreed. "I'll have to make up for that."

"It's hardly a high priority."

"All the more reason. I wouldn't want you to lay that fault at the feet of Dasnarian men also. "

We had reached about the middle of the vertical height by then, I estimated, and Andi and Rayfe dismounted in a wide apron ringed by arches and sculptures of trees. It hadn't been clear from below, but the depth of the cliff varied considerably. What had appeared to be a sheer face actually contained the length of Ordnung's practice yard in places. More so, considering the shadowed recesses beyond the doorways leading deeper into the rock. The entire cliff could be hollow, for all I knew.

Judging by the comparative stateliness of the pillars and sculptures, this would be their center of government. Indeed, a group of older Tala emerged, moving languidly but studying us with sharp, suspicious gazes. No, watching me.

I dismounted and squared my shoulders, holding my back straight. Something fluttered in the corner of my eye—Harlan's ridiculous flower. But removing it now might make it look as if I waffled in my intentions. Wishing Andi had briefed me on protocol or given me some warning that we'd face their ruling council so quickly, for surely this was a group of that sort, I decided not to bow.

"Well, Uorsin's daughter"—a white-haired woman stepped forward, addressing me without bowing either—"Annfwn did not expect to feel your feet upon her stones."

An odd way to put it. Andi and Rayfe had moved up behind me but still stood back. The other Tala counselors arranged themselves in a sort of V formation trailing from their spokesperson.

"I came in search of my youngest sister," I informed her, keeping my tone courteous but neutral.

"We know what you seek," one of the men said, face set in unfriendly lines. "You pursue what your father has long sought. We see before us his hand, reaching out to throttle the life from Annfwn."

"I am but one person, amid a host of Tala. What harm can I possibly cause you?"

"You should not have admitted her, Queen Andromeda." The woman glared at Andi over my shoulder. "You place Uorsin's viper at the heart of Annfwn."

"My sister is also Salena's daughter," Andi replied, sounding entirely unperturbed, but with a thread of steel beneath. "Annfwn is as much her home as yours."

They didn't like that, muttering to each other in their language.

"She shall not be admitted to the council session, regardless. We have information to discuss, King Rayfe, Queen Andromeda." Now she bowed, rather pointedly, to them. "It shall rest upon you, if you choose to share our secrets with a foreign monarch."

"That's perfectly understandable," I said, before Andi or Rayfe could. It seemed moot to point out that I was monarch of nothing. "Neither would I admit you to private discussions at Ordnung." I stepped to the side, to avoid turning my back on them. Behind his carefully blank expression, Harlan looked amused and Dafne seemed simply fascinated, still shimmering with the glittering enthusiasm of being in Annfwn.

I almost envied her the uncomplicated delight in it all.

"Perhaps there's a place we could wait and refresh ourselves?" I asked Andi and Rayfe. He met and held my gaze, then dipped his chin in a slight nod of acknowledgment.

Andi showed her relieved gratitude more clearly. "I'll arrange for an escort."

A young woman appeared at her elbow, though I hadn't caught the signal. Andi spoke to her in the Tala language, a development that had me raising an eyebrow and Dafne practically salivating. Taking me by the elbow, Andi led us a short distance away.

"Phyra will show you to our home and your rooms. She doesn't speak the Common Tongue—not many here do—but I've told her that you may help yourselves to whatever you need. Sorry that we can't go with you. Given the tenor of the council, we may be gone until quite late."

"Not a very friendly bunch," I commented.

"Can you blame them?" she replied with some impatience. "Most of them are of an age to have observed how Uorsin conquered their eleven neighbors and would have done the same to them, had Salena not prevented it."

"And, while you are Salena's heir, I am his. I am him." *His hand.* Why that bothered me, I wasn't certain.

Andi studied my face. "You're not him, but they don't understand that yet. Believe me, it's taken me much time to earn their trust—thank Moranu for Rayfe's unwavering faith in me—and even still . . ." She finished with a lift of her shoulders.

"Go find out the news. Settle your council. We'll leave in the morning still?"

"Yes. Dafne, there's a library you'll enjoy."

"Is it a problem if we explore a bit?" I asked her, glancing at Harlan, who nodded. Neither of us would want to cool our heels inside. "Walk around, see the sights?"

"That should be fine. Just don't skewer anyone."

"Ha-ha. Seriously—should we expect trouble?"

"No. You're here under our protection. No one would dare harm you."

"What about the elements of unrest?" I lowered my voice, in case any could understand enough to overhear.

"Elsewhere."

"Ah." Interesting. I'd figured they knew more than they'd revealed thus far. "Take your time. We'll be fine to keep ourselves occupied."

She gripped my arm. "Thank you for understanding. I never thought I'd be holding court while *you* were out playing." She made a face, then drew herself up, shrugging on her queenly authority like a cloak.

I watched her join Rayfe and go with him and their council into the inner chambers, feeling such a surge of love and pride for her that it took me a little aback.

"It's good to see her find her place," Dafne remarked.

"Yes. Yes, it is."

27

Andi and Rayfe's home turned out to be several more flights above. We walked there, the bright-eyed Phyra leading the way.

"A person could keep in good condition just walking up and down these roads all day," I remarked after we'd traveled a few of the loops, and Dafne gave me a rueful smile, more than a little out of breath and looking less delighted, more ragged.

Harlan plucked at his leather vest, to allow some air under it to his sweat-soaked shirt. "I begin to understand their custom of wearing such light clothing also." He eyed a group of long-haired young men who passed us in loose-fitting shirts with billowing sleeves and flowing trousers. "Perhaps we can borrow some."

"I doubt they have anything that will fit your mountain of a body."

He slid me a sly smile. "You seemed to enjoy it well enough last night."

Dafne studiously looked in another direction while I glared at the mercenary. He took my hand. "Don't frown so. Lady Mail-loux knows full well we spent the night together and she keeps your secrets well. If secret this is."

"I'm not frowning."

"You are." He tapped a thumb between my eyebrows. "You get this vertical line right here when you're thinking too hard."

Dafne made a soft sound of amused agreement and I batted his thumb away. To prove a point, however, I kept my hand in his as we continued to climb. Despite his accusation that I was thinking too hard, I felt strangely serene. The sunshine, flowers, the sheer, staggering beauty everywhere I looked, all conspired to create a sense of a space out of time. We could do nothing more until morning, so for the rest of the afternoon and evening, we might as well take in Annfwn.

I'd been to the seashore in Elcinea but had never had time to walk the beaches there, as so many liked to do. Looking out now over the calm, aquamarine waters of what surely had to be the Onyx Ocean—though it possessed an entirely different character here than at Windroven—I thought I might like to try it.

"If my mental map is correct, we look toward Dasnaria, somewhere over this sea."

"That's how I have it, also," Harlan replied, squinting into the distance. "Yet none of our sailing vessels have made it to this spot."

"Not even in legend?" Dafne asked.

He tipped his head. "It's possible that some tales referred to this place."

Open-air, as all the dwellings seemed to be, Andi and Rayfe's home, while grander than most, was hardly palatial. It rose several stories, with flower-draped balconies that all looked out over the serene waters. No guards appeared to be posted, but since anyone could climb in any window, you'd have to man the place with an army for any kind of effective security.

"Not at all defensible," Harlan commented, keen gaze taking in all the opportunities for trouble, just as I had.

"The Tala clearly lead a much more peaceful life than we do." Dafne sounded entirely too complacent to my ear.

"Except for that pesky business of rebels they haven't contained who clearly threaten Rayfe and Andi's rule," I reminded her. "Not to mention the suspicious-sounding death of Tosin. If Salena was Queen of the Tala before Rayfe was King, was Tosin king or consort, I wonder?"

"Does it matter?" Harlan's voice stayed mild, but some kind of annoyance crawled beneath it.

Better to clear this up now. "In the Twelve it would. For instance, were I ever to marry—which I have no intention of doing—and if I succeed to the High Throne, my husband would never be High King."

"A good thing I'm not interested in a throne, then," he returned equably. "And you're frowning again."

We'd ascended several internal staircases as we talked, and Phyra elegantly gestured Dafne toward an open doorway. She curtsied to me. "On that note, Your Highness, I think I will excuse myself to rest my tired legs. I'll be either in my rooms or in this promised library, should you have need of me."

"Coward," I muttered after her.

Phyra continued down the hallway, showed us into a large suite of rooms at the end, said something gracious sounding, and left via another door. It took me a moment to realize she wasn't coming back. Harlan looked toward the one great bed, folded his arms, and raised his eyebrows at me.

"Andi and I are going to have words," I said, wandering over to the wide windows, with more of the amazing view and a surprising amount of privacy. Only someone out at sea could look in to see us.

"She loves you and wants you happy."

"And she figures me sharing a bed with you will see to that?"

He'd moved up behind me, bracing his hands on the window ledge to bracket me with his arms. His lips brushed the back of my neck, sending shivers through me. "I love you and want you happy, too. I can sleep on the floor, if you prefer."

The tranquil sea glittered. Had my mother sat in a window like this, watching it, the way she had in the western windows of Ordnung, always gazing off toward Annfwn?

"I can't think about these things, Harlan. The future feels too far away. I need to keep my focus on the next immediate step. On the moment."

"Let's enjoy the moment, then." He kissed under my ear, in the soft, sensitive hollow. "What would you most like to do? A run on the beach? Some sparring? Stay here and make love?"

I could almost imagine that, sinking into the netting-draped bed with him and indulging in some love play with the warm breezes blowing in. The way his mouth caressed my neck, the delicious flutters that sent through me, made it seem possible. But I couldn't face coming apart again like I had the night before.

"I've never run on sand before."

"Then you're in for a treat. Let's see about changing clothes and do that."

The closet boasted a selection of the typical Tala gear, though, as I'd predicted, none were large enough to fit Harlan. He solved the problem by doffing the leather vest and using a blade to cut off a pair of trousers he'd brought. In his white sleeveless shirt and the shorts, he looked even more impressively muscular. And enticing. He raised a brow at my attention.

"Change your mind?"

"No. Though I feel silly in this getup."

None of the trousers provided would fit me, either—all ending at the knee so I looked like the quickly growing child of impoverished parents. I'd resorted to one of the filmy gowns—relieved to shuck my own stifling fighting leathers—with a flowing uneven hem and ribbon ties at the shoulders.

"You look gorgeous in it, actually. Though the sword belt diminishes the effect. It doesn't look comfortable."

I'd taken off most of my knives, keeping only a few, just in case. I hesitated to leave the sword behind, however. Not just because I felt naked without it, but I didn't like to let the Star out of my reach, especially given the great interest in it. Then again, nobody but Andi and I knew where I had it.

Harlan, with his uncanny perception, seemed to follow my

thoughts, gaze dropping to the topaz. Moving slowly, as if not to startle me, he came close enough to rub a thumb over the jewel, which still glowed with a constant heat.

"Very beautiful," he said. "And very clever."

My mouth had gone dry and I wasn't sure what to say, even had the words come easily to my tongue.

"Would you trust me to wear it for you? That way we can have it at hand, but you won't be so encumbered in the dress."

"All right," I agreed, surprising both of us. I unbuckled the belt and the gown unbunched, definitely better, unthreaded the sheath from it, and handed the sheathed sword to Harlan, feeling much as I had when he'd gazed on my bare breasts. Oddly intimate. As if he felt the same sense of ceremony, he added my sword to his belt on the opposite side from his.

Then he grinned at me and touched my cheek. "Thank you."

"I should be thanking you—you're the one acting as my page and sword bearer."

"It would be my honor." He bowed ostentatiously, a mischievous bent to his smile. "Let's go play."

Funny that he called it play—just as Andi had—because the afternoon felt that way. It took a while for me to banish the nagging sensation that I'd forgotten something, so rarely did I go without my sword. In the light gown, going barefoot because boots would not do, I also felt more free and unencumbered than—well, maybe ever.

We followed the road down the cliff face, discovering ladders here and there that let us cut through some of the endless loops. Harlan spotted them, seeing children clambering up and down and goading me to try it also, whooping in delight when he discovered a rope one that worked like a pulley system, dropping him quickly down an entire level.

No one bothered us. In fact, they gave us the studious inattention we'd encountered everywhere. A Tala version of privacy in close quarters, I suspected. The kids showed more open curiosity, tagging along behind us and then, once they grew bolder, showing us more of their shortcuts, including a final dripping series of tunnels that opened onto the shimmering sands of the beach.

It burned my feet some, having absorbed sun all day, and sucked at my leg muscles, forcing me to work harder just to walk. "I might not be doing much running," I commented, feeling the burn already. "This is more of a workout than climbing that road."

"Very good for leg strength, yes." His powerful legs churned through the loose sand, thigh muscles working easily. "In Dasnaria we have beach running as part of our training program. It weeds out the . . . less committed." He grinned and I nearly felt sorry for those soldiers. "However, we need not go through that today."

Instead, he showed me how to run where the waves had wet and dampened the sand, at the edge of the gentle surf. It felt odd, with my breasts unbound, but they aren't large, so they didn't bother me overmuch. We jogged companionably for some distance, passing more and more of the extensive cliff city. The soft, moist air made for easy running, flowing gently in and out of my lungs, as nourishing as the sunshine on my skin. After a time, however, my feet grew sore.

Ruefully, I examined the reddening sole of one foot, holding my ankle in my hand as I looked over my shoulder. "Clearly I have worn boots too much—my feet need toughening."

Harlan traced the arch, where my skin looked as pale and wrinkled as a fish, making me jump. "Ticklish? At last I've found a weakness, a chink in your formidable armor."

"Don't even think about it, or I will cut your throat as you sleep."

"Is it any wonder I've fallen in love with you?" He took my hand and guided me into the shallow water. "The salt will help."

The sun lowered toward the horizon, the sea darkening from that brilliant aquamarine to a deeper violet, as we walked back.

Other people walked as we did, some holding hands. Others in family groups, chattering and enjoying the evening. A shouting group of kids cut directly in front of us, running at top speed for the water and shape-shifting in midair into brightly colored fish that plopped into the water, leaping and swimming.

Harlan shook his head in bemusement. "I wonder when I'll become accustomed to such sights."

"I'm sure I never shall."

"If the enemy we chase possess similar abilities, they'll pose quite a challenge. I'm envisioning trained fighters with your speed and flexibility, plus the ability to shift into a lethal predator." He huffed out a breath. "I wish I had more men with me."

I felt much the same, missing my Hawks and being able to count on them. "It sounds as if Andi and Rayfe plan to accompany us—and they'll bring loyal fighters of their own." I hoped.

"I'm sorry I said anything. You weren't worrying for a while there."

"Tomorrow will bring what it will. This has been a nice afternoon. Relaxing." Something I'd never seen myself doing. "I've liked spending it with you."

He stopped and tugged me into an embrace, smiling. "I've liked it, too. An unexpected treasure." He kissed me, softly at first, then deeper when I wound my hands behind his thick neck and opened my mouth to him, to the deep, drugging sensations that swam through me. His hands roamed over me, carefully keeping to my back, my waist, the outside line of my hips, but in the thin fabric of the Tala dress, every caress penetrated to my skin as if I wore nothing at all.

Though people occasionally passed, talking softly, one man singing, their presence didn't bother me. It seemed that Harlan and I existed in an amber bubble of sunshine and heat, untouched by the rest of the world.

By the time we returned to the house high on the cliff, it had grown full dark—but Andi and Rayfe had not returned. Smiling Tala brought us a meal, so Harlan and I dined on the balcony of our rooms. We put out all the lamps, keeping only the candle on our table to eat by, all the better to enjoy the startling starscape descending to the calm waters. As with the night before, the food tasted sublime—brighter and fresher than even Ordnung could command. With such a bounty, we could relieve much of the hunger of the Twelve Kingdoms.

A thought that no doubt would make Rayfe and his Tala council feel justified in their suspicions. Still, I found it difficult to reconcile that Annfwn enjoyed so much while my own people suffered.

"Were I King of the Tala," Harlan said, in an uncanny echo of my thoughts, "I would never agree to take down the barrier. To do so would only invite pillaging of the richness of this land."

"How would you carry the goods over the mountains, though?"

He squinted out at the sea. "The oceans all connect. The magical barrier must extend all around, else the water would not be so warm. Take that barrier down and you could sail all the ships in that you pleased."

It made for an interesting puzzle. "The Twelve has never needed much of a navy, so our ships are primarily for fishing and trade—and those are located mainly on the southern and eastern coasts. I'm given to understand that sailing around the Crane Isthmus is a challenging voyage. Though I believe only the adventurers have tried it. There has never been a strong incentive to ply trade along the west coast."

"Or not one anyone knew about before."

"I really hope you two are not plotting how you'd invade Annfwn by sea," Andi said, emerging into our ring of candlelight. She looked tired and irritated.

I sat back in my chair. "Would you believe that it was more of an academic exercise?"

"Actually, from you, yes." She poured herself a glass of wine. "But do me a favor and don't let Rayfe overhear that sort of thing."

"Difficult council meeting?"

She sighed. "Yes. Certain factions . . . are not happy. News of this Temple of Deyrr has people shaken. There are some among us who know something about them. Nothing good."

"You told them about that?"

She returned my gaze steadily, without flinching. "Did you think I wouldn't?"

In truth, it hadn't occurred to me, or I might have attempted to extract a promise of secrecy from her. Water under the bridge now. "We may not have a formal alliance, beyond your marriage—which goes a long way in my mind—but I'd like to think we're on the same side of this. I'd appreciate any information or assistance your people can provide."

"I'm working on it." Her dry tone spoke volumes about the resistance she'd encountered. Her gaze fell to my sword, which I'd laid on the bench beside me. "May I see it?" she asked. She said it carefully enough that it was clear she appreciated that Harlan might not know.

I handed her the sheathed sword, pommel up, the depthless topaz gleaming like its own candle flame. "The Star of Annfwn," I said, for both their benefits, and in the interest of all being on the same side. "Whatever that means."

She rubbed the pad of her thumb over it, the same way I had a habit of doing. "It's hot."

"Has been since we crossed the border."

Raising her eyebrows at that, she held it up to the light, turning it. "And it's a perfect sphere?"

"Yes, very smooth. No facets."

"She didn't tell you anything about it when she gave it to you?"

"Not any more than I've already told you. I was young. You were still in the nursery and Ami not yet born. There might have been more that I don't remember."

"Doubtful. You remember every thrice-damned thing."

"Can you tell me more about it?"

"Nothing specific. It sort of focuses and orders magic, much like other parts of Annfwn do, so I recognize it in that way."

"You were born and she knew you were the one with the mark when she gave it to me—why didn't she give it to you instead?"

Andi handed the sword back to me and briskly rubbed her palms together, as if wiping off water. "Salena didn't do anything without a plan—long-range ones that stagger me to imagine how she followed visions from that far out. Clearly she knew you'd need this tool to focus your own magic, for something you'll need to do."

"Except I don't have—"

"I know, I know." She rose and, with an affectionate smile, surprised me by bending to plant a kiss on my brow. "You think you don't have any magic. We'll leave at dawn, so I'm off to bed in the hopes of being awake enough not to fall off Fiona."

"As if you've ever fallen off a horse in your life."

She laughed. "See? We know each other well. Good night, Captain Harlan. Rest well and be good to my sister."

"She's a very interesting woman," Harlan commented. "I did not hear her approach."

"Andi has always been very good at not being noticed when she doesn't want to be. Rather the opposite of Ami, who stands out like the sun breaching the horizon, turning night into day." I yawned, surprised that I was sleepy. The good food, better wine, sunshine, and relaxation, no doubt.

Harlan rose and blew out the candle. "Let us follow your sister's example, then. Dawn will come soon enough. Do you want me to sleep on the floor?"

"No." It would be silly, given that we'd already slept in each other's arms, more than once. "But, I don't think I—"

He stopped me with a tender brush of his fingers on my cheek.

"I read you well enough now, and you're hardly shy. When you want more of me, I'll know. Until then, I'm happy to feel you beside me."

I found a short, light gown to wear to bed. Harlan simply stripped and climbed in. After a moment's hesitation, I laid my sword next to the bed on the floor. If only the punsters could see. I thought he might have fallen asleep already, but he shifted when I slid under the sheet, extending his arm so I could snuggle against him, my head pillowed in the fold of his shoulder, which had already begun to feel natural and right.

I drifted into an easy sleep and vivid dreams.

I stood in the court at Ordnung, empty but for me. In my hand, I held the Star of Annfwn, a perfect sphere unfettered by the metal setting of the sword hilt. It burned my palm, glowing as hot and bright as the star it was named for. Though the white marble hall blazed clean and bright, shadows fluttered around the edges, disappearing when I tried to look at them directly.

I tried to draw my sword, but I couldn't seem to move. Something whispered behind me, and though I attempted to spin to face it, I couldn't. As if seeing myself from another's eyes, I realized I wore a gown fashioned of metal. Like my battle armor but welded at the joints, covering my whole body. Instead of having articulated limbs, the sleeves, bodice, and long skirt were frozen metal—appearing to flow, but rigid and unmovable. It encased me like a cage. I couldn't move no matter how I fought to, to fight the thing crawling up behind me, breathing hot on my neck.

Flinging myself awake, I found I'd turned in my sleep, so my back was to Harlan. He'd draped an arm and leg over me and breathed heavily in sleep, his warm breath the obvious trigger for my dream. Still, the dregs of the nightmare clung and I couldn't bear to lie still. Easing out from under his bulk, I slipped out the open doors to the balcony and the soft, warm night.

I poured myself some wine and paced the length of the balcony for a while, steadying my pounding heart with even breathing, walking off the dregs of the dream. If I'd known the place a little better, I'd have found a place to run a few forms, sweated out the dread those flickering shadows had left behind. Instead I finally sat and watched out over the sea.

And waited for dawn to arrive.

28

"You should have wakened me," Harlan grumbled.

"Why should we both miss sleep?" I returned mildly as I strapped on my sword and made a final check of my various blades.

"Because, Ursula, you don't have to face things alone."

"I wasn't 'facing' anything. I woke up early is all."

"What woke you?"

"Probably the fact that you were crushing me and hogging the bed. You're just annoyed that you didn't feel me get up."

"What 'annoys' me is that you continue to lie to me about how you feel." He came over and grasped my arms, searching my face. "Do you think I can't see the shadows in your face this morning, can't smell the wine on your breath or feel the tension coming off of you?"

I pulled away, shrugging off his hands. "Don't worry—I'll be fine to fight if we encounter trouble."

He barked out a laugh. "That's my last concern. You would no doubt find a way to kill all the Tala rather than fail to protect your sisters. But you're not ducking this so easily. What upset you?"

"You know exactly what's on my mind. I'm not upset." I had

to make an effort to keep my tone even. "I'm thinking ahead to the next steps."

"Those same things were on your mind last night and you fell asleep well enough. Was it a nightmare?"

"Danu, you're a stubborn man!"

"And you're a hardheaded woman. What did you dream?"

"None of your thrice-damned business."

"It is if I caused it." He looked grim. "Is it me? Did I bring back bad memories?"

"No." I should have thought of that, that he'd be concerned. "Nothing to do with that. I'm over it."

"Another untruth."

"Okay." I ran my hands through my hair, scratching my scalp to get my brain going. "We both know I'm not over it—but that's not what's bothering me. I had your typical bad dream and couldn't go back to sleep. Not a big deal."

"What was the dream?"

"Harlan." The Star against my thumb was too hot to soothe. Uncertain how else to reassure him, I went to him and rubbed my palms over his chest, the muscles warm and firm under his light shirt. "It's not you. I don't want to rehash it. Just mental garbage."

He slid his hands up my forearms, then covered my hands with his, holding them pressed against him. "Your sister has visions of the future—how do you know this wasn't something like that?"

If an armored court gown and invisible monsters in the court at Ordnung lay in my future, then I'd be in for some difficult days. "Trust me, it wasn't. Let's go. They'll be waiting for us."

"For someone who outranks everyone, you are unusually concerned about people waiting for you."

"I don't outrank Uorsin and he's a bear about being kept waiting," I surprised myself by confiding. From Harlan's sideways glance, he'd noticed the slip, too. It had never really occurred to me before how much fear of displeasing my father had shaped me that way. I didn't understand why I'd thought to say it now. Except that Harlan drew those sorts of confessions out of me. Something I needed to be wary of.

You don't have to face things alone, he'd said.

But, if I were to draw any meaning from that dream, it was that I'd been all alone.

In the end, I suspected I always would be.

Annfwn barely stirred as we rode out of the cliff city with Andi, Rayfe, and a small squad of Tala who looked suitably dangerous, with their blue eyes and feral movements. To my relief, Andi reported that Dafne had been happy to stay behind, setting herself the task of studying the Tala language.

"I warned her I've been immersed in it for nearly a year and I'm still fumbling through," Andi told me. "It's structured in a very different way."

"I learned your Common Tongue, didn't I?" Rayfe put in, with an arrogant raise of his brows, but a teasing glint in his eyes.

"Don't start with me." Andi didn't bother to look at him. "You had your whole life to learn. I've caught up pretty well."

"You've done brilliantly, my queen. As I knew you would."

She rolled her eyes but flushed with pleasure. We rode at a fast clip, easier for the streets being mostly empty. With the sun rising behind the cliff, we remained in shadow for some time, gaining the beach and riding north. We soon passed the point Harlan and I had run to, then on farther, until we finally reached the far end of the cliff city, where Tala habitation gave way to coastal marshes and flatlands. We'd been riding too fast for conversation, so I had to wait until we broke for lunch to ask any questions. Andi had clearly not wanted to discuss much while in the city, a discretion I appreciated, though I disliked not being in on the plan.

"Do we know where we're going?" I inquired, very politely, I thought.

Rayfe, however, glowered. Andi sighed and flicked him a

quelling glance. "More or less. I know this is the correct general direction. I'm hoping that as we get closer, we'll get more clues."

"Going this fast," Harlan pointed out, "does not allow for tracking."

"No, I know that." Andi pushed her hair back off her shoulders, then absently began braiding it, her brows drawn together in thought. Or something else. "We're not close enough yet for that."

Rayfe huffed with impatience. "I know you've seen the place we'll find them. We should go straight there."

"That's only one possibility, and I don't—" Her gaze drifted to Harlan before she drew it back in. "It's not ideal. I want to see how events shift as we get closer."

Something about the way she'd looked at Harlan made my blood run cold. I waited until she and I had a moment alone. "What aren't you saying?"

"Nothing. I mean . . ." She blew out a breath. "It should be no surprise to you that danger lies ahead. There are a lot of ways this plays out and it's not always clear which series of actions leads to which outcome. I want to go about this carefully."

"And Rayfe doesn't agree?"

"Rayfe is much like you." She smiled, though it was full of exasperation. "You are both creatures of action and like to be in charge. But you're both going to have to lump it and let me direct things for the time being. You'll have your time."

I studied her. "That's why you expected me. Why you wanted my help. Not because of my tracking skills or my sword arm, but because you saw I would be here."

She held up her palms, confessing her culpability. "Some events are more inevitable than others."

"And Captain Harlan—was he inevitable?"

She set a hand on my arm. "You sneer, but yes. Remember that, would you?"

The mercenary sat on a driftwood log, legs stretched out as he rested, idly polishing a knife that likely needed no cleaning.

Catching my glance, he smiled with easy affection and lifted the flat of his blade to his forehead.

"What does that mean?" Andi asked.

"I have no idea. Some sort of Dasnarian salute."

"Have you seen him use it with anyone but you?"

"No." Something that had occurred to me, also, but odd that Andi had noted it so quickly.

"Hmm."

"What?"

"You should ask him what it means."

"Maybe."

She looked amused, but also concerned. "I wish you'd let him love you, Ursula. Don't be stubborn about this."

"I'm not stopping him, am I? The mercenary does as he pleases."

With a sigh, she shook her head. "Just . . . have a little pity on those of us who love you, okay? It's not always easy."

She went to join Rayfe, leaving me to stand and wonder what she'd meant.

We rode hard all afternoon and well into the evening, breaking only at full dark to camp on the beach.

"Tomorrow," Andi declared after we'd eaten, "we'll turn inland, a few hours into morning. After that things will get interesting. Expect trouble."

"How bad?" I wanted to know.

She shrugged a little. "There are many possible outcomes— some are dire, some not as terrible. I don't see any way around it. Tomorrow marks the beginning of a difficult time for us all."

"Then we'd best enjoy ourselves while we can." Rayfe put an arm around Andi and the atmosphere noticeably thickened. "If you'll excuse us. We'll see you all in the morning."

They went off down the beach together, and the Tala squad

fell to some sort of dicing game, talking among themselves. I shook my head a little. Not that I hadn't seen it all the time, fighters pairing off to enjoy a night of lust before battle. Contemplating my little sister having a wild night of beach sex was something else.

Harlan leaned back on his elbows, not bothering to pretend he wasn't watching me, waiting for an indication of what I wanted. *Have a little pity on those of us who love you.*

Thing was, I wasn't entirely certain of the kindest way to handle him.

"Want to take a walk?" I asked him.

He smiled, entirely too pleased. "Always."

"To talk," I specified.

"We can do that." He sprang to his feet with that agility so remarkable for his size and offered me a hand up. Keeping my hand in his, he turned us in the other direction down the beach, away from where Andi and Rayfe had gone to find privacy. Idly his thumb rubbed over the back of my hand, much as I habitually touched the Star.

"What's that sort of salute you always give me?"

He slid me a glance. "Why do you want to know?"

I couldn't very well say because Andi had prompted me to find out. "Just making conversation."

"That excuse might work if you were a person who makes conversation, but you aren't. Even with apparently idle court chitchat, you always have a goal in mind."

"Fine." Was the man always right? "I wondered because it occurred to me that there's some significance to you in it. If that's so, then I should probably know what it is."

He stopped, framed my face in his hands, and kissed me, long and sweet, stealing my breath.

"What was that for?"

"For trusting me with an honest answer."

"Is this a reward system?"

"Yes." He took my hand again and resumed walking. "With

the added benefit of allowing me to take pleasure in you at the same time. And I'd thought I'd better kiss you now, in case you don't like *my* answer."

Danu. I was afraid of that. *That* was why I hadn't asked.

"It more of a pledge than a salute," he said. "The *Elskastholrr*. It's a way that a Dasnarian man offers himself to the woman he wishes to be with."

"To take to bed."

"More than that."

"How much more?"

"A lifetime's worth."

I halted and he turned to face me, placid expression, battle readiness beneath. "You did not just tell me that all along you've been offering me some sort of marriage proposal."

"Correct. I did not."

I blew out a relieved breath. Became aware that he hadn't relaxed. "What, then?"

He tucked his thumbs in his sword belt, watching me carefully. "As far as I'm concerned, I've pledged myself to you, forever."

Flabbergasted, I had no words. No breath for words. "Are you out of your mind?" I finally got out. "I told you I have no idea what the future holds. Besides, you did that first only hours after we met. Danu—we hadn't even had a real conversation at that point."

"You have a good memory. It didn't matter. I told *you* I started to fall in love the moment I watched you walk into court, kept falling as I listened to how you handled the King, and finished the job seeing you run your fighting forms. It didn't matter to me whether you'd ever return my feelings at that point. I knew how I felt and that was enough to decide me. I belong to you—heart, mind, body, and soul—whether you choose to have me or not."

"I don't believe a person can fall in love that fast."

"You don't have to. We're not talking about you. I knew how I felt and it was a simple decision to make."

"Unreal," I whispered.

He shrugged. "It's the Dasnarian way."

"A country full of madmen."

"And madwomen. It makes for many a tragic ballad."

"You laugh, but this—whatever this is between us—could end tragically." I started striding down the beach and he paced beside me. "I never asked you for this."

"That's part of what makes the pledge significant. It must be freely offered, never requested."

Which only pointed out that he'd never ask for my pledge in return. *Have a little pity on those of us who love you.* Andi must have sensed the import of the gesture somehow, which further fueled my ire.

"What if I choose another man, take another lover, take a hundred?"

"I'd still be pledged to you and only you."

I hissed the impatience through my teeth. "How do you not have thousands of randy teenagers running around pledging themselves to the cutest boys and prettiest girls?" Danu, Amelia would have had most of the population of the Twelve pledged to her.

"Not everybody does it, by any stretch. You have to have passed through the kind of training I have to be . . . I don't think you have the word. *Skablykrr.* To have demonstrated that you have the strength of character, judgment, and perseverance to make such a vow."

"Oh, great." I stopped again and threw up my hands, amazed that he had the audacity to smile at me. "Well, *I* seriously question your judgment in this."

"Why?" He sobered, catching me around the waist and pulling me to him. "You are the most incredible woman I've ever met. I never could even imagine in my wildest dreams that there might be a woman like you in the world. Is it so impossible for you to believe I could love you as I do?"

I wished to Danu that Andi's damnable words would quit ringing in my head. I wished I knew how to explain that, yes, I knew I was impossible to love, without sounding like a weakling begging to be reassured. Even Andi and Ami didn't really love me—they'd simply had no one else. I understood that.

Harlan waited me out, gently stroking my back as if I were the one who'd fatally exposed herself. As if I needed soothing.

"What if I can't ever . . . be your lover?" I finally whispered.

"You already are. A magnificent one."

"Not fully."

"That's in the eye of the beholder."

"Children. You'll want sons someday. Every man does."

"Not every man. I'd be delighted to father children—sons or daughters—with you, my fierce hawk, but it's you I want, not progeny."

"Besides, they might turn out to be shape-shifters."

He laughed. "That would make for interesting parenting."

I shook my head at him, amazed he could laugh. "I don't know what to do about this."

"How about a swim?"

I stumbled mentally. "What?"

"A swim." He set me away from him. Unbuckled his sword belt and shucked off his shirt. "The water is warm enough and I worked up a sweat today. I'm for a swim."

"How can you talk about swimming at a time like this?"

He sat, pulled off his boots, and glanced up at me, cocking his head. "Nothing has changed for me, Ursula. You're the one digesting new information. And I'm reliably informed that our idyll is nearly over. Tomorrow may bring us sorrow, so I plan to enjoy paradise while I can."

He stood, dropping his trousers so he stood naked in the shimmering starlight, all solid muscle and masculine vitality. "I won't look, if you want to join me." And with a whoop like the Tala children had made, he ran into the water, splashing and arcing into a clean, disciplined stroke that cleaved the water. I watched him swim for a while, with his signature bold strength.

Fine, then.

Before I realized I'd made the decision, I'd begun stripping off my own clothes, folding them neatly next to his cast-off ones. True to his promise, he didn't turn and look as I made my way, also naked, into the water. It made my heart ache to contemplate what he'd given up for me, would continue to miss out on, because of me. All of my jibes about purchased loyalty and he'd, without a word, given me loyalty of the deepest, most unquestioning kind.

He'd asked nothing of me, and that's exactly what I'd given him.

The water lapped warm around my ankles, slowly rising as I waded in, feeling my way along the soft, sandy bottom. When I judged it deep enough, I dove under, letting the water close over my head and bathe me with the sweet salt of Annfwn's tropical sea. Rising, I sleeked my hair back with my hands and swam to where Harlan stood shoulder deep in the lazy swells, gazing out to the horizon.

"Gorgeous, isn't it?" he said. "Now that Dafne stirred my memory, I recall tales, here and there, of a paradise like this. I'd never heard it called Annfwn, but the stories described it as such. If only all the world could have what the Tala have, without destroying this."

"Even the Tala have their problems. Food and sunshine don't solve everything."

"No." He raised his eyebrows as I moved in front of him, gaze dipping to my bare breasts, which floated at the surface while I softly treaded water. "But it goes a long way to eliminating some of the worst ones."

I put my hands on his shoulders. "I'm not tall enough to stand here."

"We can go shallower."

"That's all right—just hold me."

He gave me a delighted smile, wrapping his arms around me and spreading his feet to more firmly brace against the movement of the gentle swells. I pressed against him, the shock of full-body, skin-to-skin contact rocketing through me, sparking that fire he kindled in me. It affected him, too, and he hummed deep in his chest, hands roving over my back, hips and bottom, his cock already erect and urgent against my belly.

"You are so beautiful, Ursula," he murmured, an extension of the pleased sound he made. "Sleek and long and impossibly lovely. So full of courage. Don't blame me for loving you—I never had a chance."

"I still think you're crazy."

"I know that. I hate that it's so hard for you to believe. But I'm prepared to spend the rest of my life convincing you, if necessary."

I kissed him. Draped against him and steadied by those strong hands that never failed me, I lavished him with the best kiss I knew how to deliver. I'd improved at the skill, knowing now how he liked it when I ran my tongue inside his upper lip, how it increased his desire when I softened my mouth and opened for him to kiss me harder, a kind of plundering I delighted in allowing. The fire burned hotter, making my heart thunder, and I had to tear my mouth away to gasp in breath.

He simply moved his lips to my jaw, nipping there and laving the sting with his tongue, making me dig my nails into his flexing shoulders. Following the line of my throat, his mouth burned my skin, sizzling my blood, making me go wet and hot.

He lifted me, raising me out of the water to lavish my breasts with his tongue, and I let him hold me there, exulting in his strength, letting my head fall back so the dazzling array of stars filled my vision just as he filled that cold emptiness in my heart.

It became unbearable, the stimulation, the utter arousal of my body under his hands and lips and teeth. My heart raced as if it might burst from effort and, though I tried to steady my breathing, I lost the rhythm again and again, panting and making pleading noises. Finally I couldn't hold back and I thrashed in his grip, bending to take his mouth so he had to tip his head back to receive my desperate kisses.

"I want." I panted into his mouth. "I need."

I made no sense, but I craved so much more.

"I would give you the release you seek." His deep voice nearly growled the words. "But it may be too soon."

"I want this. Help me. Please." The fervent desire so drove me I didn't even mind that I seemed to be begging him for help.

"Can you touch yourself? Have you done that?"

Odd that I could be embarrassed, fully naked and writhing in his arms, but I buried my face in his neck, wondering if I could truly speak about this. "I did some, before . . . that time. But not after. I felt—"

"How did you feel?" He held me with such tenderness, as if he didn't feel the same mindless urgency I did. So controlled.

"I can't say it."

"Yes, you can. Lance the wound. The words are your blade. Use them to open it and let it all out. I'm here with you."

Absurd to think of words as a blade. Such simple things to confess, yet they sliced at me, old and jagged, rusty with stagnant blood.

"Dirty. I felt soiled. And it hurt."

He made a small sound. "You were so young. Of course it hurt. You were torn."

"Yes. I bled. Some. Not a lot, but I couldn't bear to think about it, so I just stuffed some cloth in there and tried to forget. Then the blood dried and it hurt even more, and when I pulled the cloth out finally, because I was afraid I'd get infected and die, it bled again."

"Oh, my hawk. Why didn't you at least see a healer?"

"I kept it secret. Told my maids my woman's time was heavy and they were all sympathetic. They gave me tea for cramps." I laughed a little into his shoulder, a watery sound.

"So brave," he murmured, kissing my temple.

"No. I was desperately afraid and miserable. Over time it stopped hurting so much and I healed. But I never touched myself there, no more than I needed to."

"Does it pain you now?"

I lifted my head and looked him in the eyes. "Not pain, but different. Aching. I want you to try again."

"It doesn't have to be tonight."

"What if tomorrow sees an end to either or both of us? I want to try. I'm tired of being a coward."

"That you could never be." He brushed my lips with his, deepened the kiss, a blacksmith stoking the fires again, thumbs caressing my nipples, and he held me afloat with his big hands spanning my rib cage. When he had me panting again, very nearly as desperate as before, he turned me in his arms. "Let's try this."

29

He had me lie back in the circle of one arm and slipped the other under my back, so I floated in the water. We kissed like that for a while, the fever burning hotter. "Touch yourself, Ursula. When you're ready. Try it a little bit."

"I don't know if I can."

"If you can't, then I certainly won't. Your body is yours first. If you can pleasure yourself, then perhaps I'll be able to also."

It was easier than I thought it might be, especially with his drugging kisses and that part of me so desperate to be touched. Keeping my focus on him, on the wild sensations he stirred in me, I slipped my hand from his neck and under the water, letting the need guide me. And found myself slick and swollen. Though part of me tensed for the pain, for the sick feelings, instead a lovely shimmering susurrus rolled up through me, a warm and nurturing wave through my body that carried me with it, like the sea around me.

I sighed out a moan and Harlan's arms tightened, his kiss intensifying. Stroking my own folds, I found the place that felt best, an almost too-piercing sensation. I tensed with it but seemed unable to stop, unwilling to back off from the sharp sweetness of it.

The need, the utter craving for release, built, and I whimpered, sighed, wanted to bite. More. I needed more. Harlan's mouth hardened on mine, demanding, his own breath coming harder. Pulling away, I gasped, "But you . . ."

"Don't worry about that. You have no idea how exciting this is for me, holding you and feeling your delight. Give yourself over to it, to me. I'm right with you. Let me feel you go over."

With that his mouth fastened on mine again, as hungry as his words, pulling on me, drinking from me, and the unbreakable tension rose hotter and higher and more intense.

And broke.

With a sharp cry, I convulsed, bowing in Harlan's arms, shattering into thousands of pieces under the hammer of the release, breaking again and again, into crumbs, then grains, at last left dissolved and languid, like so much seawater.

Harlan had gentled his kisses, making them sweet and tender, feathery brushes of his lips against mine, my cheeks, my brow.

"I knew I had to be missing something," I murmured, and his laugh rumbled through him.

"How are you?" he asked.

"Good." I levered up and turned to face him. Amazingly good, in fact, as if I'd had an excellent workout, leaving my blood running clear and fast, my body limber, full of energy. I wrapped my fingers around his erect cock and had the satisfaction of having his hands clench on me and lust burn through his deliberate gentleness. He'd be panting and pleading, too, before we were done. "I want the rest now."

"Ursula—"

"Don't argue. Unless you've changed your mind?" I stroked up and down his length, loving the way his hips moved, drawn into the rhythm. "Have you withdrawn your offer?"

"Gods no." He groaned. "It's—" Grabbing my hand, he stopped me. Not pulling it away, but holding me still. "I couldn't bear it if I hurt you. We can wait, work up to it."

"I'll tell you if it hurts. Judging by the other night, you'll know pretty fast. No, no." I cupped his cheek when he looked stricken. "This is amazing. You are amazing. That's why I want more." I turned my hand in his grip, guided his hand to my own sex. "You touch me now. A good test, yes?"

He rested the back of his hand against my thigh, not letting me tug him closer. "Are you sure?"

"Yes. Touch me. Do it."

"I won't refuse you, but we're going slowly. My way. Put your hands around my neck." He kept his hand unmoving on my thigh as I did. Then started moving it, ever so slightly, just a soft caress of his knuckles against my skin. I went to kiss him, but he stopped me. "I need to see your face," he explained, lengthening the caress, so that he drew his hand down to the curve of muscle above my knee, then drifted up higher, to the soft round at the upper end of my inner thigh.

I sighed in elation at it, at the way the heat began to build again. "Yes," I said. "More."

He chuckled. "Patience." Slowly—infuriatingly so—he gradually increased the upper end of the caress, turning so the pads of his fingers touched me, sliding up one thigh, then the other. I parted my legs, inviting him to take more, but he continued the excruciating journey, all the while watching my face as the desire rode me harder and harder.

"I can't stand any more," I grated out, my hips moving into his hand, which stubbornly refused to go where I craved it to be.

"Can't you?" He smiled, a cat with captured prey, both hungry and pleased at once. His hand rose again and I stilled, hoping he'd complete the movement and touch my folds. But he paused, nearly there. Not close enough.

"Higher," I demanded.

"As Your Highness commands," he replied and tangled his fingers in my curls, making me groan in frustration. "Too high?" He asked in an innocent tone.

"You're killing me." I managed. "Please."

"Soon." Caressing my mound, he drew his fingers down

through my curls, to the point where my nether lips parted, holding my gaze. "Yes?"

"Oh, yes."

With infinite tenderness, he slid the pad of one finger into my folds, so lightly, I might not have felt it had I not been so sensitized, my own moisture making his movement glide differently than with just water on my skin. More, his touch on me sent lightning strikes of need, far different than my own had. I cried out at the shock of it and he stilled.

"Bad?"

"Agh, no, Danu take you." I rocked my hips against his hand. "More. Harder. Move!"

He chuckled, dark and full, and pressed his whole hand against me.

I came immediately, as if he'd set spark to my tinder that had me bursting into flame. My shout of pleasure echoed in my ears and I slid my body against his big hand, the calluses an extra bite against my slick flesh, the climax pouring through me like a cleansing rain after years of drought.

I fastened my mouth on his and he let me, returning the kiss with ferocious need. Wrapping my legs around his hips, I pressed in, needing to be closer. "Inside me."

He hesitated and I bit his lower lip, not too hard, but enough to make him growl. "Don't push me. I'm trying to be gentle with you."

"I've had enough of gentle. I need hard."

"I'm not letting you bully me into something that might hurt you," he returned, but he nudged a finger into my opening, the one that ached to be filled.

"Feels good," I murmured, nipping at his neck, making him shudder, urging him to lose that careful control. He'd have none of it, though, slowly edging into me, holding my hips still with his other hand so I couldn't make him go deeper.

It drove me crazy.

"Harlan." His name came out as a desperate groan.

He laughed, breathless also. "Gods, how I've waited to hear

you say my name in that tone, whiskey hoarse with desire. But we have to go up to the beach if we don't want to make a baby."

"All right," I agreed, at this point willing to go along with whatever stipulations would get me what I wanted. I started to unwind myself from him, but his arms tightened.

"No need for that." He lifted me a little so I sat more securely with my legs wrapped around his waist and, cupping my bottom, began wading powerfully through the water.

"Much like riding a horse." The position gave me an excuse to hold on to his shoulders—and plenty of opportunity to explore his skin with my mouth. He grunted and went faster, some of that control fraying at the edges.

Gaining the drier sand, he kissed me long and hard, then set me down and rummaged through his clothes, pulling out a leather envelope.

"What is it?"

He handed me the thing, like a thin sock. "The protection. A *lind*. It stops my seed from reaching your eggs."

I eyed it dubiously. "So thin."

"Else I couldn't feel you at all." He touched my cheek. "We don't have to do this. Not yet. Not ever, if need be. Don't do it just for me."

Holding his gaze, I turned my head enough to kiss his fingers. "I want to try. Unless it would be too difficult for you if we start and I have to stop. I can't promise that—"

He pressed his fingers to my lips. "I don't need promises."

"What do you need?" I hadn't concerned myself with it before, but I wanted to know.

"I already have it. Anything more is gravy."

"Shall I put this on you?"

He took the sheath from me. "In my current state, that might end things before we get started. I'll do it." Making quick work of it, he rolled it onto his cock, then pulled me in for a kiss, setting a slow pace again with long, languid caresses. Our bodies, both still damp from the sea, slid together, heating rapidly again. He cupped my breast and I gasped, amazed that it felt so perfectly new every time and yet intimately familiar in a way that dazzled me.

He drew me down to the sand and lay back, draping me over his big body as he liked to do, hands roaming over me. "It might be best," he said, in between kisses, "if you ride me in truth—so you can control how it goes."

Some part of me that had been worrying at the thought relaxed in relief at that suggestion. I hadn't been sure I could bear to bend over and . . . I firmly put the thought away. "I'm making new images tonight," I said, then realized he'd have no idea what I meant. He seemed to follow the thought anyway.

"Do exactly as you like with me, my hawk." He folded his hands behind his neck, a banquet of masculine beauty for me to feast on.

I straddled him, working out the logistics. Lifting his cock from where it thrust against his belly, I held it in place and raised up on my knees. Harlan's lips moved, a bare whisper of his language coming out. "What are you saying?" I asked, pausing.

His gaze flicked to me, a melting glance of wild desire. "I'm reciting the dates of the Dasnarian dynasties so I don't spill too soon." He very deliberately looked away again.

It was tempting to tease him, but if we were to see this through, I knew I shouldn't. My entrance remained slick, but the head of his cock was so broad that it stretched me. I wriggled, easing him in a bit, the driving need to have him in me overcoming the rill of fear that chilled me at the twinge of pain. Danu help me, I would not let that fear stop me from so simple a thing. I'd faced far worse than this thing that countless women before me had done and enjoyed. Still, my gut clenched at the sensation of him pressing inside me there, a vague sense of illness cooling the heat that had carried me through.

"Ursula." Harlan touched my hand where I braced it on his chest. "Stop now. It's too soon."

The concern in his face tugged at my heart. So quickly he'd gone from a state of desire so fierce it forced him to recite history to distract himself from it, to this heartbreaking worry for me. Because I let my fears get in the way of the one thing he'd asked of me. By Danu, I would give it to him.

"No. I'll do this." Cleanly, without letting myself dwell further, I pushed myself down, sheathing him with my body. As if he'd indeed cleaved me with a sword, I cried out, the astonishing sensation of him filling and stretching me more extraordinary than anything that had come before. "Oh, Danu!"

Harlan sat up, wrapping arms around me, still sheathed inside me, so the motion sent ripples deep into me. "Ursula," he whispered, sounding ragged. "You're hurt."

"No." I gasped against the astounding pleasure. "It's good. So good. I didn't know."

He laughed, dark with relief, and slid his hands down my back to my hips, holding me there, then rocked himself inside me. My eyes practically rolled back in my head at the wave of exquisite sensation. I found his mouth, avid, eager for me, and kissed him as he moved deep inside me, the desire building, billowing, so that my blood boiled and I panted like a wild thing.

"Harlan." I said his name like a prayer, a vow. The heat of him set me aflame and fed me at once. The moment should last forever and I clung to him as if it could.

"Yes," he answered and held me as I came apart.

I lay against his side, in our accustomed position, my head in the fold of his shoulder as we gazed up at the stars. We hadn't spoken since we'd made love. Had held on to each other for a while, exchanged kisses, and, by mutual accord, waded into the water to clean up. He was waiting for me, I knew, to process my thoughts and feelings.

All of which seemed too enormous to parse.

I might have thought he slept, but his fingers lightly traced a caress on my arm, seeking to reassure me even now.

"What I don't understand," I finally said, "is how that could have felt so right when the other felt so wrong."

"Because the other was wrong," he replied immediately, verifying that he remained alert.

"It's the same act."

"But not the same intent."

I sighed, unsure what to think about it all. Not really wanting to think about it, in truth. "He wanted a male heir. It wasn't about me or even him. We both acted in service to the High Throne."

"He wanted to control you. Rape is an act of power and violence. What he did was wrong and he knew it."

"I'm not sure that's so. No, listen." I put my hand on his chest. "He has ever been a law unto himself. That's how he accomplished the impossible, because he answers to nothing and no one. He became High King exactly because the rules meant nothing to him, and now he's above the law. That's what makes him King."

"It's what makes him a monster."

"One you're contractually bound to serve, I have to point out."

"Not anymore."

"What does that mean?" I shifted to sit, but he held me to his side.

"*You* listen, Ursula." He sounded mean, unlike him, and I recognized the tone for a cold, burning anger. "I know you and I have different ideas about loyalty, but the *Elskastholrr* means that mine belongs to you above all things. That contract wasn't in conflict with my decision because both it and my pledge are to serve you, but it became void in my eyes the moment I learned what he'd done to you. I have no fealty, no obligation, to someone who would wound you so terribly."

"You can't just void a contract." I broke free of his hold, started to get up, but he pulled me onto his chest, holding me by the shoulders so I had to look at him.

"I can and will do whatever my pledge to you dictates."

"Well, then, I'm telling you not to break that contract."

He smiled, a grim line to his mouth making it deadly. "It doesn't work that way. My pledge was mine to give, and I did so freely, but that doesn't let you dictate to me. My agency remains mine and I decide how best to serve you."

"What are you saying, Harlan?"

"I'm saying the man is a monster and the only way you can stop me from killing him is if someone else does. Or if you kill me."

30

"I'm not hearing this."

"You heard me, Ursula. More—in your heart you know I'm right."

"I don't know any such thing." I shot the words at him. "You speak treason. Hire-sword or not, even you should respect that. Let me go." I managed to slip out of his grip, but he simply rolled over, pinning me to the sand, holding my wrists above my head so I couldn't strike at him. Even now my body warmed to his weight, the press of his naked skin to mine. But I struggled anyway, more against the thought that he'd spoken so casually, so easily, of killing Uorsin.

Not casually—no. With sure and malevolent intent.

"I told you before that I'd kill him for what he did to you."

"I didn't think you meant it."

"I always mean what I say, particularly as it concerns you."

I gave up resisting and stared him down. He calmly returned my glare. "I can't let you kill him."

"Then you'll have to kill me."

"I could." At least, I told myself that.

"I have no doubt you're physically capable of it, and that I would not be able to stop you."

"You'd just let me slaughter you."

"No." He sounded amused. "I would do my best to disarm you." As if to demonstrate, he pressed a kiss under my ear, a place that worked wonders to melt me, even as angry with him as I felt. No. More panicked at the audacity of his words. "But if it came to your life or mine, I'd choose yours."

"I don't understand you."

"Yes, you do. You just struggle against it. This is who I am, Ursula. You don't have to have me, but it is who you get if you do want me."

"I want you," I whispered. Undeniable, with my body already craving his again, hot and ready to be filled once more. More than that. I'd never known anyone like him, who understood me with one glance. *I never could imagine even in my wildest dreams that there might be a woman like you in the world.* I knew what he meant because I felt the same. Almost without thought, I arched against him and he hummed in sensual agreement, dipping his head to take my nipple in his mouth. I moaned. Tried to focus. "But I can't let you kill him."

"So I understand."

"It falls to me to protect him."

"He's not here. We are. Who knows what tomorrow will bring, yes? If we survive, we can fight about it another day."

If I had my way, we'd never discuss it again. But I also intended for us all to survive. Either way, it made this interlude that much more precious. "I want you, Harlan."

"You're not sore?" He raised his head to kiss me, then searched my face.

"No." Though I was, a little. A small thing compared to the driving need, the desperate fear that we'd have little time to enjoy each other. That I'd already wasted too much time. I fastened my teeth in the corded muscle of his throat, delighting in the shudder that ran through him. "Make me forget again."

"As you command."

He rolled off me and retrieved another of his protections and urged me over him. I resisted. "With you on top—as we just were."

"I don't want you to feel trapped."

"You didn't mind a moment ago." I pulled him down.

"True. But that wasn't sexual. I needed you to stay and finish the conversation."

"You know what I think?" I nipped his ear. "I think it's all sexual. Your weight on me is part of it. Give me more."

And with hands, mouth, and the powerful thrust of his body, he did exactly that.

I slept hard and woke up both sore and sated, blinking into Harlan's intent face. He brushed my cheek with gentle fingers and I realized that's what had awakened me. "The sun rises," he said, by way of explanation, "else I'd have let you sleep longer."

More than rising, the sun shone a good hand's width above the distant mountains. "Danu. I can't believe I slept so long. Why haven't they come looking for us?"

"No doubt wary of what state they'd find us in."

"Hmm." Naked, sticky, and both well used. Harlan bore the signs of our night together, with a number of scratches and bite marks on his chest and shoulders. I tapped one. "Should I apologize for this?"

He grinned and covered my hand with his, pressing it against his heart. "Never. Love marks such as these are a great compliment. They mean I pleased you enough that you lost yourself in the moment."

"Don't let it go to your head."

"Too late. I am full of smug self-congratulation this morning." He bent and kissed me, lingering over it. "Full of you, my lovely hawk."

I'd never been one to lie abed, usually filled with restless energy to go work out and make inroads on the day's responsibilities. Especially that day, poised on the brink of finding Ami and the babies, I should have been revving to get going. And yet, I wanted nothing more than to stay in our nest of sand and drown myself in the smell, taste, and feel of him.

Nevertheless.

I pushed him away and got to my feet. "I'm all over sand. A quick swim to clean up and we should go?"

"Duty calls," he agreed and followed me into the water.

They were all waiting on us, saddled up and ready to go. I hadn't felt the spur of it, the concern that usually pricked me. With Harlan's comments on the topic in mind, I decided not to apologize, though it had been on my tongue to do so. Instead I offered morning greetings, which were returned along with an offer of breakfast and a smile from Andi that spoke volumes.

I refused to be embarrassed.

"We've sent some of the men ahead," Rayfe told us, "to spring any traps."

"Any new insights?" I asked Andi.

She rolled her eyes, looking pained. "Nothing that makes any sense yet. Stop asking me."

"I just thought I'd check."

"If I have something useful to offer, believe me, you'll be the first to know." She'd dressed in her fighting leathers and had her hair braided back. Always a nervous fighter before, she seemed to have more confidence there now, too.

"I don't know if this is an invasive question"—I nodded particularly to Rayfe—"but in the interests of full disclosure and knowing what we're working with here—can Harlan and I expect that the rest of you might change out of human form at some point?"

"And the horses, too," Rayfe answered.

"Except for Fiona and your steeds, of course," Andi put in.

"We'll no doubt encounter same from the enemy," I pointed out. "In the press of a fight, how shall we know you from them?"

They exchanged glances. "An excellent question," Rayfe muttered.

"Part of learning to work and fight together, instead of against each other," I cheerfully agreed.

"Who knew this day would come?" Rayfe returned darkly.

"Salena," Andi said. "She knew. And she gave her daughter a tool, didn't she? Something to guide you."

"You think it will work that way?" I asked.

"I think it could. Trust in what you sense is my advice. Captain Harlan—are you willing to take your cue from Ursula?"

"Always," he replied.

Andi smiled at that, her nerves transforming into genuine affection. "I'm truly glad to hear that."

We rode inland for several hours, going at a decent clip, but slower than the day before, wending through the coastal marshlands, following an indirect path. Whether from the weight of Andi's cautions or something I sensed on another level, my skin prickled even in the sultry warmth and my blood sang at high alert. The open, flat landscape seemed as if it would hide nothing, but those kinds of places could be the most deceptive. Especially when even the wildlife was suspect because your attackers could emerge from animal form of any kind.

Despite their wild appearance, Rayfe's men maintained a discipline of their own, the scouts reporting in on a precise schedule and rotating out again. At his command, two returning scouts shifted into wolfhounds and their mounts into birds that flew above them as they coursed out, noses to the ground.

Harlan grunted softly at the display. "I keep thinking I'll get used to that." He spoke softly, also in battle readiness, as if he felt the press of the impending fight also, as if the enemy already surrounded us.

Which they might.

"You and I both." I rolled my shoulders. Hopefully if Andi did so, I'd be able to take that in stride.

"I dislike this approach." He glanced at me. "It feels ripe for ambush and it occurs to me that all three of Uorsin and Salena's heirs, plus the babies, will likely be in one place—all the better to eliminate you at once."

"It's an unsettling thought. However, in any scenario, Ami, the babies, and I would have to be together."

"Not if you let me do the rescuing."

"While I hang back and stay safe? Not happening." I pointed my chin toward Andi, who spoke with Rayfe riding a short distance ahead. He nodded at something she said and silently signaled two more men to shift into hounds, who then took off in another direction. "Besides, I suspect we'll have need of Andi's skills. I trust in what she's seen."

"A strange way to plan a battle, on the vague prognostications of a sorceress who fully admits she might be wrong."

I grinned at him. "Keeps things interesting."

A wolfhound in the distance barked, a staccato series that sent the others galloping that direction. I palmed a throwing knife and we raced after, bringing up the rear. Rayfe halted at a copse of short trees that dripped with a bloodred fruit I didn't recognize. He held up a hand to signal caution and for us to come forward.

We closed the distance, then dismounted. The Tala wolfhound sat on a patch of grass in the shade of the tree, watching with far-too-intelligent eyes. I crouched, examining the grass the dog indicated, Harlan following suit.

"I don't see anything." I kept my voice as low as possible and reached out to run my hand through the grass, but Harlan stayed me with a soft tap.

"There," he barely whispered. I frowned where he pointed,

still not seeing what he did. Tugging my elbow, he backed us out of the copse, the wolfhound coming with us. Harlan mounted, pointed, and, taking the lead now, urged his horse into a fast trot, the wolfhound at his stirrup now. I shrugged at Andi and followed. She nodded once, as if I'd confirmed something for her, she and Rayfe falling in behind us.

The attack came with no warning. None beyond the one I'd glimpsed in Andi's tense expression.

All around us, the grass seemed to explode into life, creatures from nightmares—large, toothy lizards—launching up in a disorienting rush, biting at our horses' legs with a savage attempt to hamstring them. The Tala steeds became birds, flying up, then plummeting back down to return the attack with hooked beaks and slicing talons, their erstwhile riders transforming into various snarling beasts that fell on the lizards. Andi dove from Fiona's back, becoming a large, lethal-looking cat in midair, while Fiona—exquisitely trained to Andi's signals—neatly leapt out of range, raced at top speed a short distance away, then turned to wait.

All of this I noted in the clear, cool, and infinitely slow moments of pitched battle. My stallion and Harlan's, both war trained, wheeled and stomped on the lizards. As if we'd planned it, we faced away from each other, sword arms out, creating a circle of destruction between us, the black blood of shape-shifters flying.

A mistake that the enemy chose such an extreme animal form. Shocking at first, yes, but so different from our companions that we easily discerned which was which.

Over nearly as fast as it began, the battle ended with the lizards dead around us, returning in death to the ratlike creatures Andi had said they called staymachs, sinking into the bog that had seemed to be solid ground before we rode over it.

Harlan wheeled his horse around, confirmed I'd taken no injury, and we both looked to our companions, all a milling pack of predators now. The giant black wolf that must have been Rayfe patrolled the perimeter, the wolfhounds falling in with him. The cat bounded toward Fiona, who remarkably held her ground, not flinching when Andi flowed up and out of the animal form and leapt on her back—looking exactly as she had before.

She rode up to us and raised her eyebrows, nodding at Harlan to lead us onward.

We hit two more traps like that. Each as sudden, by creatures meant to surprise and unsettle us. By Andi and Rayfe's demeanor, I gathered that they did not consider these major obstacles. We took some hits, though the injuries the Tala incurred were quickly dispensed with via shape-shifting. Harlan and I remained unscathed, though his steed had taken a nasty bite from a nest of large snakes, forcing us to stop and purge the wound of venom.

Andi held the horse calm, a knack she'd had even before, but now so honed she held the great stallion so steady it didn't move even when I opened the wound with my blade and Harlan sluiced a stinging antivenin into it.

"These are no more than preset defenses," Harlan said quietly to me. "And poorly thought out in that they only confirm our direction."

"Or cleverly herd us in the wrong one."

"The signs are there, however."

"Which signs do you follow? What did you see in the copse that sent us this way?"

He raised one eyebrow at me. "Trade secret. I look forward to you attempting to extract it from me."

"You wish."

"Oh, yes. Yes, I do."

By early evening, we'd left the marshlands behind and entered the heavily forested, rising foothills that led the way to the jagged range beyond. Very likely the range that separated us from Branli, which I'd wasted so much time and effort attempting to pass through. If we ended up pursuing into those mountains, we'd be in a fix. Snow had definitely arrived there, and Harlan and I, at least, did not have enough cold-weather gear—nor could we conveniently grow fur coats.

Abruptly, Andi reined up, frowning. Rayfe, still in wolf form, circled back, ears pricked. "Something has changed," she told us. "They're moving. A different scenario is forming."

"Can we plan ahead—be where they will be?" Harlan asked.

"Possibly."

"What changed?" I asked, feeling a curl of dread.

Andi returned the look with somber concern. "I'm not certain entirely, but they're all together and must be looping back. All the near-future scenarios now take place in the cliff city. Or near it."

Rayfe popped into human form, fully armed and dressed, which bemused me still. "Repeat that," he ordered. Andi recapitulated our conversation, confirming my suspicion that they didn't entirely understand human speech while in animal form.

"How can what the future holds have changed so decidedly?" Rayfe frowned over it.

"They're playing you," I told Andi, shaking my head at her consternation. "This Terin, our uncle, he knew Salena well, we can figure. Brother-in-law to her for how long?"

"Salena and Tosin were married nearly fifteen years," Rayfe supplied.

"And Terin likely served as a close adviser to the royal couple, I'm guessing."

"I was but a boy then, but that's how I understand it. Terin became my adviser partly because of that. For continuity." Rayfe's jaw clenched as he followed my reasoning.

"Who held the reins of government after Salena left and before you took the crown?"

"Terin." Rayfe confirmed it with a grim face.

"If he wanted to rule," Andi argued, mostly with Rayfe, "he could have competed in the trials."

"He did. I won. He lost." Rayfe lifted a shoulder and let it fall. "He said he'd only done it for his brother's memory and I believed him. He served me faithfully many years. I had no reason to doubt his loyalty in all that time."

"Until I came along." Andi chewed her lip. "I don't understand how I got the visions so wrong."

"You didn't," I told her. "You saw correctly. He made sure of it. See—your gift is the same as our mother's, and he knew her well. They no doubt spent time sorting through what she predicted and planned policy accordingly. I've only been around you with this gift for a few days and already I have a sense of how our decisions play into affecting what you see. For example, once we left the cliff city with this particular group, that eliminated some possible outcomes, right?"

With dawning realization and chagrin, Andi nodded. "I don't know why I didn't think of this."

"Because you haven't spent as much time as I have sorting through long-term strategy." All those days and nights our father had forced me to walk through battle scenarios with him. Rehashing sieges from the Great War. Planning potential reactions to various uprisings. He'd trained me well, indeed. "King Rayfe has only had the benefit of your prognostications for a relatively short time, so less practice there also. But this Terin—he knows exactly how to set up his intentions so that you'll see one set of futures. Then he abruptly altered the plan so you would see too late."

I glanced at Harlan, who nodded thoughtfully. "It's a simple strategy in the end—lure your enemy out of their stronghold so you may take possession of it."

"Though the cliff city is hardly indefensible," I answered him. "Impossible to lay siege to it."

"But as the seat of power and government, it would hold symbolic value to the Tala. Take the council hostage, intercept communications. Likely the only sort of takeover that could be effective under those physical circumstances," Harlan argued his point.

"You two terrify me," Andi interrupted us. "I know Terin's aim now."

"I'm not sure you can rely on—"

"Not from the visions, Ursula." She turned to Rayfe, fear and worry written over her countenance. "They're going for the Heart of Annfwn."

He paled. "Moranu save us all."

31

Andi and Rayfe wanted to head for the cliff city immediately, but I talked them into a short break. None of us had eaten all day, and the mossbacks, at least, I pointed out, including our non-staymach horses in the designation, needed to rest. Mostly I wanted a full explanation. Enough of this riding blind and silent. The four of us sat away from the others, to plan our next steps, though our Tala contingent visibly chafed at the delay.

"Send one of your men in bird form to provide warning to the council," I suggested.

Rayfe shook his head. "None of the ones with me can take that form."

Interesting. "The staymachs can."

"Yes," Andi put in, "but they're not that intelligent."

Right, right. "*You* can take the form of a rather large black hawk, as I recall," I pointed out to Rayfe. One that had caused considerable chaos by shattering the window in the throne room.

He laid a possessive hand on Andi's thigh. "So can Andromeda. She can take any form, as your mother could."

"As some others of our family can," Andi added.

"Can you shift back and forth, as much as you like?"

"No," Rayfe said, giving Andi a stern look, as if he spoke to an old argument. "It's as tiring as putting in hard, physical labor. Being distracted or exhausted can lead to fatal errors."

"That's not an issue at the moment," Andi inserted.

"So the pair of you could go defend this Heart, whatever it is. Get there ahead of them and we can come up from behind, trap Terin and his confederates between us."

"It's not that simple." Andi's brow knitted. "Even with Stella, I'm not sure how they think they'll get to it."

"Explain," I told her.

"Don't order me about, Ursula," she snapped. "It's a secret I can't reveal."

"You're going to have to reveal something if we're to rescue Ami and the babies. While I'm sorry for your internal politics, my aim is to rescue my sister, niece, and nephew. What happens to this Heart is immaterial to me."

"She's my sister, too." Andi glared at me.

"Losing control of the Heart would have dire consequences for the Twelve, as well," Rayfe spoke over her, running a hand down her hair, adding his glare to hers.

I hated secrets. Especially ones with dire implications.

Andi scrubbed her hands over her scalp. "I don't know why I didn't see them going for the Heart. That's big. It should be a major point in time, with many possible outcomes."

"Dire ones," I added, and Harlan flicked me an amused look.

"Okay, look." Andi leaned forward. "I want you to swear to Danu that you won't use this information against Annfwn."

Rayfe's face darkened. "Andromeda—"

"No. If she swears, she won't go back on it."

I held her gaze for a long moment, sorting the possibilities. The long-term implications of such a promise.

"Look at her," Rayfe growled, sounding remarkably wolflike. "She can't do it. There is your answer."

I didn't rise to the bait, but turned it over in my mind. All the conflicting loyalties. Salena had set all this in motion to protect Annfwn—that much seemed clear—and had expected me to be part of her plan. But there was more to it than that. She had to have known that I'd grow up wanting to protect the Twelve also. I wished I knew what she had wanted from me.

Until then, I'd have to grope my way through.

"I swear to Danu," I said slowly, "that anything you tell me about the Heart of Annfwn will be information I hold secret and will use only for the greatest good."

"As *you* see it," Rayfe snarled.

"Yes. I have no other measure to offer."

"That's good enough for me," Andi decided.

"Andromeda—she is her father's puppet."

"No." Andi seemed to be speaking to me. "She's not. She never was. I trust her."

"I'm sitting right here," I commented drily.

She ignored the tone. "The Heart of Annfwn is more a—"

"Shouldn't I step away?" Harlan interrupted.

"Why bother?" Andi gave him a distracted look. "Your pledge to Ursula will hold you to whatever she vows."

"Danu take it—you knew!" I accused her, and she gave me a bland look. "You might have warned me."

"I did warn you. Now—the Heart is not a thing so much as a place. I'm not going to tell you where it is, except that it's situated in such a way that only a shape-shifter—one with the ability to take multiple forms—can reach it. It's not exactly the source of Annfwn's magic, but it acts like a heart in truth, circulating and refreshing the magic. The right person can control the magic from there."

"Control the magic in what way?"

She sighed a little. "Among other things, the barrier."

Aha. Very interesting implications there. "The right person— one with the mark?"

"Yes."

"And Stella has the mark, but she's a babe in arms. She wouldn't be able to shape-shift to take herself to the place, would she? You didn't."

Andi's mouth twisted in a wry smile. "Not until I got to Annfwn, no. Which was a problem for me. Tala babies with strong blood can and do shape-shift in the cradle. That's part of why I wanted Stella here. It can make for some interesting moments."

Harlan glanced at me, amused, and I recalled his comment about having shape-shifter children making for interesting parenting. Not something I could get my head around.

"Okay, so Stella shifts, but she still has an infant's mind, right? She wouldn't have the ability to intelligently manipulate the Heart for years."

"Which is why this makes no sense," Andi agreed.

"What about Amelia?"

"What about her?"

"You heard Dafne—Ami has this idea that Glorianna wants her to open all of Annfwn's magic to the Twelve. She might be thinking of taking down the barrier, to restore balance or some such. Perhaps Ash and Terin have convinced her to join forces with them to do just that."

"Ash wouldn't go along," Rayfe said. "He has no love for Terin."

"You have no love for me and yet we've found common cause," I pointed out ruthlessly. "Ash is committed to freeing the Tala from the prisons of the Twelve and returning them and other by-blows with Tala blood to Annfwn. Which means bringing your barrier down."

"No, it doesn't. We were working on that already," Andi protested. "We were making great strides on my ability to consciously alter the permeability of the barrier when Ash left to—"

"To go to Ami," I filled in. "At which point Stella was abducted and made to seem as if she died. A plot like that would discourage pursuit, so it could not have been intended to lure

Ami here. She and Ash coming after Terin would have been an unintended consequence. Not predictable."

"But not entirely unwelcome."

The new voice startled me. By the time I became aware that a fox had darted in from the trees, shifted into a man, and spoken, Harlan, Rayfe, and I were all on our feet, swords drawn. The man shook his head slowly and made a tsking sound. "If I don't return very soon, unharmed, the princess and young prince will die."

"Terin, I presume."

He gave me a slight bow, full of mockery. "Your Highness. I'm surprised you don't remember me. I was a guest of Ordnung for some time while you were in residence."

I had not placed him as one of the Tala prisoners. Odd. "What happened to your perimeter guard, King Rayfe?"

"Something I would also like to know. You've laid out the stakes, Terin," Rayfe growled, looking supremely pissed. "Do you truly expect us to believe you have the Princess Amelia in your custody with no proof?"

Terin smiled, not nicely, and signaled. A wolf parted the shadows between the trees and deposited a length of bright, red-gold hair in Andi's lap. Darker rust smears marred it in places. Edging over, I crouched beside her, which also put me between her and Terin. We exchanged grave looks. Ami's hair was unmistakable. Andi touched a fingertip to the dried blood and gave a slight nod.

Danu take them all for hurting her. I let the anger flow, using it as Kaedrin had taught me so long ago. "You've signed your death warrant, Terin of the Tala."

His saucy smile faded into a grim line. "No. Salena did that. I'm just doing what she forced us into, for self-preservation. To save Annfwn. Once you believed in that," he accused Rayfe.

To his credit, Rayfe stayed calm, though his eyes glittered an unnatural blue in the shadows. He'd moved subtly to cover Andi from the other side. Harlan, though he'd remained where he was and kept his attention ostensibly on Terin, showed me in the lines of his body that he scanned the forest for signs of our guard or more of Terin's people.

"Queen Andromeda has saved Annfwn." Rayfe had an implacable expression. "The barrier is within our control again."

"While you sit cozily with Uorsin's heir," Terin sneered. "It need not be this way. The babe shall be ours entirely, free of Uorsin's taint. And you, Andromeda—you shall come with me and show me how to reach the Heart, so the babe can be taught. If you behave, you, your sisters, and the boy child can go free. You all will be allowed to leave Annfwn forever. Decide. Time is running out."

"She's not going—" Rayfe boiled with constrained violence but stopped when Andi stood and laid a hand on his arm.

"Yes, I am."

"I forbid it."

She nearly rolled her eyes. Stopped herself. "I see more now. I have to go." They exchanged a long, wordless communication, and he lowered his sword.

Andi looked to me. "Keep your blade sharp, my sister."

"Always." I turned my attention to Terin. "And the hostage exchange? When shall my sisters and nephew be returned?"

"All in good time, Uorsin's heir. Horse form, if you please, bastard niece of mine."

Without hesitation—perhaps so Rayfe couldn't stop her as he so clearly strained to do—Andi shifted into a horse, storm gray with a black mane and tail. Terin leapt onto her back and dug his heels viciously into her sides, spurring her to gallop off into the night.

Rayfe cursed low and long in his native language, then called out to the guard. None answered. Harlan gave me a small shake of his head, conveying that he'd detected nothing either while we negotiated. Rayfe picked up the skein of Ami's hair, looking grim.

"I'm following. I apologize for leaving you here, but I have no choice. I can't let them hurt her."

"Go," I told him. "We'll be on your trail."

Without another word, he shifted into hawk form, launching into the sky, black on black.

"So much I don't like about this," I commented to Harlan. "But I see no other path than to saddle up and bring Fiona with us. If we ride all night and tomorrow, perhaps finding a diagonal back to—"

The night forest exploded. We'd never sheathed our swords, but the creatures were on us with such devastating speed we nearly failed to keep them off. I palmed a dagger, nailing a wolf in the eye with it, but three more leapt at me. At my back, Harlan bellowed and swung his great sword, cleaving a clearing around us. I stepped into the space he created, which at least put one of the monster trees at our backs. Only marginally helpful, as razor-taloned birds fell on us from the branches.

After that, I became the fight. Nothing but clicking from one target to the next.

Defend, parry, attack.

Defend, parry, attack.

Defend, parry, attack.

One corner of my mind sent prayers to Danu that we would live to retreat and regroup.

Another part of me took a fierce, almost sexual joy in fighting beside Harlan. We passed targets off to each other as if we'd practiced it for years.

My speed.

His strength.

He dug in, an immovable, unassailable bulwark that sent one creature after another off bleeding into the shadows.

I spun, danced, maneuvered, guarding his flank, creating a double-bladed whirlwind that nothing penetrated.

Nothing much. I became aware of a few nasty bites singing with blood and pain when there were, at last, no more comers. I weighted back in one leg, ready to spring, surveying the twitching bodies, scanning the rustling leaves. No movement in my arc. In the corner of my eye, Harlan cut the head from a large black wolf, grunting with the effort, then performed a similar scan.

"Clear?" I asked.

"For the moment, it seems." He was out of breath. Understandable.

"We should move. Hopefully they didn't kill the horses. If we can't ride out, we'll have to find a more defensible location."

"A sound plan."

I moved forward, exercising caution, lest any of the fallen were thinking to ambush us. Harlan's tread seemed louder than usual behind me, uneven. I glanced back. "You okay?"

He nodded, grim. "Get to the horses."

The three were hobbled out where we'd left them to graze in a grassy meadow at the edge of the trees. Terrified, but unhurt. *The Tala love animals.* A foolish miss to my mind. But a stroke of luck I'd take. No doubt Terin had thought us easier to kill than that.

Harlan grunted and once again I turned back. Just in time to see him sink to his knees.

"Danu—you're injured!" In two strides, I had him under the shoulder, easing him to the ground. His arm wrapped protectively around his gut told me all I needed to know. "Stubborn man. Let me see."

"Ursula." He refused to budge his arm. "Take your steed and go."

"Not on your life."

He laughed, a hollow sound. "I'm afraid so."

Terror, keen and ice-cold, such as I'd never felt before flooded through me. "I'm not leaving you. Let me see."

I think he wouldn't have, but that unfailing strength had bled away and he couldn't resist me. Dark liver blood covered my hands before I managed to cut away his leather armor. It pulsed out, hot, fast. I pressed down to staunch the bleeding. Too much. The slick, ragged flesh shifted under my hands, sliding away.

A mortal wound.

"Don't weep, my hawk," he whispered, wrapping a hand around my wrist. "Not for me."

"Thrice-damn you," I gritted out, my vision blurry. "Don't you dare die."

"Sing for me." His voice had become thready as his lifeblood pumped into the ground.

"I won't let you die."

"Even you can't fight death, my valiant warrior. Lay my head in your lap and sing me a lullaby. You promised."

I wanted to argue I'd never promised any such thing. I wanted to badger and bully him into getting up again. But any fool could see he was dying. I'd seen enough of it to know. I rolled up his shirt and packed it into the wound anyway, to forestall death as long as possible, and then did as he asked, gently lifting his head so he could lay it in my lap.

He gazed up at me, eyes no longer sharp. "So beautiful."

I caught the sob. "I do love you. I should have said so."

"It's all right. I knew."

"Of course you did. Arrogant hire-sword."

"I wouldn't trade it. Any of it. Knowing you. Loving you. The greatest privilege of my life. Even knowing how it would end, I'd do it again."

"I'm sorry I was so hardheaded."

"You are perfect. Sing me to sleep."

So, I did. My voice croaking around the tears, I sang the only lullaby I knew.

> *Sleep deep, sleep now,*
> *Under the moon, Moranu's cowl.*
> *Danu's stars light your way*
> *To Glorianna's dawning day.*

32

I sang it three times.

He said nothing more; his breath slowed to nothing. He was gone.

I couldn't make myself check to be sure. As if, maybe if I just sat quietly, I wouldn't have to face that I'd lost him forever.

That I sat there in an open meadow under Danu's merciless stars, all alone.

"Glorianna take you, Ursula! Where are you? I know that was you croaking in that frog's voice."

Was I hallucinating? It couldn't be Ami calling out to me. "Ami?" I said, but no sound emerged. I cleared my throat. "Ami!"

"Oh, thank Glorianna!" She burst through the trees, dressed in leathers, hair cut raggedly short, carrying a dagger. Several impossible things together. But Ami it was. She ran to me and fell to her knees beside me. "Are you hurt? You're covered in blood. Ash! Come help me."

"Ash is here?" My brain felt stupid.

"Yes. Here he comes. Ash—she needs help."

"Not me." I grabbed her hands as Ash came striding up, a

bundle strapped to his chest. "Harlan. Ash, you have to heal him. Can you?"

Ami stared down at Harlan's face. "Who is he? I've never seen this man before."

"It's a really long story. Ash, please! I'll pay any price."

Ash's uncanny green eyes flashed from my face to Harlan, and he unstrapped the bundle, handed it to Ami, and knelt down. "Let me see."

"His side. I tried to stop the bleeding, but . . ."

"Essla." Ami kept her voice soft. "I think he's—"

"Don't say it." My voice cracked, along with my heart. "I can't bear to hear the words. Please try, Ash." With a sense of desperate despair, I prayed with all my might to Danu, offering her whatever she required of me. Surely she would not have guided Ash here at this moment, only to hand Harlan over to Glorianna's arms. I didn't know how to withstand that kind of crushing defeat. I'd watched Ami receive the corpse of her true love and badgered her terribly. Awful of me. "I'm sorry I was cruel to you, Ami. When you were grieving. I didn't know how it felt."

"You were right to do it. You kept me from going off the cliffs long enough to heal."

Heal. An impossible concept.

"He's alive," Ash said, sounding terse, "but barely. I need some room here."

"Wait." Ami put a hand on his shoulder. "At what cost? You can't endanger yourself."

Ash looked at me instead. "How much does he matter to you, Your Highness?"

"Everything," I admitted. I didn't even care to weigh the words, what I promised or how it might mortgage the future. None of that mattered. "I'll pay any price."

"Done, then." He nodded solemnly, but the starlight caught the craggy lines of his scarred face, showed the twist of his smile. "Now, get out of the way."

"Come on, Auntie Essla." Ami tugged me away as Ash held

Harlan's head. "He needs privacy and peace to do this. Hold your nephew and I'll fetch our packs. Is that Fiona?"

I laughed a little, that she would notice, and took the baby, trying to hold him without getting blood on his blankets. Most of it, though, had dried. We'd sat there some time. Then, exhaustion crashing over me, I folded my knees and sat where I could watch Ash work, fancying that a soft green glow emanated from his hands. Astar hiccupped and I angled my arms to better drink in his sleeping face.

"Does he do nothing but sleep?" I asked Ami when she returned, leading two horses.

"Believe me—you're grateful he's asleep. I swear he has all of your meanness and none of my sweet nature. The child is a brat."

"You don't look like a brat," I cooed at Astar and kissed him on his forehead. He smelled of milk and soft, sweet new life. Something to hold on to.

"Here." Ami tugged out one of my hands and splashed water from a canteen over it, wiping the blood away with a cloth. "Is any of this yours?"

"Some maybe. Most of it is Harlan's."

"And he is?"

My lover. My love. My unlooked-for partner for life. All the names for him tangled in my head. "A Dasnarian mercenary," I finally said, knowing he'd be amused that's what I'd settled on. "How came you to be here? Terin said he had you captive. He gave us your hair."

"As you can see, that's the only part of me that rat bastard has. Not for lack of trying." She gave me my cleaned hand back and reached for the other.

"He has Andi now. Lured with the threat to your life. Some kind of plan for her to do something with Stella. Rayfe is tracking her. We were attacked and sorely pressed. Harlan injured. They could be back anytime." The thoughts seemed to come in disconnected bursts. From a distance, I considered that I might be in shock.

"There's no Tala about. We had to stay away from the area until they cleared out."

"How do you know?"

She wrinkled her nose. "Can't you smell them? Especially Terin's lot. I can smell their particular stink a league away."

I giggled and Ami stared into my face, using the cloth to wipe the blood away, then to cool my brow.

"You're bad off, Essla," she said, a worried frown creasing her forehead. She should be rubbing it away, to prevent wrinkles, but she didn't. "What can I do for you?"

"I don't know." I looked down at Astar. "I don't know anything anymore."

She gently lifted the babe from me and I missed his warm weight immediately, a chill making me shiver. "Drink this water and lie back. Let me tend to you."

"You sound like Harlan." I did as she bade and she tucked Astar into the crook of my arm.

"Then he must be a good man."

"He is. I'm in love with him."

"Quite the development." She worked on the side away from the baby, removing my clothes in pieces, washing the various bites and scrapes she found. "You've lost a lot of blood, I think. You're hurt more than you knew. Drink more water."

"He wants to kill Uorsin, though."

"Good."

Something about her terse agreement penetrated the dreamy haze. "How can you say that?"

She moved Astar to my other side and set to work again, unbuckling my sword belt. I stopped her. "No."

"It's right here. Right by your hand. See? The topaz is glowing."

It was glowing, as if lit from within. *A star to guide you.* "The Star of Annfwn."

"Is it? A pretty name. I always figured that jewel came from Mother."

"We have to rescue Andi."

"We will, but it will help if you're not half-dead."

"Harlan died." Tears slid out of me, the stars above kaleido-scoping into a blurry, colorful wheel.

"No, honey. He's alive, remember? Ash will heal him."

"Ash saved you."

"That's right. Drink some more water and sleep for a bit, and when you wake up, he'll be waiting for you."

"He said he'd wait for me as long as I needed."

"There you go. A good man. A patient one, it sounds like. As would be necessary for anyone foolish enough to fall in love with you. Sleep now."

"Someone needs to keep watch."

"I will. I'm here. You watched over me. Let me watch over you." She covered me with a blanket, tucking it carefully around Astar.

I turned my head, to smell my nephew's hair. The Star pulsed hot in my other hand. The bright stars dimmed at the edges and I spun away into the dark.

A baby's harsh wail awakened me, though it was swiftly si-lenced. I sat bolt upright, sword in my hand, my nephew gone. "Astar!"

Ami turned, a pleased and relieved smile on her lips. She stood with a dagger in one hand and the baby in the crook of her arm, suckling at her breast. Even with her hair a ragged mess, it shone red-gold in the rising sunlight and she could have stepped out of a painting of Glorianna as mother.

"You live." She sounded wry. "Good. It was getting boring, having no one to talk to."

I got to my feet, my body a protesting mess of aches and pains. "You're standing watch alone—with nothing but a short blade and a nursing baby?"

330 • Jeffe Kennedy

"Yes, well, I thought about washing my hair and having a picnic, but this seemed like the thing to do."

The meadow rolled bright green around us, the five horses happily grazing and showing no sign of disturbance. A short distance away, Harlan lay where he'd fallen. Ash passed out beside him. I wanted to ask if he'd lived through the night, but terror of the wrong answer kept me from asking.

"He's alive," Ami said. "I think it took everything Ash had to bring him back, but—before *he* toppled over—Ash said that the Dasnarian will survive."

I nodded. Stood there a moment longer to absorb the crash of relief. Then sheathed my sword and went to him. He looked good. Normal, even, though still covered in dried blood that flaked off his skin. The area where the terrible bite had taken a chunk out of him gleamed a fresh and tender pink, soft to the touch, compared to the rest of him.

"An impressive-looking man," Ami commented from beside me, then widened her pretty violet eyes in innocence. "What? I can look."

"When did you get so earthy?"

"Good sex will do that to a girl. Wouldn't you say?"

"No comment." I sat back on my heels. "I can't believe you stood watch all night with all of us out. What would you have done if the Tala attacked? And since when do you know how to use a dagger?"

She looked a little grim. "I was really hoping not to find out. Though Ash can be awakened from the recovery sleep if needed and he's made me learn enough to stay alive until I can get to him. Still, I'm more than happy to hand guard duty over to you. If you're up to it. How do you feel?"

"I'm fine. Stiff and sore, probably not much endurance, but I can make it for a while."

Ami blinked, cocked her head. "Did you just admit to weakness?"

"Oh, shut up. Ash slept for days after healing you—are we in for that again?"

"Maybe not so long. It helps tremendously that we're inside Annfwn. And, as I said, he can be awakened enough to put him on a horse. We can strap Astar to him and he'll sleep that way." She made a face. "We've done that quite a bit, with it being just the three of us."

"I thought you were bringing your personal guard with you."

"Did. Until we had to cross the barrier. Then we were on our own. Here, now that you're awake you can take the baby and stand guard. I'll get more water and we can eat while we catch each other up." She showed me how to strap Astar's carrying bundle over my shoulders, so he lay against my chest, looking cranky to be removed from his mother's far more cushioned breast.

Experimentally, I drew my sword and checked the range of motion. Not ideal, but workable. Astar quit making those grumpy noises and waved his little fists. Moving slowly, I kept an eye on Ami as she headed down to the little stream at the border of the meadow and woods, and I worked through some basic limbering exercises. It helped banish some of the aches, though my head pounded. What were Andi and Rayfe dealing with? There would be no finding out unless we figured out how to move the mountain that was the sleeping Harlan.

"Here you go." Ami handed me a refilled canteen and transferred Astar to be buckled against her again. "Ash said you'd have a headache, losing all that blood, and to drink lots of water to replenish. He was sorry not to be able to heal you, too."

"I owe him everything already," I said simply, my gaze going to Harlan. I'd feel better when he woke up.

"So . . ." Ami sat cross-legged and set out some food—fruit and meat, mainly. "How did my heartless sister fall in love with a foreign mercenary from a country I only vaguely recall hearing about before and swap her sword for a real live man in her bed?"

"You first. Your tale is more salient to our next steps."

Her gaze flicked to Harlan. "I'm not so sure of that, but okay. After we left Windroven, Ash tracked Terin into the Wild Lands. No big surprise there."

"How did you pick up his trail?"

She smiled, radiantly lovely, but with an edge. "Mainly Tala network. Don't look like that. You know better than I, I imagine, just how many prisons hold Tala expatriates—and how many have escaped over time. The ones that can get back into Annfwn have. The ones who can't, along with the ones who haven't had the opportunity to make the journey and appeal to Andi for entry, or that have been refused entry, which is something we need to talk about, live in various states of hiding. There are ways of finding them."

"Especially for one of their number who is also an escaped convict."

"There is that." She looked at Ash and her eyes filled with both exasperation and love. "You can guess some of what he'll ask of you. I hope you're truly ready to pay his price."

"A pardon, no doubt. Which is not in my power to grant."

"Not only for him—for all the Tala prisoners. You'll have the power one day, thank Glorianna for that." Ami seemed uncertain, but made a decision. "There's something else." She rummaged in her pack and drew out the pink-gowned doll our mother had left her. Hers was far less pretty than mine and, bedraggled to begin with, had suffered from being tossed around on her journeys.

"You're carrying it around with you?" I tried not to convey how crazy I thought that was, but she glared at me.

"Yes, I do. This is why." She pricked her finger with the point of the dagger, squinching up her face, and held the bead of welling blood up near the doll's head. The pink-gold floss of it deepened into a darker red. I leaned in, to see more closely. "You try," she said, handing me the doll.

Curious, I waited until the red faded away, then simply flexed my arm enough to break open the scab on a minor wound where a talon had torn through my shirt. The head turned even deeper red, and Ami raised her brows. "Even more than me. Who'd have guessed that?"

"More what?"

"Strength of Tala blood, apparently."

"But you and I should be the same amount—same mother and father."

She shook her head. The shorter length let it curl nearly into perfect ringlets, and they bounced as she did so. "Doesn't work that way. For some reason the balance is different in different people. I bet Andi's blood would make it turn nearly black. Same with Stella. Astar has less than I do; Ash, quite a bit more. More like you, and his mother was all mossback."

I contemplated the significance of that. Ash's healing ability seemed to be another sort of shape-shifting, only turned outward. "Andi said that my fighting abilities come partly from the same thing. That what allows them to shift makes me faster and stronger."

"Why does that annoy you?"

I laughed a little, that she saw through me. "I worked hard for my skills."

"Ash is the same way, as you'll recall."

"Yes." I'd nearly killed him once. Would have, had it been any easier. Fortunately the man wielded a blade nearly as well as I did. Though I hadn't known then who he was or that Ami loved him, killing another of her true loves would have begun to look like a conspiracy. "So you used the head to find people of Tala blood and thus trailed Terin into the Wild Lands."

"Yes. He was moving with a pack and we couldn't gain on them. Always days behind." Her pretty lips pursed with frustration.

"How many?"

"It varied. Ash figured about thirty in his core group. Maybe another thirty that came and went. Scouts and so forth."

"Good to know." I mentally reviewed the bodies in the clearing and the lizards we'd killed in the ambushes. Some of those would have been staymachs and not in Ami's count. Still, we'd had to have killed at least forty.

"We tried cutting them off, but they made it across the border—we got the information on that in time to let us cross in a different place—a bit of a shortcut. One that cost us some time in the end because it was more difficult to track them inside Annfwn. When we finally caught up to them two days ago, they were ready for us."

"They ambushed you?"

"My fault. They made Stella cry. I heard her and, well, lost my head. Ash had Astar, so he was smart enough to hang back. Terin believed I was alone. He promised to give me Stella if I'd fuck him."

"In so many words?" I couldn't help but be amused to hear the foul word drip so easily from her pink mouth.

"Exactly. So I led him on, insisting on some privacy, knowing that Ash would be nearby and could more easily sneak up if Terin was distracted."

"I'm surprised Terin went for that trick."

"I can be pretty seductive when I want to." She shrugged it off. "It can be a useful weapon."

"Clever."

"Thank you." She gave me a flirtatious flutter of her lashes, then sobered. "I thought Ash wouldn't get there in time, and it wasn't easy, with his men having carried Stella off again. I had my dagger ready, in case I needed to stick him before he could, well, stick me, when Ash arrived. He nearly had him, but Terin sensed him somehow, rolled off me, and had me by the hair, using me as a shield."

"So you cut your hair."

She grimaced. "Which will take forever to regrow, but yes. Rat bastard."

"You got free, but Terin escaped with Stella, and you trailed him here and found us."

"Nearly too late," she agreed. "I can't tell you how I felt, hearing you sing that old lullaby. Gave me the chills. Though I wasn't surprised. I knew you'd find us sooner or later. Frankly I'd hoped it would be sooner."

"We had a number of delays. I wanted to be here sooner."

"I know that, and you—" She took my hand and squeezed, smiling through tears. "You came as fast as you could, just as you promised. Now that you're here, we'll get Stella back. I know it in my heart."

"Yes, we will." It had to be. "As soon as Harlan awakes, we'll get moving."

"Then you're in luck," Harlan's deep voice rumbled. "He's awake."

33

I held still for a moment, grasping for calm, sending a fervent pulse of gratitude to Danu—and Moranu, too, for her gifts of magic—finally believing it might be real.

And finally looked.

He sat up, taking in the sleeping Ash and raising an inquiring eyebrow at me. Unable to restrain myself longer, I went to him and kissed him long and hard. "Don't you ever do that to me again," I said when I could tear myself away.

"Well, if you command it, Your Highness," he replied with a broad, affectionate smile.

"I do command it. Don't make me hurt you."

"What am I promising not to do?"

"Oaf." I tried to wriggle free, but he held on, as strong as ever.

"I'm serious, my fierce hawk. What happened?" He frowned. "I remember finishing the fight. That wolf tore me open, but I had to get you to the horses before I bled out. And you . . ." He raised a hand to brush my cheek. "You said you loved me."

"Trust you to remember *that* part clearly."

He smiled at that. "You sang me a lullaby. I thought I was dying." Bemused, he let me go—though not by much, keeping one big arm around me as he sat up—and ran a hand over the healing pink skin of his side, then focused his gaze on Ami. "Princess Amelia. It's an honor to greet you. Forgive my discourtesy."

"I think, under the circumstances, you're forgiven." She cocked her head. "How did you know who I was so fast? I seriously doubt I look like any of my portraits at the moment."

"You look very like your sister." He pulled me against his side, kissing my temple. "Though somewhat less fierce."

"That was ever so," she replied. "This is Astar, currently winding up to cause a fuss, I suspect. My consort, Ash, lies there, sleeping off the healing."

"They arrived just in time," I put in. "Ash saved your life."

Harlan's visage darkened. "Raised me from the dead?"

"Not like that, no." When he only continued to frown, I framed his face in my hands. "Not like the Temple of Deyrr."

"How can you be sure? Neither of us knows their actual methods. Perhaps it's the same magic."

He had a point. I glanced at Ami and she shrugged. "No idea what you're talking about. It's your turn to fill me in anyway." She widened her eyes at my intimate entwinement with the mercenary and fluttered her long lashes, a deliberate parody of her former, more flirtatious self. "*So* much has happened."

I grimaced at her but refused to be self-conscious. Instead I turned back to Harlan and kissed him. "All that matters to me is that you're alive. Why don't you wash the blood off and have something to eat. Then we'll be on the move."

He wasn't completely mollified, but nodded, grimacing at the dried blood that saturated his trousers. Standing, he stretched, joints popping, muscles flexing.

"Here." Ami offered him the canteens and a glorious smile. "Refill these while you're at it."

"Yes, Your Highness." He took them, seeming amused by her.

"No 'highness' for me," she corrected. "Just 'princess,' or better, stick with Ami."

His gaze flicked to me with an ironic and intimate smile, reminding me how I hadn't let him call me by name. It made me feel better, to see some of his concern dissipate. Grabbing one of our packs for fresh clothes, he strode down to the stream.

Ami watched after him, speculative and admiring, then gave me an unabashed grin and lifted one shoulder. "I'm impressed, Essla. I never imagined there could be someone who could not only stand up to you, but give back as good as you dish out. Now, quick, before he comes back—tell me how this happened."

"I'm not gossiping about my love life with you."

"Yes, you are. You *owe* me for all those years of zero interest in anyone at all. I was starting to think there was something wrong with you and—What? What did I say?"

"Nothing." I shook off the tinge of sick at her words. I was over all that. "Here's the story in a nutshell."

Harlan returned before I entirely finished, falling on the food Ami offered with gusto. He took Astar and played with him while he ate, the baby cradled in the nest of his lap, absurdly tiny in comparison and wildly happy to be there. Ami and I packed up the horses as I finished the tale. Leaving out a number of more private details.

"How is it you've not told all this yet?" Harlan glanced at the high angle of the sun.

"I had to hear Ami's story first."

"And our auntie Essla has only been awake a short time herself," Ami added, taking Astar with an oof and bundling him back into his carry pack.

"Essla?" Harlan grinned at me, unabashed by my glare.

"Ami's baby name for me," I told him, turning the reproving look on her, with a similar lack of success. "She seems to have reverted to infancy just because she has her own now. Ready to load up?"

"Why have you only recently awakened?" His face had settled into that implacable look, and he scanned me. "You were injured, too, and you didn't say. Come here and let me see."

"Barely at all."

"Lost buckets of blood," Ami cheerfully spoke over me. "A couple of times I couldn't find her pulse. I was frankly terrified."

"You don't sound terrified," I said, intensifying the warning look, which she continued to blithely ignore, cooing at Astar.

"You didn't die and I'm making a practice of counting the blessings of the moment. But your man should know what you gave up for him. What a near thing it was that you had Ash heal him instead of you." She gave Harlan an angelic smile that fooled no one. "So he'll appreciate you."

Harlan stood and went to his stallion, unstrapping one of the packs again. He grabbed one of the canteens, took my hand, and tugged me away. "We need to discuss this privately."

"I'll be right here," Ami called after us, well pleased with herself. I would deal with her later.

"We need to get going," I protested. "We've lost too much time as it is."

He didn't answer right away, but his hand stayed vised on mine. When he stopped just inside the shadows of the forest and turned to face me, his pale eyes slow burning in rare anger. "Undress."

"What?"

"You heard me. Disrobe so I may tend your wounds."

"They're not that bad, and—"

"Then it won't take long. Undress yourself or I'll do it for you."

I put my hands on my hips. "I'd like to see you try."

"You're so pale you're transparent," he snapped. "I'm kicking myself for not seeing it before."

"You had other things on your mind," I pointed out in a dry tone.

"What did you give up—besides being healed yourself?"

I returned his scowl. "Nothing you need be concerned about."

"I do need to. You had no right. No right at all to put yourself in jeopardy for me."

"Oh, it only goes in one direction?"

"Yes." He wrapped his big hands in my shirt. "Because you're more important than I am. Now, the very least you can do is let me tend to you. Do I rip this off or will you undress?"

"Danu!" I broke his hold with a sharp maneuver. One that I did not want to admit lagged several beats behind my usual speed and made my head swim, then throb. "I'll undress. But let's make this snappy. We have ground to cover. Ami took care of the worst of it."

He didn't reply to that, silently retrieving supplies from his bag. I leaned against a tree to get my boots off. Fortunately for his continued good health, he did not comment when I got a little dizzy and had to sit, just gave me that accusing stare.

Heaving a sigh, he sat beside me, unwrapping Ami's bandages and running his hands lightly over my skin as he examined my many bites, lacerations, scrapes, and purpling bruises. "This is the worst one?" He prodded the wound on my thigh and I steeled myself not to wince.

"Yeah, pretty much. I think that's the one that really bled."

"No surprise. Nicked the artery." He poured some liquid over it, raising brows when I hissed at the sting. "Not so cocky now?"

I clenched my teeth. "Finish it."

Without further comment, he doctored my other open injuries, then worked in some sort of liniment around them, massaging it into my aching muscles. The man had magic hands—as he knew and used from the beginning to seduce me, I realized—and gradually my body loosened, my eyes closing of their own will, though I fought to stay alert.

"Swallow this."

I opened my eyes and wrinkled my nose at the open bottle he offered. "What is it?"

"It will help replenish your blood."

"You should have some, then."

"No." His voice had that deep, eerily calm tone it did when he was supremely pissed. "You're going to drink it all. Do it, Ursula."

"Danu, you're bossy all of a sudden." I snatched the bottle, hardened my stomach because the stuff smelled truly awful, and chugged it. "You know, if we're going to stay together, you're going to have to accept that I'm a warrior and I'll get hurt from time to time."

"I accept that about you. I love that about you." He didn't seem any less angry. "But I'll not let you sacrifice yourself for me. You think it's your duty to take care of everyone else, no matter what it costs you. Not with me. Don't ever think you have to pretend to be strong for me or hide your injuries. If we're to stay together"—he paused, for some reason amused to throw my words back at me—"then you will let me take care of you. I insist on it."

"Look, mercenary, you nearly died. You thrice-damned needed me to take care of you. I don't care if it wounds your pride."

He sighed, ran his hands over me, and tugged me onto his lap, enfolding me in the protection of his body. "It's not pride, precious Essla. I'd just far rather die than lose you."

"Well . . ." I trailed off, unutterably moved, remembering the dark despair of the night before. "I can understand that. When I thought you were dead, I wasn't sure how I could go on without you."

"I'm sorry." His voice muffled against my hair. "I'm sorry to put you through that."

"As well you should be. Don't let it happen again. I'm holding you to that command."

"I hear and obey." He touched the backs of his fingers to his forehead in the *Elskastholrr*, eyes grave. Now that I knew what it meant, the gesture drove into my heart that much more, laying me open so that I had to look away.

"Can I get dressed?"

Laughing, he let me go. "Much as I love to see you naked, it's probably for the best."

We were able to get Ash onto his horse without waking him by the simple expedient of Harlan lifting him into the saddle. Ami took up the other end of a long length of string tied to his wrist, to wake him should we need him, she explained.

"He sleeps through a strange warrior putting him on his horse, but a bit of string on his wrist will wake him?" Sounded highly dubious to me.

"You'd be surprised," Ami replied, in a wry tone she'd adopted along with her newfound steel. She checked him one last time with such tender regard and care that it surprised me. The terribly scarred, hard-edged man was the last I'd have expected her to choose, the total opposite of everything Hugh had been. But perhaps that explained it all right there.

We rode hard and fast for a while, following Ami's direction this time. She'd come to know the area quite well during their days of chasing Terin in circles. We paused fairly often, however, usually when Astar began fussing. Ami tersely informed me she had zero intention of nursing at a gallop and she'd latch the baby onto my nipple if I wanted to know how it felt. Harlan took advantage of the breaks to check my injuries and make me rest.

"I can't imagine how I managed to rest and heal before you came along," I grumped at him.

"Me neither," he retorted. "It's a wonder to me that you weren't in worse condition when I met you than you were."

Traveling in those frequent short bursts did have the advantage of letting us continue riding through the night, which meant we made the beach by dawn and—to my considerable relief— quite a bit farther south than where we'd turned inland a few days before. So far as I could tell, as the morning had dawned moist and foggy, obscuring most of the landmarks. I'd know more once it burned off, but perhaps we could make the cliff city within half a day. Andi had been in Terin's hands for far too long, and it ate at me, what we'd find when we caught up to them.

"They won't hurt her," Harlan said, changing the dressing on my thigh. The wound looked considerably better, which at least got him off my back some. "Terin needs her."

"That's what I keep telling myself about Stella." Ami looked down at a happily nursing Astar, her face showing the strain and worry she'd hidden under the saucy attitude. "I wonder if she'll even know me when I finally have her again."

"Of course she will. She nursed from you before we lost her. You're her mother. She'll know that."

Ami shrugged a little, giving me a sad smile. "I hope so."

I studied Ash, still asleep. "Should we wake him? Seems like he should have food and water."

"No, he wouldn't thank us for that." Ami shook her head at some memory. "I did that once and he nearly took my head off. He should wake soon, though, and then he'll be hungry and thirsty."

"I only nearly took your head off because I figured you for a bratty spoiled princess," Ash spoke up, opening his eyes, the green of them bright in his corrugated face. He stretched and climbed off the horse, surveying the landscape with the keen gaze of a seasoned fighter, then nodded at me. "Your Highness. Good to see you survived without my help."

"A near thing." Harlan stood and greeted Ash. "You should have healed Her Highness first, or instead."

Ash sized him up in turn. "You were in no condition to give orders and she was."

"True." He bowed. "Then take my thanks. I owe you for my life."

Ash's light green eyes flashed as they flicked to me and away again. "No you don't. The debt lies elsewhere."

Harlan's jaw firmed, but he simply nodded to Ash and returned to me, finishing the bandage and massaging the thigh muscle that had stiffened during the ride. "We shall discuss this further," he said under his breath to me.

I didn't reply. He could think what he liked. My business was my own. I'd made the agreement in extremity, yes, but I wouldn't go back and change it, even if I could.

Ash was wolfing down some food—another good reason we headed back toward the cliff city, as our supplies were growing thin—when I caught an unusual movement in the water. Large animals cutting through the swells, sleek black hides shining through the mist. "Heads up," I said softly, gratified that both men came on instant alert, flanking me as I stood. The Star in the hilt of my sword grew hotter as Ami moved up behind and to the side of me, squinting out at the water as she quickly strapped Astar into his carry pack on her chest.

"Stay behind us," I told her.

"No argument there," she muttered, but she also drew her dagger, her soft beauty sharpening with a ferocious edge.

The animal shapes disappeared and several Tala emerged from the water, standing up as if birthed from the waves. The woman in the lead, as tall as I and rangy with it, raised empty hands. "Cousins!" she called out. "Thank Moranu you're safe. We've been looking for you."

34

If the Tala woman thought we'd relax our guard at that, she was mistaken. Her cheerful smile, however, did not wane. Stopping well out of range, she bowed. "The fearsome woman with the sword must be Her Highness Ursula and the mother tiger is Princess Amelia. I'm your cousin Zynda. We've come to help."

"It would have been nice to have this help you offer back when we were beset by Terin's company and nearly killed," I commented.

Her smile dimmed considerably. "Moranu," she swore, taking in my bandaged thigh, visible below the pants I'd cut off to make Harlan's doctoring easier. And less invasive. "You're wounded. Are they still about?"

"I think we killed all the ones within reach. We haven't been bothered again. Until now."

"If you think to lump us with Terin and his ilk, think again. We"—she gestured to the several men and women standing in their own V formation behind her—"are loyal to Queen Andromeda."

"And King Rayfe?"

She grinned, not in the least bothered by my icy tone. "Him, too. But the women of Salena's line share a special bond. Beyond that, our family tends to stick together. We've long regretted not knowing Salena's daughters and it's a relief to find you well."

"Don't relax too much. Queen Andromeda is Terin's captive." I watched her closely as I said the words, looking for culpability or prior knowledge.

Instead she turned grim. "And King Rayfe?"

"Went after them. There's no word?"

She shook her head. "We thought they must be with you still, as they had not returned. What of the royal guard?"

"Dead, missing, or changed loyalties," I replied. "We were encircled without warning."

"Zyr, Chalo," she said without turning her head, and a man and woman stepped forward. They resembled Zynda, all with the long and wild black hair of the Tala, but with more deep red in it, like Andi's, their eyes a blue so dark it nearly matched her storm gray. Cousins. We had cousins. "Check out the situation, would you?" Zynda asked.

They nodded. The man, Zyr, it seemed, smiled at me and Ami. "I hope we get to meet again, Cousins." And he flashed into the shape of a large, sleek dog, as did the other woman. Both took off with lightning speed, following back on our trail.

"Weren't they some sort of water animals just now?"

"Seals, yes. Most of our family boast several forms. Everyone in this group does, which is how I chose, for best advantage." She hesitated, as if broaching a delicate subject. "You and Princess Amelia . . . cannot?"

Behind me, Ami snorted with amusement. In that, she and I understood each other. We were happy for Andi, finding her place and her magic, but neither of us felt the lack. "No, none of the four of us can. So if we're going to the Heart of Annfwn, it won't be by swimming."

Zynda's face darkened. "Why do you think that's where they've gone?"

"Terin said as much. I believe they planned to take Andi and the infant Princess Stella there."

She scrubbed her hands through her long hair, wringing it out with a long breath of resignation. "Ah, Terin. You fool."

It seemed mete to accept the truce they offered, though Harlan and Ash both kept a wary eye on our new companions. After introductions, our Tala cousins changed into horses, to better keep pace with us in our race back to the cliff city. Nobody seemed to know—or, if they did, would not say—where the Heart of Annfwn was. If it could be reached only by a shape-shifter that could take multiple forms, then it must be in an environment survivable only by certain animals, not by humans. Which meant high in the air or deep in the water.

Scanning the warm, calm sea, aquamarine again under the bright midday sun, I figured water for it. Probably deep water, since different sorts of fish lived at various depths. That's how I would hide something from shape-shifters, anyway.

Unfortunately, it would also render me and my blade worthless to Andi. The frustration ground at me, so much so that when Ami insisted on a pause to tend Astar, I growled at Harlan's attempt to make me rest and chose to pace instead. Zynda had sent several of the cousins ahead for news and had shifted to talk with one who'd just returned in bird form. I wanted to hear for myself, except that they spoke in the Tala language. I'd have to wait for the translation, which didn't ease my annoyance.

Harlan folded his arms, positioning himself to keep an eye on both me and the cousins. Ash had escorted Ami behind a stand of palm trees for a bit of privacy to nurse. "We could ride ahead," he suggested. "Leave your cousins to guard Princess Amelia."

"No." I glanced in Ami's direction, catching the bright glint of her hair.

"You don't trust them?"

"Not particularly." I sighed. "But it's not that. It's only that we keep getting separated and I have a bad feeling about . . ." I trailed off when he grinned at me. "Don't give me that. I'm not thinking I'm the only one who can protect her."

"Which you're not. She survived without you to look out for her."

"Nearly didn't. Terin could have killed her as he tried to kill me. Likely planned to after he raped her. When I think of her—" Well, clearly I couldn't even say it out loud, because my voice cracked.

Fortunately Harlan, though his face showed his compassion for me, did not try to comfort me. I would have had a difficult time maintaining composure if he had. "Then we'll be patient and keep this pace." He said it as a reminder that my frustration would bear no fruit.

Zynda approached just then. "No news," she said.

"It took that long to convey that?"

She smiled in her easy way. The Tala in general seemed remarkably difficult to needle. "It was an extensive list of all the ways in which there is no news."

"Delightful."

"So here's the thing." Zynda sobered. "I've been mulling it over. So far as I know—which is more than most do, as we of Salena's line guard this information carefully—Queen Andromeda is the only one who can enter the Heart. It's a secret passed from mother to daughter. I don't know how Salena could have guided her, however, having passed from this world so long before Andromeda returned to Annfwn."

I did, though. The doll. Secrets and messages. "Can Andi take anyone else into it?"

"I don't think so. Family lore said that each girl had to find her own way. Sort of a test. I don't think she *could* take Terin or Princess Stella into it."

"Does Terin know that?"

"On the unlikely side of possible."

"So he might try to use Stella as a form of blackmail. Send

Andi into the Heart with instructions to do something or other. But Terin's company is much weakened, unless he has greater resources than we know."

"King Rayfe is a difficult enemy, especially where his queen is concerned. He's likely nibbling at their guard from the outside and Andromeda no doubt making it difficult from within."

"They have to be holed up somewhere."

"Agreed."

How to find them? I rubbed my thumb over the Star of Annfwn, feeling it heat, and looked over to see Ami approaching.

Danu take me. How dense was my skull?

To keep Ami the same distance from me, I made her mount up on my stallion, which didn't thrill her. I had to give her credit; when I took her aside and explained the plan, she firmed her chin and agreed. Maybe she clutched my waist a bit too hard, sitting behind me. Still, the war-horse tended to jump around quite a bit more than she was used to, and I hardly blamed her.

While the others watched with bemused curiosity, we started triangulating by riding up the beach, then down again. Then into the sea up to the stallion's hocks, then well into the dunes. With us so close together, the Star heated quite warm. Had it been less than blazing noon, I had no doubt we'd see it glowing, as it had when Ami tended my wounds. However, that left little room for it to heat even more if we drew near to Andi. And how close would we have to get to her before we noticed an effect?

"I'm sure it's warmer this direction," Ami insisted, on the point closest to the cliff city.

"Are you sure that's not just because you've had your hand on it?"

She poked me in the ribs with a surprisingly pointy finger.

"Ow."

"Shut up—that didn't hurt. Give me some credit here. I'm only touching it when you get to the far point in each direction."

"Fine, fine. It's more than we had before." Next I took us on an arcing line from that point into the water and back to the dunes. "Anything?"

"Go back a bit."

Obligingly, I did. She pointed at a diagonal, south and inland. I gestured to the others, who'd mounted up and waited. The stallion lunged into a full-out run at my signal, making Ami squeal and hold so tight I nearly reminded her of my cracked ribs. We'd already argued once about having Ash heal me. I had flatly refused, saying we needed Ash as an alert fighter more than I needed having my bruises removed.

I did not want to say out loud that I wanted him at full power in case Andi, Stella, or even Rayfe needed his skills.

If no one else had considered that possibility, then they didn't need to worry also.

Harlan likely had thought of it, because he didn't argue, giving me only a long, considering look. At least he only badgered me in private, for the most part.

The rest followed us without question. Not as if any of them had a better plan. Ami and I stopped periodically to trace an arc and refocus our direction. Our cousins remained in animal form, and Astar, strapped to Ash's chest, thankfully slept. We bore more south than inland, better luck there, as I had no wish to face a pitched battle with shape-shifters in the dense woods again.

After a time, the cliffs rose in the distance, towering white as we drew nearer, silhouetted against the sparkling sea from this angle. This end had been more sparsely inhabited, for whatever arcane reasoning the Tala might use. From the inland side, the cliffs appeared to have been carved out of the tougher rock of the foothills. Probably by eons of a much harsher surf than lapped the sands now.

Darker spots showed where caves riddled the surface. A fine place to hole up.

We'd paused to orient again, when a whistling sound warned me of attack from above. I ducked and the stallion responded as he'd been trained, leaping to the side and immediately zigzagging. Ami had a better seat than I'd credited her for, because she managed not to fall off.

The phalanx of flying lizards wheeled around and dove again, met midair by a shrieking black hawk I recognized as Rayfe. Zynda and another cousin changed into raptor forms to help. So, while I managed to slice up one that came too low, reeling from a taloned swipe from our side, those of us on the ground weren't much help.

The battle ended swiftly, with several of the lizards morphing back into staymachs. One, however, remained pinned to the ground by Rayfe, who shape-shifted back into human form with his sword at the creature's throat. Handy trick, that.

"Shift!" he demanded. "By command of your king and on pain of death, shift!"

The creature thrashed under his weight, spiny tail lashing, and attempted to bring up hind claws to rake at him, something I stopped by the simple expedient of putting my blade through the base of the tail. Rayfe spared me a glance. "Thank you. About time you caught up."

"So many sights to take in."

He laughed without humor and edged his sword into the lizard's throat, blood welling out. "I'm dead serious, Osme. I wouldn't shed a tear for your death."

The lizard form wavered, then blinked into an older woman, the one from the council. Rayfe's knees pinned her shoulders and my sword speared her lower abdomen. She bared teeth at him, said something in Tala.

"In Common Tongue—you wouldn't want to be discourteous to our guests."

"Kill me. I'd rather die than watch you destroy our people."

"I'm hoping your next words are to tell me that my queen and niece enjoy continued good health."

352 • Jeffe Kennedy

"What does it matter? All is lost."

"Tell me." Rayfe had the sound of a desperate man. Harlan must have heard it, too, for he stepped up and put a bootheel on the woman's hand, leaning his considerable weight into it.

"I've little experience with shape-shifters," he commented in that eerily neutral tone he could adopt. "If you break pieces off, do they grow back?

The woman snarled at him but grimaced, focused on Rayfe. "They're fine. Terin is a fool."

"No argument there. How many in the cave?"

She firmed her lips and turned her head to the side.

"The interesting thing about shape-shifters"—Ash clapped a hand on Harlan's shoulder, his raspy voice conversational—"is that you *can* cut pieces off, but they have to shift to regrow." He crouched and set a blade at the base of the woman's pinky. "And it hurts as much as it would you or I. Of course, if they bleed to death first, it's no good. Would you like to see?"

Harlan grinned, not nicely. "I would. In the interests of learning about this fascinating new culture."

"Ten!" the woman spat.

"Who?" Rayfe put the question to her as if she'd answered immediately, as if the attendant conversation hadn't occurred. "Give me names."

Seeming to give up, she collapsed into herself, listing names, her voice grating with despair.

"You're going to lead us to them," Rayfe said when she finished. "And we'll let you live. Else I'll give you to the Dasnarian to take home for a zoo pet."

"I'm loyal to Annfwn, to the true Tala ways. Salena was a traitor and now her get will destroy us all." Her dark blue gaze burned into mine. "Foul blood runs in your veins, viper."

"This loyalty of yours means nothing," Rayfe growled. "Don't you see? It's empty. Based on stories and songs and empty ideals. People are real."

"Principles are real. The rest is nothing." She gathered herself, shouted something in Tala, and convulsed, shifting into a shredded mass of flesh, blood, and bone.

Rayfe jumped up with some sort of Tala oath, then gazed down at her. The cousins moved restlessly, looking deeply unhappy, powerfully affected.

35

"She suicided?" I asked after a moment of silence.

Blue eyes flashing hot, Rayfe nodded. "Not a pleasant way to go, but a fast and effective one. Most of us live in fear of doing it by accident. To do so deliberately . . ."

"A martyr's death," I concluded. "Meant to shake you."

Zynda glanced at the other cousins. "King Rayfe. We shall take care of the remains. Ursula assessed it fairly. No one else should know of this."

"I'm grateful. And for your assistance at this dire time."

"You might have invited us to do so." Zynda tilted her head meaningfully.

"I have enough accusations of favoritism to manage without crying to Salena's family for help." Rayfe looked to me. "How did you find us?"

Zynda flicked a glance at me. "We followed a star."

He shook his head and sighed. "All right. They're up in there somewhere. I can't sniff them out. Even now"—his gaze scanned the cliff riddled with holes from castle-sized to minute—"I'm not exactly sure which they're in."

"We may not be wizards and shape-shifters, but we have our

methods. We can find them." I glanced over my shoulder at Ami, who sat with her back to us, playing with a fussing Astar. We left the cousins to their gruesome clean-up task. Putting an arm around Ami, Ash sat beside her, and she leaned into him. I stopped to clean my sword, giving them a moment.

"Is she all right?" Rayfe inquired quietly.

"Yes." I exchanged glances with Harlan, giving him a nod of assurance, though I doubted he needed it. "Of us three, Ami has experienced the least of the crueler aspects of conflict. But she's got steel. She would not quibble with anything we do to retrieve Andi and Stella. Just don't ask her to watch."

He nodded in understanding, gaze going back to the cliffs, seething with an impatience I understood well. And yet . . . "If we get to them, do we have the numbers to overpower Terin's group swiftly?"

Rayfe glared at me. "Do you suggest leaving my queen in peril a moment longer than necessary?"

I returned the stare, evenly. "If delaying allows us to muster greater forces, yes. We can keep them pinned. They're not going anywhere and they won't hurt their hostages as long as they have hope. Think about this, King Rayfe. This is end game for them. If all is lost for their objective"—I gestured in the direction of the suicided councilor—"what's to stop Terin from killing Andi and Stella out of sheer spite? Why not strike at our hearts that way?"

Rayfe scrubbed his hands through his hair and I saw clearly the shadows of exhaustion in his face, the way fear and worry had eaten at him. Had he slept at all since Andi was taken? Likely not if he'd been focused on not losing her.

Being distracted or exhausted can lead to fatal errors.

"We have them pinned," I repeated. "They know it or they wouldn't have risked that attack. I'm hungry and I need to rest. Captain Harlan, would you ask Zynda to assign a couple of the cousins to keep watch for movement?" He gave me the *El-skastholrr* salute, with a flicker in his eyes that showed he knew and approved of what I was doing. "Ami takes forever to feed that baby," I told Rayfe. "Why don't you grab ten minutes of shut-eye? Then we'll formulate our strategy."

His face hardened and he opened his mouth to argue. I stopped him with a hand on his shoulder. "King Rayfe. You're no good to her if you're not sharp. Take a few minutes. We're here to help now."

Rayfe narrowed his eyes at me, then sat bonelessly, head propped on a log. "Andi said you always took care of everyone, whether they wanted it or not. Ten minutes." And he was out faster than Astar at his mother's breast.

"Well done," Harlan murmured as I stepped up to his side, keeping his keen gaze on the cliffside.

"Any sign of movement?"

"No, and there won't be. Terin will figure his best strategy is to stay hunkered down and try to pick us off when possible. They don't know you can use the Star to triangulate on Andi, so they think they have time."

"Figured that out, did you?"

He didn't take his eyes off the cliff, but his lips curved in satisfaction. "It heats up the more you three are in proximity to each other?"

"So it seems. I'm not sure what to make of that."

"I have no doubt you'll make something of it eventually."

"Your faith in me is sometimes alarming."

His smile twitched. "I know. Take your own advice and rest. You're no good to them if you're not sharp."

"Very funny." But my thigh throbbed and some of the deeper bruises ached, so I put my back against a tree and closed my eyes, letting my mind drift over the problem.

When we wakened him several hours later to participate in a strategy session while the cousins kept watch, Rayfe looked like he would cheerfully murder me. At least he looked capable of it now, so the lie had been worth it.

"The more I think about it, the more I figure Osme had to have lied about the number of Tala in the cave."

He cocked his head. "Possibly. Though she knew she'd suffer when we discovered it."

"Not if she'd already resolved to suicide," I pointed out. "Your threat about Dasnarian zoos put her over the edge."

Grimly he nodded a head at Harlan. "A tale we use to frighten our children with. I have no idea if it's true at all. The idea of animals in cages is appalling to us."

Harlan lifted a shoulder. "So far as I know, none of them have alternate human selves. If they do, I'm sure someone would have noted it."

I smothered a chuckle though Rayfe seemed completely unamused. I'd forgive him a lack of sense of humor, given the circumstances. "Ami and I can get close and pinpoint Andi's location, but what's to prevent Terin from snatching Stella and running?"

"Or from him killing them both?" Zynda inserted, face grave. "You mentioned that before and it's a good point."

Yes, but I'd thought better of mentioning it again.

"Stealth is better, if we can do it. Or convince him somehow that he's better off on the move than waiting us out. Can he be waiting on something? I make him as out of options at this point. In my experience, a cornered beast is a dangerous one."

Rayfe, with his glittering gaze and barely restrained violence, only proved the point. "He can't have much support left, but he's also a fanatic. He won't give up, though his group has always been in the minority."

"Zynda, you come at this from another angle—do you agree?"

My cousin cast Rayfe a cautious glance and opened her mouth.

"I know my people, Your Highness," Rayfe interrupted with a growl, sounding more like a wolf than ever.

"Do you? Did you suspect Osme before this?"

His jaw clenched over the bitterness of that betrayal, as I'd suspected.

"King Rayfe." I tried to sound gentle. "We never expect the strike from within. That's why coups of this sort can be devastatingly effective. I've studied enough of them. You're not to be blamed for trusting the people who should have been trustworthy, but take advantage now of the objective eyes and ears available to you."

"You can dispense with calling me by my title, Ursula," he ground out. "And you may be absolutely correct. Zynda?"

Zynda leaned back on one elbow, unperturbed by her king's foul humor. But then, Rayfe, for all his temper and arrogance, did not stand on much ceremony. A different style altogether from Uorsin's. Of course—a different people and a much smaller kingdom to rule. Still, interesting.

"The Tala are much like any other people," Zynda offered, as if in direct contradiction to my thoughts. "We, of Salena's family, believe Salena's daughter should be queen. Andromeda has our full support, always."

"A comfort," Rayfe remarked.

Zynda smiled easily. "As do her sisters. However, the Tala are also a superstitious people, much ruled by our animal natures. Instinctively, we believe the strongest should rule. The test that made you king is an ongoing one, Rayfe. Winning that tournament is no sinecure. You must continue to be the strongest, the cleverest, the most determined, the one most favored by Moranu, to keep your throne."

"What are you saying, Zynda?" I asked.

She held my gaze, both grimly serious and mischievous, making me wonder what animal she claimed as closest to her heart. "That the people wait and see. If Rayfe cannot rescue his queen from the likes of Terin, he is not fit to lead."

"A harsh judgment to live under."

"Are the Twelve so different, Cousin?" She shook her head

slightly. "I think not. The ruler who fails his people deserves to lose his throne."

"All three goddesses favor this effort," Ami spoke up. "Glorianna, Danu, Moranu—they work hand in hand. Andi and Stella belong with us. We just have to find the right path."

Ash laughed soundlessly under his breath and Ami elbowed him. "The goddesses work in mysterious ways. Don't forget that Glorianna granted you your greatest wish, no matter how circuitously it came about."

He looked down at her lovely face, her curls catching the waning light and her twilight eyes the same shade as the sky—and something of him went hungry as he brushed the ends of her shorn hair.

"It will grow back," she told him softly.

"I know. But I don't like the idea of you going up there, Ami."

"My daughter. My sister." She shrugged. "I can't be someone I like and not do it."

"I agree," I said, though she hadn't explicitly stated what I had in mind. "Once night falls, Ami and I will scout and get a fix on Andi's position. Stealth is the name of the game. They'll post watch, no doubt"— I glanced at Rayfe, who nodded—"but they have to be growing weary also. Osme and her trained staymachs haven't returned to them. They have to suspect we killed the guard Terin left to slaughter Harlan and me. They're possibly running out of supplies. They were moving fast and for quite some time, so they can't have carried much. Stella would need to be fed. Even with a wet nurse, they'll have to be getting nervous.

"We'll appear to leave. Zynda—appoint your best inconspicuous shifter to keep an eye for movement. If they're watching us, they've noted that we've disagreed. Rayfe—keep that angry, just-under-boiling-with-violence demeanor. You'll leave with us, unwillingly. Once we have distance, everyone who can shift picks their most unobtrusive form. Ami and I will go on foot, Ash with us to guard our backs. Captain Harlan—I'm asking you to stay back with Astar."

If I thought he'd argue the point, I was mistaken. He accepted the order with a nod. To my surprise, they all did. Even Rayfe. A crack team here, not unlike working with my Hawks. We all stood and Rayfe darkened his scowl. "I don't like it," he shouted. "Coming here with your high-handed ways, Uorsin's heir. My people won't follow you."

I stared him down coolly, my respect for him growing. "They don't have to follow, Rayfe of the Tala. They just have to get out of my way."

Once full dark fell, Ash, Ami, and I changed into the darkest clothes we had with us, then smeared our skin with mud to eliminate the pale gleam of it.

"I thought I'd hear complaints about this," I teased her.

"Oh, no. Mud is excellent to cleanse and purify the complexion," she replied easily. "Though yours is beyond such help. A pity."

She helped Harlan strap Astar onto his wide chest. We'd had to add to the length of the straps, to accommodate his girth. He should have looked absurd, swinging his massive sword to check that nothing interfered with his arc of movement, the comparatively tiny wide-eyed baby peering up at him, but he managed to look . . . heroic. He returned my gaze with a long, somber stare. Then touched the backs of his fingers to his forehead. "Danu shine her light on you, my fierce hawk. We shall await your return."

Rayfe frowned. "We should leave a man or two with you, for backup."

"You need every body you can for this mission," Harlan replied. "I will be fine. Nothing will get through me to harm the babe."

Though I knew him to be far from invulnerable, in that moment he looked it. "All in the contract to protect the royal family?" I teased him.

"As I've always promised you," he returned.

"Captain Harlan," Ami said, darting a glance at me and away. "Should we not return for some reason, don't take Astar to Ordnung."

"Ami—"

She held up a hand to cut me off. "I'm asking this of Harlan, though he owes me nothing."

"On the contrary, beyond the contract that covers you also, I owe you and your consort my life. Where would you have me take him, Princess?"

"There's a manse near Windroven, at Lianore. Take him to Lady Veronica. And if it's not safe there, then anywhere but Ordnung."

"He can stay in Annfwn, Amelia," Rayfe supplied, in a quiet voice.

She shook her head. "I'll leave it up to Captain Harlan, but if we don't return, that might not be best for him, either."

"You have my word," Harlan told her. "I give it to you as I would to Ursula."

"Thank you." She pressed a kiss to Astar's brow, then—as if on impulse—stood on tiptoe to kiss Harlan's cheek and turned quickly away. Ash brushed the tears from her cheeks, a surprisingly soft expression on his craggy face.

"Let's move out," I said, and everyone took their positions. I stepped to go, then looked back at Harlan. Danu take it. Closing the distance between us in a few strides, I kissed him long and hard, as best as I could without crushing Astar, not caring—very much—that we had an audience. "Danu keep *you*," I told him. "And woe to you if you're not hale and hearty when we return. For we will be successful."

"I do not doubt it." He cupped my head and kissed me with exquisite gentleness. "Take care of my heart, for it goes with you."

Moving in stealth goes slowly.

Easier to do solo, too, rather than hand in hand as Ami and I did. We'd experimented while waiting for nightfall and found that as long as we were in physical contact, the Star's heat remained constant. I'd had to wrap the pommel of my sword in a black silk scarf to dim the shine of the jewel, a fanciful look that Uorsin would have scorned, but there it was.

Ami proved decent at going quietly, her lithe dancer's grace making up for lack of experience. As for Ash, he moved so silently I had to stop myself from constantly checking over my shoulder to make sure he stayed with us. All the rest had taken animal form and melted into the night, eerily leaving us to feel like the only humans alive under the vast and brilliant wheel of Danu's stars.

Once we reached the cliff face, we kept to the shadows, testing each direction. The Star steadily heated under my hand until it grew burning hot, then cooled slightly. Retracing our steps, I stopped us at the point of greatest heat and we surveyed the sheer face above us. No surprise there that Terin would have picked the most difficult egress.

Word was, however, that he could take only the fox form, which meant there had to be a way to the cave for someone without wings. A snake slithered over my foot, nearly making me start. Thank Danu Ami had been looking up and didn't see it. The snake, possibly Zynda, wended a bit to the right, then up a path I hadn't seen in the dark. I let go of Ami's hand and moved hers to rest on the small of my back. She followed me up the path, Ash a knife-edged silhouette behind us. Something climbed up the cliff face and a raptor that shouldn't fly at night winged through the edge of my vision.

A baby's wail cut through the thick silence, and Ami's hands clutched convulsively on my waist as she made a small sound. She did well, for even my heart seized at it. The goddesses smiled on us indeed, for the cry came from a large cave mouth just to the left. Ash slid past us, ducking behind a rock that stood out from the cliff beside the entrance, becoming a shadow again, joined by other fluid black shapes.

I pressed a knife into Ami's hand, though she had her dagger ready, and signaled her to stay put. In the dimness, I could make out the circular prayer to Glorianna she drew in the air with her finger, which she bisected with Danu's blade and cut with Moranu's crescent. It might have been my imagination, but the Star seemed to burn hotter still.

Edging up behind Ash, I gave it a moment more, to make sure all our cohort had taken position. Then I pulled the scarf from the Star, letting it blaze bright.

36

The raptor, with a great cry, arrowed into the cave, and the rest of us stormed after.

As black as the bogs of Nemeth, the interior of the cave became an immediate tumult. Though I brandished my sword, the blazing Star my only light, I held off swinging at any animal that did not attack me first.

There were plenty of those.

Something like a boar crashed out of the shadows and into me, pinning me against the cave wall and painfully crushing my wounded thigh. With my left hand, I plunged a dagger into its eye, used that as a pivot to drive my sword through its heart.

With the boar's body as a barrier, I stayed close to the wall, willing my eyes to adjust, for the first time regretting I had no night-seeing beast to change into. The agony of my thigh coursed through my body, setting it singing with fighting fury.

Near me, Ash spun in a whirl of blades, nothing touching him. Rayfe could be any of the wolves, but I pegged him for one assailing a line of beasts forming a fanged and snarling wall across the cave. Beyond that lay my quarry, hiding behind his people, no doubt.

Don't think about him holding a blade to Andi's throat. Throttling tiny Stella, her infant body so soft and vulnerable. Only the objective.

I let myself dissolve into the mind of Danu, feeling and thinking nothing but the slice of my blades.

Defend, parry, attack, retreat, regroup.
Defend, parry, attack, retreat, regroup.
Defend, parry, attack, retreat, regroup.

I made my way forward, killing anything that attacked, dodging those that didn't. Dimly I became aware that Ash paced my progress on the other wall and two wolves guarded my back and flank.

A creature as big as a bear and fanged with it barreled out of the blackness, paw as big as my head narrowly missing my throat, claws raking the shoulder of my dagger arm as I barely ducked it. Far too fast, it swung again. Bringing up my sword, I impaled it, but the momentum carried me back, injured leg shouting with the warning of imminent collapse. I struggled against the massive weight, briefly thinking of Harlan's wrestling exhibition. Perhaps he could teach me some tricks for such eventualities.

Hot blood ran down my sword, slicking my grip. Making my hand slip.

A large black cat attacked from behind. Andi, by the flare of the Star. With a feline scream, she laid open the bear's throat with razor claws. It fell, bearing me down, and I twisted, yanking my sword free and, by the simple expedient of stomping down and leaping, cleared the final line of defense.

Terin, as wild-eyed as a cornered animal, crouched in the corner, a wailing Stella in his arms, blade held against her small body as I'd imagined far too many times.

"Stay back," he panted. "I'll kill her."

"And then what, Uncle?" I slowed my advance but did not stop. "A life—one with strong Tala blood—will be wasted. Then I'll kill you and you'll pass with all these others who died for nothing."

"You'll kill me anyway."

"Not necessarily," Rayfe growled beside me, flowing from wolf to man but sounding bestial enough to stand my hair on end. "There are other punishments for traitors. We can put you over the border in your animal form and you'll never be able to cross back. Never be a man again."

Terin laughed, the bark of a fox behind the sound. "You call me a traitor? Look to Salena and her get for that." His eyes, reflecting the glow of the Star, slid from me to my side, where Andi drew close. "We are the loyal ones. Loyal to Annfwn and all it stands for. Salena betrayed us to the outside, trapped our people there for tens of years, bereft of home. We should have killed her when she destroyed Tosin, stopped her then."

"Tosin killed himself," Andi said with gentle surety, Ash coming up beside her. Behind us, the battle sounds dropped off into the crippled silence of whimpers and the harsh breaths of recovering fighters.

"She left him no choice. A hard woman. She'd already decided to leave him, to have a child by another man. She drove the knife into his heart." His arms clenched on Stella and her fretful cries choked off. "This baby is ours. Blood price for Tosin."

"She is yours, Terin." I ignored Ash's glare, Rayfe's twitch. "Stella already belongs to Annfwn, as does Queen Andromeda. Salena paid your blood price with her life. No debt remains."

"She gave you the Star." Terin's gaze glittered on my sword and he focused on Andi. "And you have the Heart. The golden age of Annfwn has passed forever. Her borders will crumble, the magic die away. I failed. I'm sorry, Tosin." Tears tracked down his face, a gleaming trail. He looked down at the now quiet Stella. "This should have been your daughter."

"It's over now, Terin." I edged closer. "All the should-have-beens and could-have-beens. They're gone, but we live. All we can do is move forward. Make a better future for all our peoples."

"Give me the child, Uncle." Andi urged beside me. "Do not answer death with more death."

He made a harsh sound and stood, raising his chin in defiance, staring me down. "I see Salena in you. Heartless. Ruthless and without love for anyone. Go ahead, cut me down. Follow in the cold footsteps of your cruel mother."

Though I knew his words to be the taunting of the enemy in dire straits, I also tasted the truth of them. Not that I'd let that stop me. "Hand the baby over and your own people will see to whatever justice they decide."

"Kill me!" He screamed the words and, in his extremity, lost sight of Ash, who moved like a blur, knife flashing across Terin's throat and Stella falling to the stone floor.

Without thought, I dove, flying in a great leap to catch her in my hands, flipping to catch the babe across my body, letting my back hit hard on the rocks. Stella's renewed screams of fury sounded like sweet music and I lay there sending thanks to all the goddesses, trusting the others to dispatch Terin. Agony and gratitude feeling very much the same.

I let Ash carry the still wailing Stella out, needing a moment to recover my breath and strength anyway. We'd lost a number of the cousins from our side, and none of Terin's people remained alive. From the grim set of Rayfe's jaw, that was just as well.

Andi and another cousin shifted to horse form and carried Ash, Ami, and Stella back to our camp, a wolfish Rayfe pacing alongside as guard, along with several others. A few remaining cousins were too tired to risk shifting, so followed along with me on the long walk back through the early morning light.

Zynda shifted back to human, grimacing in relief as her minor wounds healed with the effort, then gave me a rueful smile. "How are you holding up, Cousin? We can rest a while before walking back. Sorry that none of us can be a horse for you."

"That's okay." Somehow riding a family member seemed uncanny and wrong. "Better for me to keep moving. Once I sit and the battle energy crashes, I'll stiffen up."

"Smart of you to bind a consort with magic hands, then."

I slid her a dark look, and she grinned in her mischievous way. "Don't look so mean," she continued. "The women of our family may be fearsome, but they're also generous of heart, mind, and body—as you clearly are. I hope you won't give Terin's words any weight."

So odd, to be considered part of a larger group, to share traits with a family besides Uorsin. "Did you—did you know my mother?" I asked.

She nodded. Then shrugged. "Barely. I was a girl when she left. And she was the Queen of the Tala, so it wasn't as if she came to the family celebrations or sat down with us at the beachside campfire. Still, I had more than a little hero worship for my famous auntie."

That made sense.

"To tell the truth, I'm surprised that you're not more, well, royal."

I raised an eyebrow at her and she gave me that unrepentant grin.

"You know, I figured, Uorsin's right hand, Heir to the Twelve Kingdoms, no animal forms—I always pictured you as more of an insane tyrant. Like your father."

"He's not a tyrant." Maybe it was letdown setting in from the fight, postbattle fatigue—I realized my slip too late.

"Isn't he? Maybe I'm wrong about him, too. So the tales of him executing anyone who stands in his way are false? The stories brought back from Tala who've escaped the prisons can be dire indeed, but those are hardly unbiased sources. And they say more than half the population is on the verge of starvation. I'm glad to hear it's not true—horrible to contemplate people living that way."

Anyone else I would have suspected of baiting me. Or exercising an agenda. Zynda, however, walked along and whistled a bright tune, as if we'd gone on a pleasant stroll instead of limping home from a pitched fight to rescue our own.

"I've always been interested to visit but also afraid to," she continued. "Maybe now that we're friends, I will. We are friends, aren't we?"

All so surreal, walking through the verdant meadow, the sky brightening as Glorianna's sun returned, fruit gleaming on the trees like jewels and the sea glinting in openings here and there. And this woman, much like me, though a few years senior, my cousin, asking to be my friend.

"Of course," I answered, though I had no idea how we'd go about that. *I see you with your subordinates, the people who turn a blind eye to what you suffer. I have not seen any friends.* It felt like years since Harlan had said that to me. Perhaps I needed to learn how to do this, too.

"Good." She smiled at me. "Gorgeous sunrise. It's going to be a lovely day."

"Aren't they all in Annfwn?"

"True enough, Cousin. It is paradise, after all."

They had a campfire going on the beach, with baskets of fish and shellfish steaming. In the aquamarine water, a seal-shaped cousin popped a head out of the swells to deliver a fish, dropping it neatly into Harlan's hands, who filled yet another basket. He'd doffed his weapons and shirt, standing knee-deep in the surf, tanned and glistening with sea spray.

Ami, sitting in the curve of Ash's arm, gave me a weepy smile, holding Stella to her breast, Astar on Ash's lap staring in fascination, reaching out for his sister with chubby hands and fighting Ash's restraining hold. Andi and Rayfe sat similarly together, on a log by the fire, deep in conversation. He had one hand wound in a long lock of her hair.

"The best part of getting to the party late is everyone else does the work," Zynda commented. "I'm taking a dip to wash off some of the battle ick. Join me?"

Harlan had caught sight of me and straightened, surveying me with that intent look that I knew measured my every scrape and contusion, taking note of my pronounced limp. I held up my palms in acknowledgment of my bruised and bloodied self and he crooked a finger at me in a come-hither.

"Never mind." Zynda laughed. "I see true love awaits."

I snorted at her but toed off my boots, rolled up my trousers, and unstrapped my ankle knives. I'd lost several and would need to replace them eventually. I could have kept the others, but after a moment's hesitation, I decided to ditch them all. I didn't care to carry any weapons at the moment. Leaving even my sword in the pile, I went to Harlan, wading into the gentle water. It burned into a few open cuts, but I ignored that, sliding gratefully under the sheltering arm he held out for me.

His lips brushed my right temple. "They said you weren't badly injured, but that's a lot of blood on your face and neck."

"No water to clean it off." I started to bend, to splash my face, but his arm tightened to stop me.

"Stay next to me a moment more," he murmured, then leaned his head against mine.

"Hard to stay behind?"

"Maybe the most difficult thing I've ever done," he agreed. "And I've faced some harrowing situations."

"I appreciated it. It meant a lot, knowing that I could count on you to protect Astar, no matter what else happened."

"I know. I'm glad for your trust in me. If you asked the same of me again, I'd do it, but . . ."

"But?"

"Please don't." His deep voice had gone so quiet I almost couldn't hear. "Just don't."

"I'm okay, really."

He let go of me to receive another fish, adding it to the bright silvered-rainbow pile in the basket. The seal opened its mouth in an oddly human smile, bobbed its head, then popped into one of the younger men, the smile staying in place as he transformed. Very odd.

"Enough?" Harlan held out the basket and the cousin nodded, giving me a little bow. "Come on, then, Essla. Wash off the blood and let me see for myself."

"That's going to scar," Ami pronounced, narrowing her eyes at a claw mark on my cheekbone, then delicately nibbling on a piece of hot fish.

"Better mine than your fair face," I returned equably. I sat in the sand, leaning against Harlan's knees as he worked the remaining strain out of my shoulders. "Or Stella's."

Ami gazed down at her daughter with lovestruck eyes. "Thank you, yes. Thanks to all of you." She gazed around the circle with damp eyes, able to look gorgeous weeping as only she could, and took Andi's hand. "I was so afraid this wouldn't end well. I owe all of you everything I am. I feared I'd never see her safe again. I'm so glad it's all over."

I waited for Andi to say it. She returned my questioning look with consideration, daring me to speak first.

Ami looked between us. "Oh, stop that, both of you, and put it out in the open."

"Don't play dumb," I retorted. "You know full well it doesn't end here. You have a decision to make."

"And you know that I think Stella needs to stay in Annfwn," Andi added.

"And you, Auntie Essla?" Ami gave me a surprisingly steely look from her pretty violet eyes. "You think I should bring them both to Ordnung. Uorsin's heir, and a spare, and a spare."

Harlan's hands on my neck stilled, and everyone fell silent, looking to me. "Oh, for Danu's sake, don't all look at me like I eat babies for breakfast."

"If only because you prefer to roast them for dinner," Ash said in a sorrowful tone.

"Very funny."

"Would you force me to bring them, Ursula?" Ami asked softly, pushing me. "The King commanded you to do so, didn't he? I mean, I appreciate you coming to help as you promised, but we also know where your primary loyalties lie and that you won't go against Uorsin's command. Would you take them from me?"

My gut chilled and I sat forward, shaking off Harlan's hands. "Did I take Astar from Windroven? Did I force you to go to Ordnung instead of going after Stella? How in the Twelve do you imagine I could force you—either of you—to do a thrice-damned thing?!"

Ami flinched a little and Andi gave me a hard look. "Don't go self-righteous on her. You know full well that you've always tried to control our lives, pushing us to do what you wanted."

That hurt. Probably because it was true. Which only made the anger rise. "Not what I wanted," I snapped. "What's best for you."

"And you're the one who decides that," Andi retorted.

"What? *You* were going to at some point?" Remembering the sense of helpless rage when Andi bungled into Rayfe and brought our father's fury down on her head, I flung a hand at him. "You think because things worked out that you weren't in terrible danger? And *you*," I said to Ami, who looked stricken, "you can sit there and ask whether I'd take your children away? When I've made myself into a traitor to the crown to help you? Everything I've done, I've done to protect you both, all these long years."

"Well, I don't know what there was to protect us from," Ami fired back.

"No. You don't. Which was precisely the point." I felt ill from the anger. Strung out from the battle still, throbbing from the scrapes and bruises, exhausted. "I need some space to breathe."

My body protested as I got to my feet, bringing my sword with me. The Star's heat diminished as I strode away from them, cooling as I withdrew.

Back to normal.

Sweat poured off me as I ran through the twelve forms. Sometimes doing them helped limber me up, increasing my energy and blood flow, burning away the restless tension. Danu's gift, to lift us up. This time, though, each movement dragged at my limbs, draining me, leaving me hollow and slow, my wounded thigh refusing to cooperate.

Finally I capitulated, stopping halfway through the seventh form to catch my breath. Then had to bend and put my hands on my knees, dropping my head to stop the dizziness that threatened to make me fall over.

"Done punishing yourself?"

I looked under my arm to where Harlan sat in the shade of a scrubby tree. "I'm not in the mood for company."

"No, you're in the mood to drive yourself into the ground. Doing a fine job of it, too."

"Leave me alone, mercenary."

"Never, Your Highness. Want some water?" He held out a canteen and I realized how parched I was. Accounted for the dizziness, no doubt.

"Danu, you're a stubborn man." But I went to sit in the shade, taking the canteen and guzzling the sweet, cool water gratefully.

"Every time you say that as if you're just discovering it. Kind of charming, really."

I huffed out a breath, shaking my head at him. "What's the buzz back at the campfire? Sorrow and consternation? More of how awful I am?"

"They don't know how much their accusations hurt you." He paused. "You need to tell them."

Envisioning myself telling my sisters they hurt my feelings, I laughed. It came out a little dry and bitter. "It's a temporary insult. Slipped under my guard because I'm tired."

"At least you admit to that part. No, I meant you need to tell them about your father and what he did to you."

The cool water turned to ice in my stomach, sharp edges digging in, slicing and drawing blood. "Absolutely not. Need I remind you of your promise not to reveal it?"

"I would not betray your trust." He said it mildly, but I'd annoyed him. Add him to the list of people pissed off at me. "But you do your sisters a disservice by not sharing this with them."

I scrubbed my hands over my scalp, my hair soaked with sweat and sticky with seawater. The cuts on my cheek throbbed in time with my leg and my whole body ached with exhaustion. If I'd had a hard time envisioning telling Andi and Ami my feelings were hurt, the prospect of speaking those words about what I'd done with our father . . . Impossible.

"That's never going to happen," I said. "It has nothing to do with the decisions I've made or have yet to make."

"Doesn't it?" Harlan kept that same patient tone but made it clear that he disagreed. "Here comes Ash."

Indeed Ash strode toward us, barefoot in the sand, in his calf-length black trousers and a billowing white shirt that covered his scars.

"I wonder what he wants."

"He's going to heal you now. Don't you dare protest." Harlan's pale eyes glittered. "I know you saved his resources in case anyone got seriously injured. Guess what? They're all safe and you're the worst of our injured, so you get the benefit of it. Don't fight me on this."

Ash stepped into the shade on the last of Harlan's words, green eyes alight with ironic humor. "Perhaps you should tie her to the tree. At least take the sword away."

"I'm fine, really, and—" I broke off at the set of Harlan's face.

"Your Highness." Ash crouched in front of me. "Your courage and resilience are never in question, but even you cannot heap injury upon injury and not suffer for it. We've already agreed to what you owe me. This will not add to it."

"Fine. But I'm not taking my clothes off for you."

He laughed soundlessly under his breath and sat cross-legged in front of me. "Not necessary."

"Shall I go?"

Ash glanced at Harlan with a sly smile. "You might want to stick around, Captain. You were passed out for your turn, so you didn't experience the rather significant side benefits of magical healing."

"Why do I not like the sound of that?" I'd wanted to hang on to being annoyed, but Ash's magic already flowed into me, with a tart snap of spring apples, refreshing, vital, and my voice came out softer. Almost immediately the aches ebbed and that core-deep exhaustion that dragged at me lessened. At the same time, a dreamy warmth overtook me, not unlike the kind stirred by Harlan's sweet, drugging kisses.

"You're more beat-up than you let on," Ash murmured, mostly to himself, looking through me the same way Andi did. "Quite a bit of internal bruising. Some bleeding. The wounded leg is severely strained. I'm amazed you stayed on your feet. You and Ami, both so thrice-damned determined not to show weakness."

"If you grew up with a father like Uorsin, you'd have learned that also." The words were out before I knew it, but neither man said anything. Maybe I'd only thought it. I floated on the sheer relief of freedom from both the pain and that sick sense of defeat that the after-battle crash always brings, no matter the outcome for your side. As the drained lethargy eased, a sparkling sense of well-being followed, burgeoning into the heat of arousal I'd felt only at Harlan's touch.

My eyes popped open to find Ash's bright-green ones gazing back with wry acknowledgment and more than a little amusement. Significant side benefits indeed. Cupping my cheek, much as Harlan liked to, he stroked a sizzling touch over the talon scores.

"You will have scars—only so much I can do there—but you'll still be prettier than I am." He took his hands away and slid them briskly together, his wry smile crooked by scar tissue. "That should take care of it. I'm off to take a nap, as was most everyone else when I left. You two should have an hour or two of privacy before we leave for Annfwn, to take the edge off that itch." He winked at me, an odd sight in his corrugated face, nodded at Harlan, and sauntered back up the beach.

37

≈

"What was that all about?" Harlan frowned after Ash.

I wrestled down the surging desire that filled me, remembering now how the other healing that fixed my cracked skull had paved the way to letting Harlan tumble me when we first entered Annfwn. Either the extent of healing made it stronger this time or Ash's particular brand of spring-sap magic had. I wouldn't have put it past him to add some extra zest on purpose, as a little payback for past insults. The only thing I knew for sure was that I wanted Harlan's hands on me with an urgency I might not be able to forestall.

Something I wasn't at all sure how to handle.

Harlan cupped my cheek, the newly healed skin there tingling at his touch, urging me to look at him. "Are you all right?"

Pressing my lips together against the moan that wanted to emerge, the need to slide myself against his body, feel him inside me, I nodded, carefully not meeting his gaze. His thumb rubbed over my bottom lip, sending a tremor through me I barely managed to squelch. I pulled back but his hand tightened on my chin. "What is it you don't want me to see?"

Knocking his hand away, I glared at him. "Ash and his thrice-damned side effects. The healing makes you hot for sex and he knew it. Don't worry—I'll work it off."

"Will you?" Face intent, hunger flaring in his gaze, he dragged me onto his lap, big hands roaming over me. "I'd like to be the one to assist with that."

I braced myself on his chest, stiff armed to hold myself back, though everything else in me longed to devour him whole. "I dislike feeling as if either of us has been manipulated into this."

His face softened. "Because of what went before?"

"What? No. I just don't like feeling . . . at the mercy of something else."

Irritation flickered into his eyes, mixing with the rising hunger. "There's nothing wrong with us wanting each other." He slid a hand up to cup my breast, thumb brushing the peaked nipple. Crumbling the last of my control. "Having each other."

With a sound of almost painful need that would have embarrassed me under other circumstances, I fell on him, voracious, devouring his hard mouth, my blood bursting into flame much like the dry driftwood of our campfire. He met me with a reflection of the same need, running hot and molten, demanding and giving at once. Hands everywhere on me, he seemed to brush my clothes away, mouth moving to each newly bared patch of skin, murmuring his Dasnarian love words.

I might forever associate the sound of his language with dark intimacy and raging desire.

Arching my back, I rode the glorious wave of sensation as he licked and kissed my bare breasts, lightly biting my nipples so I cried out, digging my nails into the hard bulge of his shoulders. He laid me back in the sand, mouth traveling down my body as he settled himself between my spread thighs.

I lifted my hips, dragging at him, urging him into me. He resisted, pushing my knees wider apart, sliding lower still, and nipping at the tendon where my inner thigh met my pelvis. "Not yet," he said against my skin. "I want to taste you. Is that all right?"

Gathering my fire-scattered thoughts, I realized what he meant to do. How exposed and open I was already and how I'd barely noticed. How much I wanted that, too. "Yes." My voice came out hoarse. "Oh, please, yes."

With a grunt of aroused agreement, he kissed the apex of my mons, then ran his tongue into my slick tissues. The sensation skewered me, so excruciatingly intense, I held still, unable to move. Part of me had still braced for the pain and the flesh memory of the nauseating sense of violation. Instead the voluptuous, deliciously keen pleasure spread through me like a balm.

"Danu," I breathed, both in prayer and gratitude. Above me, the midday sun shone down like a benediction, dappling through the green leaves, the sky beyond as aquamarine bright as the sea.

"Mmm. You taste like the sea, my Essla *cvan*." He licked me, then settled on the point of greatest pleasure, nibbling and sucking, holding my thighs wide as his agile lips and tongue worked me, as I began to thrash and writhe under the unbearable intensity.

"Oh, Harlan," I gasped, feeling helpless against this particular onslaught, on the point of a delicious surrender I couldn't resist, even had I wanted to.

"Oh, yes." He slid a thick finger inside me and pressed up, bearing down with his mouth at the same time.

And I came apart.

More intense than before, the climax took me brutally, raking me with claws that brought pure delight. My body might have broken into pieces if not held in place by Harlan's great hands, anchoring me to the earth. He didn't stop, driving me through it with mouth and touch and his sharp-edged, insistent Dasnarian words. I whimpered as the tension built again, harder, higher, and I shoved at his shoulders, close to begging.

"More," he demanded. As if triggered by it, I climaxed again, biting on the back of my hand so as not to scream out and alarm our companions. He gave me no rest, pushing me up again, relentless, fierce, as if starved for me.

"Harlan, please." I was in fact begging and didn't care, sobbing out his name and plucking at his shoulders to urge him into me. He relented, moving up my body, licking and biting on the way, devouring me bit by bit, then fastening his mouth on mine. Like the sea, indeed. He held his hips back from me, though, his cock hard and heavy against my thigh.

"I need a *lind*. Wait."

"I don't want to wait."

He laughed, a deep sound full of desire. "You also don't want me to get you with child."

"Would it be so bad?" I whispered, holding on to him, thinking of how he'd looked, broadsword in hand, staying behind with tiny Astar strapped to his chest.

Harlan went still, searching my face. "It would be miraculous," he answered. "But there's time to think of such things later."

"You said there won't be anyone else for you."

"True." He braced himself on an elbow and brushed my cheek, tender from the healing. "But you have more considerations than I do."

"Who am I kidding? There won't be anyone else for me. If only because you're the only one who'll ever put up with me."

"Don't say that. The world of men would cast themselves at your feet if they thought they stood a chance."

"I don't want anyone at my feet."

"That's where they went wrong." He kissed me, a sweet brush of his lips. "We don't have to decide now. I don't mind waiting."

"You never have minded that." I smiled at him, heart bursting with love. "But I've had a little too much of it myself."

"What about the line of succession?"

"Ami's covered that twice over. And—" I took a deep breath, let it go. "I'm tired of making decisions based on the throne. I want you, all of you. Your child, too, should we be so blessed."

"Essla," he whispered, eyes full of deep emotion, saying my name with that reverence that undid me. "Are you sure?"

"Who knows what tomorrow may bring?" I answered.

"My love." He kissed me long and deep and shifted back between my thighs. I lifted my hips and he sheathed himself in me, flesh to flesh, and we cried out as one at the sensation of joining. His big body contracted and shuddered, and he dropped his forehead against mine, breathing like a man fighting off a dozen attackers. "I'm not sure I can wait."

"Don't wait." I clenched my muscles around him and his hips flexed in reflexive response. His hand next to my head fisted, his body strained, and he broke. Losing all control, he pumped in and out of me, hard, fast, with such intensity that the wave broke over me, sending me into another climax, pummeled nearly insensible by the glorious strength and beauty of my mercenary.

We drifted awhile. Both unable to move. Lying in the dappled shade, our bodies slicked together. Barely able to draw breath under his weight, I nevertheless reveled in it, in the sensation of all his hot male skin touching me everywhere, inside and out.

He turned his head and pressed a kiss into the side of my throat. "I'm crushing you," he murmured, but he didn't move more than that.

"I like it."

He laughed. "Only you." Levering himself up onto an elbow, still joined to me, he studied my face. "Regrets?"

"Not a one. Except that we can't do it again."

"Can't we?" He smiled, lips curving with smug, so-masculine pride, and moved inside me.

I gasped, my heart shuddering into life, the deep pleasure radiating out. He moved in me slowly this time, almost lazily, watching my face, changing the angle of his thrusts until he found the one that sent me into that helpless state of desire. Beyond worrying about it now, I clung to him, giving myself over to it and to him, until my vision blurred and I fell over the edge yet again.

Andi and Ami were waiting for me when we returned, the same determined look on both their faces.

"Uh-oh," I muttered to Harlan.

"Maybe one day you'll listen to me," he replied under his breath. Then, louder: "I'll get the horses ready. Shall I carry one of the babies, Princess Amelia?"

"Thank you. I finished knitting another carryall for Stella, so now we have one for each."

"Since when do you knit that well?"

Ami widened her pretty violet eyes and fluttered her lashes, but the look in them had an edge. "I have acquired many new skills. I'm not a little girl anymore."

"Neither of us is," Andi inserted. "And the three of us are going to talk."

I scowled at Harlan, a short distance away, the sense of well-being curdling in my gut. "What did the mercenary tell you?"

"What should he have told us?" Andi countered. "You keep your own counsel well, Ursula, but it's time to share some of the burden. I have an idea what you think you were protecting us from."

"What?" Ami demanded. "Nobody ever tells me anything."

I folded my arms, daring Andi, who nodded, storm-cloud eyes darkening. "Uorsin brutalized her before all of court."

"One blow doesn't count as—"

"One that broke your nose and cracked your skull. But it wasn't just once, was it? I've been thinking back over the years, all those times that you sported breaks and bruises. From training, you always claimed," Andi continued.

"Uorsin?" Ami breathed his name, pure distress on her face. "Our father hurt you all those times?"

"Not all those times, no," I snapped. I made myself meet Andi's accusing stare. "Many of them were from opponents. That's how you learn. That's how you—"

"Grow strong," Andi finished. "Learn to get back up. I remember him saying that to you all the time. What else?"

"There is nothing else. Is the interrogation over yet?"

"Not by a long shot," Andi replied evenly, looking through me in her witchy way. "What else?"

"Isn't that bad enough?" Ami protested, knotting her fingers together. "He never once struck me. As much as he raged and blustered, I never thought he would."

"He wouldn't have—because *she* made sure of it. Isn't that right, Ursula?"

I stared her down, not answering. Not sure how to answer or to escape this line of questioning intact. The sun beat down, too hot, and sweat ran an icy trail down my spine.

"What else did he do to you?" Andi repeated the insistent question.

"What are you saying, Andi?" Ami had paled.

"Think about it. You heard some of the snide innuendos as well as I did."

"That was just talk. No one really thought any of it was true."

"Maybe we just didn't want it to be true. Did he try to force you down that path?"

"Oh, Glorianna." Ami's face crumpled. "He didn't."

I couldn't stand the expressions on their faces, the horror and pity. Dropping my head, I tried to breathe smoothly and opened my mouth to refute it, to tell them it wasn't true. Or that it was, but that it hadn't been the awful thing everyone seemed to think.

I couldn't. Instead I looked at my bare feet, long and brown against the white sand, realizing the drops of water falling onto and around them were tears.

"I can't talk about this," I finally got out.

Ami put a slender arm around my waist, leaning into me, though I still had my arms tightly folded. She smelled of sunshine, roses, and baby milk. "You don't have to, Essla."

Andi slid in on the other side, embracing both of us, the toes of her riding boots shiny and new compared to Ami's scuffed ones. "The last time we stood like this," she said, "the last time before this that we all three were together, was right before I left Ordnung. You had blood on your boots and we said good-bye."

"I remember," I managed.

"You could have told us. You *should* have told us."

"I didn't want you to know. Couldn't bear for anyone to know. I couldn't stand for you two to be hurt or to think I wouldn't be strong enough to protect you."

Ami snorted in a most unmusical, unladylike way. "Says the most heroic woman alive."

"What I want to know is," Andi said slowly, "how can you not hate him?"

"Don't you see? I couldn't, or it would all be a lie. Everything I believed in and worked for. That our mother sacrificed."

"I don't think they're the same thing, Essla," Ami whispered.

"I know. I make no sense, even to myself. I don't know what to think about anything anymore."

"I can understand that," Andi said. "What I don't understand is why you'd even consider turning more children over to him."

"I wouldn't." I wiped my cheeks. "You never gave me a chance to answer, but I won't ask either of you to go back to Ordnung. Would never force you."

"But you're going," Ami said into the silence that fell.

"I have to. I can't abandon our people. It's my path."

"That's what we thought," Andi answered.

"Which is why we're going with you," Ami added.

Surprised, I looked at them. No longer girls, indeed, but women. Queens in their own right.

"Don't argue." Andi lightly rapped her knuckles against my temple. "And don't be hardheaded. We'll go together and set things to rights. Ordnung and the Twelve are as much our responsibility as yours. We're meant to work together—see how the Star blazes?"

"I don't know why it does now when it never did before." I rubbed my thumb over the topaz, so hot it nearly burned.

"Because we've changed—we're not who we were that day I fled Ordnung," Andi said.

"I haven't changed. A great deal has happened to you two, but I'm the same person I've always been."

Ami laughed, that pure, sweet, delighted bell of a laugh that had been immortalized in more than one song, and Andi rolled her eyes.

"What?"

"Ursula." Andi shook her head slowly, as if trying to order her thoughts. "You're totally different. The sister I left behind never would have let me badger her into sharing her secret pain."

"Or fall silly in love with a foreign mercenary," Ami added with a sly smile.

"I'm not silly about it."

"You get this kind of goofy smile on your face," Andi said. "It's sweet."

"And you get all melty looking when he touches you." Ami tugged a lock of my hair. "It's nice to see. Especially . . . well, knowing now why you held yourself back from being courted."

"Does Harlan know?" Andi asked pointedly.

"Yes, he does." Ami nodded speculatively. "That's what you were talking about when you were delirious from blood loss, why he says he'll kill Uorsin if you don't."

"And you said, 'Good'—I haven't forgotten," I answered her.

"Did you?" Andi cocked her head at Ami. "I know why I want him gone from the world—even before I knew this—but I thought you still held him in high regard."

Ami shrugged. "Glorianna wills it. And don't roll your eyes at me. You either, Ursula. Not until you spend time praying to Moranu and Danu about it. See what they say."

"The goddesses don't talk to *us*," I teased her, enjoying the spark of indignation in her eyes, of feeling somewhat on level ground again.

"Yes, they do," she replied primly. "You just don't listen."

Because Ami was looking at me, Andi took the opportunity to

roll her eyes again, then pasted on an attentive smile when Ami snapped her head around to glare. "Fine. Laugh, both of you. You'll see."

Andi reached out and took my hand, squeezed it. "Are we good?"

"Yes." I took Ami's hand, too, and we all linked up. A memory came back, unbidden, of the three of us when I turned sixteen, all decked out in our party dresses, standing in a circle like this and promising to all live together in Ordnung forever. A good memory, full of more youthful naïveté than I remembered having. "We're good."

38

The Tala celebrated our return in grand style, something that seemed to surprise both Rayfe and Andi.

Perhaps Zynda had the right of it—that many had waited on the outcome of that particular power struggle, uncertain who would survive to lead, where their loyalties should lie. Now they turned out in jubilant numbers, cheering on Rayfe and Andi as if they'd won a tournament. Which, I supposed, they had in a way.

Never mind that members of this particular community had a tendency to spontaneously shift into some cavorting animal or another to express their joy. Or that one of the trainers created a dazzling array of staymachs that circled in the air, shifting in rainbows of color, rippling through various patterns that exploded in ever-growing circles.

Dafne met us at the palace—as the Common-Tongue-speaking Tala persisted in referring to Rayfe and Andi's home, either through misunderstanding of the word or to impress their foreign visitors with its importance—dressed in Tala fashion and looking radiantly happy to see us. She practically tore Stella away from Ash, weeping freely over the girl's dark curls.

She glanced up at me, cinnamon brown eyes glistening, and

nodded a little, making me think she recalled that stormy night we'd buried what we'd thought was Stella's dead body. A dark moment that neither of us expected to lead to this one.

We all bathed and changed into festive Tala outfits, whiling away the afternoon and evening on a balcony just above street level in front of the palace. It allowed us to sit in the sun, drink wine, and nibble on the various sweet and savory offerings brought by the unending parade of people and animals who strolled past. Some played music, told stories—the latter largely lost on most of us, though Dafne could already translate a surprising amount of the gist—or presented Rayfe and Andi with lovely bits of art and jewelry. Many, Zynda explained, sought to remind Andi of various family still stranded outside the barrier, and the gifts were bestowed in hope of encouraging her assistance.

"It's good to see the three of you together again," Dafne commented, as Ami, Andi, and I laughed at some joke. "I hear they plan to return to Ordnung with you."

"And you, librarian? Do you plan to return with us or stay here?"

She seemed vaguely surprised. "I assumed I'd go with you. Had you another plan?"

"I think the reasons for getting you out of Ordnung still apply to keeping you out of it. You're safer here."

"But not most useful."

"I don't know that's true. Having you learn the Tala language and study the texts here could be most useful in the long run. No matter who inherits the High Throne, he or she would benefit from your knowledge. And it might be best to let the dust settle until that time." I felt that, at least with Dafne, I did not need to spell out all that might occur. "Astar and Stella will remain here for the time being," I added. "Until we have things stabilized and the Twelve at real peace again. I'd like to appoint you regent for them, should it come to that."

She choked on her wine, Ash leaning forward to helpfully

thump her back, while Ami looked amused. Dafne threw her a look. "You knew about this plan?"

"We discussed it, yes. You're the logical choice," Ami replied.

"I'm a refugee orphan with no relation to the royal family," Dafne protested. "No noble blood that's officially recognized any longer. I can't be regent."

"The High King himself was once upon a time an upstart sailor and soldier from Elcinea. These things can be overcome," I pointed out. "And you've served as companion and faithful friend to all three of us. You offered to serve as my councilor. You're practically a half-sister. Who better to be regent? If somehow all three of us don't survive this—"

"Which doesn't bear considering," Rayfe growled, though Andi put a soothing hand on him.

"It's better to cover contingencies," Ash said. "Pretending disaster can't occur only invites the worst."

"And to have backup plans to the backup plans," Harlan agreed, as unshakable as ever.

"How would I possibly enforce it?" Dafne demanded. "I'm no warrior. I'd have no legal claim."

"Leave the legal claim to me," I told her. "I'll see that it's drawn up properly and distributed to the Twelve. Political order must be served, first and foremost. I care not if the High Throne moves to Avonlidgh"—I nodded to Ami—"but I won't see Erich or the others tear peace apart in their quest for power. As for assistance, you'll have the Tala at your back, which is not inconsiderable."

"My service would be yours, by extension." Harlan gave her a grave half bow from his chair, before settling his hand on my back again.

"And mine." Ash raised a crooked eyebrow at Rayfe, who still brooded. "Come, now, King Rayfe. Surely even you see that it's meet Salena's grandchildren should hold the throne she sacrificed so much to secure."

Rayfe's midnight blue eyes glittered and he shook his head. "I care nothing for the Twelve. If I thought it would work, I'd lock my queen up and prevent her from going."

"But you won't"—Andi glared at him—"as we've been through this."

"Annfwn needs you."

"So do my sisters. And Annfwn has Stella. Don't fight me on this, Rayfe."

"No." He sighed heavily, wound a lock of her hair around his fingers, and pulled her in for a kiss that heated rapidly, until he broke it abruptly. "I won't. Though you owe me."

She smiled, lazy and feline with it, and tugged him to his feet. "I'd better start on that debt, then."

"Best to live in the moment," Ami agreed, giving Ash a questioning glance and blushing prettily at whatever she saw in his eyes.

"I'll look in on the babies," Dafne muttered. "Sounds like I might as well get used to it."

"You don't have to take the job." I cocked my head, studying her face. "It would be a great responsibility and not one you're required to shoulder. You could go enjoy your life for a change. Travel. See the Twelve and beyond."

"You're not required to shoulder yours either." Dafne raised her brows at me. "None of you are."

"That's not true. Ami and Andi arguably don't have to go back, but it's long been my duty to see that the High Throne is secure. If not for the sake of the peace and prosperity of the Twelve, then as part of a sacred legacy from my mother."

Her bland look told me she'd noted that I'd omitted duty to Uorsin but that she would not comment there. She'd make an excellent councilor and an even better regent. "Do you ever think it's unfair—to saddle Astar and Stella with this onus, just as your parents did to you?"

"I think that not much of what we face in life is fair. I used to think of it that way sometimes, that Salena's scheming had forced us down particular paths. Now I think it's more that she trusted us to see through what she could not. Faith in the daughters she invested everything in. A different kind of loyalty." I smiled over my shoulder at Harlan. "Perhaps that my sons and daughters will also want to carry forward."

Harlan leaned forward and placed a kiss on my bare shoulder, where the filmy Tala gown fell away, kindling fire in my blood. Dafne looked thoughtful. Seemed about to say something and tucked it away.

"Something to say?" I raised one eyebrow at her. I hadn't expected her to disapprove of my relationship with Harlan, as enthusiastically as she'd pushed us together.

"Not tonight." She raised her glass of wine and toasted us, her expression warm. So much so that I doubted the concern I'd briefly glimpsed. "Before you leave in the morning, though, I have some information to share. For now, go enjoy yourselves. You've all certainly earned a bit of celebrating."

I frowned at her, ready to press, but Harlan hauled me to my feet. "I, for one, don't need to be told twice," he rumbled with amusement. "Good night, Lady Mailloux—and thank you."

He tugged me away, but I glanced back as we went inside, wondering if she felt abandoned by us. Zynda, however, had moved into my abandoned chair and seemed to be regaling her with some tale that involved much hand waving and already had her laughing.

Good.

I stood in the throne room at Ordnung, wondering where everyone had gone. It should never be this empty, with no courtiers meeting for quiet conversation or even servants polishing the floors or cleaning the sconces during the hiatus of court. Had Madeline forgotten to assign their duties?

But no—Madeline had died, her head rolling away and her blood spilling as bright as red wine across the golden marble. A sound whispered at the edge of my perception and I flinched, expecting to see her corpse. Nothing, though.

Just shadows and flickers of movement. I tried to turn to look, to face it, to draw my sword, but I couldn't move. That armored gown held me rigid. As if it had turned me into a metal statue of myself. I couldn't even look down at it this time, it clamped to me so tightly. Yet, in my mind's eye, I saw myself as if from across the room, sitting on the High Throne, platinum bright in my armored gown, my face a rictus of frenzied terror, swallowed up by it, thrashing to break free.

"Mother!" I yelled. "Mother, help me!"

"Shh . . ." Harlan ran big hands over me, holding me close. "Wake up, my Essla. Just a dream."

I blinked at him in the dark, disoriented, his skin warm and bare under my clutching fingers. "A dream?"

"A nightmare," he confirmed, turning onto his back and drawing me against his side. "You were calling for your mother."

"All that talk of legacies, no doubt." But I felt deeply shaken.

"Was it the same dream?"

The man forgot nothing. I shrugged, letting him interpret that as he would.

"Interesting, isn't it, that you have the same disturbing dream back here, where your mother lived as queen. A woman who had visions and passed that trait on to at least one of her daughters."

"This isn't a vision of the future."

"How do you know? Perhaps she's telling you something."

I laughed at that, feeling the odd panic of the dream crawling still over my skin. "I seriously doubt that."

"Tell me about it."

Knowing I wouldn't be able to go back to sleep and that he'd likely stop me if I tried to get up to sit and drink some wine, I decided to lump it and describe the dream, feeling more than a little silly as I did. But he didn't mock me, just listened quietly. As I told him, the worst of the ugly taint of it faded, receding, losing its power.

"A very interesting dream," he commented after a time.

"See? There's no such thing as an armored gown, and even if there was, I'd never wear one—so it's not a vision of the future."

"You have such a literal mind, my hawk." His fingers stroked my arm, as if I needed soothing still. "It's a metaphor."

"That I should wear more dresses?" I jibed.

He didn't rise to the bait, however. "You look lovely in dresses, it's true. I particularly like the Tala garb, which shows off your long limbs and lets me feel you move beneath. But no—such a thing would be impractical for both of its apparent purposes, yes? It fails as a gown because you cannot move. It fails as protection for the same reason. Instead it traps you. Strangles you inside it."

A shiver of unease took me. "So what is it a metaphor for?"

"I think only you can know that. Whether of your own mind or of some relic of your mother's. Both of those you would know better than anyone."

"I don't think anyone knew Salena well. She didn't let them."

"Reminds me of someone else."

"What is that supposed to mean?" *Heartless. Ruthless.*

He chuckled, running a hand down my hip. "Will you sleep now?"

"I might get up, have some wine. But you go back to sleep."

"I have a better idea." He pulled me atop him, using the increased freedom to caress me everywhere. We'd fallen asleep naked, after making love, and he seemed fully ready to engage in more. My body warmed to the idea, responding to his touch.

"Thank you for not leaving me to be alone," I whispered a long time later, and fell asleep to his big hand stroking down my spine.

In the morning, I found Dafne in the Tala library. Amused that even in this the Tala had to be different, I took in the spacious chamber lined with wooden-doored alcoves and otherwise screened only by swathes of heavy fabric stretched above. Tables scattered around the room held sparkling stones of various sizes. Dafne stood by one, carefully pinning open a scroll by weighting it with the stones.

"Seems such a system would be hard on the collection over time," I observed.

She smiled, wry. "Indeed. The Tala seem to feel that oral traditions serve as the most permanent of records, while books and scrolls are merely temporary devices to transfer that information. Rather the reverse of how we see it."

"Do you think their method works better?"

"It has its merits. However, I think we can also attribute some of Salena's . . . methods of communication to it. It might have been helpful if she'd left something as prosaic as a letter."

"An excellent point. What did you want to tell me?" I angled my head and recognized Dasnarian characters well enough now that a shadow of foreboding passed over me.

Dafne's somber expression did nothing to alleviate my growing dread. "I debated whether to tell you this, but I finally decided that if I didn't and you found I could have, you'd likely come after me with a blade."

"Okay," I said evenly, brushing the Star with my thumb. Warmish, with my sisters nearby. "What are we looking at?"

"Dasnarian dynasties. Has Captain Harlan spoken to you of his family?" She was hopeful. It showed in every line, that she hoped this would not come as a surprise to me. The dread coiled tighter.

"Some. I know he's the youngest of seven brothers." We hadn't discussed more than that, had we? Because I hadn't asked him. Believing I knew everything about him that I needed to. Letting him seduce me into trust though my initial instincts had warned me against him. My gut tightened. "What of his family?"

"It may not be significant." She sighed, eyes falling to the scroll.

"Just say it, librarian."

She traced a series of branching lines with her finger to a paragraph inscribed beside. "The Konyngrr dynasty has held the Dasnarian throne for several generations. The most recent king has seven sons. The youngest, named Harlan, with no possibility of attaining the throne, became a professional soldier and formed his own private army, called the Vervaldr."

Strangely, I felt nothing at this news. Nothing except a faint chill. *There is no place for me in Dasnaria.* I found myself nodding slowly, Dafne watching me with the caution one gives a snake. "He's a fucking prince." My voice sliced and she winced.

"It might not mean anything at all," she tried, sounding almost pleading. "I'm sure it has no bearing on his feelings for you or . . ."

I raised an eyebrow at her and she flinched. "Or why he might have so determinedly pursued the very eligible female heir to another throne? No. That would be so unlikely. Younger noble sons never take off to find a line of succession less crowded by their own brothers."

Dafne closed her eyes briefly, nodded once. "It looks bad, I know."

Even now I could be pregnant with his child. All that talk of assassinating the High King. Danu take me for a witless fool. How many women in the history of time could I have looked to for cautionary tales? I would not be the first or last to fall for a solid set of muscles, pretty promises, and the delight of being bedded, only to find herself trapped. I'd once warned Andi that she could become a blood pawn. The height of irony if that fate fell to me instead.

I wouldn't let that happen. If I did turn up pregnant, I'd abdicate all right to the throne. Perhaps I could give the child away, let it be raised somewhere in ignorance, by sheepherders as I'd once teased Ami about.

Harlan would be so long gone from our shores that he would never know. He could sail off wherever he pleased, to seek his fortune and chance at power from some other hapless princess. At the point of my sword, if need be.

"Thank you for telling me. Anything else?"

"What are you going to do about this, Ursula?" Dafne squared her shoulders. "Tell me that you'll talk to him about it first. Give him a chance to explain."

So he could lie to me again? Spew his vows and sucker me into believing he cared about me? Accuse me of withholding my secrets, my dark pain, when all along he sought to use me? "Oh, I don't think so."

I only realized I'd said the last aloud when Dafne's face fell. And I glimpsed the calculation behind it. "Don't you dare tell him, either. I forbid it."

"Ursula, I—"

"Don't disobey me on this. I would not excuse it this time."

She set her jaw, nodded.

"Why didn't you tell me last night?"

She looked desperately aggrieved. "Because I thought you would react this way and I wanted you to have at least one more night of happiness. Because he *has* done that for you. Whatever his other motives—and we still don't know what they are for sure, or if he even *has* other motives—he's been good for you. You've been happier than you've been since . . ."

"Since when?" I knew I shouldn't take my cold rage out on her, but if she meant what I thought she'd been about to say, I might not be able to leash it in.

She lifted her chin. "Since Salena died."

For some reason that hit me hard. Not what I'd expected. My mother had nothing to do with any of this.

"I'll see to the regency paperwork. Andi plans to set up a messenger chain to keep you all informed of events. Hopefully we'll send good news soon."

"What do you consider good news?"

"High King Uorsin on his throne, peace in the realm, and every last Dasnarian dead or gone from the Twelve. The world as it should be. Wish us luck with that." I turned on my heel and left, pretending not to hear her muttered oath behind me.

39

I avoided Harlan fairly easily. After all, we rode at a determined pace. With Tala scouts to clear the way and guard our party, we moved fast, gaining the border and Odfell's Pass by midday and descending immediately, to take full advantage of the remaining light. Autumn had set in on this side of the barrier, the air on the cool side after the tropical warmth of Annfwn. Andi, in particular, looked cold, breaking out a cloak almost immediately, and I realized she hadn't left Annfwn in nearly a year.

How fast time had gone. How much had happened in that year.

Once we gained the base camp, I had my Hawks to consult with and Harlan his own officers. Devious bastards, all of them, to disguise his true identity so. The news from Ordnung was not good. On the one hand, Jepp and Marskal, working in tandem with the now healthy guard outpost, had managed to reestablish regular patrols and scouting networks all the way to the township. On the other, Ordnung itself had been locked down tighter than Windroven under siege, with no one coming out and none able to get in or hail for news.

Erich—no doubt after finding Windroven empty of his quarry—

had maneuvered the armies of Avonlidgh onto the river plains west of the Danu River, within striking distance of Ordnung. Supplemented, it seemed, by forces from Nemeth and Elcinea. Duranor's army remained poised behind them, quite at home in Aerron and poised to cross the border into Mohraya. Jepp and Marskal speculated, and I agreed, that Stefan's plan would be to watch Erich and either choose a strategic moment to support his attack or trap his forces from behind, to either earn Uorsin's debt or take Ordnung for himself.

Possibly both.

Grimmer yet, those who tried to make contact with Ordnung reported back that the guard on the walls had been eerily quiet and still, not behaving as normal men and women. The township, still guarded almost entirely by Harlan's mercenaries, spoke in hushed whispers of entire contingents of raw recruits from the countryside disappearing behind the walls of the castle. Friends and relatives had not been seen in weeks and, when glimpsed, failed to respond when waved to or hailed.

They simply stood, unnaturally patient, through light and dark, in all weather conditions.

As if they'd somehow died on their feet and remained upright, living corpses. One family had managed to reclaim their daughter, it seemed, but nothing remained of her self. Just a mindless body that struggled to return to Ordnung.

Worry for his men haunted Harlan's face, and a traitorously soft part of me wanted to offer comfort. Not that I had any to give. And just a further indication of how far he'd manipulated me, that I thought of him with everything else going on.

We spent what little remained of the evening in strategy with our top lieutenants, Rayfe and Andi's Tala an odd counterpoint to the Hawks and Vervaldr, who'd intermixed and become quite familiar with each other in our absence. Without referencing Harlan, I explained what Dafne had discovered about the Temple of Deyrr and the likely explanation for the grim tales from Ordnung.

At least I could count on Harlan's lust for the High Throne to keep him and the remaining Vervaldr loyal to the effort to take out Illyria's undead guard and let us penetrate the castle. Perhaps Harlan's warnings to me about the black witch had been part of a struggle between them for supremacy, as well as a convenient method to establish trust between us. An old ploy, lulling me into believing our common enemy made us friends.

He'd positioned himself as my ally from that first day—likely before that, patiently building a scenario where I'd believe he wanted nothing more than to follow me about like a puppy. All that nonsense about the *Elskastholrr*. I burned with anger over it all, a clean, mind-clearing rage I clung to when doubts assailed me. At least Dafne had uncovered the truth before I'd made some fatal error.

A worse mistake than the ones I'd already made.

When we broke from the campfire and Harlan went to answer the call of nature, I took advantage of the opportunity to make myself scarce and bed down with some of the unattached female Hawks. Though there were fewer of those than there had been, with many of them having taken up with Dasnarian lovers. I lay awake, not even daring to get up and volunteer to take over a watch position, for fear he'd seek me out and force a confrontation.

I needed to avoid that only another day, maybe two. Once I'd killed Illyria I'd be able to have a rational conversation with Uorsin, and we'd discuss the mercenary's agenda—along with the choice of execution or banishment. I couldn't think of steps beyond that.

Just before dawn, stiff with chill and the tension of holding myself in a rigid posture to mimic sleep all night and not disturb my companions, I could stand being still not a moment more. Filled with restless tension—anticipating the coming battle, no doubt—I rose and risked a workout with some of the Hawks. Harlan would look for me, but I should be able to avoid much conversation with everyone about.

Sure enough, I'd barely made it into third form when I caught a glimpse of him, steadily working through his strengthening exercises close by. He appeared absorbed, but he had his eye on me; I felt it in the prickle of my skin. I'd have to think how best to play this. Perhaps I would have done better to sleep with him the night before, to pretend to normality, rather than arouse his suspicions.

So when I finished the twelfth form to find him waiting, I strolled past casually and smiled. A gesture he did not return. "Good morning, Captain." I kept going, but his hand shot out to stop me.

"What's going on?" he asked in a low voice.

"A great deal. I know you heard all the same reports I did."

He set his jaw. "You know that's not what I mean. Why are you avoiding me?"

"Is this about last night?" I went for distantly surprised. "I apologize. I wasn't thinking and should have said something. I thought it better to establish a bit of distance between us during this venture, for discipline's sake."

"Is that what you're calling it?" An edge now. A dangerous one.

"Yes. I'm sorry if I inadvertently insulted you. I didn't mean to."

"You have many skills, Ursula. Lying when you feel strongly about something is not one of them. You've been acting strangely since yesterday morning. I put it down to concern over the coming battle, but . . ." He broke off to study my face. "Something changed. You're going to tell me what it is."

I tried to shake him off, the rage that had been coldly building since yesterday too near the surface, but his hand tightened on my arm. "Don't you give me orders, Captain Harlan. You're going to want to take your hand off of me before I cut it off."

His pale eyes narrowed. "We're back to that, then. Why? You owe me an explanation."

"I owe you nothing!" I hissed the words between my teeth, the anger spiking.

He blinked, slowly, reassessing, taken aback. "I've hurt you.

How? What did I do?" Turning me, he took my other arm and seemed about to pull me into one of his comforting embraces, so perfectly calculated to make me feel secure and cared for. I couldn't stand a moment more.

Pivoting, I broke his hold and pulled my twin blades, sinking into a crouch. "Come at me again, mercenary, and I'll have your blood."

"Don't do this, Ursula," he warned, reflexively taking a defensive posture. Around us, interested parties gathered, keeping a safe distance.

"Afraid?" I taunted him. "Not surprising for a coward, spy, and manipulator."

"What do you accuse me of?" he demanded. "Sheath your blades and let's discuss this."

"Draw yours and let's finish this here and now." We would have to do without the Vervaldr. So be it. Better to begin that purging immediately.

"I won't draw on you." He deliberately relaxed, showing me his open palms. "I promised that and I meant it."

"Yes, because you have a greater prize in mind, don't you? Can't have me dead or incapacitated. That would ruin all of your meticulous plans."

"I have no idea what you're talking about." His eternal patience frayed at the edges and he stepped toward me, reaching out. "Calm down and—"

I struck without thinking, fresh from the forms, liquid rage fueling me. Slashing up, I caught him across the forearm, a shallow slice, but one that bled profusely. I managed to stop the continuation that would bring the blade across his throat, though he'd already turned to deflect it, trapping my arm, and we held there, a long, frozen moment, gazes locked. Slowly, he took a step back, then pressed his fingers to his forehead in the *Elskastholrr*, bright-red blood running down his arm.

"Ursula!" came Ami's voice from somewhere behind me. "What in Glorianna's name is going on?"

I became aware that Rayfe and Ash flanked me now, each with a hand on my arm.

"Easy, Your Highness," Ash murmured, the low tone making his voice scratch.

"Ask him," I spat. "Prince Harlan Konyngrr."

For a moment, Harlan looked genuinely confused. Enough that I almost could believe he was sincere. If I was a terrible liar, he was a masterful one.

"What are you talking about?" Andi, just to the side.

"He's a fucking prince of Dasnaria. Seventh in line for the throne. You put the pieces together."

Gradually Harlan's face cleared, then hardened. "Eleventh, at least. Three of my elder brothers have had sons, and that was years ago, so there's likely more. They take precedence."

"All the more reason for you to go seeking a throne elsewhere."

"Is that what you think? That all of this has been an elaborate seduction to gain access to the High Throne of the Twelve?"

"Why else keep it a secret, then? You never said a Danu-cursed word about your royal blood." A prince. Yet another power seeker. Nothing to do with me, only my rank, as always. I had wondered why he wanted me, and all the time the answer stared me in the face.

"I myself directed you to look at the Dasnarian dynasties—if you had kept reading, you would have found me eventually. As you clearly did. Why would I have pointed you there if I meant to keep my parentage secret?"

"You still never said who you really are."

"Because *this* is who I really am. This man who stands before you. A man you know well." His voice had gone deep and quiet. "It means less than nothing to me, who and what I came from. It should mean nothing to you. I've told you everything you asked to know, Ursula. I've given you my loyalty. The kind *you* value because it cannot be bought, because it is beyond price. But you deny me yours. You don't care enough to ask me to explain. Instead you pass judgment and sentence upon me. Who does that remind you of, Your Highness?"

"I want you gone." Ice coated my heart. "You and your mercenaries. I want you clear of the Twelve Kingdoms. On pain of death."

Coldly, he inclined his head. "You can command me to leave your kingdom, Your Highness, but that changes nothing for me. You know that."

"Keep your loyalty, mercenary."

"I will. Ever in my heart." He turned and walked away.

For the rest of the day, everyone steered clear of me except when necessary, which suited me fine. Ami tried to talk to me once but quickly abandoned the field when I snarled at her. There were plenty of conversations to have, reports to receive, and instructions to give. It felt good to get back in rhythm with my Hawks. As the day went on, I felt more my usual self and less like whoever I'd become in Annfwn.

I had never been the kind of woman to wear flimsy dresses and cavort with her lover on the beach. The more time passed, the more it felt like a dream. Or like it had happened to someone else. By the time I caught my first sight of Ordnung's towers, I had the entire episode relegated to foolishness. Andi and Ami had practically said so. *The sister I left behind never would have . . . Silly in love . . .*

We camped within an hour's ride of the walls that night. In the dark before dawn, we'd finish discreetly encircling the castle, hopefully penetrating the walls before Erich's scouts caught wind of us. Uorsin might yet open the gates to us, his three daughters, if we asked entrance, as he wouldn't for others. No sense escalating a conflict that might be avoided. If, however, we were refused or encountered no response, we'd be in position to tighten the net and attack.

My eyes burned from not sleeping the night before, hardly an unusual occurrence for me. At least in the past. A missed night or two had never made much difference for me before, but I'd grown soft that way also. Accustomed to the indulgences Harlan had lulled me into. The gritty surreality brought on by that, by my outburst of the morning—had I ever been so boilingly angry? Not hurt. He was wrong. I wouldn't let it be that—and worry over what the next day would hold, all of it combined to keep me on edge. With all the planning done, I had nothing to do but check my weapons and gear, to sharpen my already keen-edged blades. My neck tight as steel, I rolled my head on my shoulders to loosen it and accidentally caught Harlan's implacable gaze from across the campfire.

Oddly enough, he sat with Ash, and they seemed to be deep in conversation. It mattered not to me.

"Come walk with me." Andi, standing beside me, held out her hand. On the other side of the fire, Rayfe went to join Ash and Harlan, passing a flask of something, and the men, all three, burst into laughter at some joke. It put my teeth on edge.

"I don't think—"

"It wasn't a request, Ursula."

With a hiss of exasperation, I stood and followed her into the dark. The waxing moon rose over the valley below, Moranu's perfect crescent, gilding Andi's profile with a silver glow. Danu's stars above glittered with cold fire, brittle and sharp in comparison.

"I think I know you as well as anyone," she began and glanced at me with a smile, though it had a sad tilt. "An unhappy thought, as I feel I don't know you as well as I might. You've been very alone—much more than I ever realized. I never really thought about what it was like for you, when Salena died. How it would have hit you the worst. That you felt betrayed by her death."

"She hardly betrayed me by dying, Andi."

"But she did. She abandoned you to him with her death. Leaving you unprotected for him to mold and abuse. Ami and I had you, but who took care of you? No one, I think."

It hurt to think about it. "I took care of myself. And it doesn't matter. All ancient history."

"It's not." She faced me. "Don't you see, Ursula? You look for everyone to betray you, to leave you, to fail to love you. Our father has you thinking that everything is about the High Throne, that this power is all that matters. That he—maybe even you—are somehow not people at the core. That you're not driven by love and insecurity and fear like everyone else is."

"Did the mercenary ask you to speak with me?"

She laughed, a huff of angry air. "No. Harlan has spoken to no one all day until now that I can see, and then only because Ash and Rayfe feel for him, having their own experiences with Salena's daughters. He's quietly bleeding to death inside. Just as you are. I swear to Moranu I'd like to knock your hard heads together."

"I can't ignore the evidence, Andi."

"Then think about your thrice-damned evidence! Does he behave like a man hungry for power? Because you and I know very well what that looks like. If that's Harlan's long-term plan, he picked a much more indirect route than he could have. I have seen nothing about him that indicates he's anything other than completely straightforward. As far as I can tell, he goes after what he wants with declared and open intent."

And had from the moment I met him. Still. "I have a responsibility to the High Throne, to keeping the peace of the Twelve. I might point out that this is not something you've ever understood, much as I tried to get you to take your responsibilities seriously."

"Don't try to pick a fight with me, too. Nothing will stop any of us from being at your side tomorrow, no matter how you might attempt to shield us or push us away. Try to keep in mind that we're all on your side. There is an enemy and it's not any of the people here tonight."

"Is that witchy wisdom?" I sneered, then realized she'd already gone.

The deployment went with perfect dispatch and well-oiled silence, Rayfe, Harlan, and I each coordinating our arm of our combined forces. We sent them ahead, then moved at a brisk pace down to the high road. As the sky pinkened with dawn, we stayed out of sight of the main gates, waiting for sunrise to make our grand entrance.

Andi, Ami, and Rayfe had all donned garments worthy of a state visit. Andi and Rayfe were elegant in glossy Tala black, both with their long hair loose and wild, while Ash wore dark fighting leathers, managing to look quite lethal, guarding Ami's back. She was in an amazing gown of the purple and gold of Avonlidgh, embroidered with Glorianna's pink roses.

"How in the Twelve did you have that thing packed?" I muttered at her, and she gave me a sweet smile. Someone had trimmed up her hair and it fell in glossy, perfect ringlets.

"Andi had it whipped up for me. The Tala have such artistry in these things. Presentation is important."

I glanced down at my own battered leathers, much the worse for the wear of the last weeks. "Alas for that."

"No worries there." She looked me over. "You've never needed fine clothes to outshine us all. You make an impression just by being." Her gaze flicked past me. "Ah," she breathed. "And here's your perfect accessory."

Harlan, in full Vervaldr regalia, mounted on his impressive battle stallion, pulled up behind me with a nod.

"Captain Harlan." I spoke through my teeth. "Why are you here?"

He gazed back at me, his face set in granite lines, showing no emotion. "It's where I belong."

I opened my mouth to say something about the contract, but the dangerous glint in his eye changed my mind. Instead, I deliberately raised a shoulder and let it fall, then turned my back on him.

The sun edged a fiery golden curve over the valley, and the Temple of Glorianna rang bells, the dawn hymn going up, though thinly, as if too few voices supported it. Ami drew Glorianna's circle in the air. Then once again added Moranu's crescent and bisected them with Danu's blade, invoking all three goddesses and asking their protection and benediction. Finished, she nodded to me.

The same sun would set at the other side of what almost certainly would be a pivotal day in history. I wondered if I'd survive to see it.

Taking a deep breath, I straightened my spine.

And led them to the gates of Ordnung.

40

My skin crawled at the sight.

One hundred times worse than the unease with which I'd viewed Ordnung upon my return from Windroven. The walls, as reported, were densely populated with unmoving guards. With weapons trained upon us, they presented a formidable defense.

The corpse-rot gray of their faces instilled a deeper fear.

I resisted glancing back at Harlan, though I guessed at his growing anger, for a number of the dead guard indeed wore Vervaldr colors. Victors from a few skirmishes reported the dead could be incapacitated by losing heads or limbs but that they seemed to live on regardless. It would be a question for later, how to give them true death.

For now I wanted them off my walls, this smear on the face of what should be the Twelve's shining glory.

I reined up, Andi and Ami flanking me, half a horse length behind, Rayfe and Ash similarly arrayed just beside them. Harlan rode at my back.

It's where I belong.

At least I could trust in his investment to keep me alive. Shaking it off, I called out. "All hail, High King Uorsin! His daughters have returned, to pay him fealty."

Rayfe made a disparaging snort at that, but I ignored him.

"As Princesses of the Realm, along with our consorts, we request entry into Ordnung."

None of the dead guard moved. Nothing moved anywhere, except Glorianna's rays angling to dance on the still white towers, no pennants flying. Superstitiously, with a pang of irrational dread, I imagined everyone inside Ordnung like this. Gray and rotten with *deyrr*.

Then, slowly and without sound, the gates opened. No other notice was given. They simply swung wide, a maw gaping into a silent, empty outer courtyard.

Keeping my head high, I rode forward.

No one spoke, though Rayfe growled under his breath, the sound of a cornered wolf. A feeling I understood on a visceral level. We rode through the courtyard, the only sound the clopping of the horses' hooves, the creak of our tack. Foreboding crawled along my spine, and for a wild, desperate moment, I imagined turning tail and running, back to the tranquil beach at Annfwn, to the delight of Harlan's arms and the delicious pleasure he'd given me.

Despite myself, I looked back at him, and rather than the rigidly carved lines of emotionless fury, instead I glimpsed what might have been compassion.

Andi caught my eye as I faced forward again, storm-gray eyes glittering with silver, the thunderstorm of magic gathering around her, a potent charge poised to strike. She shielded us with a light version of the Annfwn barrier, lest the mind magic make us forget what we came to do. She dipped her chin and squared her own shoulders. On my other side, Ami rode wreathed in Glorianna's rays, gloriously lovely, radiant in her determination. She smiled at me, beauty and steel both in her visage.

The Star blazed scorching hot against my palm and I began to hope that we might yet triumph.

Tempting as it was to ride directly into court, we dismounted at the inner doors. With no one to hand our mounts off to, we left them standing in place, reins tied off and ready. Except for Rayfe's steed, who transformed into a sleek wolfhound, waist high and pacing at his heel.

We entered the castle itself, the urns of flowers dead and wilted, untended. Autumn leaves blew through the halls and no servants followed after to sweep them away. The place reeked of death, of *deyrr*, perhaps.

I should never have left.

The doors to the throne room stood open, and there, at least, some semblance of normality greeted us. Packed with people as it should be, the room stayed strangely silent, but for the rustling of the courtiers turning their heads to take us in. Their gazes grabbed at me with desperation. None said a word, but they silently pleaded for help. But in the way a mortally wounded warrior begs for swift death, not to be saved. Because he already knows there's no possibility to hope otherwise.

The reason was obvious. At the end of the center aisle, Illyria, banked-coal eyes dead in her face, draped herself over the High Throne, fouling it with her presence. She wore Salena's rubies and my Heir's Circlet around her brow. Wearing a collar like a dog and chained to the dais, Derodotur crouched at her feet, not even raising his head to look at us. Ranks of undead guard stood around and behind her, a grating despair in their faces, despite the menace of their drawn weapons.

We walked toward her, Andi and Ami close beside me, their sun and moon magic like a bolstering force that kept me upright.

"Illyria." I made her name an accusation. No dancing around this. "Where is High King Uorsin?"

"He is . . . meditating." Her reply slithered out between lush lips curved in a triumphant smile. "What could possibly have brought you back, Princess? Or, I should say, Princesses. There is nothing for you here any longer."

"On the contrary, there is nothing for you here," I answered. "Remove your foul self from the High Throne or we shall take you from it."

She laughed, genuinely amused. "For your impertinence, I'll have tribute. The Star of Annfwn blazes at your side. So unpleasant of you to have stolen it from me. So accommodating of you to walk into my trap. Salena's line ends here."

My turn to laugh. "Your arrogance is a disease, Illyria. A blindness that keeps you from seeing that you've already lost. Step down, admit your defeat."

She pretended to sneer, but she didn't quite manage to keep her indolent pose. "And what army do you bring against me— you, your sisters, a cripple, a wild man, and a hire-sword?"

"More than you know. Even now you've been surrounded with my forces, the Hawks along with the consolidated outposts of Mohraya."

"Avonlidgh's elite guard," Ami added.

"And the might of the Tala," Rayfe snarled. "Who've taken Ordnung before and can again."

"The Vervaldr also stand with Her Highness, rightful heir to the High Throne." Harlan spoke behind me, and her eyes flicked to him in irritation.

"Harlan Konyngrr, the temple's gold shines as bright as any here. Name your price."

"It's one you cannot reach. I have taken the *Elskastholrr*."

If anything could spark in her dead eyes, the astonishment nearly did so. "You'll join the ranks of my undead guard, then, after you watch your beloved die."

"Step down, Illyria," I commanded her. "I shall not tell you a third time."

"No, you won't." She smiled, not a pleasant one, and lifted a hand, twisted it.

My heart cramped and my vision went dark at the edges.

Someone in the court broke into hysterical sobbing, and I found I couldn't move. My sword would not come to hand, and I nearly fell. But Ami took my arm, warm light streaming into me, and Andi's thundercloud thickened, coalesced. A bolt of blue lightning forked from above, stabbing Illyria and knocking her back in the throne.

The fist on my heart released even as Illyria's dead guard lurched forward. Rayfe and Ash drew swords, laying into them. Concentrating, as we'd discussed, on disarming and delimbing them. They came apart in a hideous way, corrupt blood spraying.

Glorianna's rose window shattered and giant black raptors poured in, swooping down to rake talons over the dead guards' eyes. Disable would be the name of the game. Rayfe tossed me a wicked grin over his shoulder, insufferably pleased with himself to have broken that window twice. To my surprise, I found myself grinning back.

We'd have words later. I focused in on Illyria, who stared at Andi. "What are you?" she demanded.

"I am Salena's daughter," Andi answered. "With the might of Moranu behind me."

I stepped up to the throne, hit a wall like Annfwn's invisible barrier. "Andi?"

Illyria regained some confidence. "So much for Moranu's might. You cannot reach me. Mind your backs."

A wail of horrified screaming went up as the dead poured in the doors behind us. With a roar, Harlan swung his broadsword, cleaving through two, three at a time. "Take her out, now!" he shouted at me.

Blue lightning stabbed at the invisible wall with no effect and I threw myself against it to no avail. Behind it, Illyria wrapped a bejeweled hand around Derodotur's throat and squeezed. Rather than resisting, he sat passively, mindless. Already dead. I gathered myself to try again and Ami set a slim hand on my arm.

"I am also Salena's daughter," she said, in a voice like temple bells, "and Glorianna's avatar. You deprive the dead of the surcease of her arms." She reached up to run her lovely fingers down the surface of the barrier and it became visible. Rotten with death magic and dripping blood. Under her light touch, it pinkened, going from blood red to rose, then shattered into thousands of rose petals, falling into a scented heap.

Moving my fastest, I leapt over them and ran my blade straight into Illyria's black heart.

With no effect.

She smiled and blew me a little kiss. "You can't kill me, Salena's daughter. Uorsin's daughter. Daughter of failure. For I am beyond death."

"I am Salena's daughter," I sneered at her and, with my left hand, stabbed a dagger through the arm that held Derodotur. He fell, collapsing without a sound. "I wield Danu's blade. Amelia? Andromeda?" They stepped up and laid hands over the sword hilt. The Star of Annfwn blazed. "I don't need to kill you. In Mohraya we burn our dead."

Illyria screamed as the blade heated, the skin around it scorching and peeling back black and dissolving into ash. The gaping wound grew, widening, and I followed it with the sword, carving away at her as her blood-curdling screams vaporized with the loss of her lungs, cleaving up to demolish her throat and into her twisted brain. Beside me, Ami gagged, but she kept her hand on mine. A silver-blue light shimmered from Andi, clearing the ash and stench of corruption away. Until nothing remained of Illyria except for her twitching arm, still pinned to the throne, and a tumble of limbs and jewels tangled in her sparkling skirts.

"Glorianna take and keep her." Amelia finally released her death grip on my hand and drew the circle of Glorianna in the air. "Though even the goddess of love will be hard-pressed to embrace this one."

Andi wrapped her cloak around her hand and pulled the Heir's circlet from the ashes, wiping it clean. Then held it out. "It's cool enough."

I hesitated. Uorsin had taken it from me. It wasn't for me to decide.

With a huff of impatience, Amelia took it from her and fitted it over my brow. "Glorianna wills it," she said in a fierce tone. "She told me so."

The hall was in chaos. With a nod to me, Andi changed form into a big cat, joining Rayfe to methodically slice the mindless masses into harmless pieces. Harlan and Ash fought side by side, a mound of dismembered undead piling high around them.

It appeared the plan had worked, with some of the winged Tala shifting back to open the gates. Hawks, Vervaldr, Mohrayans, and even people of the township, armed with whatever they could lay hands on, all fought down the undead guard. Even Ambassador Laurenne had taken up a long kitchen knife, using it to grim effect.

There was no triumph in this victory. We slaughtered our own people to win this battle. It made me sick at heart. Made me wish I could dispatch Illyria again. A hideous demise for each of these.

"They were dead before we got here," Ami said to me, her eyes dark with horror. "That's all the comfort I can take. We'll have so many to mourn, to send to the bower of Glorianna's arms. How could Uorsin let this happen?"

I didn't know. Perhaps he, too, would be one of her animated dead. In the furious beat of my heart, I found the wish that he would be. The alternative was too terrible to face.

And yet, it fell to me to do it.

I left Ami on the dais, as well protected there as anywhere. Uorsin would be in his rooms, most likely. Locked or barricaded in. Signaling to a few of my Hawks, including Marskal and Jepp, I jogged back down the center aisle, dodging severed limbs that crawled and grabbed disconcertingly.

Taking a moment, I found Lise. "Start a bonfire. Go to the

Temple and get the priests from wherever they're hiding and have them begin funeral rites."

She nodded, gulping down the sickness I also felt. I turned and found Harlan beside me. "Stay here," I ordered him.

"No. I go with you."

"I don't want you with me."

"You've made that clear," he returned, emotionless but for that enduring gleam of injury in his eyes and under it that slow burn of anger. "As I have made my position clear. You will not confront your father alone."

I gestured at my team of lean, lethal Hawks, poised to follow me. "I'm not alone."

"Nevertheless."

I briefly considered ordering him imprisoned in the dungeons, but we needed every pair of able hands. "I want you to promise me something. Right now."

"I've already promised you everything."

"Enough with that. Swear that you'll leave the Twelve when I order it, that you'll cease your designs on the throne and go."

"You already said this."

"Yes, and you did not agree. I didn't miss that. Swear it."

He hesitated fractionally. "I swear I will depart when you command it, Your Highness."

"Don't think that I won't."

Harlan didn't reply to that, just returned my gaze evenly, a mountain of placid strength, spattered in gore. Absurdly, I wanted to touch him, to break through that wall between us, though I'd been the one to put it there.

Instead I focused on the next fight and went to see the High King.

41

No soldiers stood guard outside the massive doors to Uorsin's chambers. The torches blazed, but no other signs of life were in evidence. Barred from the inside, not from without. I pulled the lever for the internal bell, doubting it would do much good. If he had barricaded himself in, he'd have no way of knowing it was me and not Illyria who'd come for him.

Without much hope, I pounded with the side of my fist, shouting for him. Bruising my hand. Harlan folded his around mine, drawing it away.

"Let me." He made considerably more sound with his mighty fist, to no more avail. "I've never been inside the High King's rooms. He can't hear us?"

I shook my head, ready to gnash my teeth with frustration. "Walls, doors, all too thick."

"Windows?"

"None. It's a secure room."

"Battering ram on the doors."

"Might be our only option. It will take a while." I gestured at the narrow space, explicitly intended to prevent exactly that. No space to maneuver or to gain momentum. "The doors are iron. And there's three sets."

"A thorough defense."

I knew it sounded odd, the level of paranoia. It had bothered me, too, watching it grow over the years as Uorsin added levels of protection. But the current situation proved he'd been right to do it. Didn't it?

"How is he getting food and water?"

"I don't know. I haven't been here, remember? By the looks of people, no one's eaten for days." Being pissed wouldn't help. I rolled my head on my shoulders, stopping abruptly when I remembered he'd take it as a tell. "He has a stockpile, in case this very thing happens."

"So what would he do? How would he know a crisis is over and emerge to see to his people?"

Under his question lay the implicit accusation that he'd abandoned his throne to Illyria.

"He could be dead or incapacitated," I retorted, as if Harlan had spoken the words aloud. Defending him against my own insidious doubts. "We have to get in there."

Instead of arguing with me, he studied the doors. "Often the entrance is the strongest part, because attackers focus on that. Would another way in be weaker—ceiling or floors?"

"Possible." I ran the layout of Ordnung in my head, what lay on the other sides of the chamber walls. Madeline would have known better. I put away the pang of her untimely death, the first of this avalanche. Derodotur would have likely known, having lived here so long. Or Zevondeth. If she still lived. "I can get that information. In the meantime, order must be restored."

I dispatched one of the Hawks to round up the housekeeping staff, find the most senior persons still in possession of their mortal senses, and find out the last time anyone had brought food to the King. And to get the kitchen going if it wasn't. We had several armies and a decimated castle population to feed. I seriously wondered how we'd do it. At least someone else could be dealing with that problem. "If Ami isn't working with the Temple on the funeral rites, have her look in on the food situation," I added. "She's had experience with this sort of thing.

"Marskal, if Andi's capable, get her to shift back to human form and have her take over research. I wish we had Dafne, but Andi might know of other librarians. Find someone who knows the building plan for Ordnung. I'll find out if Zevondeth still lives and what she knows. Jepp, collect your scouts and let's find out if there's movement out there. Let the people stuck in the township know that they can leave for their homes, but to be wary of running afoul of the encamped armies or their patrols. Send any Vervaldr here to report to Captain Harlan for reassignment. Maybe Rayfe and Ash will help with organizing our defenses, in case Erich sees this as an opportunity to attack. See if anyone knows where Lord Percy is. Odds on, he's been dead a while, but I need to know. I want six guards on these doors at all times—arrange the rotation however you think best. If there's any sign at all from within, send for me immediately."

What else?

"Oh, and get someone to roust the maids and start cleanup of the gore—this place reeks and that can't be healthy. The last thing we need is for people to take ill on top of everything else. Speaking of which, someone will need to dig more latrines to accommodate all these people."

Fortunately my Hawks were accustomed to handling many tasks of living and dying and so took no affront at being go-between to the serving staff. With a last pound on the doors, to continued lack of response, I turned to find Harlan with an odd smile on his lips. "What?"

"You're countermanding the King's commands."

"I'm handling things in his absence the best way I know how. We can't feed and house all those people. Better that they get to their homes. And we need the Vervaldr here. If only for latrine duty."

"Is there any aspect of running this castle or kingdom you don't personally handle?"

"Yes—the dozen or so tasks I just delegated." At a brisk pace, I headed for Zevondeth's rooms, praying to Danu that she still lived. In the real way.

"I don't know what's wrong with me that I can be so utterly in love with you and find you so admirable, when you've tried and condemned me for something I never did, that you refuse to even discuss."

"It demonstrates your continued poor judgment. And don't start with that—you won't get under my defenses again."

"Yet, you did not attempt to assign me a task, send me away."

"Even I know when to stop banging my head against a wall."

"Do you?" His tone of voice warned me, but I didn't spin out of his reach quite in time. Lulled, as I had been lately, into letting him get too close. Always a mistake, as I would inevitably lose once within grappling distance. He had me backed up against the stones of the hallway, wrists pinned so I couldn't draw, heat burning in his pale gaze. "We'll have this out, you and I."

"This is not the time."

"When better? You'll be informed if Uorsin pokes his nose out. Lady Zevondeth is going nowhere in the next few moments. You've neatly avoided being alone with me until now, and if I know you, which I believe I do, you'll no doubt make sure of it in the future. Then, before I've had a chance to talk to you, you'll have found an excuse to order me away."

"I should have done it already."

"Then why haven't you?"

My heart ached from it all—the deaths, the starving faces, all the horrors, the tangled nest of uncertainty about my father, the bitter rage against Harlan, the agonizing sense of betrayal—I felt bruised and battered and supremely unable to stand up to any of it.

"I want you to go." I meant it to sound hard, but it came out with an edge of pleading. He heard it, too, because his gaze softened.

"Ursula." Harlan breathed my name like a prayer. "Essla. My hawk. I'm sorry. You don't want my apology, but you have it. It never once occurred to me that my family would mean anything to you. I left that so long ago that I forget most of the time that was ever part of my life. None of it means anything to me—until the moment I realized you thought I'd betrayed you. I never would. I couldn't. I love you far too much. Not for a throne. For you."

You look for everyone to betray you, to leave you, to fail to love you.

I stared at him as if he'd taken a blade to my gut and opened me up. And pressed my lips together against the hurt. I'd thought I'd been angry at him, but no. No, it was worse. I was my father's daughter. My father, barricaded in his chambers, while his people suffered. *Our father has you thinking that everything is about the High Throne, that this power is all that matters.*

"I don't know what to say," I whispered, as if we could be overheard.

"Just say you'll give me time to prove myself to you."

I laughed a little, a bit of a sob behind it. "You've proven yourself over and over. I'm the one who's failed." Over and over.

"No." He let go of my wrists but stopped shy of touching my face, his hands fluttering a whisper away. "I'm filthy or I'd hold you. You've never failed because you've never stopped trying. You never will. All those people who look to you to save them know it."

"I don't know either what's wrong with you that you love me. How you can."

"I know. But I do. You can trust in that. Always."

"I need you to promise me one more thing."

Wary, he waited.

"I understand that it's part of taking care of me for you, but I want you to swear that you won't attempt to kill the King."

His jaw tightened. "You ask a great deal."

"I'm asking you to trust me to handle this the best way I know how."

"I do so swear," he ground out. "Only by way of demonstrating that you are more important to me than anything else."

I didn't care about the filth that coated us both, I flung myself against the bulwark of his body, kissing him and clinging, impossibly starved for him, even after such a brief time.

"How did I get through before you?" I wondered aloud, when I pulled away for breath.

"I've long questioned that," he replied with a wry smile.

"I'm sorry, too. That I'm so hardheaded. That I didn't talk to you."

"It's part of who you are—for good and ill. It gives you this spine of steel"—he ran his hands up my back—"but can encase and trap you, as in your nightmare. Your stubbornness should be a strength, not a crippling handicap."

"Yes." Something about that niggled at me. I set it aside to cook, but not so far that I'd forget to think about it. "I have to talk to Zevondeth, if she still lives."

"Then let's go."

Della refused to even open the doors this time. Fortunately they were far easier to breech than Uorsin's, especially with my personal battering ram. Harlan broke through with the second heave of his powerful shoulders, neatly clearing away the furniture that had been stacked against it. Harlan checked the bedchamber and emerged almost immediately, shaking his head that Zevondeth was not inside.

Della's shrill screams hurt my ears, and I was tempted to run her through with my blade just to shut her up. We could hardly afford to lose more lives, however. The experience also made me wonder how many people were similarly barricaded in the untold rooms, towers, and crannies of Ordnung, too frightened to emerge. The castle had been bursting at the seams when we left, and surely

Illyria hadn't had time to work her death magic on them all. Who knew how long that magic took, but she'd made so many of her dead guard.

Where and how had she been doing it, anyway? Something else to see to. It made me weary just contemplating it.

"Here now!" I tried for a verbal slap, to break through Della's hysteria. "You know who I am."

"Ye-ee-ess," she sobbed. "But you could be one of *them*!" She started weeping in great gulps.

"Look at me." I took her by the arms, dirtying her pretty dress, but oh, well. "Do I look undead? I'm Her Highness Ursula and you are bound to obey me. Now, I command you to calm down and listen."

She whitened but also shut down the hysterics.

"Better. Does Lady Zevondeth live?"

"I do, no thanks to you, missy. Stop tormenting Della."

I eyed the wall that Zevondeth had apparently materialized through. "Magic or false panel?" I asked her.

"As if I'd tell you. I might need it, should you follow entirely in your tyrant of a father's footsteps." Zevondeth drew herself up to her full height, which wasn't saying much, milky eyes unnaturally keen on my face. Alert, sane, and whole.

"You're looking considerably better than the last time I saw you."

"You're looking a bit worse for wear. The babies?" she demanded.

"Safe and well. High King Uorsin?" I tossed back.

She grimaced. "Thrice-damned fool. Cowering in his safe room while the one real accomplishment of his miserable life crumbles. So far as I know he lives."

"Do you know how I can get into his rooms? He doesn't answer hails."

"Have you asked that black witch Illyria?"

"I would have, but she was too busy turning to ash while skewered with the Star of Annfwn."

A smile cracked Zevondeth's lined face, all the more disconcerting for the way it distorted the map of wrinkles. "Good girl. I knew you'd find the way to use it. Salena told you what you must do, then?"

Maybe not so sane. "Salena died, Lady Zevondeth. Has been dead coming on twenty years."

"I'm not a demented idiot," Zevondeth snapped and, leaning heavily on her cane, made her way to the fireplace.

"The last time we spoke, you—"

"Camouflage." She glared in my direction and cocked her head. "Best way to hide out from the Practitioners of Deyrr, to be beneath their notice."

"You knew who she was?"

"Tried to warn you, didn't I? More the fool you for not listening. Will you take the rest of my advice now?"

I slid a cautious glance at Harlan, who listened with interest, and was glad I'd elicited his promise.

He seeks the soldiers you cannot kill, to save himself from your avenging sword. But he won't escape it. It's his destiny and yours.

"That may not be necessary. Illyria is destroyed and her magic fading."

Zevondeth shook her head and muttered under her breath. She took something from the mantel and made her way to me, then set a trio of glass vials on the table. "We shall make a trade, then. I'll tell you a way into Uorsin's self-imposed prison in exchange for your blood." Faster than she should have been, she snagged my wrist and struck out with a small, sharp knife.

Not faster than I could move, however, easily slipping her grip even as Harlan stepped forward. "Here, now," he barked.

She grinned at him, showing missing teeth and total fearlessness. "No blood. No information."

"Take mine, then."

"You're a handsome one, Captain Harlan of Dasnaria, and

your blood no doubt stalwart, but I need hers." She pointed at the vials. "To complete the set. One, two, three. The soil, the seed, and you."

"I don't understand."

"A bow alone is useless. Even a drawn bow is useless. Fit an arrow to it and you have something."

"I'm the arrow."

She nodded. "Danu's blade, poised to strike. Give me your blood, child, and you will see."

The doll will help you see and so will Lady Zevondeth. When she asks for your blood, give it to her and do as she tells you, even if it makes no sense.

"Fine."

"Ursula, you—"

"No, Harlan. It's all right. I think I need to do this. *I* will do it." Taking the blade from Zevondeth, I made a cut on my left forearm, where the small wound wouldn't interfere with gripping my weapons. My blood dripped bright into the glass container she handed me. It was cold, unnaturally so. And in those milky white eyes I glimpsed a canny glitter. She took the vial, gnarled fingers catching it gingerly, fitted it into the little rack, between the other two, the ones that held Ami's and Andi's blood, and said some sort of prayer over it.

Or spell.

Then she presented it to me with a bow. "With this I divest myself of an old obligation," she intoned. "Give my regards to Salena." As if that had removed the starch from her bones, she visibly withered and her gaze went truly blind, hand groping in the air. Della neatly inserted herself under it, helping Zevondeth toward the bedroom. "So cold," the old woman whimpered.

"We'll light a fire and get you under the blankets," Della crooned.

"Wait—what am I to do with this?" I called after them. I

thought Zevondeth wouldn't answer. Then she slapped a hand on the doorframe and looked back at me, opaque eyes as bright as a bird's.

"Remember," she said.

"What about the way to Uorsin?"

She pointed at the vials, then disappeared into the bedroom.

42

Remember. Remember what? Something Salena had told me, surely. But, Danu take it, if I hadn't thought of this important thing in all these years, then how was I to force myself to recall it now? I even retrieved the doll, tempted to tear the thrice-damned thing apart, knowing full well it contained nothing more than it ever had.

I paced a restless circuit in my rooms, throwing my mind back to conversations with my mother, holding aside all the memories of my father that threatened to overpower them, at the same time willing someone to come and tell me Uorsin had emerged. I should really be down helping with the cleanup, overseeing that all the undead were dispatched, and dismantling whatever Illyria had used to make them. The smoke of burning flesh sweetened with the funeral oil of Glorianna's rites filtered in the window, reminding me of all that went on that needed tending to.

Remember what? I thought of my early childhood and Mother brushing my hair, then Uorsin shattering the teacups. No. I thought of her pregnant with Andi, staring off to the west and Uorsin knocking me cold with the flat of his blade. No, no. And then she was gone and he . . . No, no, no!

I couldn't evoke one set of memories without drowning in the others, and it made my head ache.

"Ursula." Harlan was prying my fingers from my skull. "Essla," he repeated, holding my hands in his, gaze boring into mine with such concern that I realized he'd been trying to talk to me for a while. Had I forgotten he was there?

"I'm fine."

He didn't bother to argue. "The more you strain for this memory, the more it will elude you. Sit."

I let him seat me and thought longingly of some wine. Going behind me, he worked the tight cords of my neck. "Tell me your favorite memory of her."

"I've thought about that one and—"

"Shh. Relax. Just tell me about it. How old were you?"

"Seven. My seventh birthday."

"Ah. I bet you were adorable."

I had to laugh. "Not exactly. I got my growth early, so I was too tall, knobby kneed and clumsy with it." A noise from the hall caught my attention. Had Uorsin emerged? Had something happened? But whoever it was passed by.

"How did you celebrate? What season is your natal day?"

"Midsummer. We went on a picnic, just the two of us. It was never only the two of us, really."

"Next summer perhaps you and I should do that on your birthday. How old will you be?"

I had to think about it. "Twenty-nine." It seemed impossible to imagine, both my age and the prospect of a summer when I might picnic with Harlan. "This is a waste of time. Let's try a battering ram."

"They're trying it. We'll get word if there's news. You can't force your way through everything, my hawk. Tell me about the birthday picnic. What else made it special?"

"She gave me the Star that day. Told me I would need it. She said . . ." My gaze went to the topaz gleaming in the light, embedded in the hilt of my sword, lying next to the sprawled doll, with her stuffing hanging out, and the three vials of blood.

The doll will help you see.

A star to guide you.

Interesting, isn't it, that you have the same disturbing dream back here, where your mother lived as queen.

Follow your dreams.

When I rose, Harlan didn't stop me. I made my way back to the bookshelf, to the foolish doll bed I'd made and kept her in, hidden away with other girlish things. And withdrew the gown I hadn't bothered to put back on her the last time. Silver, dulled by time, but silver. Like the armored gown. What had happened in the dream? I'd been like the doll, dressed in the gown, unable to move, to draw my sword, to touch the jewel, the Star she'd given me.

"Would you help me?" He immediately stepped to my side. I handed him my sword. "Can you pry the jewel out?"

He frowned, rotating it, running a big thumb over the forged metal that held it in place. "It will take some strength."

"Good thing I know someone who's got some."

He grunted, mind absorbed in the problem, then took the sword to the stone windowsill, setting it so the hilt faced in, and unsheathed his big-bladed knife. Shoulders flexing, he worked at the setting, the metal gradually giving way under his might. He slipped twice, scoring the stone and likely ruining his blade. From that day on I would forever see those stone scars and remember how he did what I asked without question or complaint.

With a creak of metal fatigue, the setting gave way, the topaz sphere popping out to hit the floor and roll to my feet. I took it up and, remembering how the head of Ami's doll had turned red in response to blood, set the Star inside my doll's head. Then I opened the three vials and poured our combined blood over the jewel, letting it soak in.

Nothing happened. The dull edge of panic began to set in.

I wiped sweat from my forehead, aware of being overheated from Zevondeth's rooms, forgetting that my hands were covered in blood. It tingled against my skin, like Ash's healing, like Andi's magic. I stared at my hand, bright with my blood, with that of my sisters. It was not enough to have the blood on me. No holding what I had to do at arm's length. Steeling myself, I licked the blood from my hands.

I stood in the empty throne room of Ordnung. It rung with silence and for a moment I thought everyone had died. But no, someone sat on the High Throne behind me. Uorsin? I tried to turn to see, sickness rising at the thought of him behind me, hurting me. But no. I couldn't move, for I wore that silver-plated gown. Throttling me. Holding me trapped.

"Let it be your strength," a voice said. My mother's voice. Hearing it sliced at my heart, and all I wanted was to see her face again. "Move through, not against, my daughter."

On the doll, the silver gown was only cloth, worn thin by time. I stopped fighting it. Accepted it and the fit. And turned. And moved.

Salena smiled at me from the High Throne. A new one, made of carved wood inlaid with jeweled fruits and flowers as I'd seen in Annfwn. Her hair cascaded dark around her, and her eyes, lit with love for me, glowed nearly silver.

"I'm so proud of you, Ursula. Your path has been a long and difficult one. I would have spared you, if I could."

"So you said once." Some bitterness edged up the back of my throat. "I suppose even you couldn't see everything that would occur."

"But I did." Her face contorted with grief. "Not soon enough. And when the future shifted, when I saw what could happen to you, I tried to stop it."

"When? I don't understand." I took a step toward her. "This is a dream."

"Dreams are just a different reality. I died, yes, but I'm still nearby."

"In the bower of Glorianna's arms?" I couldn't help saying it, imagining Ami glaring at me for it.

Salena made a wry face I recognized as one of Andi's expressions. "I don't think Glorianna would have me—or that Moranu would release me to her. But no, I'm closer than that. I've always been with you."

"The Star," I realized.

"Yes. When I saw the probability of my death, I anchored myself to it. It's not an exact thing, but it's worked well enough. It's let me create messages for your sisters. And to stay, for the end game."

"What is that?"

She regarded me steadily. "I think you know."

"This was your game. Never mine. Why didn't you finish it?"

"The time had to be right. You three had to be ready. You, my daughters, can do what I could not."

"Do what? What did you hope to accomplish by leaving everything and everyone behind?"

"Only the King can save the land. That is his sacred duty. His destiny. Ask Andromeda—if she's come into her own, she'll see the truth of it. Ask Amelia—if she's come into her own, she'll know how to do it. All the land requires this. Annfwn, the Twelve, the greater world. Danu's blade lit by Glorianna's mercy will set Moranu's magic free."

"I don't know what to do." I pleaded with her, and my dress began to feel tight, restrictive.

"No man or woman is above the law, and the world is greater than all else. Your loyalty belongs to the world first. Andromeda knows of wisdom and sacrifice. Amelia brings the love that's needed. You are the blade that cuts through the knots and lances the wound. You know what to do. You always have."

"I don't know." I fought against the hardening gown. "I can't even get to Uorsin."

She smiled. Not at all nicely.

"Leave that to me."

I shoved hard against the confining armored gown and met with the rock-hard wall of Harlan's chest. He grunted, a break in the Dasnarian lullaby he picked up again, singing it softly as if I weren't thrashing like a wild woman in his arms.

Going still, I tried to assimilate what had happened, and he tipped my chin up in a panicked grip, relaxing when he looked into my eyes.

"You're back. I was terrified you never would be."

He admitted to such things so easily. Not something I could understand, maybe ever. And yet it made him no weaker in my eyes. Stronger really.

"How long was I out?"

"Hours." He nodded at the window, the autumn dusk falling sooner. In another hour or so the sun would set and the waxing moon rise to light the fields.

Harvest time. I shivered, wondering if I could face what lay ahead. I would have to consult with Andi and Ami about my dream. What Salena had told me.

A bellow of rage, not unlike that of a wounded bear, echoed down the corridors. I knew what it was before Marskal flung open the doors to my chambers, not even blinking at the sight of me entangled on Harlan's lap.

"Captain." He nodded instead of saluting. "He's out."

"Heading which way?"

"Throne room." He stopped me at the door with a hand on my arm. "He injured Jepp—nearly gutted her. And a maid bringing food. I think he's out of his mind."

"Danu." I took a moment to send a fervent prayer for her guidance. The pommel of my sword was jagged metal now. Nothing to be done for it. But I needed to keep the Star with me, of that much I was certain. Another bellow, followed by distant screams, raked down my spine. Without much time to consider, I put it in my mouth and swallowed.

Far from choking me, it went down smoothly, burning warm

in my gut and dissolving the old fears, the new terrors. I would face what lay ahead because I had to.

I raced through the halls, Harlan at my back, as always.

The throne room stood nearly empty. Not unnaturally so, but because everyone had fled. The gore and shattered glass had been cleaned away. Perhaps superstitiously, I looked to the thrones, the familiar lineup of five. No single throne of vines and flowers.

No Salena. Of course not.

The Star burned in my stomach. Uorsin, unkempt as a madman, stood in the center of the room, sword pointed at Amelia's belly as he shouted incoherently about his heir. Andi and Rayfe, both with weapons in their hands, restrained Ash, who seemed about to explode with rage, his green eyes bright even from my vantage point.

Andi, seeming unsurprised to see me skid in, gave me a solemn nod.

"High King Uorsin!" I called out.

Though I hadn't spoken that loudly, my voice nevertheless cut through his shouts. He spun and stared at me with fury in his eyes.

"Traitor," he growled, gaze going to the circlet still banding my brow. "Think you to assassinate me along with my queen?"

"Not your queen, but an enemy of the Twelve," I replied. "She killed even Derodotur, your most faithful companion and adviser. She was the enemy, not us. How can you not see that?"

"She would have opened the doors to Annfwn. My destiny. She only needed the Star and she could have given me what your mother refused to. You had it all along, didn't you? Never did I think you'd betray me. My eldest. My heir."

"I've never betrayed you. I've only ever acted for the good of the High Throne."

"I *am* the High Throne!" He thundered the words. "You might as well question the sun as doubt me."

"You're a man." As I said the words, the truth came clear. "A human being. And the High Throne is only as good as the person who sits on it. You have not done good by our people. I'm asking you to abdicate."

He seemed to froth with rage. "Are you?" Uorsin's voice had gone that dead quiet. "So you can have the power? You're no better than I am."

"Or Astar or Stella," I answered him. "It cannot be yours any longer. You're not worthy of it."

"Who are you to pass judgment on me?" He strode toward me and raised a fist to backhand me. Before I thought, before I knew it—I blocked the blow with the streaming strength of the combined blood within me, sidestepping so that he faltered under his own momentum. The astonishment in his face spoke volumes, as if he barely recognized me. With a sense of clean relief, I knew that it came from not knowing me at all.

I'd never been anyone to him. No one real. Just the son I wasn't.

"Who am I to judge you? I'm the person you raised to treasure what Ordnung and the High Throne stood for above all else. I'm the daughter you taught to value peace and strength used to protect the weak. I'm the heir you created with Salena, Queen of the Tala. By her hand and by your own standards, I judge you and find you wanting. You are not worthy of the High Throne.

"You once said to me you thought you'd done your best by me. This is my best."

"I'll kill you," he growled. "As I should have killed you in your cradle. As I killed your witch-whore of a mother."

The admission sliced my heart. A clean blow opening an old wound. I'd known. All along. So many things I'd tried not to know. No more. Only Danu's bright truth.

"She tried to kill me and failed," Uorsin raged. "You'll fail also and die like she did." He lunged at me, breaking the shock, and I barely parried. His reach, his strength—even crazed—far exceeded mine. I needed distance and worked to create some for myself.

Defend, parry, attack, retreat, regroup.

For several minutes, we exchanged strikes and I chanted the

mantra to myself. The jagged metal of my pommel dug into my wrist, my blood slickening my grip. But his rage worked against him, and my conviction worked for me. It seemed Danu slowed time and guided my blade, allowing me time to strategize, to maneuver him, to become aware that the other five had formed a loose circle around us. Andi's magic thickened the air, readying itself. Ami caught my eye and pointed to the doors, walking in that direction and looking back over her shoulder at me.

I wasn't alone in this.

Defend, parry, attack, retreat, regroup.

The blood sang in my veins, the Star burning in my belly. To guide me by.

I pressed Uorsin that direction, leading, then pushing, as we circled each other. He landed strikes on me here and there, but I didn't feel them. Only the sense of purpose. "Abdicate your throne, Uorsin. For the good of the realm."

Andromeda knows of wisdom and sacrifice. Amelia brings the love that's needed. You are the blade that cuts through the knots and lances the wound. You know what to do.

"Never!" he bellowed. Fear in his eyes, Uorsin backed, struggling to fend me off. I fenced him in, driving him to the grassy courtyard outside the arcade.

Uorsin's breathing flowed ragged and yet he hurled garbled threats still, cursing us, promising retribution. He stumbled, falling to his knees on the grass, the point of my sword at his heart. Andi and Ami stood across from me, opposite points on our triad, Rayfe and Ash behind them, just as I knew Harlan guarded my own back.

"Abdicate," I repeated. "For the peace of the Twelve."

The shadows drew long and purple, Glorianna's sun setting on the peaks behind us and Moranu's moon rising over the walls.

Above him and beside me, my sisters waited for the world to be righted.

"Never," he shouted at me. "I am the King! You'll have to kill me first."

"Abdicate," I told him, for the third and final time. "Or I will kill you, for the good of the world."

"You won't be able to. I'm your King."

"I have to kill you, because you are the King. And you are the one who failed. Failed your sacred duty. This is your redemption. By Danu's sword."

"Under Moranu's moon," Andi intoned.

"Glorianna receives you," Amelia finished.

With a clean thrust of my blade, I killed my father.

Then stood over him while the earth drank in his blood. In a wave, magic crashed over and through me, taking my consciousness with it.

43

I awoke in my own bed, ringed by candles.

Disconcertingly, it wasn't Harlan's grave gaze that greeted me, but Ash's uncanny green one, bright in his scarred face.

"The King is dead," he told me. Then inclined his head. "Long live the High Queen." He gave me his twisted half smile. "She's awake!" he called over his shoulder.

Harlan arrived first, taking my hand and pressing a kiss to my palm, where it burned clear through me. Andi and Ami, both looking tired but at peace, followed. Rayfe leaned against the doorway, blue eyes feral as they rested on Andi.

"He's really dead." I saw my father's face in my mind, the terror and resignation as I'd spoken his sentence. *I have to kill you, because you are the King.* "We have to bring the babies over. Amelia, you can act as regent. Unless you prefer to take the crown. I assume, Andi, that you can't, since you have to stay in Annfwn."

"Actually, I don't have to stay in Annfwn necessarily—the barrier no longer divides it from the Twelve."

"Which," Ash inserted, wiping his hands clean, "lets you off of one hook. But I expect you to repay your debt by releasing the Tala prisoners from all the prisons."

"There would be chaos, pillaging," I protested, struggling up, Harlan assisting.

"We'll work it out," Rayfe replied. "We'll set up escorts for the worst and deal with them in Annfwn." He grimaced. "We can make a treaty over it, if you prefer, High Queen Ursula."

"I can't be queen. I have to be executed. No one is above the law."

"Perhaps not, but who will pass that judgment?" Amelia asked. "The land accepted the sacrifice and you're the highest mortal power we have over the Thirteen Kingdoms. Glorianna save us all."

"Thirteen?"

"Like it or not"—Rayfe's hard gaze flicked to Andi, who returned it calmly—"the ritual you three performed connected Annfwn to the Twelve. The Heart now extends over the entire empire. *Your* empire, it appears, though I think it could be argued that Annfwn annexed the Twelve, rather than the other way around."

"They were never meant to be divided." Ami gave him a radiant smile. "The goddesses—and Salena—brought this about. You can't fight the will of the Three."

"Besides"—Andi went to him and slid her arms around his waist, leaning in—"the Heart is anchored in the Star, which seems to be inside our High Queen. You would hate being High King, anyway. Ursula lives for this stuff. Moranu knows she'll be sorting out logistics for years to come while we run on the beach." She tossed me a smug smile.

"Apparently I'm Queen of Avonlidgh." Ami frowned. "Word is Erich died on the battlefield. Duranor's forces attacked and defeated them within hours. Stefan pledges fealty to the high crown and already sent a list of possible rewards for his support. Ash and I will have to travel to Windroven to settle things after Dafne brings the babies over. Then we can come back here and help as need be."

"We'll help, too." Andi leaned her head against Rayfe's shoulder, smiling as he wound his fingers in her hair. "It will take me

438 • Jeffe Kennedy

some time to learn how the magic will disperse and how I should direct it. I'll need to know where to send it first."

"Aerron," I answered. "Can you shift the weather and restore the rainfall? If we could bring it gradually into the southern regions first, maybe over the course of a few months, to give the ground time to soften and saturate, then—"

Andi laughed and held up a hand. "How about we wait until morning."

"After all, we have a coronation to plan." Ami clapped her hands. "Which means new dresses for you!"

"Danu take me." I let my head drop back and it nestled neatly into the fold of Harlan's shoulder.

He stroked my hair back from my forehead. "You did well, my hawk. Tomorrow is soon enough to solve the world's problems."

I looked up into his solemn face. "I killed my father. The King."

"You did what you had to do. Tomorrow you will do the same. And every day after that. It's who you are."

"With you at my back."

He smiled "Always. *Elskastholrr.*"

Heedless of the others, grateful not to be alone in this, I drew him down for a kiss. "*Elskastholrr.*"